Elemental

Elemental

THE TSUNAMI RELIEF ANTHOLOGY

*Stories of
Science Fiction
and Fantasy*

Edited by Steven Savile
and Alethea Kontis

Introduction by
Arthur C. Clarke

A TOM DOHERTY ASSOCIATES BOOK
New York

TOR®

This is a work of fiction. All the characters and events portrayed in these stories are either fictitious or are used fictitiously.

ELEMENTAL: THE TSUNAMI RELIEF ANTHOLOGY

This book is printed on acid-free paper.

Edited by Steven Savile and Alethea Kontis

A Tor Book
Published by Tom Doherty Associates, LLC
175 Fifth Avenue
New York, NY 10010

www.tor.com

Tor® is a registered trademark of Tom Doherty Associates, LLC.

Library of Congress Cataloging-in-Publication Data

Elemental : the Tsunami relief anthology : stories of science fiction and fantasy / [edited by] Steven Savile and Alethea Kontis.—1st ed.
    p. cm.
  ISBN 0-765-31562-9 (hc)
  EAN 978-0-765-31562-5 (hc)
  ISBN 0-765-31563-7 (tpbk)
  EAN 978-0-765-31563-2 (tpbk)
    1. Science fiction, American. 2. Fantasy fiction, American. 3. Science fiction, English.
  4. Fantasy fiction, English. I. Savile, Steven. II. Kontis, Alethea.
  PS648.S3E544 2006
  813'.087608—dc22
                                                                    2005034486

First Edition: May 2006

Printed in the United States of America

0 9 8 7 6 5 4 3 2 1

Copyright Acknowledgments

Contents

Acknowledgments

Elemental owes a debt of gratitude to more people than it is possible to list on one page.

We would like to thank Tom Doherty and David Hartwell for their vision, support, and belief every step of the way.

We tip our hats to Christine Jaeger, Priscilla Flores, Toni Weisskopf, and Elena Stokes—some of the greatest cheerleaders the world will ever know.

To Denis Wong, Jodi Rosoff, and Steve Calcutt for all their time and hard work.

To Janet Lee, our last-minute angel in the whirlwind.

To Michael Whelan, for a cover that made dreams come true.

To our parents and friends, who lived with us during the months it took for the germ of an idea to grow into the book you hold in your hands.

To Luc Reid and the members of the Codex Writers Group, who hold a very special place in our hearts. Without them we would never have met, and this book would not have happened. Their friendship saves us from testing one of the absolutes: nothing can survive in a vacuum.

Elemental wouldn't be the amazing book it is without the generosity of the writers who donated their time and talent, so to them we say again thank you, and to the countless others who have shown their support in so many ways. It has been, and continues to be, an uplifting and humbling experience.

Three of the first writers we approached are no longer with us, and it is to these three that we would like to dedicate this anthology. In the spirit that they inspired us, we can only hope that this book inspires you.

Jack L. Chalker, Andre Norton, and Robert Sheckley

Shapers of dreams
Inspirers
Friends in the great spirit of adventure

Introduction

Once and Future Tsunamis

BY ARTHUR C. CLARKE

Although the devastating tsunami struck coastal areas even a few kilometers away from Colombo, I have so far not ventured out to see any of its damage. I am not sure if I can bear to look at what the killer waves have done to my favorite beaches in Unawatuna, Hikkaduwa, and elsewhere along Sri Lanka's southern coast. But I have been watching with mounting horror and grief the disaster's television coverage. The New Year dawned with the Global Family closely following the unfolding tragedy via satellite television and on the Web. As the grim images from Aceh, Chennai, Galle, and elsewhere replaced the traditional scenes of celebrations, I realized that it will soon be 60 years since I invented the communications satellite (in *Wireless World,* October 1945).

I was also reminded of what Bernard Kouchner, former French health minister and first UN governor of Kosovo, once said: "Where there is no camera, there is no humanitarian intervention." Indeed, how many of the millions of men and women who donated generously for disaster relief would have done so if they had merely read about it in the newspapers? In the coming weeks, the media's coverage of the disaster will be analyzed and critiqued. Nature's fury presented the media with an unfolding human drama of gigantic proportions that is usually the domain of Hollywood screenwriters. As a noted media watcher in the U.S., Danny Schechter, remarked: "This is not reality television. This is reality on television."

Speaking of movies, when *The Day After Tomorrow* was showing in Colombo last summer, some people asked me if such a calamity could befall Sri Lanka. Without debating the scientific merits of the movie, I said that Nature always had a few tricks up her sleeve. Little did I imagine that before the year ended, killer waves forty feet high would lash the coast of Sri Lanka, leaving an unprecedented trail of destruction in my adopted country. For millions of Sri Lankans, the day after Christmas was a living nightmare that mimicked *The Day After Tomorrow*. As Sri Lanka struggles to come to terms with the multiple impacts of this tragedy, we confront a massive humanitarian crisis involving over one million displaced persons. The first priority is to provide emergency shelter and relief. As soon as possible thereafter, we must create conditions that will enable the affected people to return to normal lives and livelihoods. In spite of all its progress, science can only give us a few hours' warning—at the most—of an incoming tsunami. And as we now know, there were no systems in place in the Indian Ocean countries to broadcast that warning to millions of coastal dwellers. As we raise our heads from this blow, we must address the long-term issues of better preparedness. That includes effective warning systems that work well just when they are needed. The tsunami, in its wake, brought its share of conspiracy theories and speculations. Among the latter kind was the suggestion that I had foreseen this disaster. The Boxing Day disaster reminded me that I had, in fact, written about another tsunami that Sri Lanka had experienced more than a century ago. In my first book about Ceylon, *The Reefs of Taprobane* (1957), this is what I wrote:

One August day in 1883, the water suddenly started to drain out of Galle harbour. Within a few minutes, the sea bed was exposed for hundreds of feet from shore. Myriads of fish were flopping around in their death agonies, and many wrecks, from small fishing boats to large iron steamers, were miraculously uncovered by the water that had concealed them for years. "But the inhabitants of Galle did not stop to stare and wonder. They knew what to expect, and rushed to high ground as quickly as they could. Fortunately for the town and its people, the sea did not return in the usual tidal wave; perhaps because Galle was on the far, sheltered side of the island, it came back smoothly and without violence, like a swiftly incoming tide. "It was many days before the people of Galle learned why the sea had so suddenly deserted their harbor, when they heard for the first time the doom-laden name of Krakatoa.

These words were written too long ago for me to locate my original notes, but I am intrigued: How did the people of Galle in 1883 know big waves were coming up soon after the sea receded? What made them rush to high ground? In contrast, in twenty-first-century Sri Lanka, this simple fact was unknown to most people. No one knows exactly how many men, women, and children perished on December 26 because they rushed out to see the suddenly receding sea. But that number must indeed be high. Referring to the Krakatoa-inspired tsunami, I had also written in 1957:

> It was a moment unique in recorded history, and one which will probably never come again. I would have given anything to have been present then with a camera, but would probably have been too terrified to use it.

Well, never say never. This time round, there were plenty of holidaymakers armed with video cameras on the beach. Many of them just could not resist the temptation to capture the moment—alas, some cameras and their owners added to the grim statistics. What survived makes this probably the most widely filmed natural disaster in history. Devastating as they are, disasters have been a favorite element of storytellers over millennia. In my own science fiction, I have conjured many and varied disasters that happen just when everything is going according to plan. A tsunami arrives toward the end of the story in *Childhood's End* (1953). In *The Ghost from the Grand Banks* (1990), an ambitious plan to raise the *Titanic* is completely wrecked by a massive storm in the north Atlantic. *The Songs of Distant Earth* (1986) suggested a planetary rescue plan for the ultimate disaster: the end of the world. However, in terms of scientific research and policy action inspired, *Rendezvous with Rama* (1973) may yet turn out to be my one piece of writing that one day saves the most number of lives. *Rama* opens with an asteroid impact on Europe which obliterates northern Italy—on the morning of 11 September 2077. (I am still spooked by randomly choosing this date, and claim no powers of prescience.) I cannot recall what turned my attention to the possible danger of asteroid impacts. It was quite an old idea in science fiction, and one that science now takes very seriously. Life-threatening impacts are more frequent than many people realize: there were three known major impacts during the twentieth century alone (Siberia in 1908 and 1947, and Brazil in 1930)—damage was minimal in all cases as, miraculously, they happened in uninhabited areas. It is only a matter of time before our luck runs out. In *Rama*, I introduced a new concept. I argued that as soon as the technology permitted, we should set up powerful radar and optical search systems to detect Earth-threatening objects. The name I suggested was Spaceguard, which, together with Spacewatch, has now been widely accepted. Today, astronomers scan the skies in both hemispheres looking for rogue asteroids and comets. The fact that these efforts are woefully underfunded—and that some rely on private funding—says how little the bean counters in governments appreciate the value of this work.

When the possible consequences of asteroid impacts on Earth are discussed, people seem to be comforted by the fact that two-thirds of the planet's surface is ocean. In fact, we should worry more: an ocean impact can multiply damage by triggering the mother of all tsunamis. Duncan Steel, an authority on the subject, has done some terrifying calculations. He took a modest-sized space rock, 200 meters in diameter, colliding with Earth at a typical speed of 19 kilometers per second. As it is brought to a halt, it releases kinetic energy in an explosion equal to 600 megatons of TNT—ten times the yield of the most powerful nuclear weapon tested (underground). Even though only about 10 percent of this energy would be transferred to the tsunami, such waves will carry this massive energy over long distances to coasts far away. They can therefore cause much more diffused destruction than would have resulted from a land impact. In the latter, the interaction between the blast wave and the irregularities of the ground (hills, buildings, trees) limits the area damaged. On the ocean, the wave propagates until it runs into land.

Contrary to popular belief, we science fiction writers don't predict the future—we try to prevent undesirable futures. In the wake of the Asian tsunami, scientists and governments are scrambling to set up systems to monitor and warn us of future disasters. Let's keep an eye on the skies even as we worry about the next hazard from the depths.

Although he lost his diving school in the recent tsunami, Sir Arthur Clarke has no plans to leave Sri Lanka again. He thanks Nalaka Gunawardene for his support in writing this essay.

Elemental

Report from the Near Future:

Crystallization

BY DAVID GERROLD

David Gerrold started writing professionally in 1967. His first sale was the "Trouble with Tribbles" episode of *Star Trek*. Within five years, he had published seven novels, two books about television production, three anthologies, and a short story collection. He was nominated for the Hugo and Nebula Awards six times in four years. Since 1967, he has published more than forty books. Several of his novels are considered classics, including *The Man Who Folded Himself*, *When HARLIE Was One*, and the four books in *The War Against the Chtorr*.

Gerrold has written episodes for more than a dozen different television series, including *Star Trek*, *Star Trek Animated*, *Twilight Zone*, *Land of the Lost*, *Babylon 5*, *Sliders*, *Logan's Run*, and *Tales from the Darkside*. He has had columns in six different magazines and two Web sites, including *Starlog*, *Galileo*, *Profiles*, *PC-Techniques*, *Visual Developer*, *Yahoo*, and *GalaxyOnline*. In 1995, he won the Hugo and Nebula awards for "The Martian Child," an autobiographical tale of his son's adoption.

David Gerrold lives with his son in Northridge, California. Learn more about Gerrold at his Web site: www.gerrold.com.

It's that moment when a liquid solidifies, when the temperature drops or the pressure rises and the substance finally stops flowing, it slows down, it turns to slush—to mud, it hardens, it finally becomes impenetrable. . . .

For the first few hours after the Los Angeles freeway system crystallized, most people believed the problem was temporary and that traffic would eventually start flowing again. Even for the first few days, they believed they could eventually chip their way out of the concretized arteries.

The slush of Los Angeles traffic had been slower than sluggish for years, churning through looped spaghetti concrete channels in a lumpy stream of metal and plastic peristalsis, in a persistent state of uncertain hesitation, punctuated only occasionally by forward-jerking movements and uneven painful surges, a textbook demonstration of socio-technical constipation and definitely no place for a stick shift.

The city engineers had been aware of the potential for crystallization for nearly two decades, but no one had ever taken the warnings seriously, and eventually even they began to assume that their own projections of crystallization were situational artifacts occurring whenever the simulators reached the limits of their ability to process the rapid flows of data.

Unfortunately, only the data was flowing rapidly. One desperate afternoon, even that stopped. The air-conditioning broke down in the central monitoring station. The temperature rose uncomfortably. Fans didn't help. The computers began shutting down in self-defense. The screens went blank, or declared, "No signal." Blind and deaf, the traffic engineers could neither monitor nor prescribe.

The rest was inevitable.

Outside, in the place where the facts didn't care about simulation, events took on a terrifying momentum of their own. It was Friday, early afternoon on a three-day holiday weekend. Temperatures in the basin had peaked at 106 degrees shortly after one p.m. Add to that a localized gas shortage acerbated by higher than usual oil prices, a high degree of situational stress about the staggering economy, a disturbing series of terrorist bombings in the mideast, and three days of overheated shock-jock nattering about a particularly scandalous high-profile murder trial, and crystallization was no longer a question of if or when, but *where*.

Surprisingly, it did not begin on the freeway. Not exactly. Although a freeway was involved. The first hardening in the traffic flow began in the San Fernando Valley where Burbank Blvd. intersected with Sepulveda. Always a sluggish intersection, today it revealed its true capacity for horror. An overweight, overstressed soccer mom with two screaming children in the backseat of her SUV and a cell phone pressed to her ear, her attention everywhere but on the road in front of her, abruptly became aware of a motorcyclist coming up out of the blind spot on her right. Startled, she swerved left, forcing two teenagers in a dropped Honda Civic (don't ask) to brake suddenly. The empty tanker truck that shouldn't have been in the same lane behind them braked, swerved, and jackknifed sideways into a city bus, effectively blocking all three northbound lanes of Sepulveda and the middle two lanes of Burbank.

Almost immediately traffic stopped on both boulevards, backing up on Burbank as far east as Van Nuys Blvd. and as far west as Woodley. Sepulveda froze all the way north to Sherman Way and as far south as Ventura Blvd. When the traffic at the intersection of Ventura and Sepulveda froze, the crystallization of the surface streets began to spread east and west on Ventura Blvd. as well. In the horror about to happen, there would be no alternative routes.

The 405 freeway stretches north across the San Fernando Valley; the heaviest used access ramps are at Burbank Blvd., just slightly east of the fatal intersection and up a slight incline. The northbound and southbound access ramps represent two additional intersections to interrupt Burbank's westward flow—it's a wasps' nest of lanes, contradictory traffic signals, and intermittent left-turn arrows. Even at three in the morning, it takes ninety seconds to negotiate this ganglionic nightmare in any direction. During crush hour, wise drivers bring a book or a magazine. Teenage boys change the radio station and readjust themselves in their jeans. Grown men pick their noses and think about business. Teenage girls turn their rearview mirrors and fix their makeup. Everyone else is on the phone, their attention two or ten or a thousand miles away. Watching the road is optional, something that only sissies and old ladies ever do.

On any ordinary afternoon, traffic feeding into the northbound Burbank offramp would start backing up by two p.m. By five, it would be backed up two miles south, all the way to the 405/101 interchange. This day, however, traffic was even more manic than usual. As soon as the critical intersection of Burbank and Sepulveda hardened, the crystallization of the 405 began spreading southward as fast as new cars arrived and joined the creeping boundaries of the linear parking lot.

Imagine the intersection of the 405 and the 101 as a cross. The entire northwest quadrant is the Sepulveda dam basin. For two miles west, there are only two surface avenues that go north through the basin to the neighborhoods beyond, Haskell and Balboa. For two miles north, there is only one westward access—Burbank. But there are over a million residents northwest of the intersection and their *only* access from the south or east is through this interchange—or through the intersections of Ventura and Sepulveda, or Burbank and Sepulveda. As quickly as Sepulveda clogged, all of the intersections and all of the surrounding surface avenues began to solidify as well. Within forty minutes, an area ten miles square had crystallized.

The 405 and the 101 freeways only exacerbated the situation, feeding more cars into this black hole of traffic from all four compass points. With no place to go, the traffic ground to a halt both north and south on the 405 and very quickly after east and west on the 101 as well.

With the computers down, Cal-Trans was unable to post warning bulletins on the freeway alert signs. Instead, an Amber Alert was posted to look out for a suspected kidnapper driving a black Ford Explorer, license number, etc. It was this particular (alleged) kidnapper's bad luck to be caught on the 101 westbound at Vineland. Traffic came to a halt with the SUV pocketed between a stretch limo on the left and a battered Plymouth pickup on the right, piled high with tree branches and driven by three Mexican gardeners whose command of English was limited. Behind the pickup truck, however, was a distracted mother, whose eleven-year-old son had read the Amber Alert only a few moments before and who was now intently watching all of the traffic around on the promise of a ten-dollar bill from his mother if he spotted the suspect Explorer—but only if he kept absolutely quiet while he did, so his mother could listen to her deadbeat ex-husband (who apparently operated out of the bizarre belief that a good excuse is always an acceptable substitute for a tangible result) explain why his child-support check would be late again.

In the middle of this conversation, the eleven-year-old suddenly began shouting and pointing. Despite his mother's annoyed refusal to accept the obvious—that she now owed her son ten dollars that she did not have—she eventually accepted that indeed, the suspect's vehicle was only a few yards ahead in the next lane over. By then, owing to a repeat of the same Amber Alert news bulletin on static-riven KFWB, the inhabitants of two other vehicles had also spotted the Explorer. One driver was already calling 911. The other driver and his two passengers (all of them new enlistees on leave from the marine base at El Toro and on their way to visit the Tarzana-based fiancée of the driver) exited their own SUV, two of them carrying baseball bats kept in the vehicle for occasional trips into West Hollywood for gay-bashing. With traffic temporarily halted—or so they believed (that it was temporary)—they approached the Explorer on foot. The suspected kidnapper panicked, tried to hit the gas, tried to force his way between a lime-green Volkswagen Beetle and a 1988 Honda Civic driven by a harried college student whose car insurance had just been canceled, and the result was a three-way crunch, with three soon-to-be-ex-marines banging on the hood and fenders of the locked Explorer with baseball bats. They had just escalated to smashing windows when the first officers arrived on scene and ordered them to stand down.

From there, the situation metamorphosed into a police standoff as even more motorcycle officers came racing up the still empty shoulders of the freeway, followed by the warbling and flashing cruisers of the California Highway Patrol and the Los Angeles Police Department. Very quickly, this nexus of confusion and rage was surrounded by armed officers, all of them crouching behind automobile fenders with guns drawn, while two police helicopters and three news choppers circled overhead and terrified drivers in all directions evacuated their vehicles, crawling quickly away through the lanes on their hands and knees—including the harried mother, still on her cell phone, and her eleven-year-old son who whined loudly that he wanted to stay and see the kidnapper get shot. The suspected kidnapper, his vehicle permanently jammed between the Volkswagen and the Honda, was unable to extricate himself from the vehicle and sat there helplessly while police ordered him to get out with his hands up.

The irony of the situation was that the Amber Alert had been posted with the wrong license number. The driver was not a kidnapper; his only relationship to the kidnapping was that he drove a black Ford Explorer. He had only tried to flee because he had seen three angry men coming toward his vehicle with baseball bats.

Nevertheless, innocent or guilty, this particular blood clot in the arterial flow of urban commerce effectively shut down the 101 in both directions, trapping even more drivers in their cars. Some of them turned off their engines and got out to smoke, leaning against their fenders or lifting themselves up to sit on the still-warm hoods of their rapidly depreciating vehicles.

Meanwhile, the clotting of the freeway system spread south and east with pernicious speed. East along the 134 toward the 5, and southward down the 101, which was already terminal. It took less than an hour for the crystallization of the system to hit the nexus of the Pasadena, Harbor, and Hollywood freeways. The four-level interchange, one of the first in the nation, was in easy view of the mayor's office in the nearby city hall, a building that, contrary to popular belief, had *not* been destroyed in the 1953 attack of George Pal's Martians and their manta-ray-shaped war machines.

With the news media now reporting that the 101 and 405 freeways were impassable and that drivers were advised to seek alternate routes—of which there were either few or none, the best thing to do was find a movie theater or a motel and wait for the weekend. Starting at city-center, the northward crush of traffic tried to force its way up the 5, an overstressed artery that crawled along the east side of Griffith Park; the results were predictable and immediate—another nexus of crystallization. Nothing moved. The clotting of the Los Angeles freeway system was now irreversible. Within another hour, the 10, most of the 110, and a large part of the 210 were equally out of commission as were most of the surrounding surface streets. Too many cars, not enough road.

Unable to feed their traffic flows into the northward and westward traffic channels, the 710 and the 605 also began to solidify. Crystallization spread like ice across the surface of a lake, creeping steadily and inevitably toward a frozen stillness. As fast as new cars arrived at the outward edges of the solidification, that's how fast it spread.

And there were still four hours until sunset.

Most drivers, unaware of the scale of the growing catastrophe, unable to comprehend or believe that their trusted freeway system had finally, utterly, and completely failed them, remained in their cars, existing in a state of quiet desperation—or quiet domestication—most of them still believed that it was just a matter of time until traffic began easing forward again.

The Zen master Solomon Short is quoted as saying, "No pebble ever takes responsibility for the whole avalanche." Nowhere was this as evident as it was when the disaster escalated to its next stage.

Start with the sweltering heat. It's the fifth day of a heat wave with no end in sight. There's no wind; the air is stagnant and brown. People are tired, uncomfortable, cranky, and selfish. Unwilling to be uncomfortable, every driver in a vehicle with air-conditioning has rolled up his windows and has his air conditioner turned on full blast. To power his air conditioner, he's running his engine. Half a million vehicles. All those engines create a furnace of additional heat at ground level, encouraging even more drivers to keep their engines running and their air conditioners blasting.

Frozen in time, as inert as the dead air above them, a million and a half cars and trucks and buses, idling impatiently, every second burning tens of thousands of gallons of gasoline into hot exhaust; as the sun's rays bake the day, various chemical transformations occur. The exhaust becomes a rising cloud of air pollution. All those restless waiting vehicles spew a cumulative soup of toxic fumes into the brown smoky air of the basin, aggregating into an already deadly miasma that lays across the inert afternoon like a smothering blanket—and triggering the next stage of the catastrophe.

Sitting alone, stuck and frustrated, desperate and angry, people begin to demonstrate irrational behavior. Some people begin honking incessantly, triggering even more stress in the people around them. Some drivers turn up their music—too loud. The hyperamplified subwoofers broadcast rhythmic pulses that feel like body punches to people in vehicles many lengths ahead and behind. Arguments begin. Fights break out. Windows get smashed with golf clubs. Ramming incidents occur. Even individuals uninvolved experience increased levels of stress. A few have panic attacks. Others suffer respiratory distress. Others go into full-blown asthma attacks. Then it gets worse. Kosh's corollary to Short's observation: The avalanche has already started; it is too late for the pebbles to vote.

Despite the efforts of social historians, an accurate account of the events of the day remains impossible; too many events, too many scattered and confused accounts. What is certain, however, is that once the cascade of failures began, each breakdown triggered the next; but the most catastrophic of all was the failure of the telephone system.

Stuck on the freeways, with relief from the sun still hours away, people began flipping open their cell phones and calling home, calling for help, calling ambulances and fire trucks and police, even calling Cal-Trans and the city councilmen and the Governor's office to complain. As the channels overloaded, the system began dumping calls to clear bandwidth; people began calling their service providers to complain. In self-defense, the network went into emergency procedures and shut itself down. The result—increased feelings of alienation and isolation among those trapped in the crystallized traffic. The arteries became linear madhouses of desperate frustration. Increasing numbers of people lost control of their bladders and bowels, adding to their individual discomfort, both physical and emotional.

As the afternoon wore on, two pregnant women went into labor and a third miscarried. Two people enroute to hospitals died in the ambulances that could not get through. A burly farmworker, one of several crammed into the back of a pickup truck, experienced debilitating food poisoning, a combination of projectile vomiting and near-projectile diarrhea that expelled more than two liters of fluid out of his body in less than thirty minutes. A fifty-six-year-old type-A studio executive experienced crushing chest pains that left him gasping for breath and too weak to cry for help. No help was available anyway. Even where calls for help could still be made from emergency call boxes, impatient drivers had already filled both shoulders of the highway in their desperate attempts to escape. The rescue vehicles couldn't get in and the medevac choppers had no place to land.

By mid-afternoon, a significant number of vehicles had run out of gas. Even under the best of circumstances, a single stalled automobile in a middle lane could back up traffic in all four lanes for miles. Under these circumstances, with hundreds of dead vehicles scattered throughout the system and more dying every minute, the crystallization had become complete. The vehicular arteries were solid and terminally impassible. The patient was dead, although it would be several days before any of the specialists would admit it.

But on some unconscious level, some people were already getting a visceral sense of what had happened. Maybe their survival instincts were kicking in, or maybe they were simply overcome by frustration—but it was the final moment of breakdown, the recognition that the system had failed and could not repair itself. Drivers started getting out of their cars. They locked them up, out of some optimistic belief that they would eventually have the chance to come back and retrieve them, then they left them where they were. They gathered what belongings they could carry and abandoned their metal sanctuaries. First one or two, then a few more, and finally a veritable flood of refugees, they hiked between the sweltering lanes toward the nearest off-ramp and their separate illusions of relief.

Not all drivers were that easily persuaded. They sat and waited in desperate hope, afraid to leave, afraid to let go of their attachment to their vehicles, afraid to disconnect from pernicious false identity—*I am my car*—that pervades Los Angeles culture. Still believing that this was only temporary, they sat in their cars, their engines still running, their air conditioners still blasting. (Even today, all these years later, archaeologists are still finding mummified bodies in some vehicles, including many varieties of small animals.)

Some engineers argue that even up to this point, the Los Angeles freeway system might have been saved, if only the next phase of the disaster could have been prevented. Others argue that the next moments were inevitable from the first beginnings of the crystallization process. Computer simulations have given us no clear answer.

It was this simple. All of those automobiles, all of those desperate drivers too attached to their metal and plastic personalities, unwilling to leave the technological illusion of identity, security, and safety, they sat in their wombs of music, unaware that their engine temperatures were steadily, inexorably rising. The automobile engine is designed to cool itself while in motion; it needs a steady flow of air through its radiator so it can dissipate excess heat. But now, immobilized, all of those engines running without any chance of cooling, the temperatures around them rising, overheating was inevitable. The first vehicle caught fire at 3:31. Like a good idea occurring to many people simultaneously, within the next half hour, thirteen more vehicles began to smolder, and soon, flames were licking out from under the hoods of seven of them.

But the fire trucks couldn't get to them. The shoulders were jammed. Cars with plastic gas tanks exploded with surprising fury, and the fires began to spread, leaping from vehicle to vehicle with alarming speed. Drivers who only moments before had been completely resistant to leaving the comfort of their sedans panicked and fled. Soon, there were firestorms. The biggest raged on the 405 where it intersected with the 101, at the heart of the first big clot in the system. Another firestorm flickered to life further south on the 405 where it intersected with the 10. A third fire exploded just west of where the 10 intersected with the

110 and also where it fed into the 5. In a very short time, the two fires met in the middle and expanded into a terrifying wall of flame that cut across the heart of the city.

Aerial tanker drops helped to slow down the flames, but it wasn't enough. Before the end of the 7:00 news broadcast, the governor had declared the city a disaster area. All across the world, people clustered around television screens, mesmerized by an event that was both incomprehensible and horrific. Los Angeles was choking to death on its own vomit. Like a great beast shuddering to a halt, the city of the angels was collapsing and shutting down.

Even after the fires were contained, even after the last smoldering embers were extinguished, most of the inhabitants of the city continued to believe that normalcy could be restored, that someday traffic would flow again. Maybe they believed this because there were still pockets of mobility scattered throughout the urban sprawl, quiet neighborhoods where housewives could still drive to the corner market for milk and bread and eggs; but by the fourth day, as the stores began to run out of perishables, the problem of resupply became critical. How could the city feed its stranded millions?

Despite promises from local, state, and federal authorities that the freeways could be restored and working again within a few days, well, maybe two weeks at the most—all right, full recovery was probably at least a month or two away, but the city could function and survive, just a little more time, that's all we need—despite all the promises and reassurances, by the middle of the week many Angelenos were beginning to experience growing fear, frustration, and skepticism.

The city hadn't yet succumbed to panic, but the seeds were growing. Many of those who lived on the edges of the city, especially those who had access to uncongested avenues, began evacuating themselves voluntarily to other communities. In the first week alone, Orange County took in over 40,000 refugees, San Bernardino accepted 50,000; many went to the homes of friends and relatives, others went to hotels, the most desperate camped out in tent cities erected on the grounds of local high schools, colleges, and the parking lots of several major malls. But there were still over five million people within the affected areas of the city.

At least twenty thousand came out on motorcycles or motor scooters; while the trip through the surface streets was slow, it wasn't impossible. Many more rode out of the disaster area by train. Metro-Link borrowed trains from as far away as Seattle to ferry passengers from Union Station to refugee camps in Santa Barbara, San Diego, and Palmdale.

Even more came out of the frozen zone by subway and light rail. The Green Line and the Gold Line and the Blue Line were major arteries. The Red Line funneled people from the mid–San Fernando Valley down to Union Station, where they could transfer to the other colors of the rainbow, or to other trains that would take them even farther out.

A few people, not a significant number, escaped by helicopter. Van Nuys Airport and LAX became hubs of activity for those who could reach them, with planes landing and taking off as fast as the overstressed controllers could open flight paths in the sky. The lack of aviation fuel deliveries to the airports meant that planes had to fly in carrying enough fuel for their outward journeys. All of the airports in the zone were given double-black stars, an unprecedented new classification which meant that travel to or from was at-your-own-risk. It meant limited-to-zero availability of rescue and emergency vehicles and facilities.

But the refugees from deeper inside the disaster zone, where there was no access to rail or air, had the most difficulty extricating themselves. Some refugees walked as far as ten miles to reach a subway station, or a Metro-Link access. Amtrak brought in emergency trains on freight lines, putting up awnings and tents and benches to create makeshift stations at convenient street-crossings and overpasses. The crowds gathered and waited. Many arrived with bicycles, overloaded with their belongings. Red Cross helicopters lowered food and water to the waiting masses.

The disaster maps showed that almost every neighborhood within an area bounded by the 5 on the east, the 405 on the west, the 118 on the north, and the 105 on the south was pretty much immobilized to some degree or other, with tendrils of crystallization extending linearly outward from all of these routes.

While surface streets provided some relief, the spillover from the network of hardened freeways had choked most of the city's major thoroughfares. The streets were full of cars; the only reason the city had functioned before was that not every car was on the road at the same time. Now that the city was immobilized, a panic-stricken populace rushed to their automobiles to make their escape. Evacuation didn't solve the problem, it exacerbated it. Broadcasting information on viable routes out of the city was self-defeating. As soon as a route was cleared and announced, it clogged up within minutes.

On Thursday, seven days after crystallization, as part of a larger disaster-relief package, the Republican-controlled Congress passed the Insurance Emergency Relief bill, declaring the disaster an act of God, thereby freeing automobile insurers from billions of dollars of exposure. This allowed the state to declare all abandoned vehicles a public nuisance and begin the wholesale removal of freeway blockages. The outrage that followed was not limited to the survivors of the disaster.

Leaders of the Democratic party were quick to point out that the Republicans had abandoned the protection of property rights in favor of the rights of big government. While not exactly a wedge issue, it did open the door for further political divisions. The Democrats portrayed themselves as the Party of Opportunity and painted the Republicans as the Party of Opportunists. The destruction of a million automobiles was seen as a gift to an automobile industry that would clearly benefit from the need to replace those lost vehicles. The bottom line, the Democrats insisted, was that the Greedy Old Party had no heart, they had abandoned the people of Southern California in favor of protecting the interests of their corporate sponsors. The Republican Congress tried to backpedal, but the damage had already been done.

Meanwhile, estimates of the time to full recovery now varied from six months to three years. The cranes and tow trucks necessary to clear the streets would have to work their way slowly to the center of the disaster and there were no computer simulations capable of the necessary extrapolations. Where to put the extracted vehicles and how to get them there complicated the issue.

The cars couldn't be removed from the freeways, because there was no place to put them. Trying to save all these autos for their owners' eventual return meant finding storage space for them and logging their locations in a master database. Perhaps the surviving cars could be transported out to some wide-empty space out in the desert, from which owners could reclaim them. For a fee. Maybe. But did anyone really want to risk putting all these vehicles back into circulation where they could just clog the system again? The arguments were just beginning. (Some people advocated that this disaster represented an opportunity to remodel Los Angeles's dependency on automobiles and replace or augment the freeways with more light rail systems. But that particular alternative was not only an expensive proposition, it was not an immediate solution to anything.)

Even though the Vehicle Reclamation teams were now authorized to pile up cars in great towering pyramids of metal and glass and plastic wherever they found a big enough parking lot, there was enormous reluctance to do so. All those automobiles represented billions of dollars that nobody wanted to discard casually, especially not the far-removed owners. On the other hand, by the time the reclamation teams reached the majority of affected vehicles most of them would have rusted into near-total uselessness.

On the brighter side, the Los Angeles County Air Pollution Control District announced that air pollution levels for the basin had dropped dramatically. The air was cleaner than it had been since 1955 when the county finally outlawed backyard incinerators. An awkward spokesman embarrassedly announced that this was the direct result of taking a million and a half vehicles off the road, except that of course, those million and a half vehicles were still *on* the road. Just not moving anymore. But this was the *good* news. It was now safe to breathe in Los Angeles again.

Despite that incentive, the flood of refugees streaming out of the city continued, straining the resources of surrounding counties beyond the breaking point. By now, the first waves of escapees from the zone were spreading out across the continent, bringing with them sordid tales of nonvehicular terror and enough digital camera photos, phone-camera photos, and handycam videos to keep the news agencies happy for weeks. Even after the continuing live coverage abated and regular programming resumed, the networks still scheduled ongoing special reports. This was as much an opportunity as a necessity. Universal, Warner Bros., Fox, Disney, and Paramount all had their lots within the frozen zone. The production of at least sixteen major television series—including, ironically, *The O.C.*, were shut down. Although there were finished episodes of all prime-time series in the pipeline, once those were aired, new episodes would not be available until new production facilities were established, or until transportation to existing facilities could be resumed.

Every news and current events show from *60 Minutes* to *Nova* began multipart examinations of the collapse of an entire city, with alarming speculations about the possibility of similar crystallizations occurring elsewhere. Real estate values in small towns and rural areas began to climb.

The days stretched into weeks as refugees continued to stream out of the zone, sometimes as many as a hundred thousand a day. The nightly news kept a running tally on the numbers; the flood showed no signs of abating; but each succeeding day, those who had successfully escaped from L.A. seemed more and more despairing and desperate. While not quite ragged, they looked hungry and haggard, thin and wan. Many had gone for a week or more without fresh fruits and vegetables, fresh milk and other perishables. They had exchanged their tan healthy presence for more sallow dispirited complexions. The surrounding counties continued to absorb as many as they could, exporting the overflow to the rest of the nation as fast as transportation could be arranged. Amtrak borrowed Pullman cars from Canada and Mexico, and converted over a hundred freight cars into makeshift passenger units. A number of Jewish families refused to board anything that looked like a boxcar.

Entering the fourth week of the disaster, as it became apparent that this was the new normal, disaster recovery teams entering the frozen zone discovered a startling fact—some people had created ways to survive their transformed circumstances. The most amazing finding was that some Angelenos had given up their dependency on their cars and learned how to *walk*. (No, that is not a misprint. The word is *walk*.) Computer analysis of urban residential zones revealed that more than 35 percent of all residential dwellings in Los Angeles had access to supermarkets, pharmacies, banks, and other essential services within a radius of ten blocks or less. For these people, walking might be an inconvenience, but it was easier than giving up their homes. Reports from the zone suggested that in some places, neighborhoods were reinventing themselves as actual communities.

Satellite maps revealed that fully 10 percent of those who were refusing to leave their homes were planting gardens in their backyards or on their front lawns. Others were creating a new economy using bicycles and motorcycles to transship goods from subway and light rail stations into the otherwise unreachable interior of the zone. Simulations projected that 20 percent of the city's population could survive without automobile access, possibly more if enough streets could be cleared so that trucks could deliver goods to local communities—but if enough streets could be cleared, the automobiles would return.

Surprisingly—or maybe not so surprisingly—a small but growing number of people liked the new normal, and were starting to voice the opinion that they did *not* want the automobiles to return. They actually liked being able to see the Hollywood Hills clearly. They liked the way the air smelled in the morning. They liked working in the garden, walking to the corner store, actually talking to their neighbors, and living at a less frenetic pace.

Teams of sociologists who studied the phenomenon—now called disvehiclization—observed that it was not simply a rejection of the automobile, but of the entire technological cocoon that had enveloped daily life. The disvehiclized person was also more likely to leave his or her cell phone off, turning it on only for limited periods each day; the disvehiclized person rarely watched television; he or she also cut back on computer time, accessing the Internet only for essential news or shopping services.

But not everybody could afford disvehiclization; it was a luxury of the retired, and of those who could work from their homes. Those who still depended on day jobs could not survive without transportation. While the subway, light rail, and emergency bus lines were able to provide some measure of service, they were simply not designed to handle the traffic load, nor did they provide the degree of coverage necessary to the entire basin. In the first month alone, over a million people emigrated from Los Angeles to surrounding counties.

In Orange County, rents soared first, demand far exceeded supply. Real estate values followed quickly. Automobile sales took off as well, both new and used; individuals who felt their lives were dependent on their mobility were quick to replace their lost cars. For the first few weeks, car dealers all across the nation were shipping as many vehicles as they could into Ventura, San Bernardino, Santa Clarita, and Orange counties.

Commentators have called this influx of additional vehicles onto the avenues and highways of the counties surrounding Los Angeles the "squeezed mud" effect. Squeeze a handful of mud, it oozes out between your fingers; squeeze Los Angeles, and the traffic oozes out in all directions across the state. Cal-Trans projects that the post-crystallization era will see at least an additional million vehicles on the highways of the four counties surrounding Los Angeles.

Cal-Trans officials are also quick to point out that the recent stoppages on the 22, the 55, and the 91 are only localized anomalies, and not representative of any larger process. There is absolutely no reason to fear crystallization in Orange County. Absolutely no reason at all.

And Tomorrow and

BY ADAM ROBERTS

Adam Roberts is a professor of nineteenth-century literature at Royal Holloway, University of London. He has published six novels under his own name: *Salt* (2000), *On* (2001), *Stone* (2002), *Polystom* (2003), *The Snow* (2004), and *Gradisil* (2005), and is responsible for the parodies of A.R.R.R. Roberts: *The Soddit* (2003), *The McAtrix Derided* (2003), *The Sellamillion* (2004), *The Va Dinci Cod* (2005), and *Star Warped* (2005). Roberts is an SF critic and reviewer, and he has a wealth of short fiction and academic publications to his credit.

" 'And Tomorrow and' is a comic piece," Roberts said, "although not an especially cheery or giggly one. I was intrigued by the disjunction between, on the one hand, the Gordian-knot vehemence with which Macbeth unleashes violence upon the things that restrict him, and, on the other, the pedantically legalistic terms of the prophecy that is his eventual undoing. But I was more intrigued by the comic possibilities of reading this most bloody and murderous of Shakespeare's plays as an articulation of a very modern sort of heroism, the refusal to simply crumple, the refusal to give up, the discovery of a strenuous and dark Joy in the face of extinction. I was also struck that the pedantic and legalistic prophecies that doom Macbeth wouldn't stand up to ten minutes of cross-examination in a court of law by any half-decent contracts lawyer."

Find more about Adam Roberts at www.adamroberts.com.

ACT I

The castle had been abandoned by almost all of its inhabitants. Its population had decided, little point in staying only to be slaughtered by the English army, and so they crept out by ones and twos throughout the night, and they made what peace they could with the enemy. Some even begged to join Malcolm's troop, so as to be on the winning side in the morrow's inevitable English victory. When Macbeth awoke, with only Seyton in attendance, he found his halls deserted, his battlements unguarded. "Let them fly!" he blustered, striding up the stone stairs to survey the scene from the top of his tallest tower. "I bear a charméd life. I need them not!"

He looked down upon the investing force: a mass of humanity stretching as far as the eye could see. They had thrown down the boughs and branches that they had taken from Birnam Wood, and now stood in serried ranks, their armor and their weapons glittering in the morning sunlight.

"It looks bad sir," said Seyton, in a miserable voice.

"Nonsense!" boomed Macbeth. "We cannot be defeated."

"But the charm, sir," said Seyton, cringing a little as if expecting Macbeth to strike him in his furious frustration. "Has it not tricked you? It said you would never vanquished be, till Great Birnam Wood should come to high Dunsinane hill."

"Indeed it *did*," said Macbeth, with enormous self-satisfaction.

"And we need but look, sir!" said Seyton, indicating the host that lay spread before them. "Malcolm's army has brought Birnam Wood hither!"

"Seyton, Seyton, Seyton," said Macbeth, genially. He clasped his servant about the shoulders and gave the top of his head a little rub with the knuckles of his right hand. "You've got to *pay* more *attention*. The one crucial thing about magical prophecies is that they are enormously and pedantically *precise*. So, what—Malcolm's army cut down a few boughs and carried them along to Dunsinane! That's *hardly* the same thing as the forest moving! Ask yourself this . . . if you were a mapmaker—"

"Mapmaker," repeated Seyton, nodding uncertainly.

"—yes, if you were *making a map*—for the sake of argument, you know—and you were making a map of Scotland, where would you put Birnam Wood? Over there on the distant hill"—he pointed to the horizon where the blue-green forest still lay like a cloud against the horizon— "the location of the *trunks* and *roots* and most of the *foliage*? Or here at Dunsinane, where a few thousand branches and leaves have been carried?"

"Um," said Seyton, tentatively offering his answer like a schoolchild before a stern schoolmaster, "the first one?"

"Exactly! Birnam *Wood* is still on the *hill*. The prophecy has not been fulfilled. I am, accordingly, *un*worried."

From below came the sound of repeated thuds. Malcolm's sappers, in the unusual position of being able to work without resistance from castle defenders, were knocking down the main gate with a large battering ram. "Right," said Macbeth. "Better put on some armor. Not that I need it. More for the show of it than anything."

With a great crash the gate gave way.

By the time he got downstairs, armored and besworded, Macbeth's main courtyard was filled with several hundred English soldiers. At the front of this fierce crowd were Macduff and young Siward. Siward made a rush at Macbeth, hurrying up the stone stairway to engage the Scottish king. Macbeth chopped his head off with a single stroke of his sword.

The crowd in the courtyard hissed their disapproval.

Rather relishing the theatricality of it, Macbeth cried out: "Begone, Macduff! You cannot kill me!"

The general hissing turned into a general laughing.

"Do you boast so?" said Macduff, cockily, throwing his sword from hand to hand and starting up the stairs. "We outnumber you, fiendish tyrant! Outnumber you considerably."

"What you've got to keep in mind," said Macbeth, "is that I bear a charméd life that must not yield to one of woman born. Actually."

"Ha!" cried Macduff. "Ah! Ha! Well!" He seemed very pleased with himself. "Despair thy charm," he said. "And let the angel that thou still hast served tell thee, Macduff—that's *me*—was from his mother's womb untimely *ripped*!' He stuck his chest out.

"You were still born of woman, though, weren't you?" Macbeth pointed out.

The courtyard had fallen silent.

"You what?" said Macduff.

"Born of woman nevertheless. Born—you. Woman—your mother."

"Ah no, but Macduff was from his mother's womb untimely *ripped*..."

"Yes yes, Caesarian section, named after Julius Caesar, the Roman emperor who was born via a surgical incision into the wall of the abdomen rather than through the birth canal," said Macbeth. "Yes we all know about that. But it's still a form of *birth*, isn't it? You're still *born*, and *of woman*.'

"No I wasn't."

"Yes you were."

"Wasn't."

"What would you call it then? Are you really asserting that being born by Caesarian section is not *being born?*"

"Um," said Macduff, a little confusedly. "Untimely ripped... um..."

"I tell you what," said Macbeth. "Let's pop along to the castle library, and look it up in a dictionary. That'll decide the matter."

"All right," said Macduff, brightening.

So they made their way to the library, stacked floor to ceiling with dusty folios and quartos and octavos. There Macbeth pulled the *Dictionarius* from its resting place, plonked it on a desk and turned its heavy pages.

"Here you go," said Macbeth, with his finger on the relevant definition. "*Sectura Caesaris* 'form of birth in which the infant is delivered through an incision in the mother's uterus and abdominal wall rather than the more conventional birth canal.' There you are—'a form of birth.' In other words: you are still born of woman, regardless of whatever obstetric interventions happened to be used at the birth. You might as well say that the use of *forceps* meant that you were no longer 'born of woman'!"

"Well..." said Macduff, scratching his chin. "I suppose you're right..."

"Have at you!" said Macbeth, standing back and raising his sword.

Twenty people had followed the two of them to the library; and so it was that twenty people watched Macbeth and Macduff fight for about a minute and a half, clanging their swords together vehemently and grunting, until Macbeth swung a blow that Macduff failed to intercept, cleaved through his helm and split his head open. Macduff dropped to the floor dead.

"Right," said Macbeth, cheerily. "Who's next?"

ACT II

It took Macbeth less than five minutes to cut his way through the soldiers in the library. No matter how they swung or stabbed, their swords always slid away from Macbeth's body. It was, as one of them observed (just prior to having his leg fatally severed with a lunging swordstroke, such that he fell and quickly bled to death) the *weirdest* thing.

Macbeth, his armor smeared with blood, strode along the corridor and out into the courtyard. With a cheer the crowd there surged toward him; but he was not dismayed. It was, from his point of view, a simple matter to stand his ground hacking and chopping targets as they presented themselves. His assailers soon discovered that swords aimed howsoever accurately and forcefully would glide from his armor as if they had been merely glancing blows wielded infirmly. When a hundred had fallen and Macbeth was still unscathed, the heart rather went out of the advance party. A few tried upping the general mood of heroic battle by yelling war cries and running at Macbeth. Many more retreated precipitously through the main gate.

Macbeth followed them.

The carnage that ensued passed rapidly through various stages, being by turns astonishing, distressing, and, ultimately, frankly, rather boring. Wherever Macbeth walked, his sword brought death to dozens. When its blade was too chipped to cut effectively, he simply threw it aside and picked up a sword from one of the many corpses he had created.

At the beginning of this assault by one single attacker, Malcolm ordered a general charge. But from his vantage point of being on horse-back on the hill, he realized—though he could scarcely credit it—that not one of the swords, maces, arrows, or spears aimed at Macbeth was able to pierce his skin. His casualties began to mount up. He changed tactics: ordering a phalanx of men to press forward in the hopes of tramping or crushing the singleton enemy. But that was equally ineffective, and after two score men or more had been slain the phalanx as a whole broke up. Malcolm issued another order for a general crush, and the entire army—tens of thousands of men—surrounded Macbeth and tried to press in. There followed a quarter of an hour of uncertain alarum. But Malcolm soon became aware that a great circular wall of his own dead soldiers was being piled around Macbeth.

By the end of the day Macbeth had single-handedly killed over eight hundred men. This slaughter had tired him out, and he made his way back into the castle—which was, of course, wholly overrun by Malcolm's soldiers—mounted the stairs to his chamber, and went to sleep in his bed. "Now!" cried Malcolm, when this news was relayed to him. "Kill him in his bed! Stab him! Smother him while he snores!"

But no matter how they tried, none of the men under Malcolm's command were able to force the life out of the supine body of Macbeth. Blades skittered harmlessly off his skin. The pillow placed over his face, and even partially stuffed into his mouth, prevented him from breathing; but the lack of air in no way incommoded the sleeping man. They piled great stones on him, but no matter how great the weight Macbeth's body was uncrushable.

Finally the dawn came and Macbeth awoke, yawning and stretching. After a little light breakfast of poisoned bread and adulterated kippers (neither malign substance having any effect upon him) he resumed killing. He took it easier on this second day, careful not to wear himself out; and accordingly he worked longer and more efficiently: by dusk he had killed over a thousand men. Malcolm's army, hugely discouraged, was starting to melt away; deserters slinking back to Birnam Wood and away to the south.

On the third day Macbeth killed another thousand, along with Malcolm himself. After that it was a simple matter to either kill off or else chase away the remnants of the army, and by dusk of this day the place was his.

It fell to Macbeth himself to clear away all the corpses. He had, after all, no servants—Seyton had been hanged from a gibbet on the first day's battle—and he could not command any. So over a period of a week or so he dug a large pit at the rear of the castle and dragged the thousands of bodies into it.

ACT III

Life settled down a bit after that. He found that he didn't *need* to eat; although he was still aware of hunger, and still capable of deriving sensual pleasure from good food. So he scavenged the nearby countryside and occupied himself with wandering about the empty castle, cooking himself food, heating himself bath water, thinking, sleeping.

He pondered the charms that protected him, meditating the precise limits the witches had established. They had not, for instance, said that 'no *man* of woman born can harm Macbeth' (which would have left open the chance that a *woman*, or *child*, of woman-born could kill him): they had specified *none* of woman born. That seemed safe enough. The other charm was even more heartening: *Macbeth shall never vanquished be,* they had said, *until Birnam Wood to high Dunsinane castle shall come against him.* Vanquished meant killed by an enemy; but it also, he reasoned, meant poisoned, killed by sickness, laid low by old age, or any of the consequences of mortal existence. Until the wood actually uprooted itself and travelled wholesale to his castle, none of these fates could befall him. That was indeed a powerful charm.

After three months a second army came to beseige his castle. This time it was led by the English king Edward in person; and he brought with him, in addition to many soldiers, a huge assemblage of holy men, wizards, magi, and people otherwise magically inclined who had promised to undo the charm that preserved Macbeth's life.

Macbeth rather welcomed the distraction. Life had settled into quite a tedious rut.

He made sure, this time, to do all his killing outside the castle walls, so as not to leave himself the awkward job of clearing dead bodies out of his corridors, rooms and stairwells afterward. And he especially took pleasure in slaughtering the magicians, most of whom were armed with nothing more than wands, books of spells, and crucifixes. Macbeth found and killed King Edward himself on day four, but it took a whole week for the army as a whole to become discouraged. Eventually the whole force broke up and fled, apart from a few hardened types who threw themselves at Macbeth's feet and pledged allegiance to him as the Witch King of the North. He swore them into his service.

ACT IV

Every now and again, over the ensuing hundred years or so, Macbeth would gather around him a band of followers—men either in awe of his magic immunity, or else simply prepared to follow any figure in authority if the financial inducements were strong enough. But these groupings never added up to an army, and since none of the people who followed him were gifted with his invulnerability, they tended to get slaughtered in battle. His initial plan—to reclaim the throne of Scotland by war and by the sword—was, he came to realize, unattainable. People feared him, and a few would do his will; but most shunned him, would not follow him. He found himself thoroughly isolated.

Eventually he stopped accumulating bands of followers and struck out by himself.

He roamed about for many years, searching Scotland for the witches in the hope of extracting from them some useful magical fillip that would enhance his fortunes. But they seemed to have departed the land.

His search was fruitless. He returned to Dunsinane castle to find that it had been claimed, in his absence, by the Thane of Aberdeen and his retinue. It didn't take Macbeth long to kill off, or chase away, those interlopers.

For several decades after this, he sat in his castle alone. The people in the local villages established a mode of uneasy coexistence with him: they brought him offerings of food, wine, books, and whatever else he asked for; but they otherwise left him alone and went about their own business. Macbeth grew accustomed to the solitude, and even came rather to relish it. He had learned to despise ordinary humanity, with their ridiculous fleshly vulnerability, their habit of dropping dead at the slightest scratch, the inevitability of their physical aging, decay, and death. He wondered why it was he had ever wanted to rule over such starveling creatures. It seemed to him now as a butcher sitting in a throne and gathering his swine around him as courtiers. Mortal glory was no longer of interest to him.

The castle began to decay around him. He undertook some repairs himself, single-handed; but no amount of rampaging around the local villages like a fairy-story ogre—no amount of railing and yelling—could persuade the villagers to help him. None of them was prepared to come and work as his servant, at even the highest pay. Rather they fled away, took refuge in the hills until he had departed.

Increasingly reclusive, Macbeth devoted himself to gathering together and reading the world's many books. Word spread of this mysterious hermit-laird (though by now most people had forgotten his name) who paid handsomely in gold for any book of curious lore or magical promise. Book traders made their way to the castle, pocketed their fees, and hurried away again, glad to be gone. When Macbeth's gold was exhausted, he strode out into the larger world and ransacked and robbed and extorted until his fortune was restored. He hoped, by accumulating the world's largest library of magical arcana, and by decades of dedicated study, to master the same supernatural skills that the witches themselves had possessed. Why should he track down those wild women and beg them for favors, when he could command the magic himself?

But no matter how much he studied and practiced, he could not develop magical ability.

More than this, he realized that the charm had changed him. He decided to found a dynasty, reasoning that even if his children grew old and died he could still live as patriarch over his own grandchild, great-grandchildren, more distant descendents yet and on into the abyss of future time. He could persuade no woman willingly to marry him of course, but it was a simple matter to abduct likely looking specimens from the locality. But no matter how long he kept them, and no matter what he did, not one of them became pregnant with his offspring. He realized that whatever it was that was acting upon his body to preserve it from death and harm was also preventing him from fathering children.

At this he fell into a depression for several decades; barely moving from his chamber, letting his hair and beard and nails grow to prodigious lengths. He attempted to kill himself—an honorable, warrior's death, falling on his own sword like Mark Anthony. But he was himself born of woman, and incapable of harming himself.

After that he did various things. He spent much of the thirteenth century traveling the world; first as an anonymous foot soldier of the crusades, and thereafter as a curious tourist walking and riding to Cathay, to Siberia, over the ice to Alaska, and across the great plains of the New World. If I were to detail his adventures, this story would stretch through thousands of pages, and marvelous though the adventures were, they would come to seem tedious to you. He roamed through Central and South America, and finally traveled back to Europe on one of Cortez's ships. Bored of travel, he made his way back to Scotland. Once again his castle had been occupied, but he disposed of the family living there and retook possession.

For a decade or so this reinstallation in his own home provided him with various distractions. Enraged villagers, and later religiously devout armies, came to destroy him—now once again infamous (after many decades of anonymity) far and wide as a devil in human form, a warlock who had sold his soul to the devil, and many like phrases. They burned his castle around him, but the flames did not bother him. Instead he walked amongst them bringing death with his sword. Eventually they fled. They always fled eventually. It took Macbeth a decade to rebuild Dunsinane, working entirely by himself, but he found he quite enjoyed the work.

In the year 1666 he became intrigued by the idea that the world might be about to end. Traveling preachers assured the world that the apocalypse promised by Saint John was imminent. Would his charm survive the end of the world? He thought about this a great deal and decided it would not. He had come to the conclusion that the operative part of his charm—the "none of woman born shall harm Macbeth"—was the *woman*. Mary, mother of God, had been a virgin. Therefore she was a girl rather than a woman: and Christ was not of woman born. At his second coming, Macbeth decided, there would exist in the world a person capable of destroying him—an end he looked forward to with complete equanimity. But 1666 turned into 1667, and then into 1668, and the end of the world did not come. Macbeth reconciled himself to a genuinely immortal life. He discovered that immortality tasted not of glory, not even especially of life. It was a gray sort of experience, neither markedly happy nor sad. It was the life stones experience. It was the reason they were so silent and unmoved. It was the existence of the ocean itself, changeless though restless, chafing yet moveless. It was Macbeth's existence.

ACT V

There was a knocking at the door.

Nobody had knocked at his door for a decade or more. His last visitor had been the census taker, and Macbeth—who had learned this lesson from experience long before—had disposed of him swiftly rather than risk having his precious solitude disturbed. Maps marked Dunsinane as a folly; Macbeth had gone to great lengths to dig out underground dwellings and knock down much of the upper portion, so as not to be too conspicuous from the air. What with the reforestation of pretty much the whole of Scotland following the European Act of '57 his home was well hidden: off the ramblers trails and not listed in any land tax spreadsheets.

So who was knocking?

He clambered up the stairs to the main hall and pulled open the door. Outside, standing in the rain (Macbeth, sequestered in his underground laboratory, had not even realized it was raining) was a man. He was wearing the latest in bodymorph clothes, a purple plastic cape that rolled into a seam of his shirt as he stepped over the threshold, and dynstripes in his hair.

"May I come in?" he asked, politely enough.

"I don't welcome visitors," said Macbeth.

"That's as may be, sir," said the man. "But I have official accreditation." He held out a laminated badge for Macbeth's perusal; an animated glyph of the man's face smiled and nodded at him repeatedly from the badge. "And the legal right of entry."

Macbeth thought of killing him there and then, but he held back. He hadn't talked to another human being in two years. He was curious as to what errand had brought this official individual so deep into the woods.

As he shut the door behind him he asked, "So what is it you want?"

"Are you, sir, a relation of the *Macbeth* family?" the man asked.

Now this was a startling thing. The people of this part of Scotland had long, long ago forgotten Macbeth's name and true identity. He lived, where he was not entirely forgotten, as a kind of legend; stories of an ogre who could not be killed, of a wizard with the gift of immortality. "How do you know that name?"

"Databases worldwide have been linked and cross-Web searched," the man said in a slightly sing-song voice. "Various anomalies have been detected. It is my job—assigned me by my parent company, McDF Inc.—to investigate these. The deeds to this property have not been filed in eleven hundred years. The last listed owner was a Mr. Macbeth. I am here to discover whether this property is still in the possession of that family, in order to register it for Poll Tax, Land Reclamation Tax, and various other government and EU duties."

This told Macbeth all he needed to know. This taxman would have to die or Macbeth's life would be disturbed, and he hated disturbance. He reached this conclusion with a heavy heart. The youthful enthusiasm for slaughter had long since passed from his breast. Now, from his immortal perspective, the mayfly humans who were born, grew, and died all around him were objects rather of pity than scorn. Still, necessity overrode his compassion. If it must be done (as, of course, it *must*) it was well it was done quickly.

He pulled a sword from the wall and squared up to the puny individual. "I'm afraid," he announced, "that I cannot be disturbed by taxes and duties. I value my solitude."

"I must warn you, sir," said the taxman, holding up one finger in a slightly prissy gesture, "that I am licensed to defend myself from unprovoked attack. My parent company, having invested thirty-eight million Euros in my development, are legally entitled to preserve their investment from unnecessary harm."

Macbeth only shook his head. He swung the sword. The blade crashed against the man's shoulder; instead of severing it as Macbeth expected, the collision resulted in a series of sparks and fizzes, and a scattering of gray smoke into the air.

"You have caused several thousand Euros damage," said the strange man, "to my right arm. I must inform you that my manufacturers, McDF Inc., are legally entitled to recover that sum from your bank account."

Puzzling, Macbeth wrenched the sword free and lifted it for another sweep, aiming this time at the taxman's head.

"I do apologize for this, sir," the taxman said, with a mournful expression on his face. He pointed a finger at Macbeth. The end of the finger clicked out and swiveled to the side. With a loud *thwup* sound a projectile launched itself from the hollow digit and smashed into Macbeth's chest. More astonished than in pain, he dropped his sword and collapsed backward onto the stone flags.

The strange taxman, leaning over him now, was speaking into a communicator of some kind. "Please send a medical team at once. Unmarked and unnamed property, located near the center of Greater Birnam Wood. Lock onto my signal. Please hurry; subject is badly wounded." He peered down at Macbeth, who was already losing focus in his eyes, with the sheer oddness of this feeling—these smashed ribs—this blood (which had stayed safely in his veins through all these centuries) spilling onto the floor. It was, he had to admit, and despite the pain involved, a feeling something like—release.

"I do apologize for doing that, sir," the taxman was saying. "I have called an air ambulance to assist. I do hope, sir, that they arrive here before you die."

"Oh I do hope," said Macbeth, in a gaspy voice, "not."

Abductio ad Absurdum

BY ESTHER M. FRIESNER

Esther M. Friesner is an author, poet, short story writer, editor, and self-proclaimed Queen of the Hamsters. Perhaps best known for editing the ever-popular Chicks in Chainmail series of anthologies (*Chicks in Chainmail, Chicks N' Chained Males, Did You Say Chicks?, The Chick Is in the Mail,* and *Turn the Other Chick*), Friesner most recently teamed up with fellow funnyman Robert Asprin for the novel *E. Godz.* She has won the Nebula Award twice, for her short stories "Death and the Librarian" and "A Birth Day."

According to Friesner, "Abductio ad Absurdum" was written as the result of one too many TV programs and/or tabloid stories about alien abductions. "I had reached my saturation point when it came to media coverage of the ongoing set-to between Evolutionists and Creationists," she says. "And so, in an effort to forget that there was nothing good on TV I began to wonder: How long *has* this alien abduction thing been going on? Besides aliens, what other beings have been known to snatch up earthlings? Even those humans who share a common cause seem unable to set aside competition in favor of cooperation. How would beings that are supposed to be superior to humans deal with such a situation? What if *everyone* was right about what happened Way Back When? Am I going to have fun writing about this?" The answer to the last question being affirmative, the rest is history.

Esther Friesner lives in Connecticut with her husband, two children, two rambunctious cats, and a fluctuating population of hamsters.

"I beg your pardon," said the alien. "There appears to have been some mistake."

"I should say so," his unwilling guest replied with an indignant snort. He made a great business of shaking the rumples out of his robes and brushing invisible specks of dust from his person. "And you've made it."

The alien's luminous blue skin went watery green, a sure sign of embarrassment. Probing himself sheepishly with one barbed tentacle, he sidled over to the viewing panel of the little scout ship, his slime trail minty with dismay. "I can't for the lives of me understand what went wrong," he bubbled, all five eyes sliding wildly over the surface of his head, searching the banks of screens and telltales for the elusive answer. "I was aiming for the brown, hairy one. You're neither, if you don't mind my saying so."

"Bah," was all the answer the visitor deigned to return. One toss of his head and his long, golden curls took on a life of their own, filling the control pod with the radiance of a thousand dawns.

"Oh my. You can do—you're certainly not—What else might you be able to—? Dear me." The calculated display of celestial splendor threw the alien for more of a loop than the one he was already riding. At a complete loss, he sucked a tentacle nervously, forgetting about the barbs, and cut his rubbery lip badly.

His abrupt cry of pain wrought a radical change in his conscripted guest. Light flared from the visitor's hand, a spout of flame that congealed into the dimensions of a sword, but when the fire dimmed, the object showed itself to be no more than an olive branch. Waving the lithe bit of greenery in a no-nonsense-now manner, the alien's abductee seized his captor's oozing face and declared, "Let me see that. I'm a trained professional. Healing's my specialty, not these ridiculous reconnaissance assignments."

The alien eyed his captive charily, three of them firmly fixed on the visitor, a pair left over to mind the ship's controls. The olive branch whisked across his lips, leaving a pleasant tingling sensation in its wake and filling his scent receptors with the rich perfume of the homeworld jungles. He gave a little shudder of ecstacy and molted in spite of himself.

The visitor jumped back, his disgust plain to see. "What was *that* all about?" he demanded, toeing the alien's sloughed skin with one golden-sandaled foot.

The alien went positively emerald out of sheer mortification. As with many species, he immediately sought to counteract his discomfiture by going on the offensive. (*It Is Better to Bluff Than to Squirm* is a dictum embroidered on samplers all across the universe and outnumbers *Home*

Sweet Home by a factor of a trillion and three.) His whole attitude toward his peculiar guest turned crisp and curt. "Look, I don't have time for this," he said. "I've got a job to do; a job *you're* delaying."

"And what do you think *I'm* supposed to be doing with *my* time?" came the testy reply. "Planting fig trees? I was just about to Reveal myself to the chosen creatoid when *zap!*—I'm jerked right off the earth to *this* Himforsaken place. Not that He isn't everywhere, of course, but you get my meaning," he added quickly.

"Uh . . . sure I do," said the alien, who didn't. "But what's a . . . creatoid?"

The visitor sighed, and the smaller plumes edging his mighty wings riffled delicately in the breeze. "A creatoid is something that *He* created, naturally. Only it's something that—well—something that's not *exactly* like the rest of His creations. You see, most of His work's got a fairly straightforward purpose, a clear-cut and obvious use or function. It's there for a *reason.* Trees give fruit and shade and a nice place for cats to sharpen their claws. Mosquitoes give frogs something to eat, frogs feed storks, storks bring babies. Otters and dolphins and larks make joy more than just a word, even if the Word *did* get here before the otter. Platypuses are comic relief and Tyrannosaurs keep the rest of them on their toes—those of them that have toes. But *these* things, these creatoids—" He sighed again.

"Which ones?" The alien glided back to the viewing panel. It was filled with a glowing, golden vista of the wide African savannah. Vast herds of herbivores meandered lazily across the plain. Steel-muscled packs of predators crouched in the tall grass, awaiting developments. In the foreground, a lone, brown, hairy being huddled in the branches of the only tree to be seen for a hundred yards around. Her tiny, bright eyes scanned the horizon anxiously. At the foot of the tree lay a number of bones, including a skull showing the same aggressively overdeveloped brow-ridges as her own. All bore the marks of a big cat's busy jaws and all were proof of how right she was to be vigilant, terrified, and arboreal.

"*That's* the one!" the alien's guest exclaimed, delighted. "That's my assigned creatoid right there!"

"That one's *your* target too?" asked the alien.

"Too?" This was not the sort of Revelation to which the visitor was accustomed. "You don't mean it. What business could you possibly have with something like *that?*"

"Hey, I just get my orders from the group-supes and if I know what's good for me I follow them, no questions asked. What I was told to do was come to this planet and check out certain designated life-forms for any signs of potential higher intelligence that might prove worthwhile for us to nurture, develop, and encourage."

"Why?"

"I told you, I don't ask questions. What were *you* supposed to do with that—*creatoid*—before you got in my way?"

"It's like I was saying: Where I come from, at the moment we're none of us too sure why He bothered creating something like that, so my superiors commanded me to descend and investigate. I've got to find out what *use* it is. Not that we're questioning His grand design or anything, perish the thought, but we *would* like to have a clue as to whether we should ignore it, sustain it, or accidentally-on-purpose smite it out of existence before things get *too* far out of hand. And so, if you'll excuse me—" There was a burst of light and the alien felt momentarily trapped within the heart of a C-major chord before regaining full use of his senses. When most of his eyes could once more focus, he found himself alone in the scout ship.

The alien was rather miffed. Usually the beings he brought aboard were powerless to leave until he was through studying them. This was the first time that one of his subjects had left of its own will, under its own figurative steam. He checked the view panel. Yes, there it was, wings and all, back on the savannah, standing among the bones at the foot of the solitary tree. It seemed smaller than it had been on board ship, *much* smaller, shrewmouse-small, so small that the brown, hairy thing up the tree didn't even notice its presence below.

"Clever," the alien muttered. "Less likely to scare off your target, that way. And you're a nimble little bugger, aren't you? Flashing here, there, and everywhere like that, getting right in the way of my snag-beam when I was trying to lay hold of that—that—creatoid-thingy. Well, young teleporter-me-lad, you may be fast and you may be clever, but you're not going to muck up *my* service record. I saw her first."

The alien hunted up a portable, tentacle-held model of the aforementioned snag-beam, checked it out and strapped it on. "*This* way I won't miss," he told himself, his newly healed lip taut with a grim smile. "There's nothing like the up-close-and-personal touch."

He slid over to another part of the ship's controls, flickered his barbs over buttons, switches, sensors and knobbly things, then stepped into the center of the glowing disc that materialized in the middle of the deck. The light was cool and smelled of vanillaworms, a superfluous sensory input that allowed the traveler to relax and forget about the fact that his disassembled particles were being spewed through space. It was also mildly hallucinogenic.

The alien enjoyed a good snort of vanillaworm as much as the next entity. He was always sad when the light of the translocator beam faded and the trip was over, but work awaited. Thick grass cushioned his bulk until his gravitation adjusters kicked in, making his atmospheriskin crackle loudly. He was right under the tree and ready for business.

It was just then that his former visitor chose to rear up to a magnificent height, bringing him eye-level with the creature in the branches. "Be not afraid!" the alien's erstwhile guest declared cheerily, extending an olive branch that became the biggest banana the young world had ever seen.

It was history's worst case of bad timing since the last comet strike. The creature in the tree looked from winged messenger to blue blob, from titanic banana to bells-and-whistles ray gun, bared her fangs, let out a screech that got the attention of every pack of giant hyenas on the plains, and launched herself from the branches. She hit the ground running on all fours, but soon picked up speed and was skimming along on her hind limbs until she was no more than a speck in the distance.

The alien and his former guest exchanged a significant look. "That does it. I quit," the alien said at last. "I'm going home and I'm going to tell them that the creatures were all extinct when I got here."

"But that's a lie," the visitor chided.

"The truth is as much a matter of *when* as it is of *what*," the alien countered. "I live a long way away from here. Who's to say what the truth will be by the time I get home? I mean, come on, honestly, do you think something *that* weak and scrawny's got what it takes to survive much longer?" He picked up a chewed-over legbone and used it to point in the direction his elusive target had bolted. "No claws, no horns, and did you get a look at those sorry excuses for fangs? Pitiful."

The visitor shrugged his mighty wings and absently took a bite of the banana. "I suppose you're right. But still, *I* can't lie about this to my superiors. We've got all sorts of administrative policies in place against stuff like that. They're going to insist I come back and do something about that critter, Who knows what. Maybe I'll get lucky. Maybe by the time they do decide what to do about it, it *will* be extinct."

"You can always hope," the alien suggested amiably.

"And pray." The visitor stopped chewing a mouthful of banana long enough to notice that he'd been snacking on his symbol of office. "Want some?" he asked, blushing.

It was a slip that never should have happened. It was an action forbidden by every basic regulation in the alien's training, but the higgledy-piggledy state of his mission made him forgetful and careless. He took the fruit and ate of it, relishing its sweetness. Only then did the full knowledge of what he'd done hit him.

"Oh, my God!" he cried.

"Your what?" asked the visitor.

The alien wasn't listening. "What have I done? I'm contaminated! Doomed! I consumed extraplanetary nourishment! Who knows what sort of microbes it's carrying? Even if it doesn't kill me, I can't go home again and risk introducing potentially fatal organisms to my people. I'm an exile, an outcast forever!" He began to leak copiously.

The visitor was abashed. "The sin is mine," he said, full of contrition. "I was the one who enticed you to eat it."

"That's not going to make a lot of difference to my group-supes," the alien blubbered.

The visitor nibbled his lower lip and cast a mindful glance skywards. "I probably shouldn't even be suggesting this to you, but . . . do you *have* to tell them about it?"

"You know nothing of our reentry procedures, so save your breath. The first thing they do to you is run you through a battery of diagnostic devices that can tell what your eggmom had for breakfast the day she extruded you. If I *tried* to return, they'd immolate me before I could finish saying, 'But it wasn't my fault!' I don't *want* to be immolated."

"You won't have to be," the visitor said, suddenly sanguine. "Listen, I've got an idea: If you can't go home again, why not stay? It's not such a bad world. I can make one or two little changes to your body so that you won't have any problems living here."

"You could do that?" The alien's tears were already hardening to chunks of amber.

"I *said* I'm a healer. Healing changes your body, so why shouldn't changing your body count as healing? Now let me see . . ." He rolled up the sleeves of his resplendent gold and silver robes and set to work. "First I'll fix it so you can breathe the air, drink the water, eat the food, the whole basic package. Now then, the gravity's a bit more than you're used to, so we'll have to go with a low-slung chassis, something simple yet elegant, not too fussy—I'm working without an olive branch here, and I never was much of an artist, but still . . . there! Done."

The alien tasted the air with his freshly forked tongue and swayed from side to side, surveying the scaly length of his new body. "Not bad. I look like one of my old tentacles. But what's with the four little legs?" he asked. "I mean, these stomach muscles can take me anywhere I want to go, so what's the *point*?"

"Most of the land-creatoids I've seen have them," the visitor said. "I was just going along with the trend. If you don't like them, we can try getting them removed later on. Happy?"

"I guess," the alien allowed grudgingly. "I'd be happier if I had somewhere a bit safer to live, though. Have you smelled the air? It reeks of carnivores, and in case you hadn't noticed, I'm carnal. I don't think these dinky little legs are going to outrun any halfway healthy meat-eater."

"Where would you like to live?"

"Oh, I don't know. Some nice, green garden spot with a lot more trees and bushes and plants. Especially trees. It's always safer in the trees."

The visitor bent down and picked up the alien, draping him around his neck. "I know just the place," he said, heading east. "Very tranquil, very safe, and not too many other inhabitants, none of them carnivores. A little isolated, but that's all to the good. I just hope you won't find it too, well, boring."

"Don't worry about me," the alien said with a hissy chuckle. "If it becomes too tedious, I can always do a spot of recreational research with any accessible subjects. Most experiments are nothing more than minor variations on the universal theme of 'What do you suppose would happen to *this* if I did *that*?' I'll find what to keep me busy, never fear. Once a scientist, always a scientist."

For some reason known but to the Source of otters, anthropoids, angels, and aliens alike, the new-made serpent's words made the visitor shudder to the roots of his shining wings.

In the Matter of Fallen Angels

BY JACQUELINE CAREY

Jacqueline Carey is the best-selling author of the critically acclaimed Kushiel's Legacy trilogy of fantasy novels (*Kushiel's Dart, Kushiel's Choice,* and *Kushiel's Avatar*) and The Sundering epic fantasy duology (*Banewreaker* and *Godslayer*). Her short stories have appeared in the anthologies *Emerald Magic: Great Tales of Irish Fantasy* and *I-94: A Collection of Southwest Michigan Writers.* She has also written a nonfiction coffee-table book on Angels entitled *Angels: Celestial Spirits in Art & Legend.*

Over the course of writing *Angels* and developing the theology woven into the setting of the Kushiel's Legacy series, Carey did a fair bit of research into angelology. "In the Matter of Fallen Angels" has absolutely nothing to do with any of it. Rather, it was inspired by the distant memory of reading a short story by Gabriel Garcia Marquez, "A Very Old Man with Enormous Wings," a piece of magic realism that uses the manifestation of the miraculous to explore unattractive aspects of human nature. "In the Matter of Fallen Angels" utilizes a similar device in an inverse manner. It's a much lighter and more modest piece, surreal and absurd. And although it's centered on the extraordinary, in the end, it's the ordinary, simple joys and rhythms of small-town life that it celebrates.

Jacqueline Carey lives in Michigan. You can find out more about Jacqueline Carey and her work at www.jacquelinecarey.com.

No one could ever say for sure when it happened, that is, whether it happened before midnight or after or on the stroke. Even religion was no help in the matter, because if you read the event one way it was likely that it happened on the Sabbath, but if you read it the other then it was likely that it happened after, and who knew what it meant if it happened on the crux?

And there's always heat lightning at night in the summer in these parts. Sometimes it flickers all night long and maybe that night it was an omen of great portent, but it seemed just like any old summer night in Utopia. If you had walked around town that evening and asked if anyone thought that an angel would fall to earth behind Garrett Ainsworth's general store, everyone would have laughed. Utopia may be a two-horse town in the middle of nowhere, but the people who live there aren't crazy and most of them even have satellite dishes.

It was one of those mornings when it seems like the atmosphere has cleared its throat overnight and awakened to sing the sun up into a robin's-egg blue sky, fine and bright and promising that all things are possible, which is exactly what Quinn Parnell was thinking on his way to the General—what everyone in Utopia called the general store—for a cup of coffee and a quick catch-up on the weekend's news before his office hours started. Because he was an atheist as well as the town lawyer, the parameters in which the anything Quinn felt was possible might occur did not extend to include the supernatural. What he thought was that it was the sort of morning on which you might buy a winning lottery ticket or suddenly fall in love with a woman you've seen every day for ten years. And because this is the sort of morning it was, when Quinn first saw that no one was sitting on the General's porch drinking coffee and exchanging gossip, he thought that Garrett Ainsworth had woken up with fly-fishing fever and closed shop for the day.

This was something that happened without warning three or four times a year, a sort of Norman Rockwell syndrome. Utopia was prone to sudden attacks of rural quaintness. It was that small a town.

But today this was not the case, and when Quinn reached the porch he saw that the General was open, and when he went inside he found that the General was deserted. A fresh pot of coffee sat full and untouched on the burner. The cold storage units hummed. The ceiling fan rotated on low speed, creating eddies in the dust motes that hung in the slanting beams of the early morning sun. Quinn was standing in the main aisle and rubbing his chin when the screen door at the rear of the store creaked open.

"Quinn," said Bobby MacReary, who did construction work when there was any to be had and played backgammon at the General all day when there was not. He wore a very peculiar expression this morning. "Come here."

Garrett Ainsworth lived above the General and his backyard was a large, fenced lot. At the far end it bordered Foxglove Creek and was shady and green. The area right behind the General was barren dirt sporting a barbecue pit, two picnic tables and, this morning, the recumbent form of a fallen angel.

"I'll be damned," Old Man Stoat was saying as Quinn followed Bobby out the back door. It sounded as though he were saying it for the fiftieth time already that morning, which he was. Garrett Ainsworth had his hands shoved deep in his pockets and wasn't saying anything, but then he was always more of a listener than a talker.

The angel at first glance looked like a toppled statue, except for the wings. It was lying on its side and would have been facing them, only its left wing covered its face so they couldn't see it. It was not moving.

"What the hell is it?" Quinn asked.

"Can't be sure," said Garrett Ainsworth, "but it looks like an angel."

This was true. It looked exactly like, and like nothing but, an angel.

"Is it alive?" asked Quinn.

"I think so," Garrett said. He also wore a very peculiar expression on his face.

Except for a length of dazzlingly white cloth artfully girded about its loins, the angel was naked. Its contours were heroic and masculine. Its flesh possessed the hard translucency of marble and its hair was a bronze that glowed like a Greek shield in the light of the morning sun over the plains of Marathon.

"Maybe I'd better fetch Reverend Plunkett," said Bobby MacReary, and disappeared into the General. The angel did not move at the sound of the screen door banging shut. Its wings were a thousand shades of white, from the snowy whiteness of its down feathers to the ivory of its massive pinions, which were dove-gray at the shaft.

"I'll be damned," said Old Man Stoat again and spat tobacco juice into the dust. The angel's ribcage rose and fell slowly, steadily and almost imperceptibly, the way marble would if it could breathe. Quinn's knees turned to water faster than a priest could transubstantiate wine and he sat down in the dirt.

"This is not happening," Quinn said very calmly, and as everyone knows did not say much else for quite some time.

Bobby MacReary came back with Reverend Plunkett, who was puffing heavily from hurrying. His black hair shone with Brylcreem and his cherubic mouth shaped an O of surprise when he saw the angel.

"How did this get here?" he demanded.

Garrett Ainsworth shrugged and looked at the sky. "Fell, I guess."

After this things began to get a bit out of hand. At the insistence of Reverend Plunkett, because it was a *fallen* angel, Bobby MacReary went to the lumberyard to buy chicken wire and 2 × 4s to construct a coop around the angel. He told everyone he saw and by the time he had built the coop, a good-sized crowd had gathered in the General's backyard, where the angel had not stirred and Quinn still sat in the dirt and stared unbelieving. Everyone was very nice about it and careful not to bump into him, recognizing what a difficult time Quinn must be having with this as an atheist.

The Utopia Chapter of the League of Women Voters decided to put aside their opposition to supporting stereotypical views of feminine domesticity and brought sandwiches and lemonade. Doc Hayward brought his stethoscope and listened gingerly to the angel's heartbeat, said it sounded fine, and wouldn't do anything else. Bobby MacReary, who liked running errands, went to fetch Doc Farnsworth, who was the county veterinarian, but Doc Farnsworth was drunk and wouldn't believe him, which everybody said was just as well.

At around 11:00 a.m. the Reverend D.J. Breedlove and most of his congregation showed up. The two Reverends got into a shouting match, which always happened anyway. The choir from Mount Zion Baptist Church, which was accustomed to doing without its spiritual leader whenever he and Reverend Plunkett encountered one another, sang a couple gospel hymns that really got the backyard rollicking but didn't stir the angel, so they broke it off and went to have some lemonade. Someone had the idea to send Bobby MacReary to fetch Solly Morgan, who had a dry-cleaning business and was Jewish, but it turned out that the angel didn't respond to Hebrew any more than it had to hymns. Solly Morgan shrugged and patted Quinn sympathetically on the shoulder and went over to play backgammon with Bobby MacReary.

All in all, nothing really happened the first day except that most everyone had a good time and Garrett Ainsworth sold all his luncheon meats and most of his frozen lemonade to the League of Women Voters. When it started to get dark and no one could talk Quinn Parnell into going home, they decided to leave him to keep watch over the angel. Miss Jessamine Brown, who led Reverend Breedlove's choir and ran the boarding house over on Elm Street, brought Quinn a blanket and a thermos of soup even though it was eighty degrees with the sun down, because her grandma always said that soup nourished a body.

Nothing really happened on the second day or the third day either, except that the sun rose in the east and set in the west and the shadow of the coop that Bobby MacReary built moved across the angel. At least this is what most people, who got in the habit of coming in shifts instead of staying all day, thought. Quinn Parnell, who stayed, saw what happened. He saw how the angel's body slowly acquired gravity and he witnessed the adamant made flesh. As the hours wore into one another and the sun completed two measured circuits, the alabaster skin took on a subtle flush of humanity. The bronze corona of the angel's hair, seen from the back of its head like a shield-in-the-sun, dimmed to a tawny brown. Its wings; well, if you have ever seen a swan close up that looked as pristine and white as a bridal bouquet from far away, you will know how its feathers looked, disheveled and a little discoloured.

These are the things that Quinn saw happen, and usually when change happens gradually, it is easiest to see it by leaving for a while and coming back, but this does not necessarily apply in the matter of fallen angels.

After a while Quinn got to talking and being able to carry on conversations about ordinary things, like the weather and what the weather was like this time last year and how Bob Angler finally had his license pulled for drunk driving and the Jacksons' youngest boy Will was going off to MIT in a few weeks and wasn't that amazing, and he could talk about these things sitting in the dirt in Garrett Ainsworth's backyard, but the only thing he could say when they asked him when he was going home was, "When it does."

And that was pretty much all that happened on the second day and the third day, but on the fourth day things changed again just when everyone was getting used to the way they were, because when the sun rose and threw the shadow of the cottonwood trees cool and verdant and westward along the banks of Foxglove Creek, the angel was standing.

This is what Garrett Ainsworth saw when he walked out his back door that morning: Quinn Parnell sitting Indian-style in the dirt, wrapped in Miss Jessamine's crocheted blanket, staring at the coop. And the angel, standing. Not moving but standing, its head turned in the direction of the sun, its wings neither folded nor spread but lifted, half-open, the way a bird's will do sometimes when it is roosting to remind itself that it is a creature of flight.

Early morning sunlight filtering greenly through the leaves of the cottonwood trees cast a honeycombed pattern of shadow through the chicken wire onto the angel's skin. Garrett Ainsworth stopped and stood and unconsciously ran his tongue around the inside of his mouth, feeling for a loose tooth, a loose connection, some tripped circuit breaker that he could reset and go back to yesterday when the angel that had fallen in his backyard was still faceless and like to stay that way. When this didn't work he asked Quinn Parnell, "When?"

Quinn shrugged his crocheted-blanketed shoulders, his bestubbled face haggard in the morning light. Across town someone's dog was barking in a steady, measured cadence, a distant, yelping metronome. "Well," said Garrett Ainsworth and sucked his teeth meditatively one last time, "I'll fetch us a couple cups of coffee."

Pretty soon the regulars started to show, and everyone who came helped himself or herself to a cup of coffee and put a quarter in the kitty. Used to be Garrett would ring up coffee like a regular sale, but not lately. Anyway, people mostly stayed honest about their coffee donations, what with the angel and all.

Somehow it made a big difference that the angel was standing, at least for a while. The kids who had been tossing a Frisbee around yesterday didn't today, although Bobby MacReary still played backgammon with anyone who would stand him a game. Old Man Stoat even got so he would step around to the back of the coop to spit.

Of course the main thing was that everyone wanted to look at the angel's face, which was no problem really since all you had to do was walk right up and look at it. Mrs. Patsy Tucker fell over in a dead faint when she looked at it, but after they laid her out on one of the picnic tables—all 240 pounds of her squeezed into a flowery summer dress—and Doc Hayward examined her, he told Claire Williams privately that Patsy Tucker was a hypochondriac, which everyone knew anyway, and that he doubted it was any accident that she fainted right when Hank Baldwin was right there to catch her. In any case, she came to pretty quick after they put a cold compress on her forehead and chafed her wrists.

What did the angel do? Nothing. Even when Betty and Jack DeKalb's boy Rick, who was already a terror at seven, tossed a clod of dirt at it. Even when Rick howled while his mother hauled him off by the arm, swatting his behind at every other step: Nothing. It just stood there like a half-answered prayer by a homoerotic Pygmalion, tracking the sun degree after slow degree.

Since no one knew what to expect, this behavior did not seem unduly strange and perhaps in fact was not so for angels fallen in either the literal or metaphorical sense. The angel's eyes were suited for gazing at the sun, at once fierce and fiery and distant the way a hawk's are, but altogether different. Its face was very beautiful in a way that seemed very simple and almost indifferent to itself, and so could almost be taken for granted; the brow was fair and broad, a graceful expanse over which the tawny locks tumbled in classic disarray, the nose straight in the manner one sees in profiles on ancient coins.

In other words, it looked pretty much like an angel ought to.

Hilary Putney-Smoot, who was the oldest woman in Utopia and a delightfully eccentric soul even in the early stages of senility, brought her art class of children ages 8–12 to paint the fallen angel that afternoon. A few parents secretly hoped that this would prompt a budding Raphael to emerge among their offspring, but this did not occur and the parents of Hilary Putney-Smoot's pupils sighed inwardly, smiled and exclaimed, and hung the paintings on refrigerators with magnets or in dimly lit hallways if the paintings were matted as was the case with the older children. Many years later they would realize that these paintings, long since consigned to attics and scrapbooks, grown brittle, faded and dusty with age, were the only visual documentation of the angel and they would wonder why no one took photographs or videos and whether it was possible that such a thing had occurred after all.

The angel took no more notice of the young artists than it had of the hurled clod of dirt, though of course everyone noticed how it took no notice. The two Reverends got into another shouting match about it, as by this time they had become firmly entrenched in opposing opinions, with Reverend Plunkett maintaining that the angel was a damned soul newly cast out of Heaven contemplating its future as a foul fiend eternally tormented in the bowels of Hell and Reverend Breedlove just as adamantly insisting that the angel had merely lost its way and was being visited on Utopia to remind everyone that we are all lambs of God lost on the way and should like the angel spend our time in humble contemplation of the Almighty and the mysterious sublimity of His design to bring grace and redemption to the human heart.

Since neither explanation seemed particularly satisfying, nobody bothered to take sides and the fourth day wound down with the Reverends declaring a truce due to heat prostration and Hilary Putney-Smoot packing art supplies away in an old tacklebox with arthritic hands and a twinkle in her eye because even though she didn't know that she'd had her dress on inside-out all day, she had noticed something about her young pupils that no one else had. "My dear," she whispered in Quinn Parnell's ear, "they all painted the angel, but not a one of them painted the coop!"

That night, which was the fourth night or possibly the fifth, depending of course on the indeterminable factor of exactly when the angel had arrived, it rained. It didn't rain hard, but it was enough to make Quinn pull Miss Jessamine's crocheted blanket over his head like a hood. Through the murky darkness he could see that the angel had not moved. The rain damped down the dust, which gave off an acrid tang. Quinn sighed, huddled, and dozed.

The sun rose on the fifth day to burn off the residue of the night's rain and nothing was changed except that Quinn smelled like wet wool for a few hours. That morning Claire Williams declared that she was sick and tired of Quinn's mangy dog act and that if he couldn't behave like a man at least he could look like one, and she upped and went into the General and purchased a men's battery-powered shaver and borrowed a hand mirror from Garrett Ainsworth and came back out and stuck the mirror in Quinn's left hand and the shaver in his shirt pocket. And of course everyone wondered about that, because everyone knew that pretty, acerbic Claire Williams had been married to a hotshot prosecutor in Boston for seven years before moving back to Utopia alone where she took over the weekly newspaper and never spoke about the divorce. Now this, and Quinn a lawyer too.

The nature of a small town being what it is, no one asked Claire Williams directly about her sudden concern over Quinn Parnell's personal appearance. They didn't ask her why no coverage of the fallen angel had appeared in yesterday's issue of *The Utopian Weekly* either, but that was another matter. There was news and then there was news, and this was not the sort of news one printed in the paper, because if that happened the next thing you know the town would be crawling with FBI agents and men in mirrored sunglasses from a division of the United States Air Force that doesn't exist on any official records and therefore cannot possibly have a hangar full of UFOs somewhere in the deserts of Nevada or a laboratory where bizarre experiments are practiced on alleged extraterrestrials, and then you'd have reporters from the *National Enquirer* and *The Sun* and *Weekly World News* digging through your garbage and Geraldo Rivera on your doorstep and the Vatican on the phone all day long. In the matter of fallen angels, this goes without saying.

Apart from Claire Williams and Quinn shaving his face as meekly as one of Reverend Breedlove's lambs, the most exciting event by far to mark day five of the angel was the afternoon arrival of Old Man Stoat's granddaughter Angie, who unexpectedly returned from having run away with a tattoo artist with no fixed address and a vintage Harley-Davidson Knucklehead with bottle-green fenders.

What Angie Stoat said when she saw the angel, after she screeched to a halt in front of the General with Metallica blaring from the enormous speakers she'd installed in the Chevy S-10 pickup truck that she'd bought with the money from her parents' life insurance policy and that everyone figured she'd sold on the road, after she threw open the back door of the General and barged prodigally back into life in Utopia, was, "Holy shit!" Which was, all things considered, an honest reaction.

In any case, it gave everyone plenty to talk about, especially after Angie and Old Man Stoat got into a shouting match fit to rival anything the Reverends could dish out, and all the while the angel never blinked one celestial lash. It ended with Angie storming off, screen door banging, Chevy tires squealing, and everyone agreeing that gossip-wise day five was the best yet, while Old Man Stoat sat on a corner of a picnic bench mumbling around a wad of Skoal so large that no one, not even Bobby MacReary, could understand a word he said.

No one knew if Angie's leaving meant that she was gone temporarily or for good again, but the fact was she had only driven as far as the levee a few miles downriver where all the teenagers hung out and drank beer and hillbilly lemonade and hooked up and broke up in endless adolescent geometries, all of which Angie had run away from once already.

What awoke Quinn from his vigilant, blanket-huddled doze in the small hours of the night was that Angie Stoat cursed softly when she bruised her hip bumping into the corner of a picnic table.

It was not raining that night and the moon was gibbous, nearly full, drenching the landscape in the sort of milky, pearls-on-black-velvet luminosity that drives poets to put words on paper. Quinn watched Angie Stoat stand before the coop, her fingers curling into the chicken wire. He watched her step back and kick off her boots decisively, strip off the faded blue jeans and the sleeveless black T-shirt that said "Zeke's Custom Shop" on the front, watched her unlatch the coop and walk in naked. She had a tattoo of a dagger entwined with ivy on her right shoulder blade and her naked body twined about the angel's like ivy in the moonlight, limbs winding, one pale hand seeking to turn the angel's face from its moon-fixed gaze, shadow-tangled hair spilling like ink over the angel's shoulder, mouth seeking heat.

To what avail? None. The angel stood firm in the moonlight, legs planted like columns, head tilted; maybe, just maybe, Quinn thought he saw the angel's wings quiver faintly when Angie Stoat disengaged herself with a short, rueful laugh, but that could have been a shivery trick of the silvery moon. She stood hugging herself and regarding the angel, then stepped out of the coop, latching the door behind her. Naked by moonlight Angie looked only seventeen—which she was—and too thin with shadows pooling in the hollows of her loins and revealing the frailty of her ribcage; but her skin was silver in the moonlight and when she stretched up her arms to put on her T-shirt her nipples were as dark as plums.

Leaving, Angie Stoat caught Quinn's wakeful eye and paused and smiled an ambiguous smile that was neither triumphant nor defeated and was definitely not seventeen years old. "You would have tried it too," she said with a shrug, and strode off into the night on her long, lean, blue-jeanned legs. Quinn blinked his bleary eyes and settled back into his doze, not entirely sure he had ever awakened.

So passed the fifth night, which may well have been the sixth, and it cannot be considered odd that neither Quinn Parnell nor Angie Stoat ever spoke of what was seen and done in those dark, mercuric hours, for a glance exchanged by moonlight is both conspiratorial and a secret of the most fragile sort that may be destroyed by a single word.

On the sixth day the heat was worse, causing the air to shimmer and the cottonwood seeds to burst their pods and drift about the backyard like the down of molting swans. It was in fact too hot to do anything but gossip, and that languidly. Garrett Ainsworth brought out a couple of patio umbrellas to provide shade and gave out free ice for the coolers, since by now everyone just brought whatever refreshments they wanted. A lot of the parents brought Kool-Aid for the kids because it was cheaper than pop, and Hilary Putney-Smoot brought fresh mint from her herb garden for all the people who set out jars and made sun tea. Everyone took turns making sure that Quinn had something to drink and didn't dehydrate in the heat. Despite having shaved yesterday, he was looking more haggard today and a few people like Claire Williams and Garrett Ainsworth were beginning to wonder privately if it wasn't time to start worrying about him. If they had known what happened last night, they might have guessed that Quinn was suffering from lack of sleep and a voyeurist's hangover, but they would have been wrong. Quinn's increased preoccupation had in fact nothing to do with Angie Stoat's attempted celestial seduction and everything to do with the angel's slow deterioration.

It was still Quinn who stayed, you see, and Quinn who noticed how the angel's tawny locks hung now lank and untended, how the angel's sculpted torso rose and fell with the effort of respiration, how it carried its wings imperceptibly lower and the feathers hung limp in the torpid heat. The once-dazzlingly-white cloth that girded its loins was merely white, no whiter than the cottonwood seeds blowing about the yard and catching in the chicken wire. The angel's naked feet were grimy with dust and there was a streak of dirt on one bare shoulder where little Rick DeKalb had thrown a dirt-clod at it. Because he could not give voice to these things, Quinn stayed silent and suffered a grinding pain in his heart that he knew to be an intimation of mortality not his own.

The main debate in Garrett Ainsworth's backyard that day was whether or not any events of a miraculous nature had occurred in Utopia since the angel had arrived. There was Miss Jessamine's nasturtium, which had unexpectedly revived, and Del Danby's black labrador retriever Lucy that had given birth to a litter of no less than twelve pups on Tuesday, but these were rather dubious as miracles go. There was Angie Stoat's prodigal return, of course, but this was not as miraculous as would be, say, her graduating from high school on time next spring. Madoc Jones claimed to have heard the voice of God in the woods behind the old Oosterberg place, but everyone knew he went out into the woods to hunt for hallucinogenic mushrooms, so that didn't really count. Besides, he was Welsh.

In the early evening hours it cooled off a bit, and Patsy Tucker donated the usage of her croquet set for anyone who was interested in playing, which it turned out was quite a few. Bobby MacCreary fell in the creek trying to make a tricky shot after Claire Williams knocked his ball out of the course, but declared that it was refreshing and jumped in again to prove it. After that a lot of the kids wanted to jump in the creek, but then Bobby MacReary discovered he had a leech on his ankle and almost passed out when Garrett pulled it off, and after that no one wanted to go in the creek. Claire Williams won three out of four games of croquet and admitted that she and her husband used to play it a great deal at their friends the VanderKemps's summer house and then her lips compressed into a thin line and she wouldn't say anything more about it.

Around 7:30 p.m. Bob Angler—who wasn't supposed to be driving—and a couple of his friends pulled up with a mess of brook trout and a keg of beer and organized a fish fry. All in all, despite the heat it turned out that the sixth day was a good one and everyone except Quinn went home after dark declaring that they didn't remember when they'd had so much fun. Which was a good thing since this would be the last day, although of course no one knew this at the time.

That night the moon rose full, and it was so round and perfect that you knew last night's moon had only been for practice. For a long time after dark, sounds of life could still be heard throughout the town, people shouting, cars passing, doors slamming, and occasionally music, which was not surprising what with it being Saturday night and a full moon. But after a while, in the hours between when the latest revelers went to bed and the earliest risers rose from it, everything became silent and still. The moon was at its apex then, small and bright and high overhead, lifting the angel's regard to its own apex with raised chin, barethroated and vulnerable in the moonlight.

And it was then that Quinn Parnell got up. All his joints were stiff and made clicking sounds when he moved and the muscles in his legs were knotted and cramped. He hobbled over to the coop like an old, old man and supported himself by hooking his fingers in the chicken wire the way Angie Stoat had done, and he stared at the angel.

And slowly, slowly—though not compared to how it followed the orbit of sun and moon—the angel lowered its moon-fixed gaze and looked Quinn full in the face. Its wings quivered, for sure this time, raising a little breeze that stirred the bits of cottonwood seed stuck in the chicken wire.

How long did they stand staring at one another? Quinn never knew, only that he never ever forgot it and never ever told another living soul. When he could look away he did, and unlatched the coop with hands that trembled before turning his back and hobbling away on painracked legs. When he reached the farther picnic table, he stopped and waited.

There was no sound and no change in the subtle moonlight, but presently a brief wind sprang up and died again, and Quinn waited another full minute afterward before turning around and seeing that the coop was empty and there was no sign of an angel anywhere in Garrett Ainsworth's backyard.

It took a while, but after that things pretty much went back to normal.

Tiger in the Night

BY BRIAN ALDISS

Brian W. Aldiss started publishing stories in 1954. His first science fiction novel, *Non-Stop*, was released in 1955. More than fifty years later he is still filling our bookshelves with tales of spectacular worlds, now with more than forty novels and 300 short stories to his credit. His short story "Supertoys Last All Summer Long" was the inspiration for the 2001 Steven Spielberg film *A.I.* Aldiss has also written several volumes of poetry, as well as highly acclaimed critical works on both writing and science fiction.

A resident of the United Kingdom, Aldiss has won the Hugo Award, Nebula Award, British Science Fiction Award, and John W. Campbell Memorial Award. He was honored as SFWA Grand Master in 1999 and has three times been Guest of Honor or Toastmaster of the World Science Fiction Convention. In 2004 he was inducted into the Science Fiction and Fantasy Hall of Fame. In June 2005, he was awarded The Most Excellent Order of the British Empire for "services to literature."

Brian Aldiss lives in Oxford, England. Visit his Web site at www.brian waldiss.com.

It's three o'clock in the morning by the parish clock when there comes a knock at my door.

"Don't go, Will," says my wife. But I heeded not the wishes of women in my young days. Up I get. The Lord God lashes me on, just to squeeze a line of verse from me.

A ragged-trousered boy stands at my door, shivering in the dark.

"It ain't yet cleared, mister," he says.

"Lead on," I say. Off we go through the night, and he goes barefoot.

I ask him why his mother cannot find him shoes in which to walk the streets of our capital.

He says, "Ain't got no shoes. Ain't got no mother."

The streets are all but deserted, cold, damp, cruel.

So we come to the walls of the zoo.

"It ain't yet cleared," he says again.

I toss him a farthing and I climb the wall, as I could do in my young days.

How black is the night—and blacker yet inside the zoo.

I stand there. I wait. Devil a star overhead.

A man approaches with a bull's-eye lantern burning dim. All I see is the dull illumination and his dull face. He's tall and clean-shaven. I know him for a respectable man, though I hold respectability to be a poor enough quality. Nor do I like him because of his trade: but I did him a favor once and now he repays me.

"It's not yet been cleared," he tells me. "This is illegal in the eyes of the law, Will." He calls me Will. I call him Mr. Phipps.

"Let's trust that the eyes of the law are blind," I tell him.

We make our way along between cages. All about are sounds of animal suffering, low cries, snuffles, moans: the sighs and gasps of those who should be free. Which is superior, I wonder—those who cage or those who are caged? I smell the odors of their droppings. I am pained by their pain. The bars gleam like drawn bayonets as we pass by.

We come to a certain shed, where Mr. Phipps says, "It's not dangerous. I have him pent."

Then in the stinking dark he sticks out a hand to me, a hand narrow and pale such as belonged to Judas Iscariot. I place a half-sovereign on his palm and he opens the shed door.

Oh, but it's black there, black as our sins, a cruel black where no good ever came looking. No half-sovereign would ever admit a caring deity here!

The light from the lantern illumines the tiger's head. Its eyes burn as if from another star.

I cannot breathe for the wonder of that pent head. In its great beautiful skull burn cunning and ferocity, uncontaminated by intellect.

Mr. Phipps is explaining. "It's the wars, Will. That damned Napoleon!" He indicates the imprisoned animal. "They snatched him from a French place—a menagerie, they told me. Smuggled him over here, drugged, in a chest. It ain't legal so far. I got to try for a sustificate. It ain't yet cleared."

I don't listen to him. I stare at the great beast. It makes no sound. The tiger, the dumb tiger, speaks a different language of a different world. He seems to exude both hate and love and things beyond. His head has been wedged between two bars. He has a collar clamped to one bar. In order to express his discomfort, his body constantly shifts position, sitting, standing, crouching, crouching, standing, sitting. The wonderful composition of stripes and colors burns even in the dimness, burns into my soul.

That the Lord God made such a creature! Not for us but for itself, for its savage mate. It is of unearthly beauty—and all about it should be the solace of green and striped foliage, the boundless freedoms of the savannah.

Not this loathesome hut, these vile bars.

I burst into tears. Savage tears, tears that burn.

"Be a man, Will," says Mr. Phipps.

But who would desire to be a man when men do such cruel things?

"Let it go free," I say. My voice chokes.

"What? Have this brute at liberty to roam our green and pleasant land? It would eat everyone. You're mad in the head, Will, always were."

I take a final look at this masterpiece of nature and then I run from there.

My soul cries out at the villainy of it, the injustice.

For years, I suffer in spirit with that glorious cat, and can say nothing. Then a verse bursts forth from my mind, as God willed.

What immortal hand or eye
Will aid you in that dreadful sty?
Man forges prisons, forges laws—
You the freedom of your jaws.

No, it will never do! A poor lame thing. At least in verse I can liberate the splendid creature. I destroy that verse and write instead—

Tiger, tiger, burning bright,
In the forests of the night,
What immortal hand or eye
Could frame thy dreadful symmetry?

The strange case of Jared Spoon,

who went to pieces for love.

BY STEL PAVLOU

Stel Pavlou makes stuff up for a living. So far he's made up a movie and two novels: He wrote and coproduced the feature film *The 51st State*, starring Samuel L. Jackson and Robert Carlyle, and penned both *Decipher* (2002) and *Gene* (2004). He hopes to make a few more things up before anyone catches on and stops him.

When asked about the origin of "Jared Spoon," Pavlou playfully replied: "I like Kurt Vonnegut stories. What got me into SF was Vonnegut, Adams, Dali, and Escher. Not because I wanted to be like them, but rather I saw in their surrealistic noodlings something very familiar. I was then promptly told by publishers that I was derivative and I've been writing in a different voice ever since. Well, this is a journey back to my starting point. My early love affair with juxtaposition. She's insightful and sardonic, and what a pair of tits."

Pavlou lives in Rochester, New York. Visit his Web site at www.stelpavlou.com.

One day she just took a knife to him.

She said, "I'm gonna stick this to ya if you look at me that way again."

He was shocked, obviously. He had a mouthful of lunch.

"What way?"

"Or how about I cut off a finger? Yeah, one of ya fuckin' fingers. See how you like that?"

So he wiped his mouth on the napkin. Set his sandwich down. Almost like, should he get out of this alive it would be nice to get back to the sandwich.

In the end she didn't stab him with it. She threw it at him. It took a lobe clean off.

It bled a lot.

He responded with a kind of Parkinson's twitch.

She didn't have a name after that.

He called her Girl 77. There was no telling how many personalities she really had rattling around in that wonderfully packaged though fucked-up brain of hers. If he had to sit and count them all he'd say seventy-seven was a good guesstimate, but don't quote him. She was full of surprises. That was why he loved her.

That was the day Jared Spoon decided to quit smoking.

The letter read: *My dearest, darling Jared.*

Immediately he had the impression this was not from anybody he knew.

The letter continued: *I am going to send you something. I don't want you to be alarmed. I am going to send you something very intimate. I want you to know it is sent out of love. Please keep it in your safe place until I instruct you otherwise. We shall be together very soon, my love. Yours deeply and intimately, Girl 77.*

Jared Spoon shuddered at the thought of his safe place.

He watched Girl 77 rocking quietly on the floor.

We shall be together *very soon?* How much sooner than already being together did she want?

He decided he should put more of an effort into making a lasting impression on her.

Jared Spoon used patches at first.

After a while he ran out of places to put them and slapped them on the back of his neck.

Herb Foresight thought they made him look like an armadillo. Jared Spoon didn't bother setting him straight. Herb Foresight was an idiot.

There is no health warning on a packet of nicotine patches.

At first he waited until nothing arrived. By then he was up to six patches a day!

Still Girl 77 said nothing about a delivery.

At last he was free from the burden of options!

He stood across the room to ask his question and hoped she wouldn't beat the snot out of him for disturbing her.

He said, "Girl 77, what happened to that thing you were going to send me?"

He waited for her lolloping form to come galloping across the carpet poised to club him one. Instead, she remained inert.

Girl 77 denied everything.

"I deny everything," she said.

"Huh?"

She denied knowing him.

"How can you deny knowing me?"

"Who are you?"

"Are you serious?"

"Please leave."

"You want me to leave?"

She denied even asking him to leave.

She said, "I didn't ask you to leave."

She marched into the bedroom and returned dragging a large black suitcase behind her. "This is not your suitcase. I did not pack it."

Jared Spoon was at a loss. This was his apartment. He asked if he should just stay a while.

She denied she could speak any English.

"I no speak English," she said.

The Sennadril plastic cigarette substitute took away the craving for a cigarette by mimicking the look and feel of a real one, thus satiating the body's habitual need to keep placing flammable objects in the mouth.

Herb Foresight thought he looked like he'd stuffed a pen in his mouth. He said, "You taking notes?"

Jared Spoon set the suitcase down on the kitchen table and drummed his fingers on it.

"What's in the case?"

"Girl 77 gave it to me."

"That's about right. She's got nothing but baggage and she's always giving it to you. You need to stop."

Jared Spoon said, "She's not something I can quit."

"You quit smoking."

"But not nicotine."

Herb Foresight scratched his chin. He understood very few things in this world. This too was not one of them. "You're doing this out of love?"

"I'm doing this out of desperation. I want to make her happy."

"By moving out?"

"She'll have forgotten by the morning."

"She threw you out on your stitched-up ear, my friend."

"She just needs her medication."

Drugs he understood. "Drugs. Jesus Christ, Jared. I can get you drugs. Anything you want, you just ask. You know that. What's she into? Blips? I can get a good deal on Blips, Nuts, Gloob, say the word."

"Not *drugs*," Jared Spoon corrected. "Medication. Peptoglycomol B, Frinzadrine, and Nitrinol. You think you can come up with that?"

"I can't even say that."

"She needs it for her head."

"So you're doin' this for head."

"For love."

Jared Spoon smuggled drugs for Herb Foresight once. He kept them in his safe place. He kept so many things in his safe place it became uncomfortable.

Girl 77 said she might be crazy but you couldn't pay her enough to put anything up *her* bum-bum.

He kipped on the couch that night.

It stank.

It was covered in leather and polished with wax. Every time he rolled over it sounded like a fart.

He dreamed he was lowing. Cud obsessed in a grazing field with the rest of them. Ruminating on his part in this endless piebald queue. Shuffling onwards to the place where the shotgun sounds were made.

It was enough to make him bolt from the couch and into the darkness scream: "Moo!"

The address on the parcel read: *Jared Spoon, 40116, No. 3.*

This was not his toothbrush.

This was wrapped in brown paper and taped at both ends.

Jared Spoon decided that perhaps it would have been for the best if he had checked his suitcase before leaving home.

He peeled away the layers to find a sturdy silver box and a note which read: *My dearest, darling Jared. So it begins!*

Jared Spoon took umbrage. Surely this was not where it began but where it continued?

A swift exhumation of the contents suggested it was neither. This was where it veered wildly off at a tangent and ploughed catastrophically into the ground leaving nothing but the depressing smell of singed artichokes.

Herb Foresight said, "What's that?"

His homeless, ear-stitched friend prodded the vacuum-packed plastic lump with a finger. "It's a foot in a box."

"A foot?"

"In a box."

"What size?"

"What?"

"What size is it?"

"A size eight, I think. Why?"

"Might help track down the owner."

"You think its size will be the deciding factor?"

"What are you going to do with it?"

Jared Spoon said, "Well I'm buggered if I'm putting it up my bum-bum."

Jared Spoon sat on the toilet clutching his head.

Nicozing chewing gum came in six *incredible* flavors. Spearmint, peppermint, freshmint, coolmint, aquamint, and menthol.

All of them produced the same incredible side effects! Mouth ulcers, jaw ache, dizziness, headache, and upset stomach.

Try as he might, he couldn't blame his squits on the chewing gum.

How many more pieces of this poor unfortunate footless person would be paying him a visit?

Jared Spoon went home to discover that the answer was three and a bit.

Herb Foresight stood in Jared Spoon's kitchen and peered down at the deep freezer in awe.

"Fuck me, she's been busy."

"There's nearly half a person in here."

"Just like your girlfriend."

Jared Spoon said, "That's uncalled for."

He stashed the new vacuum-packed appendage in with the peas and closed the lid.

"All week they've just kept coming. Yesterday it was a gall bladder with a note that read: *This is how much I love you.*"

"A gall bladder is a lot of love."

Jared Spoon chewed on his fingernails and nervously paced the two-meter-square patch of linoleum.

"Do you think it's a good thing that she finally trusts me?"

"I don't think she even knows you moved back in, my friend. You need to talk to her. This is getting out of hand."

"She comes, she goes. She never says a word. Where's she getting these things?"

Herb Foresight had a theory. "From people," he said. "From people."

This had to stop.

So far he'd tried patches, pens, gum. Nothing had worked.

Herb Foresight said there was this pill he could try that would make him chunder if he so much as looked at a cigarette.

Jared Spoon said he wasn't convinced by it. Nobody ever caught cancer of the eyeballs from looking at a cigarette.

He contemplated abstinence instead.

The invitation read: *My dearest, darling Girl 77.*

With any luck that would get her attention.

The invitation continued: *I have received your intimates and I have kept them in a place that's almost as safe as the other one. Why don't you come to dinner and we can moo about them? Yours as ever, Jared Spoon.*

He was hesitant, he had to admit. Meal times were when she got feisty and he owned knives. So he lit scented candles to try to soften the mood.

They didn't help.

She said, "Are you a nancy boy?"

"What? No."

"It would explain a lot."

"I've done everything you asked."

"Well, you're out of luck, nancy boy. I didn't ask you to do anything."

"I kept your intimates safe."

Girl 77 seemed genuinely perplexed. She said, "What the fuck are you talking about?"

Jared Spoon said, "In the freezer."

The discussion didn't go as planned.

Girl 77 took one look at the collected vacuum-packed works of mystery person, eyed the burning candles arranged around the table, and screamed, "Satanist!"

Jared Spoon stumbled to his feet. "I just wanted to make you happy."

"How would this make me happy, you fucking loony?"

She bolted from the apartment. "I'm going to tell," she said. "I'm going to tell everyone!"

In the event she told no one.

She ran out into the road and was hit by a bus.

Seven people came to the funeral.

Originally they'd come for somebody else's, but it started pissing down and they needed somewhere to go. They huddled inside the chapel and did their best to be moved by the eulogy.

They wouldn't leave after that.

They said it was impolite not to follow through on the whole occasion. So they followed Jared Spoon all the way home.

They stood in front of the TV and reminisced about the life of the woman in the photo frame. Jared Spoon didn't know her either. He'd only just bought it but it seemed to make them happy.

He found a packet of biscuits and put them on a plate.

They remarked on what a fine spread it was. She would have loved it, they said.

That was the day Jared Spoon started smoking again.

The form read: *Please sign and date to acknowledge receipt of your parcel.*

Jared Spoon eyed the package with dread. *Another one?* Perhaps this was her last gift to him. He said: "When was this posted?"

The delivery driver checked his log. "This morning."

"That can't be right."

"Why not?"

"She's dead."

"So what's the problem?"

"Getting to a Post Office I should imagine."

The delivery driver didn't understand. He wasn't paid to understand. Though that was frankly evidence of nothing, he wasn't paid to tap dance either.

"Look, mate," he said. "Do you want it or not?"

Jared Spoon thought about it before asking that one question he probably should have asked to begin with. "Who sent it?"

The delivery driver checked his log again. "Dunno," he said. "But there's a return address if you want."

"Please."

"The Second Vonnegut and Fowler Institute of Cloneography."

"You may call me Ersatz," said Mister Ersatz Ersatz.

Jared Spoon sat across the office from him, his bodily collection piled up on a cart and said, "What if I don't want to?"

"What is it you do here?" Jared Spoon said.

With a broad welcoming smile, Mr. Ersatz Ersatz said, "We're like Kinko's for people."

"Is it usual for someone to photocopy their arse and post it out?"

Mr. Ersatz Ersatz seemed genuinely befuddled. "Did you receive an arse in the post?"

"No. I got a foot, among other things."

"And very well it suits you too."

"It's not mine. I didn't request anything. None of these bits and pieces are my bits and pieces."

"Well whose bits and pieces are they?"

Jared Spoon said the answer to that question was why he had come here.

They took a test.

By *they*, I mean neither Jared Spoon nor Mr. Ersatz Ersatz. But somebody. Probably somebody who worked for Mr. Ersatz Ersatz.

The results led to merchandise that lived down on the sixty-fifth floor.

Jared Spoon looked like he'd seen a ghost.

A handicapped ghost with parts of two legs, a foot and a gall bladder missing, and dragging a life support machine around behind her on an umbilical, but a ghost nonetheless.

He said, "My God, she looks just like Girl 77. How is this possible?"

"She wanted to be perfect for you, Mr. Spoon. She wanted to show you how much she really loved you. She filled a capsule with the only personality she had that made the slightest bit of sense and rammed it up the tubes of this delightful little photocopy and was all ready to make the switch until we hit a snag."

Jared Spoon watched her lolloping form amble around the room. "She's perfect . . ."

"Perfectly penniless."

"This girl doesn't belong to anybody?"

"She belongs to us. Only she doesn't want to. You see she loves you, Mr. Spoon, just as much as Girl 77 did. We're very good, you see. She loves you so much she's willing to do anything."

Jared Spoon finally understood. "She's been smuggling herself out a piece at a time."

"Yes. And I'm afraid that puts you in a bit of a bind."

"Me? Why?"

"We're talking theft, Mr. Spoon. That's very serious."

"You're going to have her arrested?"

"Her? We can't very well charge our merchandise with stealing our merchandise. That would just be silly. No, we're going to have you arrested."

"For what?"

"Receiving stolen goods. You did receive goods, did you not?"

"Yes."

"They were stolen, were they not?"

"Not by me."

"But by somebody!"

"If you say so."

"I do say so."

"I didn't know they were stolen."

"That's no excuse!"

"I believed they were legitimate and accepted them in good faith."

"Faith has nothing to do with it! We are men of science are we not?"

"You're a man of science. I'm a man of no fixed employment."

Mr. Ersatz Ersatz pondered on this.

Jared Spoon said, "Surely we can come to an arrangement?"

Mr. Ersatz Ersatz grinned from ear to ear. "How's your credit rating?"

One day she just took a knife to him.

She said, "I'm gonna cut that up for ya. I'm never gonna let you eat that way again."

He was shocked, obviously. He had a mouthful of lunch.

"What way?"

"Or how about I cook you some fish fingers? Yeah, some funky fish fingers. See how you like that?"

So he wiped his mouth on the napkin. Set his sandwich down. Almost like, should he get a good meal out of this it would still be nice to get back to the sandwich.

In the end she didn't cut it up for him. She threw something amazing together instead.

It was hot.

He responded with a kind of Parkinson's twitch.

She didn't have a name after that.

He called her Jigsaw Janet.

When they'd finished stitching her back together he took her home and they spent the most wonderful love-filled days together.

They never argued. They never disagreed. She was perfect.

And by Friday, he was bored out of his brains.

She found him out on the front steps, a black suitcase by his side, puffing furiously on a long Sobranie Black Russian. Cigarettes for hard bastards who laughed at their lungs. There was nothing like the real thing.

Jigsaw Janet sat quietly down beside him. "It's over, isn't it?" she said.

"I'm afraid so."

"Why? Don't you love me?"

"No," said Jared Spoon. "I find you derivative."

The Solipsist at Dinner

BY LARRY NIVEN

Larry Niven has been a staple of the science fiction community since his first story, "The Coldest Place," debuted in 1964. In 1970, Niven published the first novel in the award-winning Ringworld series (*Ringworld, The Ringworld Engineers, The Ringworld Throne,* and *Ringworld's Children*)—reputedly one of the greatest science fiction series of all time. The Ringworld titles, however, make up only a small portion of his famous Known Space world of future history, which in itself contains more than thirty short stories and novels. Niven is also the creator of the shared-world Man-Kzin War series. He most recently coauthored (with Brenda Cooper) the novel *Building Harlequin's Moon.*

In a departure from the hard-core science fiction he is best known for, Niven addresses one of writing's biggest metaphysical questions in "The Solipsist at Dinner." Does everything really exist, or is the world we know simply a figment of our imagination? "You might say I've been thinking about this topic for forty or fifty years," Niven says. "The storytelling generation ahead of my own all had something to say on the subject. Everybody has a solipsist lurking inside him—that level of arrogance is a normal part of humanity—but the universe keeps swatting it down."

Niven lives in Chatsworth, California, with his wife, Marilyn, cat, Amelia, and several fish.

Wayne Morris had ordered a spicy tuna hand roll, extra chili. He tried a piece and managed to swallow it, but there were tears in his eyes. "Wow. That's powerful."

Nero grinned at him. "You said you were getting to like it that way. Too much?"

Wayne took another bite. His eyes were still tearing up, but he savored it. Then he said, "It's just that the whole world seems to be getting a little blurry."

"Like what?"

"Well, my eyesight. Sense of taste. Hearing."

Nero laughed and wiggled his bushy black eyebrows. "That's just what everyone says when he gets older! You're near seventy."

"Like, I hear a ringing. It's always there. Sometimes I don't notice it, but if I listen—" He listened and heard the ringing, a steady bell tone.

"It's called tinnitus." Nero raised his voice slightly, enunciating a little more carefully. The sushi restaurant was noisy, particularly at the counter. "Lots of people get tinnitus. You get it young if you work in a noisy environment, like if you're an artillery officer or a movie critic."

"I don't care what it's called, it's still distracting. I have to crank the volume up when I'm listening to TV. Sharon hates it. My sense of taste is going too. I like things spicy. As a kid I wouldn't have touched this stuff I'm eating now. And when I'm driving at night, all the lights are colored blobs. Everything else is a little blurry too, except—"

"That's normal too. Except? Something isn't blurry?"

"Clouds, trees, they look okay. I finally figured out that anything fractal looks okay because I don't *expect* sharp edges and geometric shapes. My mind extrapolates."

"That's a cute notion. Might even be true. Eyes are funny."

"What I think is that my imagination is failing."

Nero shrugged his eyebrows at him. Wayne said, "There's a philosophical position called solipsism. It means—"

"I know what it means. There's nothing else in the universe, there's just you. Everything else is your imagination. Philosophical position, my ass."

"Well, it is. I think, therefore I am, but what about the rest of you? It's internally consistent and impossible to disprove."

"When I was a kid," Nero said, "all the science fiction writers wrote stories about . . . vampires, time travel, robots, faster than light travel, all that stuff—"

"Heinlein. Whatever Robert Heinlein wrote, everyone else had to imitate."

"And solipsism. Everyone wrote a solipsism story. They were all sort of alike. I mean, if you take it seriously, what have you got? No protagonists, no background, no external conflict—"

"Yeah. Forty years I've been writing short stories and I never did anything with that." Wayne got the sushi chef's attention and ordered a California roll. "If I had it to do all over again I'd imagine a better short story market."

"You'd be God," Nero said suddenly. "And God's imagination would be failing. Wow. Think how powerful your imagination must have been, before you imagined you were a baby."

"Think how screwy the laws of physics would be getting, right about now."

"An expanding universe, speeding up. Einstein's jigger factor gone all wrong. Dark matter. Dark energy. All just metaphors for death?"

The sushi chef set their order in front of them: rice wrapped around avocado, bits of vegetable, and fish treated to imitate crab. Wayne mixed wasabi with soy sauce. He said, "Might be more interesting the other way around. First I'm God. I create a universe. I wait. Eventually there's intelligence. Intelligence starts evolving ideas about the universe. I incorporate the good ones."

"You mean, for awhile there really was a steady-state universe?"

"And a Zodiac. God was using star patterns for blackboard diagrams, a scheme for mapping out lives. Later there were black holes that didn't evaporate until Hawking changed his mind. It's all a collaboration! There was a nasty simplistic Hell at first, but then Dante started adding details. Since then everybody wants to improve on Dante, so now Hell is horrendously complicated."

"God wouldn't need much of an imagination at all," Nero said. "Just a sense of consistency. It doesn't start with a Big Bang. It starts with Eden and then *blooms*."

They went through the California roll, then ordered monkfish liver. Wayne asked, "Who dreams up diseases?"

"Oh . . . there'd be shamans, and then shamans would need to explain why people hurt. Now it's priests on one side and medical researchers—" Nero looked up. "Something?"

"I'm positive on prostate cancer."

"Damn."

He'd been trying to put it out of his head. "I went back to Doctor Wells this morning. Positive. My morbid imagination at work."

"Well, yeah, a solipsist would think that. Now you'll have to dream up a psychiatrist to cure you of thinking you've got cancer."

"Maybe—"

"Sorry. I shouldn't be making fun—"

"Maybe I should dream up a friend. A psychiatrist is just a hired friend anyway, right?"

"Have you talked to Sharon about this?"

Wayne covered his ears. The tinnitus surged.

He dreaded telling his wife. He didn't have enough friends. Maybe he'd taken this solipsistic stuff too seriously when he was younger. He didn't believe it now, and as for Nero, Nero had worked in a novel, long ago. Wayne had killed him off in the sequel and he wasn't plausible today, Nero with his funny-hat eyebrows.

It was time to stop talking to imaginary characters, time to talk to Sharon. Wayne paid the bill and left.

The Wager

BY KINLEY MacGREGOR

Urban legend has it that Sherrilyn Kenyon and Kinley MacGregor arm wrestled to see who would be in this anthology . . . and Kinley won.

Sherrilyn Kenyon is the *New York Times* best-selling author who reigns supreme over the paranormal worlds of her Dream-, Were-, and Dark-Hunters. She is also the creator of the Bureau of American Defense series, the first novel of which (*BAD Attitude*) launched in fall 2005. Her alter ego, Kinley MacGregor, takes credit for The Brotherhood of the Sword books, the MacAllister series, and many others. Between them they have more than twenty books in print, as well as countless stories, articles, and essays in collections and magazines around the world.

"The Wager" is set in Kinley MacGregor's new Lords of Avalon series (beginning in 2006 with *Sword of Darkness*)—an alternate-Arthurian fantasy of epic proportions. In the days after the battle of Camlann, Arthur is taken to the isle of Avalon. The sacred objects of Camelot that gave him his power have been scattered to protect them from evil. The Round Table is fractured. The good guys have retreated to Avalon to serve their fallen king and the surviving Penmerlin who came forward after Arthur's Merlin mysteriously vanished. The evil Morgan le Fey has taken over Camelot and placed a new Pendragon on the throne. The former Knights of the Round Table are now the Lords of Avalon, and they will do whatever is necessary to stop the Pendragon from succeeding.

Sherrilyn Kenyon lives just outside Nashville, Tennessee. Visit her Web site at www.sherrilynkenyon.com.

It'd been a long, cold . . .

Millennium.

Thomas paused as he penned those words. Surely it wasn't that long. Was it? Frowning, he looked at the calendar on his PDA that Merlin had brought to him from what future man would call the twenty-first century and gave a low whistle.

It hadn't been quite that long, even though he lived in a land where time had no real meaning. It only felt like it, and therefore he left the word on the paper. It sounded better than saying just a few centuries—and that was what writing was all about, he'd learned. The truth was important, but not so much as keeping his audience entertained. News bored people, but stories . . .

That was where the money was. At least for people other than him. There was no money here, nor much of anything else.

But he was digressing. Millennium or not, it had been way too long since he'd last been free.

He who bargains with the devil pays with eternity. His dear old mangled mother had been fond of the saying. Too bad he hadn't been better at listening—but then that was the problem with "conversation." So many times even when you paused for a breath you weren't really listening to the other person so much as planning your next speech. Of course, he'd been a cocky youth.

What did some old crone know about anything anyway? he used to think. He was Thomas Malory. *Sir* Thomas Malory—couldn't forget the Sir part. That was all-important.

In his day that Sir had meant that he was a man with standing. A man with prospects.

A man with no friggin' clue (Thom really liked the vernacular Percival had taught him from other centuries. There was just such color to some of the later phraseology . . . but now to return to what he'd been thinking).

Life had begun easy enough for him. He'd been born into a well-to-do family. A *nice* family . . . Nice incidentally was a four-lettered word. Look it up, it really was. It meant to be agreeable. Pleasant. Courteous.

Boring.

Like any good youth worth his salt, he'd run as far away from nice as he could. Nice was for the weak (another four-lettered word). It was for a doddering fool (see how everything vile led back to four letters [even vile was four letters]).

And Thomas was anything but a fool. Or so he'd thought.

Until the day he'd met *her* (Please insert footnote here that in French, *la douleur,* i.e., pain, is feminine). There was a reason for that. Women, not money, were the root of all evil (it was a trick of their gender that "woman" was five and not four letters, but then "girl" was four letters too. This was done to throw us poor men off so that we wouldn't realize just how corrupt and detrimental they were).

But back to the point of our story. Women were the root of all evil. No doubt. Or at the very least the fall of every good man.

And Thom should know. He'd been doing quite well for himself until that fateful day when *she* had shown herself to him. Like a vision of heaven, she'd been crossing the street wearing a gown of blue. Or maybe it was green. Hell, after all these centuries it could have been brown. The color hadn't mattered at the time because in truth he'd been picturing her naked in his mind.

And he'd learned one very important lesson. Never picture a woman naked when she was capable of reading your mind. At least not unless you were seriously into masochism.

Thom wasn't. Then again, given his current predicament, perhaps he was.

Only a true masochist would dart across the street to meet and fall in love with Merlin.

Thom paused in his writing. "Now, good reader, before you think me odd. Let me explain. You see Merlin in ancient Britain wasn't a name. It was a title and the one who bore that title could be either male or female. And my Merlin was a beautiful blond angel who just happens to be a little less than forgiving. How do I know? See first paragraph where I talk about being imprisoned for a millennium . . . give or take a few centuries which still doesn't sound quite as impressive as millennium."

Thom felt a little better after uttering that speech. Though not much. How could any man feel better while stuck in a hole?

For it was true. Hell had no fury greater than a woman's wrath.

"That's what having a beer with your buddies will get you."

Well, in his case it was more like a keg of ale. But that would be jumping ahead of the story.

Sighing at himself, Thom dipped his quill in ink and returned to his vellum sheet. It was true, he had other means of writing things down, but since it all began with a quill and vellum, he wanted this diatribe to be captured the same way. After all, this was his version of the story. Or more simply, this was the truth of the matter. While others only speculated, he knew the truth.

And no, the truth would not set him free. Only Merlin could do that and well, that was an entirely different story from this one.

This story began with a poor besotted man seeing his Aphrodite across the street. She had paused in her walk and was looking about as if she'd lost something.

Me, he'd thought. *You have lost me and I am right here.*

With no thought except to hear the sound of his beloved's voice before she started on her way again, he'd headed toward her only to nearly die under the hooves of a horse as he stepped out in front of a carter. Thom not-so-deftly dodged the carter and landed extremely unceremoniously in a trough.

Drenched, but still besotted by Cupid's whim, Thom attempted to wring himself dry before he again headed toward her . . . this time a bit more cautious of traffic.

He couldn't breathe. Couldn't think. Couldn't dry the damn stench of the reeking water off his clothes. All he could do was watch his Calypso as she waited (he told himself) for him to claim her.

As he drew near her, a million clever thoughts and introductions popped eagerly into his mind. He was going to sweep her off her feet with witty repartee. She would be bedazzled by his nimble, elegant tongue (in more ways than one if everything went according to plan).

And then she had looked at him. Those brilliant blue . . . or maybe they were green . . . eyes had pierced him with curiosity.

Thom had drawn a deep breath, opened his mouth to speak, to woo her with his charm, when all of a sudden his cleverness abandoned him.

Nothing. His mind was blank. Worthless. Aggravating.

"Greetings." Even he cringed as that simple, stupid word had tumbled out of his lips.

"Greetings, good sir."

Her voice had been clear and soft. Like the song of an angel. She'd stood there for a moment, looking expectantly at him while his heart pounded, his forehead beaded with sweat.

Speak, Thom, speak.

"Nice day, eh?"

"Very nice."

Aye, he was a fool. One who no longer bore any trace of his shriveled manhood. Wanting to save whatever dignity he possessed (which at this point was in the negative digits), Thom nodded. "I just thought I'd point it out to you, fair maiden. Good day."

Cringing even more, he'd started away from her only to pause as he caught sight of something strange.

Now, being a rational human being, he'd thought it an unusually large bird. Let's face it, in fifteenth-century England, everyone spoke of dragons, but no one had really thought to ever see one.

And yet there it was in the sky. Like a giant . . . dragon. Which it was. Large and black with big red bulbous eyes and gleaming scales, it had circled above them, blocking out the sun.

Thomas, being a coward, had wanted to run, but, being a lusty man, he quickly saw an opportunity to woo his fair lady with dashing actions instead of a feeble tongue. After all, what woman wouldn't swoon over a dragonslayer?

That had been the idea.

At least until the dragon kicked his ass. With one swipe of a talon, the dragon had batted him into the building. Thom had fallen to the street and every part of his body had throbbed and ached.

It was awful. Or so he'd thought until the woman had placed her hand on his forehead. One minute he'd been lying on the street reeking of trough water, and in the next he'd found himself lying on a large, gilded bed.

"Where am I?"

"Sh," his angel had said. "You have been poisoned by the dragon. Lie still and give my touch time to heal you or you will surely die."

(Note to self. I should have started moving about, thrashing wildly.)

Not wanting to die (because I was stupid), Thom had done as she asked. He had lain there, looking up into her perfectly sculpted features. She was beauty and grace.

"Have you a name, my lady?"

"Merlin."

That had been the last name he would have ever attributed to a woman so comely. "Merlin?"

"Aye. Now be still."

For the first time in all of his life, Thom had obeyed. He'd closed his eyes and inhaled the fresh, sweet scent of lilac that clung to the bed he laid in. He wondered if this was Merlin's bed and then he wondered of other things that men and women could do in a bed . . . especially together.

"Stop that."

He opened his eyes at the reprimand from his Aphrodite. "Stop what?"

"Those thoughts," she'd said sharply. "I hear every one of them and they disturb me."

"Disturb you how?"

"I am the Penmerlin and I must remain chaste. Thoughts such as those do not belong in my head."

"They're not in your head, my lady, they're in mine and if they offend you, perhaps you should keep to yourself."

She'd gifted him with a dazzling smile. "You are a bold one, Thom. Perhaps I should have let the mandrake take you."

"Mandrake?" As in the root?

"The dragon," she'd explained. "His kind have the ability to take either the form of man or dragon, hence their name."

Well that certainly explained that, however other matters had been rather vague in his mind. "But he wasn't after me. He was after you. Why?"

"Because I was on the trail of a very special Merlin and the mandrake sensed me. That is why I so seldom venture to the world of man. When one possesses as much magic as I do, it is too easy for other magical beasts to find you."

That made sense to him. "You are enemies."

She nodded. "He works for Morgan le Fey."

Thom'd had the audacity to laugh at that. "The sister of King Arthur."

Merlin hadn't joined in his laughter. "Aye, the very same."

The serious look on her face and the tone of her voice had instantly sobered him. "You're not jesting."

"Nay. The tales of Arthur are real, but they are not quite what the minstrels tell. Arthur's world was vast and his battles are still being waged, not only in this time, but in future ones as well."

In that moment, Thom wasn't sure what enraptured him most. The stunning creature he longed to bed or the idea that Camelot really had existed.

Over the course of the next few days while he healed from his attack, Thom had stayed in the fabled isle of Avalon and listened to Merlin's stories of Arthur and his knights.

But more than that, he'd seen them. At least those who still lived. There for a week, he'd walked amongst the legends and shook the hands of fables. He'd learned that Merlin was only one of her kind. Others like her had been sent out into the world of man to be hidden from Morgan who wanted to use those Merlins and the sacred objects they protected for evil.

It was a frightening battle they waged. One that held no regard for time or beings. And in the end, the very fate of the world rested in the hands of the victor.

"I wish to be one of you," Thom had finally confessed to Merlin on the evening of his eighth day. "I want to help save the world."

Her eyes had turned dull. "That isn't your destiny, Thom. You must return to the world of man and be as you were."

She made that sound simple enough, but he wasn't the same man who had come to Avalon. His time here had changed him. "How can I ever be as I was now that I know the truth?"

She'd stepped away from him. "You will be as you were, Thom . . . I promise."

And then everything had gone blurry. His eyesight had failed until he found himself encased in darkness.

Thom awakened the next morning to find himself back in England, in his own house . . . his own bed.

He'd tried desperately to return to Avalon, only to have everyone tell him that'd he'd dreamed it all.

"You've been here the whole time," his housekeeper had sworn.

But he hadn't believed it. How could he? This wasn't some illness that had befallen him. It wasn't.

It was real (another four letter word that often led men to disaster).

Eventually Thom had convinced himself that they were right and he'd dreamed it all. The land of Merlins had only existed in his mind. Where else could it have been?

And so he'd returned to his old ways. He'd gambled, he'd fought, he'd wenched, and most of all he'd drunk and drunk and drunk.

Until *that* night.

It was a night (another noun that was five letters in English and four in French. There were times when the French were greatly astute). Thom had wandered off to his favorite tavern that was filled with many of his less than proper friends. As the night passed, and they'd fallen deep into their cups, Geoffrey or maybe it'd been Henry or Richard had begun to place a wager.

He who told the best tale would win a purse of coin (not the four letters here).

No one knew how much coin was in the purse because they were all too drunk to care. Instead they had begun with their stories before a small group of wenches who were their judges.

Thom, too drunk to notice that a man had drawn near their table, had fondled his wench while the others went on before him.

"That's all well and nice," he'd said as Richard finished up some retelling of one of Chaucer's tales (the man was far from original). "But I, Thomas Malory . . . *Sir* Thomas Malory can beat you all."

"Of course you can, Thom," Geoffrey had said with a laugh and a belch. "You always *think* you can."

"No, no, there is no think . . . I'm too drunk for that. This is all about doing." He'd held his cup out to be refilled before he'd started the story. At first he'd meant to tell the story of a farming mishap his father had told him of, but before he could think better of it (drinking usually had this effect), out had come the whole matter of the King Arthur Merlin had told him about.

Or at least some of it. Being Thom, who liked to embellish all truth, he'd taken some liberties. He'd changed a few things, but basically he'd kept to the story. After all, what harm could come of it? He'd dreamed it all anyway, and it was an interesting tale.

And the next thing he'd known, he'd won that wager and taken home a purse which later proved to only contain two rocks and some lint. A paltry prize indeed.

Then, before he'd even known what had happened, people had started coming up to him and speaking of a book he'd written. Thom, not being a fool to let such fame bypass him, had played along at first. Until he'd seen the book himself. There it was, in all beautiful glory. His name.

No man had ever destroyed his life more quickly than Thom did the instant that book became commonly available.

One instant he'd been in his own bed and the next he'd been in a small, tiny, infinitesimal cell with an angry blond angel glaring at him.

"Do I know you?" he'd asked her.

She'd glared at him. Out of nowhere, *the* book had appeared. "How could you do this?"

Now at this time, self-preservation had caused Thom to ask the one question that had been getting men into trouble for centuries. "Do what?"

And just like countless men before him (and after him, is this not true, men?) he learned too late that he should have remained completely silent.

"You have unleashed our secret, Thomas. Doom to you for it, because with this book you have exposed us to those who want us dead."

Suddenly, his dream returned to him and he remembered every bit of it. Most of all, he remembered that it wasn't a dream.

The Lords of Avalon were all real . . . just as Morgan was. And as Merlin led the remnants of the Knights of the Round Table, Morgen led her Cercle du Damné. Two halves fighting for the world.

But that left Thom with just one question. "If you had all that magic, Merlin, why didn't you know about the book that would be written if you returned me to the world?"

With those words uttered, he'd learned that there truly was a worse question to ask a woman than A) her age, B) her weight, and C) do what?

"Please note that here I rot and here I stay until Merlin cools down."

Thom looked down at the PDA and sighed. Time might not have any real meaning in Avalon, but it meant a whole hell of a lot to him.

Expedition, with Recipes

Joe Haldeman wanted to be an astronaut when he grew up. He went on to get a BS
in astronomy . . . and an MFA in writing. He sold his first story in 1969, while he
was still in the army, post-Vietnam, and his book *The Forever War* won the Hugo,
Nebula, and Ditmar Awards as Best Science Fiction Novel of 1975. A full-time writer
for more than twenty-five years now, Haldeman's most recent novels include:
Guardian (2002), *Camouflage* (2004), and *Old Twentieth* (2005). He has published
short stories and novellas, songs and poetry, articles and editorials—and appears in
about twenty languages, including Klingon, which he suspects will generate letters he
won't want to answer. He is on the National Space Society Board of Advisors, and
currently works as an adjunct professor at the Massachusetts Institute of Technology.

"Expedition, with Recipes" is a hidden gem, written during the early years of
Haldeman's illustrious career but never published. "It was a classic failure of commu-
nication," said Haldeman. "A woman who worked for a UNICEF magazine was
looking for five or six science fiction writers to each do a story, under 2,000 words,
about 'children and food in the future.' When you tell a science fiction writer to write
a story, he naturally types out a piece of fiction. But the woman had wanted a 'story'
in newspaper parlance, a nonfiction piece. I wrote 'Expedition' that day, and sent it
off. A few months later, I got a small check, but the story never appeared."

Joe Haldeman lives in Florida. Learn more at his Web site: http://home.earthlink.
net/~haldeman.

RICE 2075

1 c. rice
2 c. water, boiled and filtered

Prepare rice in the usual manner. Serves 10.

There were many places to play, when there was time to play.
They liked best playing in the City, of course, since their parents for-

bade it. But you had to have at least a dozen kids to go in there, because of the dogs and cats. And sometimes the people you saw there,
the drifters.

They met at a bend in the river, where a collapsed railroad bridge af-
forded a broken passageway across the rapids. It led to the ashes and
fascinating rubble of the City.

Fifteen children squatted, hidden, behind the riverbank. The thawing
mud under their shoes squeaked every time someone shifted his weight.
They ranged in age from eight or nine to about twelve.

"Where's Danny? We can't wait much longer," Francine whispered.
She was the oldest, and would lead the expedition if Danny didn't show
up.

"Can't go without Danny," another said. Which was more practical
than loyal; Danny had the only gun.

"He'll make it," Steve said. He was Danny's best friend. He raised
himself cautiously to peer over the riverbank.

"*Don't do that*," Francine said. "What did I tell you?"

"I'm careful," Steve protested. The sentry who guarded the entrance
to their commune was a good quarter-mile away; Francine was being
overcautious.

He didn't see anything. Francine passed the time by telling a story, a
cautionary tale, to the three new kids. To the others, too. This was the
first expedition since fall, and some of them might have forgotten.

The story was about the importance of staying together. A few
years before, a girl had wandered away from the group. They
searched for her every afternoon for a week, and finally found her
dress and a pile of bones beside the remains of a campfire. Someone
had eaten her.

"How do they know it was a person?" one of the new kids said.
"Maybe the dogs got her."

Francine was ready for that, and dropped her voice even lower. "The
dogs wouldn't have undressed her. Her dress was bloody but not torn.

"And the dogs would have left her head attached."

COCKROACHES WITH SALT

10–20 cockroaches, large
2 tsp. salt (if available; optional)

Reserve insects, live, until you have a sufficient number. Put salt in a pan with a tight-fitting lid, and get the pan very hot before adding insects.

The cockroaches are done when the legs come off easily, though some prefer to cook them longer. They may be shelled before eating.

Danny showed up and explained that he was late because the gun had been buried on the other side of the commune. (The gun was a .22 rifle, automatic, with a broken stock. The original owner had killed seven dogs with it, but the rest of the pack had dragged him or her down before the rifle could be reloaded.)

They crossed the river single file, Danny leading. No one fell in, and there were no perils waiting at the opposite bank.

"Where to this time?" Steve asked.

"I've been thinking," Danny said. "We've been wasting time, looking through the stores. That's the first place anybody'd look. We never find more than a can or two." He pointed to his right. "Maybe we'll find some houses down there. Never been—"

"You know what happened the last time we tried houses," Francine said.

"We've got a gun this time."

"We never even saw the one who killed Melissa."

"Don't argue." They started down the road. Two large cats stalked them on either flank. One still showed some trace of Siamese parentage, and growled at them. The cats were fearless but prudent; they would attack and kill a single child, perhaps, but knew not to attack a group.

Besides, cats had no trouble finding food in the City.

RAT

Some rats
Water
Ashes
Salt

Slit the rats' throats immediately after killing, and hang by their tails to bleed. When bled, immerse in boiling water to which a handful of ashes has been added. Scald the rats for about a half-hour, then remove and scrape the hair off with a dull knife. Eviscerate and soak in salt water overnight (the heads may be removed and used for stock). Parboil in salt water until tender, and then bake or fry.

They came into a suburban area, where fire-gutted ruins fronted broad expanses of weed. Dark red jumbles of rust stood in driveways and carports.

Finally, one house looked promising. The top floor had burned and collapsed, but the ground floor seemed in fairly good condition. Through a broken window, they could see the white gleam of a refrigerator.

They picked their way carefully through the rubble, into the kitchen. The refrigerator yielded nothing but dry gray fluff and old crockery. But there was a pantry full of canned goods. No freeze-dried food, unfortunately. They knew from experience that most of the canned goods would be spoiled.

The first twenty or so cans gave up nothing but parti-colored rot. "Why don't we just kill the cats?" one of the newcomers asked.

"We tried that once," Francine said. "Everybody got sick, like to died."

Danny picked up the gun and slipped the safety off. "Think I heard something," he said. Actually, he just wanted some fresh air. If they found any food, they'd save him a portion.

The dogs almost got him.

He opened the front door and a large, gaunt mastiff, leader of the pack, sprang to its feet and charged. He shot it once in the head and jumped back through the door, slamming it. "Dogs!"

The pack started howling and barking, all on their feet now and milling around.

"Shoot them," somebody said.

"We only have fifteen or sixteen bullets left," Danny said. "Can't waste them." Besides, there were twice that many dogs.

All the children were crowded up against the windows. A large dog started to drag away the mastiff's carcass. Then another bounded over to fight him for it.

"Maybe this," Danny muttered. He took careful aim and killed those two dogs in quick succession. One of them died slowly, with a great deal of noise. The other dogs started to back away. He fired a third time, at a dog on the outskirts of the pack. The bullet just nicked it, but it yelped and ran. That was enough; the whole pack broke up and scattered in panic.

"Have to work fast, now. Who's got the coals?"

"We do." A brother and sister had tin cans full of ash.

"Start a fire out front while me and Steve skin those dogs. Everybody else hunt up wood."

"No wet or rotten wood," Francine said. "We don't want no smoke."

"They know that," Danny said. "You go try and find some water."

She did find some, in the basement hot water heater. They used it to rinse out the carcasses after they had skinned and gutted them. By that time, the fires had roared up and settled back to a bank of hot coals.

They put the dogs on crude spits and roasted them. With the first meat smells, many of the children started crying with hunger and dryly retching. It had been a long winter.

Danny carved pieces off the outside as soon as they were done. "We have to eat it all now," he said. "You know what happens if we try to take any of it back."

The summer and spring before, they had tried to bring roasted dogs back to the commune. One time, a gang of teenagers had jumped them as they came off the bridge. The other time, they hid the meat up in a tree, but the oldsters found out about it somehow and took it for the communal pot. Which meant the kids got very little.

Up in the sentry tower, a man squinted through binoculars. "Here they come," he said to the other man. "Across the railroad bridge."

"All there?"

"There were sixteen when they . . . looks like they're missing two—no, rear guard, coming up. That's Danny Bondini, with the rifle."

"Have any food?"

"Can't tell. Nothing big."

"Wonder what they shot at."

"God knows. Guess it wasn't those dogs we heard."

"Well. We won't stop them this time. Maybe they'll bring something back tomorrow."

"With luck."

SURVIVAL 2075

Assorted men, aged 13–45
Assorted women, aged 13–45
Assorted old people
Assorted children
Limited food supply

Feed the men and women first. If any is left over, give it to such of the old people as are still useful—then to the children, who can forage for themselves, and besides are easily replaced.

Tough Love 3001

Juliet Marillier is the author of the award-winning Sevenwaters trilogy (*Daughter of the Forest, Son of the Shadows, Child of the Prophecy*) and the Saga of the Light Isles novels (*Wolfskin* and *Foxmask*). Her latest book, *The Dark Mirror*, is the first in the Bridei Chronicles. She has also published short fiction in various venues—her "In Coed Celyddon" appears alongside fellow Australian writers Garth Nix and Isobelle Carmody in the YA anthology *The Road to Camelot*, edited by Sophie Masson.

"Tough Love 3001" arose from Marillier's first experience of running a critique group in which she had a mixed bunch of authors—including one fantasy novelist and several people with literary pretensions. "Ultimately, without a natural gift as a story-teller and that essential quality I call 'heart,' no amount of literary technique is going to make a person a good writer," she says. "I learned—painfully—that making something positive out of a critique group is less to do with understanding structure, style, characterization, and so on, and far more to do with breaking down prejudices and tending to wounded egos. The rampant snobbery about so-called genre fiction was a challenge to deal with. Eventually I decided I'd better stop beating myself up after class and release some of my feelings into a piece of writing. When I showed the story to the critique group, the only one who 'got it' was the fantasy writer."

Marillier lives in a hundred-year-old cottage by the Swan River in Guildford, Western Australia. You can learn more about her work on her Web site: www.vianet. net.au/~marill.

This story is dedicated to the eight participants in the 2004 Tough Love *critique course held at the Katharine Susannah Prichard Writer's Centre in Western Australia.*

It's also dedicated to Neil Gaiman, a prince among storytellers.

Ground rules, I said, suppressing a sigh of exasperation. The buzz of eight Unispeak Translators died down and a small sea of eyes, bulging, faceted, retractable, feline, globular, turned in my direction. There was a silence of complete incomprehension.

"Ground rules allow us to maximize the value of our limited number of sessions." The sigh came out despite me. Of all the groups I'd been given for Tough Love since they brought me here from the twenty-first century to run it, this was the motleyest crew of students I'd ever clapped eyes on. I suspected the short course they'd come from all over the galaxy to attend would be just long enough to make a slight dent in the shining armor of false expectations each of them wore today. Who the hell were they? What did they imagine they would get out of this? Not for the first time, I pondered the wisdom of quitting a tenured position at the University of Western Australia for this. I had burned my bridges. Time travel being what it is, there was no going back. The *Intergalactic Voyager* did have state-of-the-art teaching facilities. It did have a bar stocked with every alcoholic drink this side of Alpha Centauri. Its students, on the other hand . . .

An attenuated, multiocular creature was saying something. The Unispeak model I have is the V28: it's programmed to convey style as well as meaning when it translates. This voice was genteel and nervous.

"You mean, keep left? Wash hands after using the facilities? No walking on the syntho-turf?"

I found a smile. "Those are rules, certainly. We might start with something about respecting one another's work, or not interrupting."

They considered this awhile. The one who had spoken quivered her antennae anxiously.

I said, "Perhaps we could go around the circle, and everyone could think of one ground rule."

Silence. For a bunch of individuals who were supposed to be writers, this was not a promising start.

"Be on time?" I suggested. "Wear pink socks?"

They looked blank; I had baffled them. A few seconds passed, then a creature of robust build with a mass of tentacles began to quiver uncontrollably, emitting a series of guttural sobs. "Ah-ha-ha-ho-ho!" my

Unispeak translated. "Very good! Pink socks! I so adore the humor of the absurd! May I contribute?"

"Be my guest," I said, marker pen at the ready. I make a point of using antique technology (repro, that is) for my Tough Love classes. The students find my pens and whiteboard as fascinating as I would quills and parchment. I could see it was going to take more than a few colored Textas to get this lot's creative juices flowing.

"Um," said Tentacles, "let me see now. Be courteous to the teacher? Bow on entry?"

I wrote, *Be courteous*, on the whiteboard. They could all read English; it was a requirement of entry to my course. Unfortunately, some of them were anatomically incapable of speaking it. "Thank you," I said. " 'Bowing is perhaps too culture-specific. Any more?' "

"Even when bored witless, one should not sleep in class," offered a participant whose appearance was markedly sluglike.

I wondered if the Unispeak had been programmed with a sense of humor; insouciance touched with ennui made this voice sound like those old recordings of Noel Coward. "Indeed," I said, writing it on the board. "You won't be getting much sleep at night, either. I'll be setting you daily writing and reading tasks, and you'll all have a piece ready for critique by your allocated session." I wrote, *Do your homework.* "Now," I said, turning to face their expectant eyes, "we're going to go around the circle and introduce ourselves."

There was a ripple of movement which I took to indicate agreement.

"Good. I'm Annie Scott, and as you know I was headhunted from the early twenty-first to run this course. Back then I was a university lecturer in creative writing and literary criticism. This is quite similar."

A collective sigh; the eyes rolled, blinked, flashed in what I decided to interpret as appreciation.

"Your turn," I said, glancing at Tentacles, who seemed the boldest.

He gave his name. Even via the Unispeak it was unpronounceable. "Difficult, I know," he said politely. "You may call me Dickens, if you prefer. I am a fervent admirer of that great writer, Charles Dickens."

"Dickens. Right," I said.

The introductions went on. Dickens had started a trend for literary pseudonyms. By the time we were around the circle we had Brontë, the one with the antennae; Seth the slug; Saramago, whose maniacal grin displayed three rows of pointed teeth; terribly tall, one-eyed Atwood; and Winton, who was vaguely humanoid. Two retained their own names: K'gruz and Armahalon. Armahalon had just sung us a formal greeting of a profoundly cerebral kind when I realized there was a ninth chair in the circle, and that it, too, was occupied. The table at which my students sat had obscured this final attendee; only the tips of its ears could be seen above the edge. I moved closer and peered down, trying not to seem rude. Eight students was standard. That was all they were paying me for.

The creature sat quietly. It was pea-green and slightly fuzzy, like a cheap velour toy. There was a look about it that suggested a dog, or perhaps a corporeally challenged elephant, or one of those things you used to see in wildlife documentaries clinging to trees and looking helpless. The ears were enormous, fragile and winglike. The eyes were liquid and mournful. I had absolutely no idea whether it was an aspiring writer or some trendy kind of lap pet.

"Er . . ." I ventured, "whose is this?"

The students peered down, and the little creature turned its forlorn gaze up at them.

Atwood shuddered. "I'm here to critique, not to be shed on," she murmured.

"If we're talking lap pets," Saramago put in, "give me a Zardonian bog-troll any day. Best alarm system in the Galaxy. And they keep your feet so warm at night."

"What will we discuss today, Teacher?" asked Seth in a voice like a bubbling mud pool.

"Call me Annie, please. Tomorrow we'll start critiquing one another's work. Today we'll practice on a piece by an established author, to ease you in. Critiquing is like walking on a wire. Some writers are utterly delusional about the nature and quality of their own work. Be honest, but temper your honesty with compassion. When someone critiques your writing, it can feel as if they're hurting your beloved child."

"Ah, yes," enthused Dickens, swirling his tentacles in a show of agreement. "Beloved child, yes. Better if we tell soothing lies?"

"You must tell truths expressed with understanding and kindness," I told him.

K'gruz was wearing a full-body protective suit with a filter mechanism; his Unispeak appeared to be hard-wired directly into his head. The voice emerged from a speaker. "I cannot be kind about Saramago's work!" K'gruz exclaimed. "He writes by hand, and he uses green ink secreted from his own disgusting glands. How can one take such a writer seriously? The presentation is entirely unprofessional. As for his *oeuvre* itself, it stinks more richly than the filth with which he sets it down. The concepts, the themes, the woeful lack of punctuation . . . where can I start?" If K'gruz had possessed eyebrows, at that point they would have arched extravagantly. As it was, he managed an expressive shrug that made his suit and its contents ripple.

I opened my mouth to intervene before Saramago decided to use his teeth, but the ladylike Brontë cut in.

"Ink? Ink is nothing! There is no point to any of it if we cannot divine a *resonance*, a *truth*, a *transcendence*, a—"

"Don't kid yourself," growled K'gruz. "Your own work is nothing more than an inflated piece of fluff, hardly good enough for a quickvid on a short-hop interplanetary transit of the less salubrious kind. You're in no position to question literary—"

"Friends, friends!" Seth was trying to make peace. "Ground rules, please—" but nobody was listening. Saramago was snapping his teeth, Brontë's antennae were trembling with indignation, Armahalon had one foot on the table, revealing scythelike toenails that were none too clean, and Winton was leaning back in his chair, laughing hysterically. Atwood was taking notes.

"Excuse me—" I said.

"Class, please—" I cried out.

"Stop acting like a bunch of spoiled infants!" I yelled.

"Alas, teacher," Dickens spoke in my ear, "I fear this Tough Love is no more than a battleground for exhausted ideas."

Under different circumstances I'd have complimented him on his turn of phrase. Things were getting nastier by the second. Saramago had sunk his teeth into the nearest available object, which was Brontë's hand; she was emitting little shrill cries of outrage. K'gruz was fiddling with a dial on his protective suit, from which a thin stream of evil-smelling yellow vapor was hissing forth. Seth and Armahalon were locked in an embrace that had nothing at all to do with interspecies attraction. Even Winton was getting in a random uppercut here and there. Atwood's digits were tapping away overtime on her Personal Recording Device (PRD). She had the new model, the one that communicates direct with a Unispeak and reads your work back to you in your language of choice. So much for green ink. I was being paid a fortune to run this, and my class had degenerated into a whistling, shrieking, punching, gasping free-for-all.

<<onceuponatimeinakingdomdfarfarawaytherelivedaprincessina towerofglass>>

The stream of sound pierced my skull at a decibel level designed to induce rapid-onset insanity. It was clear from the sudden stillness and agonized expressions of the others that it had hit them the same way.

<<awickedsorcererhadlockedherupandthrownawaythekeyheronly companionswerethelittlebirdsoftheforestrobinwrenjayowlthrushand swallowarewedonenow?>>

The agony ended. Wincing, we took our hands off our aural receptors.

"Who did that?" I asked shakily. It had been the most unthinkable kind of interruption, a violent mind-assault of the kind generally employed only in situations of military interrogation. I hadn't thought I'd need to put *No torture* in the ground rules.

Eight sets of eyes swiveled toward the handbag-sized creature, which turned its liquid gaze on me and spoke in a tone now mellow and musical.

"Sorry, Teacher. I considered you a damsel in distress, and was compelled to attempt a rescue."

I wrote *No mind-blasts* on the whiteboard. "And your name is?" I snapped.

"Ne'il." The sound was delivered on a mournful, falling cadence. A neat glottal stop divided it into two clear syllables.

"Neil?" asked Atwood. "Who Neil?"

"O'Neill?" suggested Seth. "Eugene O'Neill?"

I waited. Very probably, Green Handbag had stolen a march on me.

"Wait a minute." Brontë was scratching her head; it was an impressive sight. I had never seen such flexible antennae. "He forced a story into us with his beastly mind-blast. A *fairy tale.*" She glared at Ne'il accusingly.

"Ne'il Gae-munn," he said, making a little song of it.

"Neil Gay-mun?" Winton echoed. "Who the heck was he?"

I saw the shudder go through Brontë's whole body; the cold disapproval enter Armahalon's eyes.

"Some of you know Neil Gaiman's work, I see." I ignored the chill in the air and went on gamely. "This is quite a coincidence, unless, of course, our friend here has psychic abilities. The story we're going to look at now is one of Gaiman's. It's coming through on your PRDs now; please read it silently and we'll discuss it when you're finished."

There was a mutinous quality about the ensuing silence. After a little, Brontë spoke. "This exercise is a waste of time for me. I can't comment on this kind of thing. I don't understand the conventions."

"If I had known we were going to discuss *genre* fiction," Armahalon delivered the offending word with brittle distaste, "I would never have enrolled for the class."

"I, too, am a literary writer," Dickens put in apologetically.

"This is for children," growled K'gruz. "Stepmothers, dwarves, magic fruit . . . It can have nothing at all to do with an advanced class in literary critique."

I waited.

Seth was a fast reader; he was already well into the story. "For children? Oh, I do not think so," he said. "It is a dark tale. Unsettling."

"I need coffee," Saramago declared, rising to his feet. "Call me when we get to—"

"Sit down!" I said. "I'm in charge here. Read the story. Ne'il, why aren't you reading? You are a participant in the group, aren't you?"

He smiled beatifically, and I imagined Yoda saying, *Old am I.* "I know the tale," he said. " 'Snow, Glass, Apples,' yes?"

"All the same—"

"By heart," he said. "Is not that the home of all good tales: the heart?"

"Some would disagree with you," I told him in an undertone, for the class had been hooked by the story and was reading avidly now. "Some would say the intellect. Or even the soul."

"Mmm," Ne'il said, his eyes luminous. "Or the balls?"

I looked at him.

"Or anatomical equivalent," he said, glancing around the table. There was perhaps one and a half sets of testicles between the lot of us.

"Good joke," I whispered. "We're seriously lacking in humor here. Do you think I can teach this lot to laugh at themselves? Can they find their own hearts, and one another's?"

"If hearts they have," Ne'il said, grinning, "find them we will."

It was a grueling few days. Each student was different. Each was compelled by dreams, hopes, delusions; each was full of insecurity and prejudice, envy and bias. They knew their stuff, that was, the narrow personal corridor of fiction writing each had decided was worthy of his or her in-depth study. Some had real talent. Dickens had written a huge novel of nineteenth-century London, full of sly humor and unforgettable characters. Saramago surprised us with a piece in which comparative religion was studied through father/son relationships. I was impressed that a being with so many teeth at his disposal was the intergalactic equivalent of a humanist. Brontë's work was lightweight, Armahalon's impenetrably deep. Winton spent his nights in the bar and turned up late for class until I called him a slacker. The next day he brought us a delicate piece of short fiction, a gem of stylistic simplicity.

"Ah," Ne'il said. "You are a storyteller."

By the second day they were forming reluctant bonds. By the third day they were going to the bar en masse to down the brew of their choice and argue late into the night about Eliot Perlman's use of the second person and whether magic realism was just a particularly pretentious form of genre fiction. By the final day most of them had seen their own work with new eyes. Brontë was the exception; she hugged her piece defensively, refusing to change a single word. Atwood was restructuring her picaresque epic into a verse novel. K'gruz had reduced the number of breast references in his manuscript from fifty-four to twelve, and found synonyms for *pert* and *perky*.

Ne'il had submitted no written work at all. Every night as the members of Tough Love 3001 gathered in the *Intergalactic Voyager*'s smoky watering hole, he would sit amongst them and tell a story. They were tales of dragons and heroes, of hardship and quest, of self-discovery and heartbreak. They were myths, legends, sagas, and fairy tales. They were, without a doubt, genre fiction. From the moment the diminutive green narrator opened his mouth to the time when he said "and they lived happily ever after," not a soul in that bar made so much as a squeak, a rustle, a sigh. Ne'il had them in the palm of his hand, or anatomical equivalent.

———

At the final class, I thanked them for their dedication and hard work and was able to say quite truthfully that I was sorry the course was over. They offered grave compliments in return: they had learned much, they would never forget me, they would be back next year.

"Where's Ne'il?" I asked, seeing the ninth chair was empty. "Has his shuttle left already? He didn't say good-bye."

"Alas, we do not know," said Dickens. "Perhaps he has exhausted his fund of tales. All good things come to an end. Annie, we wish to present you with this gift in token of our appreciation."

I'd been rather hoping for a bottle of wine or perhaps a flask of the powerful *k'grech* they brewed on K'gruz's home planet. This silver-wrapped parcel was more the size and shape of a cake, or maybe a hat. I tore off the ribbon and the shiny paper and choked in horror.

It was a handbag. It was fuzzy and green, velourlike in texture, and had a cosy rotundity of form. The handle was constructed from two large, ear-shaped flaps knotted together.

"We made it for you," Armahalon said in his humming tones.

"We made it all together," said Saramago, showing his teeth.

"I've never liked fantasy," observed K'gruz. "All those dragons and women in gauze and leather. It's so . . . so . . . ."

I clapped my hands over my mouth, wondering if I could make it to the gleaming toilet facilities of the *Intergalactic Voyager* before I spewed up my breakfast all over the floor. Stars spun before my eyes; my knees buckled.

"Dickens, fetch water," a familiar voice murmured somewhere close by. "Our attempt at humor has misfired. Annie, do not cry."

"You should read more nonfiction, Annie," said Atwood drily. "Didn't you know Ne'il's species shed their skins every full moon?"

I opened my eyes. There beside me on the floor was Ne'il, or at least I assumed it was he; his new skin was a delicate shade of mauve.

"It's closer to lilac," he corrected, smiling. "See, you taught them to laugh."

"That wasn't funny!" I snapped as my heartbeat returned to normal. "I thought—"

"Ah," said Ne'il, "you forgot my name. Is not the sweetest of fairy tales tinged with darkness? Such duality lies at the heart of all experience: light and shadow, safe reality and fearsome imagining, fruitful summer and fallow winter. Has not the most charming of Gae-munn's work a tiny touch of horror?"

"What?" gasped Brontë, looking truly affronted. "Fantasy *and* horror? You mean there's such a thing as—*double-genre?*"

"Never mind," I said. "Write your stories, dream your dreams, work hard, and come back next year if you can. And if I don't see you again, live happily ever after."

The bag was heavy. When I got back to my room I discovered it held three squat miniflasks of top quality *k'grech,* guaranteed to blow out the drinker's eyeballs. My students had passed with flying colors.

Chanting the Violet Dog Down

A Tale of Noreela

BY TIM LEBBON

Tim Lebbon's novels include *Desolation*, *Berserk*, *The Nature of Balance*, *Face*, and *Until She Sleeps*. His work has been published in dozens of anthologies and magazines, including *The Year's Best Fantasy & Horror*. He has won a Bram Stoker Award, a Tombstone Award, and two British Fantasy Awards, as well as being nominated for a World Fantasy Award. Lebbon is one of the young stars in the resurgence of speculative fiction in the UK; a number of his stories are being developed for film and television, and he has recently finished working with Mike Mignola on a new Hellboy project. You can read more about Lebbon's work at www.timlebbon.net.

Lebbon is never afraid of writing a "difficult" story. Characters in his world suffer and hurt in ways most of us can only imagine—and if we are actually honest with ourselves would never want to imagine. His signature on a story inevitably means that the reader is going to share some of that suffering. "Chanting the Violet Dog Down" is no exception. It offers a unique glimpse into the dark heart of Noreela, the setting for Lebbon's most recent novel, *Dusk,* and its forthcoming sequel, *Dawn* (Bantam Dell). The land is in turmoil. Noreela itself is dying. The first stage of that long slow death is the fading of the magic that bound the bones of the world together, and with it, its powers to keep the stuff of nightmares at bay. The Mourners from the Temple of Lament do their best to help the dead find rest, but sometimes their best is not enough. There's a wealth of information about the Mourners, the Violet Dogs, and the many wonders of Noreela on the dedicated Web site at www.noreela.com.

Lebbon lives in Monmouthshire, Wales.

The Mourner stared down at the empty graves, and began to wonder why.

She had come a long way to be here and now that she realized her trip was wasted, there was little to do but turn and head for home. There were no dead to dwell over, no wraiths to chant down to peace with her strange songs . . . only a field of ragged holes, soil humped beside them like recumbent loved ones grieving lost friends.

She walked slowly across the field. It had snowed last night, and the rough bottoms of the graves were coated with a virgin layer. The soil piled around them still broke surface, as though warm enough to melt any snow that settled there. The Mourner knelt, scooped up a mixed handful of snow and soil and let it fall between her fingers. Cold. She closed her eyes and delved inward, but it was cold in there as well.

The only footprints were her own.

She stood and hugged her cloak around her. A cool breeze blew in from the north, agitating the forest that bounded the northern edge of the field and shaking snow from the leafless limbs. It fell in dusty sprays, creating false movement in the shadows. The Mourner sighed and tried to look deeper.

She had walked two hundred miles from Long Marrakash, stopping only to eat and once to sleep, and all the way she had been dwelling on the period of Mourning to come. In the Temple of Lament she had been touched by the sense of death from this place; a virulent disease had wiped out most of the small village of Kinead, and she had collected her meager belongings and gone to serve as its Mourner. She and others like her drifted to and fro across the north of Noreela, out to sites of great loss and back again, like tides of blood in a great living thing; the Temple of Lament its heart, the places of death its fading extremities. It was ironic that as the land slowed down, so its blood flowed faster.

The walk had been long, the going harsh, and those hours and days of introspection had served to sharpen her mind.

Now she was cold and tired, and her mental preparation had formed a weight inside, a pressure craving release. She had been expecting several days of mourning, yet she had found only empty holes in the ground. The bodies had gone elsewhere, and she could sense no wraiths to chant down.

She walked back and forth across the field, looking down into each rough hole but finding only more snow. She was well versed in death and she could see that these graves, though opened up and spread across the ground, were still relatively new. Whatever had once occupied them had been buried weeks, perhaps even days before. There were no loose bones here, no scraps of rotten clothing, no mad wraiths skimming beneath the surface of the world as they tried to come to terms with living no more. And with every breath she took, the Mourner sensed the scent of fresh death on the air.

She scanned the foliage bounding the graveyard, the shadows beneath the trees, searching for observers or signs of the absent dead. There were none. She was alone with these waiting holes.

"Death can go nowhere on its own," she whispered, and a breeze snatched her words away like rare birds. She heard their echo, though there was nothing to echo from.

She left the empty graveyard and headed through the trees for Kinead.

Perhaps before the Cataclysmic War two centuries before Kinead might have been a happy, healthy village. But like many places across Noreela since that terrible War ended, this village was falling into ruin. Stone buildings were patched and repaired with timber, and timber dwellings were rotting into the ground. The frozen stream was black as night, the two tracks passing through the village were filled with potholes, and a large machine stood motionless at the crossroads, its hollowed stone and metal carcass exposed to the elements. A skull raven sat atop the dead machine, watching the Mourner as she walked slowly into the silence.

There were no signs of life. Snow blanketed the village, its surface pristine and untouched by anything other than a few lonely, hungry birds. The door to the tavern was wedged open by a chair lying on its back. The Mourner passed by, glancing inside but unable to make out any detail. It was dark in there. She could smell spilled ale and rotten food. She closed her eyes; still no wraiths.

"Where are you?" she said. The village did not answer.

She moved to one of the stone dwellings, mounted its terrace, and stood before the door. There was a red smudge on the dark timber, as if something bloody had been thrown against it. She looked around her feet but the terrace was empty. A small nudge from her boot opened the door with a creak of frozen hinges. She held her breath, probing inside for the owner's wraith but finding nothing. She could smell only must and age, not the stench of rot. No bodies here.

The people of Kinead were dead, their diseased passing rapid and painful enough to have been felt at the Temple of Lament. Every death was different, and the Mourner could recall the sense of Kinead's doom settling across her mind like a slayer spider's corrosive web. *Something unnatural*, she had thought, but that idea was not new. Much that happened in Noreela these days was strange.

During her journey from Long Marrakash, the bodies of Kinead's dead had been exhumed and taken away. With them, still attached by the shock of death and their fear of the endless Black that awaited them, their wraiths.

Taken where? the Mourner thought. *And why?*

"You're here!" The voice held both wonder and dread. "I knew you would rise from the hollow field, I knew you'd come, I could smell you down there, hear you, *taste* you!"

The Mourner turned around and saw the naked man. He was standing shivering beside the dead machine, his skin gray in some places, red and purple in others where the cold had killed his flesh. He had a long beard clotted with blood, and in one feeble hand he carried a rusty sword. His fingers seemed to merge with the handle as though he could never let go.

"Who are you?" the Mourner asked. "Where are the dead? I'm here from Lament to mourn and chant them down."

"Lament?" the man said. He frowned, took a couple of faltering steps, and went to his knees. He held the sword up before him. "You're not the Violet Dog?"

Violet Dog! The words surprised the Mourner; so filled with dread yet uttered infrequently, and heard even less.

"No," the Mourner said, remembering long lonely periods spent reading in her room at Lament. "There are no Violet Dogs. They're a story from before history."

The man looked at her, his eyes surprisingly bright in a face so wan. He seemed to be searching for something. She lowered her cloak's hood and let him see her face, and his eyes went wide. "Are you a Mourner?"

"I am," she said.

"Then what of the Violet Dog?" The man looked around as if expecting someone or something else to join in the conversation.

The Mourner did not reply. Instead she pulled one hand from the wide sleeve of her cloak and delved inside for her knife. She plucked it from the strap around her waist and held it at the ready. The man was weak, almost dead, and he seemed to pose no real threat. But the air was filled with violence. She looked left and right around the village, and for the first time she saw and recognized the red splashes on many of the doors. Hand prints, in paint or blood. Perhaps they were signs of those households having fallen victim to the disease, or . . .

The Violet Dogs enjoy the taste of pain. They savor the tang of fear in the flesh, and they may mark their victims days or weeks before taking them. Words the Mourner had read long ago in forgotten books, yet now they came to her unannounced.

"Death-whore!" The man came at her. He was surprisingly fast, jumping to his feet and covering the distance between them before the Mourner could lift her knife. He struck her across the forehead with the sword's hilt and fell on her as she stumbled back, pushing her down into the snow. It soaked quickly through her cloak, making her as cold as the dead. The man grinned down.

"Leave those wraiths where they flail and suffer," he said. Spittle dribbled from his mouth and landed on her face. It was warm. She saw fever in his eyes, and she wondered how long he had left.

"I came here to—"

"You're not needed," the man said. "*It* needs them, the Violet Dog, and it will be here to claim their rotting corpses soon."

"There are no—"

"Violet Dogs?"

The Mourner tried to shift but the man held her down. Thin though he was, naked and half-dead from cold and disease, still he found strength in his madness. *Perhaps he'll kill me*, the Mourner thought. She glanced at his hands, looking at his nails to see whether they held grave dirt beneath them. But his nails were all torn off. And the sword raised in his right hand was not darkened by rust after all.

"Maybe," he said. He drew close, the stubbled black flesh of his chin scraping the Mourner's cool lips. "Maybe not for a while. But the land is changing. And I know at least one of the secrets it's thrown up." He stood, turned, and ran.

By the time the Mourner lifted herself from the ground, the man had vanished. He knew Kinead, she did not, and there was no chance of finding him.

So where are the dead? she thought. She closed her eyes and calmed herself by listening for newly dead wraiths, but she heard only the background mumble that was evident almost anywhere in the land. Whispers from before history began, louder mutters from those dead these past few years, these were wraiths either at peace or with voices grown distant over time. *Where are you?* she thought. She expected and received no reply.

She considered going back to the field of open graves. Perhaps there she would find clues to the dead villagers' location: drag marks in the ground, a splayed corpse pointing the way. But she was tired, hungry, and thirsty, and it had started snowing again.

And there was something else. Though the rest of the village remained completely silent—the movement of the air itself dampened by the snow—she felt observed. The unsettling sensation had been growing since discovering the empty graves, and it had reached a new intensity the moment the naked madman left her lying on the ground. She scanned the village; windows, doorways, shadows beside leaning buildings and beneath leafless trees, rooftops and the spaces beneath stilted homes. She could see no one else. Even the skull raven had gone from atop the dead machine, though she had not heard it fly away. The living had gone from this place, yet the mystery remained: the dead had vanished too.

The Mourner closed her eyes but sensed only time paying her attention, stretching out behind much farther than it ever could before. History was so rich and full, and the future held no certainties. The Cataclysmic War had seen to that.

The snow thickened, the first brief flurries replaced quickly with fat, wet flakes. The sky promised much more to come. The Mourner looked at the red hand prints on the doors of Kinead's buildings, certain that the madman had put them there yet still disturbed by their presence. Virtually every door she saw had a print, and one that did not—across from the frozen stream, a run-down dwelling that seemed to have a tree growing from its roof had suffered a recent fire. Its timber walls had fallen in, and the tree growing through its remains was charred black.

I wonder if the Violet Dog has come back to claim its victims, she thought, then shook her head and sighed. There *were* no Violet Dogs. Even if they *had* ever existed, it had been so long ago that there was only doubt and myth about their existence now, not fact. She had read books, yes, and heard occasional rumors of them when she came out into the world to mourn, and once she had met a woman in Pavisse who claimed to know where one was buried. But the woman had died soon after from Plague, and the Mourner had left Pavisse several days later exhausted from mourning so many thousands of dead.

She had forgotten the woman's mention of the Violet Dogs, until now.

The Mourner turned and looked at the tavern. It was the only building with an open door. She would not feel right forcing her way into any of the homes, dead though their owners were. As she approached the tavern entrance, she avoided looking at the front of the door. Inside there would be food and drink and somewhere to rest, and she did not need foolish superstition to trouble her while she decided what to do next.

The villagers were dead, and to chant down their troubled wraiths, first she had to find them.

As she tried to pull the jammed door closed behind her, the Mourner heard the man shouting from elsewhere in the village: "It will make you one of them as well, Mourner!"

The stench of rotwine permeated the tavern. Beneath that lay the memory of a million conversations, all of Noreela's history—true and not so true—discussed here over food and drink, while all the time the land wore down, dragging its people with it.

The Mourner leaned against the bar, exhausted. A clay mug toppled to the floor and shattered. She held her breath and listened for a reaction. None came, not even the sound of a startled rat scurrying for cover.

"The graveyard is empty," the Mourner said. Living in such solitude at the Temple of Lament meant that she was used to her own company, and talking to herself made her feel less alone. It could also give life to places never meant to fall silent. "Something dug up the recently dead and took them away. The naked madman . . . though he looks almost dead himself. Frostbite. Disease. And where or what is the hollow field?" She leaned over the bar and found an unopened bottle of rotwine. She hated the vile drink, but right now she needed something to wet her dry insides. She was unused to fear, and the attack had shaken her more than she cared to admit.

She popped the cork and drank, wincing at the taste but welcoming the warmth that spread quickly through her body. Even the sound of her swallowing seemed loud.

"And the Violet Dogs," she said. But she spoke no more, because their name seemed to hang in the atmosphere of this place, giving a ghost to the myth.

The Mourner busied herself finding food. There was a stew in a huge pan in the tavern's kitchens, but it had developed a surface mold that puffed a haze of spores as she leaned in to sniff. She found a few sour apples, however, and a loaf of bread that was just edible after she had removed its hardened crusts. She sat at a table in the corner of the tavern, ate and drank, and before long her vision started fluttering between the tavern, and somewhere else.

The tavern: wood oiled black by spilled ale, bar polished smooth by decades of patrons, the air heavy and still and possessed of a ghostly shine from snow reflecting through the two small windows.

Somewhere else: a large open plain leading down to the sea, a collection of timber dwellings huddled in a small valley, and in the distant port a forest of tall masts sailing in.

Here, and there. Present, and past. The Mourner's head nodded forward, and though she fought against it she could not prevent sleep from taking her away.

There is panic in the village. A rider had come from the port, spreading news of invaders from the sea, though he quickly rode on before anyone could glean more sense from him. So the villagers stand at the western approach and stare down at the port, where flames sprout in several places and smoke rises into the still autumn air, and the shapes rushing outward are too fast to be the town's fleeing inhabitants.

In the port, a hundred strange ships bob at anchor.

We should leave, someone says.

We can't leave, this is our home and we should fight, comes the reply.

I'm scared, a child says, and the adults realize too late where their duties lie.

The red tide swarms up the shallow hillsides from the port, screeching and yelling, wailing and crying out words that no one here understands. Their legs are long and muscled, arms thin and spindly, bare torsos red with tattoos or spilled blood, and their heads are doglike with teeth as long as a man's finger. They stand twice the height of any villager. They are incredibly fast. And their intent is obvious.

The first Violet Dog reaches the village and buries an ax in a woman's face. The other villagers are fleeing now, some of them taking up puny weapons against the attackers, and even as the last of them is killed, so the woman with the axed head rises from the ground and sets off with a shambling gait toward the east. She is dead, but somehow she finds the breath to scream.

The Mourner sprang awake. A scream had stirred her, and she wondered whether it was her own.

She rubbed at her temples to try and work the dregs of the nightmare from her mind. She had many dreams and almost always recalled them, but as she came around this one scattered away, and she was happy to let it go.

Violet Dogs, she thought. *I read about them once, that's why the dream was so vivid.* She frowned, feeling the dream dissipate into a background sense of death gone wrong. *And the madman thought I was one.*

The bottle of rotwine lay spilled on the table, contents still glugging from the broken neck. The remains of her second apple had turned brown. The light from outside had faded, but she could tell by its stillness that it was still snowing heavily. She stood and went to the door, ready to open it and see whether anything had changed.

They'll be there, she thought, *the dead, standing in the street and staring at me, and before them will be the sick naked man, dead now but still much, much better.*

"Out of my damn head!" the Mourner said. She closed her eyes and breathed deeply, holding her hands by her sides and bowing her head. The dream had faded, but its impression remained.

She opened the door. Snow fell thick, already obscuring her footprints to and fro across the track. She wondered what other strange trails were also hidden beneath earlier falls. There was no sign of the man, and no dead villagers stood rooted in the deepening snow. Wherever they were, their wraiths still needed chanting down.

The Mourner left the tavern and pulled the door closed behind her. It was colder than it had been, the snow deeper, and the only sound was the crunching of snow underfoot.

She started searching before even realizing the choice she had made. She could have easily returned to the Temple of Lament in Long Marrakash, but in doing so she would be abandoning the lost dead of Kinead. Few people were ever ready to die.

The Mourner guessed that they must be somewhere in the fields beyond the village. There were not many buildings large enough to hide them all together, and if she closed her eyes and tried to hear their wraiths, there was only the usual background mutter. Nothing new. Fresh wraiths remained very close to their former flesh, and she would have to find one to help the other. So she headed south, planning on circling the village. She kept a wary eye open for the madman.

Her first circle of the village revealed no hints of where the dead had been taken. The snow had lessened slightly, and though that meant she could see further in the fading light, the fresh fall still made the going difficult. Her feet were cold, and she stopped every few hundred steps to sit and rub some warmth back into her toes. No fresh footprints crossed her path.

She moved out a few hundred paces and started a second circle, and she was a quarter-way around when she entered a small copse of trees. She slowed, then stopped, because something was wrong.

The Mourner closed her eyes and listened for wraiths. Nothing. Her own labored breaths sounded unreasonably loud, and trying to slow her breathing made it louder. She looked behind her. Nobody followed. Yet she was being observed. It was the same sensation she'd had when the naked man fled, an idea that she was the center of something's attention, the focus of all its thought.

"Being foolish now," she said. She walked on. "Just that poor dying man, spouting his madness while the disease eats him from the inside out. That's all. There's nothing else out here." She continued, muttering words of comfort and considering how she could barricade the tavern door that evening.

And then the Mourner found the hollow field. She emerged from a copse of trees, pushing her way through a dense wall of undergrowth that had taken on the weight of snow and ice, and the land vanished before her. She stepped back into the embrace of vegetation, suddenly grateful for its spiky touch through her heavy robe. Though bare of leaves it was alive. Before here, in the hollow in the ground, nothing lived.

It was larger than a single field, perhaps two thousand steps across, and surrounded by trees and bushes heavy with snow. Its sides sloped down toward its center, maybe three hundred paces lower than where she now stood. They were formed of smooth, bare rock. Nothing grew down there, and when the snow landed it instantly melted away, forming small streams that trickled down toward the black throat at the hollow's base. A cave? A hole? The Mourner did not know, and she felt no inclination to find out. The village dead needed her. And there was the fear. Because the madman had mentioned this hollow field in the same breath as a Violet Dog, and the Mourner could still remember that woman in Pavisse raging that she knew where one of those mythical creatures was buried.

She turned her back on that place and started pushing back through the trees, her sense of direction subsumed by the simple need to be going *away* from the hollow field. A while later, still surrounded by trees, she heard the first sounds of the dead in her mind.

The Mourner came to a stop with the sweat of fear trickling down her sides.

The wraiths of the dead were crying. They were very quiet, but knowing they were there seemed to make them easier to hear. She closed her eyes and welcomed them in, showing them that she had a song to chant them down. Even then they barely calmed. They raged and whirled in her mind. There were many of them, and they were mad and frightened. Usually the dead feared nothing.

The Mourner started forward, pushing through the trees that grew close together, stepping high to avoid her clothing becoming entangled in the spiky shrubs around their trunks.

Violet Dogs, she thought, those creatures still on her mind. *They're a myth. Living-dead invaders from somewhere out of the land. There are stories, but no proof. Rough dreams for adults mourning the world gone bad. Nightmares for children, threatened with the Violet Dogs to make them behave.* She moved toward the moaning dead, wondering what she would find.

When she parted the final overhanging branches she saw the field, its strange crop, and the naked man dragging himself from one planted corpse to another.

"There's no such thing as a Violet Dog," the Mourner said.

The man seemed to be ignoring her. He was tending his grotesque crop, still naked and crawling from one dead villager to the next. His skin was purple with the rot of disease. The sword had vanished.

There were over a hundred corpses planted across the field. They were fixed to heavy sticks thrust down into the ground, tied by their burial clothes or wrapped around with rope. Most heads bowed down, though a couple had tilted back to stare at the sky with hollowed eye-sockets. Some of the bodies—those that looked as though they had never been buried—bore terrible wounds to their faces and necks.

The Mourner's head was filled with the awful muttering and moaning of their wraiths, though the field itself was silent but for the constant crawl of the madman.

The field was all but bare of snow. The muck was churned up, and puddles of brown water filled dips in the frozen ground. He must have dragged the bodies here one by one, digging them out of their fresh graves and hauling them through the village and the small forest to this dreadful place. Though subsequent snowfalls had covered the drag trails through Kinead, here the snow did not have a chance, because the man never stopped moving. He reached the planted feet of one corpse, ran his rough hands up the dead woman's legs, shook to make sure she was secure, and then moved on to the next.

The Mourner closed her eyes and listened to the wraiths. Still attached, still waiting to be chanted down to peace, they were being tormented by this man's unnatural intent.

"You're doing this for nothing," she said. "There's no Violet Dog to accept your offering. The hollow field was made by a swallow hole. I've heard of them. They're appearing across Noreela now that magic has gone and the land is winding down." She waited for the man to react, but he kept on crawling. The field was painfully silent. "Do you hear me?"

The Mourner stepped forward, emerging from the trees and becoming the second living thing in the field. The man stopped and stared at her, pulling back leathery lips to reveal his few remaining teeth. His left arm seemed to give out and he fell into the mud. He lowered his head and rested it on the ground, hissing, writhing, making strange patterns in the wet earth.

The Mourner closed her eyes, and the man's wraith was already screaming.

"You're dying," she said.

"I don't care. The Violet Dog will be here soon, and it will wake the dead. My mother, my father, my brothers, and my wife. It *will* wake them!" He started sobbing into the wet soil.

"And you?" the Mourner asked. "When you die, do you want to be woken?"

The man looked up, raised himself on outstretched arms. "Of course," he said.

The Mourner shook her head. "The disease has made you mad. The disease, and that thing in the field you can't explain, it's driven you to distraction and—"

"It spoke to me," the man said. His voice was growing weaker. "It told me what to do. I sat in the hollow field for a whole day when the last of my family and friends died. I sat next to the hole, and I was being watched, and it gave me hope."

"Where's the hope in being living-dead?" the Mourner said. "That's what they did, you know, or so it's said. They took life and then remade their victims in their own image. Dead, but walking. There's no hope in that."

"You have no idea. You never lost anything like I have!"

"I never *had* anything like you. No family, no lover. I've always been a Mourner." *I've always been alone,* she thought. But that was more than she ever wanted to say. She closed her eyes and sighed, blocking out the wraiths. She would get to them soon.

"Don't you feel it?" he asked. "You do. You know it's there. And it'll have your soul too."

She turned away from the dying man and walked through the field of corpses. She started at the farthest corner where an old man was tied to a dead tree. Signs of the disease that had killed him were evident, and she quickly found his wraith. Her chant was low and fast, and the wraith calmed and went down into the earth, below this plane and into the next. The corpse looked the same, but the noise in the Mourner's mind was slightly lessened.

She went from body to body, chanting their wraiths down and setting them at peace. She always kept one eye on the man writhing in the mud. He tried to pull himself after her, and occasionally he shouted. But his words were making less sense than ever, his language distorted into a dialect she did not know, and eventually he lay still.

It took her until the sun was dipping to the west to reach the final wraith. It was still raging, and she recognized the man's madness in its violent twisting. All the other wraiths had wanted to be given peace, but this one still awaited the touch of the Violet Dog. However he had come to know about those monsters, he had been so obsessed that his wraith still craved resurrection in rotting flesh.

The Mourner began her chant, low and fast, and she knew that it would take until morning.

___

After she chanted the dead madman's wraith down, she had another nightmare:

The Violet Dogs are attacking a town on the Cantrass Plains. They swarm in from the west, slaughtering horses and sheebok to begin with, then setting into the town's defenders. The people raise a valiant defense, but it is over in a matter of hours. The Violet Dogs wait in the defeated town for a while, eating those dead people too mutilated to rise again, resting, turning their faces to the sun as if challenging its brightness. Many of the dead have already risen and started their shambolic march to the east. They are the Violet Dogs' advance army, sent on to bear the brunt of any more sustained defenses that other towns may offer. But the outcome, inevitably, will be the same.

The town in ruins, the Violet Dogs streak out across the landscape, like a flow of blood heading east. None of them remain behind. They come, they destroy and kill, and then they move on. Their victims rise again. There seems to be no rhyme or reason to their assault, other than to spread the contagion with which they are afflicted.

The Mourner woke up wondering whether the Violet Dogs had ever been truly alive.

She knew that she should bury the dead, but at the same time the thought came, *Why bother?* They were at peace, and moving them from an upright stick to a hole in the ground would do nothing to benefit them. Her job was done. She could leave the corpses to carrion.

And yet the Mourner was not yet ready to head back to Long Marrakash. Something drew her east, not west. Something she had to see, to know, and hopefully to understand. So she went that way, pushing through the trees and undergrowth until she stood on the edge of the hollow field once again, and she tried to imagine just what had driven Kinead's single survivor mad. She had heard of swallow holes in the land, pits that sucked in their surroundings, but she had never seen one until now, and she never truly believed. *It's the land wearing down,* another Mourner had once told her. *It's Noreela eating itself as it dies.*

She started walking down the gentle rocky slope toward the base of the hollow. The snow had started again, and now it was settling on the stone, damping the sound of her footsteps. It felt as though she was walking into air that grew thicker with each step, the coldness offering a resistance she had never felt before. Fear, she supposed, could do that even to a Mourner.

Something cried out above her, and when she looked up she saw a flock of skull ravens flying west to east. They came in over the fields and then swerved, passing around the great bowl in the land instead of straight across it.

She was perhaps halfway to the base of the hollow now, and with every step something inside was urging her to turn and flee. Fear built up, but she could deal with that. A lifetime filled with death had given her a particular insight into that emotion. The thing telling her to turn around was something deeper, darker, less well known. Something more basic.

A hundred steps from the hole at the center of the hollow, the Mourner stopped and fell to her knees. She smelled age and rot and something worse than death. She cried out and tried to back away, but her legs seemed fixed to the ground by the cold, held there as if the cold itself were an attractive force. She waved her arms and leaned to the left, the right. Still she did not move. She could only go forward. Her knees scraped across the sharp rock, staining the snow red. She struggled to her feet again and walked the final few steps, and even there, leaning over the edge and looking down, breathing in the stink of ages as though the land itself were rotting, still she could not see.

As the Mourner fled Kinead, the hollow in the ground and the field of corpses, something intruded into her mind and gave her images of cold and darkness that she could never understand. She did not even take time to collect food and clothing from the village. The snow had increased and she walked into a blizzard, yet the pull of the Temple of Lament was already strong. There lay safety and peace, and a loneliness she knew of old.

"No such things as Violet Dogs," the Mourner said, and the sound of her voice gave comfort. Deadened though it was by the heavy snow, tinged with the fear that she could not shake off, still she started talking, repeating that phrase for as long as it sounded true.

In a very short time she could talk no more.

Butterflies Like Jewels

BY ERIC NYLUND

Eric Nylund has a bachelor's degree in chemistry and a master's degree in chemical physics. He has published five novels: virtual reality thrillers *A Signal Shattered* and *Signal to Noise*; contemporary fantasy novels *Pawn's Dream* and *Dry Water* (nominated for the 1997 World Fantasy Award); and the science fantasy novel *A Game of Universe*. He has also written books for the Halo game universe, including *Halo: The Fall of Reach* and *Halo: First Strike*.

Eric Nylund lives near Seattle with his wife, author Syne Mitchell.

Man will analyze, calculate with microscopic precision, and narrow his perception until one day he will be able to measure everything in his ever-shrinking universe . . . and be able to imagine *exactly nothing.*

—last telegram from Sir Eustace Carter Van Diem
(of the famed Lost Nile Expedition) to the
Royal Geographic Society, 16 March 1841.

Dr. Robert Lang wished he could take the old man anywhere else; the mountains, a beach, he'd even have settled for a night at a bowling alley.

The room had a single bed, a rack of electric bio-monitors, a dust-covered television suspended in the corner, and nothing else to get in the way of the attending staff. It felt like a prison cell—not a private room in the most prestigious elder-care facility in the country.

The man in bed was emaciated, his skin taut and his eyes recessed in their sockets. The last thing Dr. Lang wanted to do was bother him with questions, but he had no choice.

He pulled a chair next to the bed and sat.

"Mr. Van Diem? Sir?"

The old man's eyes fluttered open and focused on the young doctor sitting by his side. His thin lips quavered into a smile. "None of my nurses wear such sad expressions. I appreciate the sentimentality, Dr. Lang."

He reached out and touched Lang's hand. And as if he had felt something unexpected, he suddenly looked at the doctor's hands. "Are you an artist?"

Fifteen years ago, Lang had painted. But he quit art when he'd fallen in love with his one required science class: biology. Before he could blink, he found himself a premed major, up to his eyeballs in student loans, and at Oceanview as a resident. He knew helping people was his life's work . . . but sometimes he missed being able to make his imaginings real and create whole worlds on canvass.

"Yes, a long time ago."

Van Diem nodded and withdrew his hand.

"Are you well enough to talk, sir?"

"Ah." Van Diem struggled to shift his frail frame higher upon his pillow. "You wish to discuss Dr. Ambrose."

"You were the last to see him." Dr. Lang resisted the impulse to add the word *alive* to the end of this statement.

It had been six days since Ambrose went missing in the middle of his rounds. His Mercedes remained in the parking garage, his coffee half-drunk on his desk; they even found his notes in this room, halted mid-sentence.

"Do you remember anything?" Lang asked, leaning closer. "Something perhaps you forgot to tell the police?"

"Are you my doctor, now?" Van Diem's hazel eyes lit like tiny candles, and he sat straighter. "Anything we discuss is covered by doctor-patient confidentiality?"

Lang wasn't sure what he meant. He glanced at Van Diem's chart. There was no mention of senility, Alzheimer's, or other dementia in the hundred-four-year-old man.

"Of course," he said.

Unless, Lang failed to state, a life was at stake. And one was: Lang's.

The police had him marked as their prime suspect in Dr. Ambrose's disappearance. His arguments with Ambrose were well known to the staff. There had been a scuffle last month over a nurse. Everyone hated Ambrose. He was indifferent to his patients' suffering, molested the nurses, and enjoyed playing God. Lang, however, had been the only one on the staff who had communicated his feelings with his fists.

His animosity for the man must have been obvious to the detectives when they had interviewed him.

Van Diem cleared his throat, startling Dr. Lang from his wandering thoughts.

"You were somewhere else, young man?"

"Yes, I'm sorry."

The old man stared into Lang's eyes, unblinking.

Van Diem was another mystery. According to his records he came to Oceanview Convalescent Home thirty years ago. In his commitment statement, he said he needed peace and quiet before he continued his journey. He had no previous medical records. No social security number. His bills were paid from a Cayman Islands account.

Dr. Lang took a pen from his coat and flipped open his notepad. "Ambrose saw you on his rounds, and then? Did he leave? Was there anyone with him?"

"Yes. He came. He left. Alone. Not." Van Diem's voice was a rustle of dry leaves. He inhaled. "I smell tobacco and vanilla bean." His gaze drifted to Lang's lab coat pocket. "You have a pipe?"

Lang wondered how Van Diem could smell such a thing, but nonetheless fished Dr. Ambrose's pipe from his pocket. It was a meerschaum. The white stone was carved into an elephant's head, trunk flowing into the stem, and large ears folded against the body of the bowl. Lang could make out tiny wrinkles in the animal's skin so lifelike that he half expected its soulful eyes to blink.

"I found it in the hall, in the ashcan." Lang shrugged. "I should turn it over to the police, I suppose. They could swab it for DNA—"

Van Diem grabbed Lang's wrist and drew him close. "No!" He looked at his hand, talon-like, grasping Lang. He frowned and released the doctor.

Lang rubbed his wrist, astonished at the old man's strength.

"My apologies, Dr. Lang, but you must not give that to the police. It is mine."

Lang had never imagined someone so old could have moved so fast. Psychotic mania triggered by what? The pipe? He dared not question him further.

"I'd better leave. I'm upsetting you."

"No. Please." Van Diem exhaled and his body seemed to collapse beneath the rumpled sheet. "I'll tell you where Dr. Ambrose is."

He closed his eyes and fell silent.

Dr. Lang waited, eager to hear more, but after a full minute of silence, he feared that he had triggered a stroke in Van Diem. He reached for the man's wrist.

Trancelike, Van Diem spoke: "I will show you where he is, doctor. Yes, that is the only way. But you must bring my expedition bag from storage. The pipe, too. And bring matches . . . plenty of matches."

At midnight, Dr. Lang descended into the basement of Oceanview. He'd never come here before; he didn't like the dark. His overactive imagination, he supposed.

But he had been motivated by the old man's queer insistence . . . that, and a tip from his lawyer that the DA intended to file charges against him in the morning.

So he'd come down here; he had to find Ambrose. Even a long shot was worth following. Whatever he found, it had to use it carefully—jog Van Diem's memory and discover Ambrose's whereabouts—but he didn't want to risk getting the old man too excited. It might kill someone his age.

Lang flicked on the lights; dim forty-watt bulbs hung like necrotic fruit throughout the half-acre chamber. Rows of shelving stretched to the ceiling and cast a matrix of shadows. It smelled of concrete and rat piss.

He quieted his irrational fears and entered.

Boxes on the shelves bore dated tags and Lang strode back in time, thirty years, until he found one marked: Diem, V. / Personal Effects No.: 98456.

Dust coated everything in this basement . . . and there were scuffs around this box as if it had been recently moved.

He considered calling the police and have them dust for fingerprints. But what if they didn't care? What if they did and there was nothing to this? They could take him into custody and he'd never get another chance to see what Van Diem wanted so badly.

Lang snapped on a pair of latex gloves and eased the box to the floor.

Inside was a leather bag, blackened with age, and if Lang wasn't mistaken, made from rhinoceros hide. It bore several scars and a bullet hole.

He gingerly opened the bag; the leather creaked. Inside there were two side layers that hinged open to reveal dozens of individual compartments. Within the center space was a rotten butterfly net. There were moldering maps with notes handwritten in Arabic. Inside the smaller compartments were beetles, butterflies, worms, in jars filled with alcohol, others pinned, and some held by tiny mechanical pincers to immobilize their legs.

What did an entomologist's collection kit have to do with Ambrose's disappearance? Despite what it said on Van Diem's chart, Lang now doubted the old man's mental faculties.

He closed the bag and picked it up. It felt heavier than it had before.

Lang crept back upstairs, and carefully looked up and down the halls to make sure no one was there. Every fourth fluorescent light was on, flickering, leaving dollops of shuddering illumination on the blue and gray tiles. He slinked past a cart full of uneaten creamed chicken, rice, and lime Jell-O.

He slipped into Van Diem's room without knocking. To his surprise the old man was awake, reading a magazine.

Van Diem spied the bag in Lang's hand and sat up.

"I brought what you wanted." Lang set the bag on the bed, which groaned under its weight.

Lang noticed a new nightstand that hadn't been there this afternoon. On it were scientific journals: *Physical Review D, Topics in Topology,* and *Biochemical Clinical Psychology.*

Van Diem dragged the bag into his lap.

From under his covers more magazines spilled open onto the floor. Lang bent to pick them up, finding dog-eared articles such as: "Unstable N-Manifolds Key to Stability," "Signal Structure of Chemically Imbalanced Neurons," "Wavefunction Probability Distribution and the Many-Worlds Theorem."

Fishing through the bag, Van Diem said, "Now we find Ambrose. You will help me."

"He wanted what was in your bag?"

"Yes and no. The bag, my mind. Ambrose asked for answers . . . no, that's not accurate. He tricked the answers from me." Van Diem smoothed a hand over his head, through wispy white hair that Lang was certain had not been there this morning. "My pipe? Did you bring it as well?"

Lang wasn't sure letting him have the pipe was a good idea. Then again, the old man was talking; he wasn't making much sense, but perhaps he could sort the fiction from the fantasy of Van Diem's sudden mania. And besides, Lang had already tampered with potential evidence; there was no going back now.

He produced the meerschaum pipe and handed it to Van Diem.

The old man turned it over in his trembling hands, inspecting the white carved stone as if it were a precision instrument, caressing the wrinkles of the elephant's trunk.

"You can't smoke in the building. I'll get a wheelchair—"

"Be good enough to strike me a light," Van Diem said, "would you?"

Lang considered. What harm could it do? There was no pure oxygen in the room, and he'd be here to watch. And did he really want the orderlies and the outside security cameras to see him wheeling around the centenarian for a midnight smoke?

He opened the window and then fumbled through his pocket and handed Van Diem a pack of wooden matches.

"Ah, good, matches. Infinitely better than a lighter. A moment please."

Van Diem opened his expedition bag and removed maps dotted with islands and Greek symbols, a dried toad, and a case of impaled butterflies with wings of opal, then halted when he found an ivory vial. He uncorked it and dumped its contents into his hand: three thumb-sized satin green moths. He then packed the creatures into the bowl of the meerschaum pipe.

"Perception is the key." Van Diem struck a match and watched the fire blossom; flames mirrored in his eyes. He touched the match to the dead insects and sucked the heat through the pipe. The creatures glowed, and their legs moved in the heat. They crackled and popped. They looked disturbingly alive, wriggling in the flames.

One puff, a second, and he inhaled deeply. Blue smoke curled from his lips and nose and the bowl. It smelled of vinegar and vanilla.

He exhaled, saying, "Most see only the faintest film of reality that surrounds them."

The air thickened and the smoke, rather than dissipating, remained curled and baroque tendrils of faintly luminescent fumes that caressed the air.

"There is so much more."

The smoky veils parted . . . and the room changed.

Lang blinked once, twice, three times, unsure if he saw correctly.

Van Diem's bed grew four posts and a canopy of red velvet. The blue and gray tiled floor rippled into hard stripes of stained oak. Shadowy Rembrandts in gilt frames pushed their way through the mint green paint of the walls. Gas lamps with Tiffany glass flickered on.

Van Diem's eyes were dark green, and they looked like two small beetles.

Lang stood immobile, choking on half-formed words, trying to assemble a coherent thought. And then one bubbled to the forefront of his conscious mind: panic.

He ran for the room's door, ripped it open, and sprinted down the hall, knocking over the cart piled with leftover dinners. Recovering, he made a mad dash to his office.

Behind him, Van Diem chuckled.

Lang paced in his office, behind its locked door, trying to work the terror from his body. He marched to his rosewood desk, back to the wall of reference books, and then to his desk where he sat and logged onto his computer.

Hallucination. It had to have been a psychotropic chemical carried by the smoke. It had happened too rapidly, though, like no hallucinogenic agent he knew. And those beetles in Van Diem's bag were thirty years old. What drug remained potent for so long?

Lang punched up the hospital's database and opened Van Diem's file. The old man was the key to this. It was the same nondata posted on his chart.

There had to be data on the man somewhere. No one existed in an information vacuum in this day and age.

Lang went online, typed "Edward Van Diem" into a search engine, and pressed ENTER.

He inhaled deeply, waiting for his query to bounce across the Internet. He could still smell vinegar and vanilla. In his peripheral vision he saw ripples, looked and saw only the dark wood grain of his walnut desk.

An aftereffect of the drug?

His computer screen blinked and Lang saw hundreds of search matches—but not for the "Edward Van Diem" he had typed, rather for one "Sir Eustace Carter Van Diem."

There were links to the history of African exploration, lists of controversial knighthoods granted in nineteenth-century England, the home page of the Royal Geographical Society, famous archeological digs in the Valley of the Kings, and accounts of lost expeditions to find the headwaters of the Nile.

Lang opened a page at random.

A tin daguerreotype appeared on screen. In it a spry elderly man in khakis and pith helmet stood between Zulu warriors who towered over him, their hands on his shoulders. The warriors brandished spears and were bedecked with feathers, smiles, and little else. The old man smiled, too. He held a Westly-Richards elephant rifle in one hand . . . and cradled a pipe in the other.

Lang magnified the image.

The pipe was white meerschaum, its bowl carved into the shape of an elephant.

Could Edward Van Diem be this man's grandson? He scrolled his magnified screen to the face. The resemblance was uncanny.

Lang wasn't sure what was going on, but hallucinations or not, Van Diem was talking now, and Lang had to hear what he had to say.

He licked his lips, his mouth suddenly dry. He'd listen to Van Diem, but he'd take a few precautions.

Lang unlocked the drawer in his cedar desk, grabbed the snub-nosed .38 there, and shoved it into his coat pocket. Just in case. He wasn't going to let whatever happened to Ambrose happen to him . . . if he could help it.

"Come in, come in, Doctor. You are late for tea."

Lang's eyes registered what used to be Van Diem's room, but he failed to comprehend what he saw. He stood half in and half out of the doorway. He stood half in and half out of another world.

A chandelier of a thousand cut crystals hung from the ceiling thirty feet above the polished cream-and-pink checkerboard floor. The three facing walls were green glass, with round portals cut into them that led to gardens filled with Olympian statues and flashing fountains. And upon the horizon stood towers of aquamarine luminous in the afternoon sun. Zeppelins glided smoothly by with metallic skins, and Big Ben, ornate with silver, struck four in the afternoon.

Van Diem sat in a chair of bleached wicker and a table was within arm's reach. The smoldering meerschaum pipe rested upon it, next to his expedition bag. Butterflies swarmed from the open bag: red ones with ghostly blue spots, green ones so small they appeared as tiny emeralds gleaming in the afternoon light, others of plain white with holes in their wings like pieces of flying lace, and ones with foot-long feathery antenna and tails of fog.

Lang watched, unable to move.

Van Diem took his pipe and puffed upon it. A Queen Anne loveseat appeared.

No, it didn't appear; Lang just saw it—as if it had always been there, and he'd never noticed it before.

"Please sit, Doctor. I would like to share a few things before we find Dr. Ambrose."

Lang wanted to move, but his body was numb. He reached into his pocket and touched the pistol, a scrap of reality to anchor himself. He tasted metal in his mouth, and smelled the gun oil.

"None of this is real," he whispered.

Van Diem appeared a man of fifty. Coppery hair crowned his head, and he wore satin black pants and a long coat trimmed with gold brocade.

"Reality is," Van Diem said, "malleable. That is what I learned in Africa, when I met the Sinjuro people, the butterfly people, the people who live in their dreams."

Lang recognized this younger incarnation of the old man. "Sir Eustace Carter Van Diem . . . ," he said.

Van Diem smiled the same smile he wore in the tin daguerreotype taken over a century ago. "I knew you were smart."

He picked up the pipe and lit it. The cloud of butterflies about him thickened, shimmered with colors and motion, confetti thrown into the air that never landed.

"I apologize for the suddenness of all this, young man, seeing reality unveiled is unsettling. And, I'm afraid, it is entirely my fault."

Lang found he could again move; he turned, but the door that had been behind him was gone. In its place was a wall of green glass and beyond a metropolis with spires and domes of gold, a river of glittering silver, and farther still, a palace that gleamed like a million brilliant-cut diamonds. He closed his eyes, knowing this was only hallucination, the door was still there . . . along with the rest of the hospital. It had to be. Eyes shut, he tried to step back into the corridor, but felt only smooth glass.

Butterflies landed upon his arms, coiling and uncoiling their spiral tongues. He shook them off.

Van Diem motioned him to the loveseat, and Lang, not knowing what else to do, stumbled to it and sat.

"Ambrose discovered my previous explorations as well," Van Diem said. "At first he asked me simple questions about my name and where I was born. I remembered, at least, enough to keep him probing until he found my bag, field journals, and pipe." He held the smoldering pipe tighter. "It was only then that I saw the darkness in the man's heart, but, alas, by then it was too late."

He sucked on the pipe until the bowl glowed red. One of the fluttering insects, attracted to the light, flew into the bowl, sizzled, and made a great cloud of blue smoke. The air rippled.

Van Diem stared at Lang and frowned. "I see from your sour expression that you are having a difficult time." He sighed. "Perhaps a scientific explanation would better suit an educated mind? How quantum mechanics postulates that for every potential microscopic outcome there are alternate realities born? And infinite possibilities to pick amongst? A slight push with the mind—wavefunctions perturbate, tunnel, shift, and well, here we are."

Fossilized trilobites scuttled through the stone checkerboard floor.

Lang grasped part of Van Diem's explanation. The room took on a solidity it didn't have before, feeling more real now.

"But," Lang said, twisting his hands together, "quantum mechanics only works on a microscopic scale. This is different."

Van Diem consulted his pocket watch. "Time grows short. We shall save the philosophical implications of existence for another day. I must explain about Dr. Ambrose." He stood, and looked thirty now, a mop of red hair falling over his brown eyes. "But it is an explanation I will impart as we move."

Lang stood and backed away. "I can't. . . ."

"Come, come, man," Van Diem said, his brows bunching together. "You have taken the first step. You have the proper mental facilities. A lesser man could never have entered this room and survived with a shred of his sanity intact." He pointed at him. "Observe."

Lang's lab coat was gone. Instead, he wore a doublet and hose, and the 38 snubnose had become a silver flintlock tucked into a wide black leather belt. A cape of dark gray cascaded off his shoulders and down his back.

Lang smoothed his hands over the velvety material. If this was hallucination, it was like nothing he had ever read of. It reminded him of how he felt when he had painted; he'd imagine, and with a brushstroke it would be created. How different was this? It was something he desired to explore more.

"All right," Lang whispered. "I think I can keep an open mind."

Van Diem found his smile again. "Good." He walked over and clapped Lang on the shoulder. "Some think that having an open mind is a form of madness. But you shall learn it is so much more."

He led Lang through a portal in the glass wall, through a garden of fountains, past water that shot up in wavering columns and glistening buxom nymphs that splashed one another in the wading pools.

Lang and Van Diem descended a set of winding steps, back and forth, switchbacking down into the city.

A blanket of fog settled around them as the sun set.

The buildings were slender structures with Victorian ironwork and painted lavender, crimson, with roofs covered in slate. The people on the streets wore togas, Civil War Cavalry uniforms, business suits, body paint, and one who passed them had on a white space suit with the helmet tucked under her arm.

Lang pulled his cloak tighter about himself to ward off their too-curious stares.

A tabby wearing a fedora and one lime-green boot on its hind leg brushed against Van Diem.

"Fish?" the cat asked.

Van Diem patted its haunch, and then took a puff of his pipe. A school of carp swam out of the mist, spied the cat, and darted away.

The tabby scrambled after them.

"Ambrose is here?" Lang asked, shooing a butterfly from his lips.

Van Diem pointed to a footbridge that arched over a black river. "There."

The structures in that part of the city leaned against one another, tilting at odd angles. They had broken windows and weeds grew between cobblestones. The streets were deserted. The house Van Diem indicated had been charred by fire—save the door, which was lacquered red and embossed with a Chinese dragon.

"When Ambrose glimpsed the true nature of reality," Van Diem said, "he wanted to use it to gather power and women"—his face twisted in revulsion—"and money, of all the filthy things."

Lang could imagine. Ambrose was the kind of man who, given three wishes, would wish for more wishes. And given control over his personal reality . . . Lang wasn't sure he wanted to find out what he did with it.

"He refused to let me guide him or heed my warnings. Now he teeters on the brink of perversity."

A chill slithered up Lang's spine. "Why not leave him alone?"

"It is not just his reality he will shape. Once he exhausts his dark fantasies here, he will return to Oceanview and make your hospital and its patients his playthings. Then he will take your world."

The chill in Lang's spine crystallized into solid icy fear.

"And stopping him is a task that now falls to you, doctor.

"Me?! Why me?"

Van Diem sighed and looked weakened by the weight of his words. "I have tried to enter his mind," he said, "and failed. I do not understand its dark passages. He and I come from different times and worlds. And even if I did eventually confront him, how could I defeat such a man? I would challenge him to an honorable duel. Do you think him gentleman enough to oblige me?"

Lang knew the instant Van Diem turned his back to count out ten paces for a Victorian duel, Ambrose would shoot him.

"No."

Van Diem held out his meerschaum pipe. "I no longer need this. Take it." He plucked three butterflies from the air and set them upon Lang's cloak. "Besides," he said, "you have another reason to find Dr. Ambrose? Some legal matter?"

"Yeah, I suppose I do."

Lang took Van Diem's pipe. It was still warm and the instant he touched it, his fear melted. He knew he'd have to face Dr. Ambrose. Alone.

The elephant carved into the meerschaum seemed to grin at Lang.

Lang pushed past the golden dragon door and into a hotel lobby. Loose floorboards creaked and overhead timbers shifted as if the entire place might collapse if he sneezed. Hallways led in every direction: passages lined with mirrors, tunnels that were pitch dark and cobwebbed, and corridors of stone that flickered with smoky torches.

The lobby had one occupant, a shaved gorilla in a red and silver robe. The creature stood blocking Lang's path. It reeked of musk and High Karate aftershave.

"How may I serve you, O Wise Master?" the simian growled. Its massive hand rested upon a sheathed scimitar as long as Lang was tall.

Lang repressed the urge to back away from the monstrosity. Then he recognized the hawk nose of Ambrose upon the creature—as if it were his long-lost Neanderthal ancestor.

He knew the rest of its face as well; he'd seen it in his nightmares. It had appeared in Lang's dreams at tax time, encouraging him to cheat, and when he had to choose between a practice in lucrative plastic surgery or geriatrics. The gorilla's name was Greed.

Lang inhaled, gathering his bravado.

"It's not you who can serve me," Lang said as he struck a match and lit the pipe. "It's I who will help you."

Lang searched his childhood for pirate stories and treasure chests filled with doubloons.

One of the three butterflies upon his cloak fluttered free and spiraled into the fire. It burned in a flash of flame and pink smoke.

In Lang's left hand, he felt the weight and cold of coins.

He offered them to the robed ape, who expectantly held out both hands.

"A little something for your retirement fund." Lang spilled the doubloons into its grasping palms. "Now, if you can point the way to Dr. Ambrose?"

"Of course, sir," it grumbled and nodded to a stone tunnel.

The coins in the ape's hands overflowed. For every one he dropped three more appeared, clattering and rolling across the floor.

It crouched to pick these up, but more appeared. The ape shifted its hoarded coins into the lap of its robe, but this only caused more to spill—and more coins appeared, until he was knee deep in the metal, struggling to hold it all.

Lang left it there to drown in his riches, and entered the tunnel.

The black basalt passage sucked the light from the torches set every six paces into its walls.

Lang looked back and saw the entrance seal behind him. A spike of smothering claustrophobia stabbed him, making him dizzy and nauseated.

He knelt and put his head between his knees and took a few deep breaths.

There he saw tracks in the dirt: loafers, size thirteen. They could have been Ambrose's . . . but they faded with every step until they vanished.

Lang brushed the dirt away and found a gray tile, and then a blue one. Another gray and another blue made an alternating pattern. It was the floor from Oceanview.

Lang stood and set his feet firmly upon the gritty tiles, shuffling forward.

Surrounding him he heard the grinding of stone over stone, but he didn't focus on that. Instead, he closed his eyes and imagined the smells of Mercurochrome and bedpans, the sounds of heart monitors and the whispered gossip of nurses.

Lang bumped into something, opened his eyes, and saw the service cart he had knocked into earlier that evening. It still held plates with half-eaten creamed chicken, rice, and lime Jell-O.

Lang spied Ambrose's office and eased toward it, ducking around the open door.

The room was empty, dust in the corners, and the windows painted black.

Not here? Where would he be? If this were Lang's fantasy, he'd have taken the corner office upstairs, the one with the million-dollar view of the coast. The office of the Chief of Staff.

Lang crept to the stairs and plodded up three flights to the administrative floor. The halls were deserted. The odor of burning tar lingered in the air.

The door to the Chief of Staff's office was shut, but beyond the frosted window Lang saw shadows and the flicker of flames.

He eased it open.

The walls were red daub, the floor dirt. A hookah powered by greasy pumps and rusted steel chambers sat in the center, taking up most of the space in the once-executive office. Ambrose sat cross-legged before it and sucked without joy or appreciation, chewing the end of the tube.

His skin was sallow and drawn tight, and his hair had fallen out and lay scattered about him.

Lightning flashed and Lang's attention was drawn to the window. The glass had been shattered, and outside black frothy waves clawed at the coast. Lightning lanced the towering waves and he thought he caught a split-second glimpse of tentacles the size of skyscrapers rising from the water.

"I thought someone might figure it all out," Ambrose croaked. "I'm glad it was you."

Beetles covered Ambrose, crawling over his scalp and into his ears. There were fat ruby-red ones, slender green ones, black behemoths the size of his fist with rhinoceros horns, and ladybugs with heart-shaped speckles. They crawled on the floor, walls, and ceiling,

A yellow scarab landed on Lang's arm and he brushed it off.

Ambrose grasped a plump red beetle and set the squirming creature into the bowl. He incinerated the thing, inhaled, and exhaled an oily smoke. "Better you than the police, some hospital administrator, or the old man. You, at least, might be able to understand me."

"You have to stop," Lang whispered.

"Why?" Ambrose coughed a laugh. "I've just started."

Lang hefted Van Diem's pipe. "I've just started too," he said.

That had been a threat, not a statement, and Ambrose understood his intent perfectly.

Ambrose narrowed his watery gaze. "We've had our differences in the past, Lang, but you have the talent to appreciate what's at stake. We can split the universe. *Not fifty-fifty*, of course, but with you as a"—he considered—"a junior partner. Think of all the things we can do. All the things we can take!"

Lang wondered if he could use the power and not be twisted by it. He could end war, rid the world of famine, cure the sick. . . .

"Let me show you how it's done," Ambrose said. He inhaled and his chest purred, thick with phlegm. His eyes were solid black and fixed upon Lang.

. . . and if it had been *anyone* other than Ambrose, he might have been tempted.

"I don't think so," Lang said.

Neither Ambrose nor Lang moved for a heartbeat.

Ambrose's lips quavered about the nozzle of the hookah in a half-formed smile. He then snatched a beetle from the air with inhuman speed and crunched it into the bowl.

Lang grabbed for his box of matches, fumbled them open . . . and the matches and meerschaum pipe dropped to the floor.

Flame popped from Ambrose's index finger and he lit the insect; it screamed. He drew smoke into the hookah's chamber, and then sucked the smoke into his body.

The daub walls stretched and pinged into black metal and spikes extruded. Iron Maidens dangled from hooks.

Lang smelled blood and charred meat.

"Too slow," Ambrose cooed. "I win. Now we have fun."

Lang wasn't scared, though. Fire boiled in his blood. Ambrose won? Not in a million years would he let that happen. If he wanted a real fight, he'd get one—and not a fair duel like Sir Eustace Carter Van Diem would have offered, either.

No, this evening, Lang fought to win.

"Split *this* fifty-fifty." Lang drew his flintlock, cocked it, and squeezed the trigger.

In another reality, an old man by the name of Van Diem passed on in the middle of the night from natural causes. And in some other reality, Dr. Lang shot and killed Dr. Ambrose, was subsequently tried, convicted, and sentenced to the gas chamber.

But those were realities Dr. Robert Lang, Chief of Staff of the Oceanview Senior Care Center, did not care to pursue. There were more important things on his mind.

He paused to admire the half-finished oil painting on the easel. It was a fantasy of the ocean, a city floating off the coast with mermaids and dolphins splashing in the surf.

It was silly, but it made him smile. He'd have to visit the place one day.

In the meantime, he had rounds to perform and sick patients to comfort. He also had tea scheduled this afternoon with Van Diem . . . and after hours, who knew what they'd discover in their explorations?

He lit his meerschaum pipe and inhaled a rich vanilla smoke.

Outside the picture window of his office, monarch butterflies swarmed against the glass, struggling to get in, their fluttering wings in the sunlight looking like jewels.

Perfection

BY LYNN FLEWELLING

Lynn Flewelling is best known for her two fantasy novel series: the ongoing Nightrunner books (*Luck in the Shadows, Stalking Darkness,* and *Traitor's Moon*) and the Tamír trilogy (*The Bone Doll's Twin* and *Hidden Warrior,* with the concluding volume forthcoming in 2006). Set in a politically complex mythical world, Flewelling's tales blend the classic elements of high fantasy with cloak and dagger mystery, gender and sexuality, the supernatural, and more than a dash of humor. Flewelling's books have been translated into more than a dozen languages and her articles on writing have appeared in *Writer's Digest, Speculations,* and several books.

Flewelling thinks mostly in novel lengths, but she does manage the occasional short story. "Perfection" is set in a far-off corner of her fantasy world, but differs considerably from her usual tone. The idea for the story came to Flewelling after rereading some of Edwardian satirist Saki's short stories. "I love his wry twists and turns, subtle sarcasm and unexpected revelations," she explains. "I'm also fascinated by ancient technologies. It's amazing, the gadgets and engineering marvels people came up with in what we consider pretechnology societies. The idea for 'Perfection' just took root one day and pulled all these elements together."

Lynn Flewelling lives in East Aurora, New York.

Looking into the Emperor's face for the first time, Myriel knew the rumors were all true.

In deference to her age and reputation, she had been allowed a low chair below the golden dais. The master builder bowed deeply, then sat and rubbed absently at her aching knees. *He will begin as they all do,* she thought, and was not mistaken.

"In my youth, Mistress Myriel, I visited the temple you designed for Queen Arclia," the Emperor told her, leaning forward, elbows on his knees. "I remember the mechanical birds you created, that sang at dawn each day."

Myriel found herself staring at his hands as he talked. He was a lean, sharp-eyed man, scarred from years of conquest, yet his hands were large, fine, expressive. Hands that might just as easily have been trained to the artist's brush or chisel.

"During my first great campaign I captured the pleasure gardens you laid out in Lower Ankgar," he went on. "More recently, I passed the hot weeks of summer in the new palace you built for the King of Zengat. Some claim you are a wizard, the way you force stone to your will."

"It takes no force, August Majesty, merely an understanding of the nature and limits of my materials," she replied.

The Emperor's ministers frowned and whispered behind him, shocked at her audacity, but the Emperor smiled knowingly. They were both masters of their chosen crafts; a show of false modesty would be pointless.

"Is it right, do you think, that the kings who serve me should be better sheltered than their emperor?" he asked.

"Certainly not, August Majesty."

"Then build me a palace, Mistress Myriel, one such as the world has never seen! Create devices and delights that will illuminate the memory of my reign through the ages. The wealth of the Empire and her finest craftsmen are at your command, in return for your greatest work. Give me a palace that will never be outshone. Give me—perfection!"

Such naked vanity in that long face! She saw it in most of her patrons. "Make mine the best, the largest, the greatest!" they all demanded, like children clamoring at a baker's booth. But there was more in this man's eyes than mere ego. The public buildings he'd commissioned during his reign were unparalleled in grace and opulence, and spoke of an artist's soul.

This devourer of lands and kingdoms went on, using his fine hands to paint images on the air—joists and buttressing, incised plasterwork, hypocausts, atriums, and gardens. He understood perfectly how a well-conceived structure created its own unique magic without any wizardly tricks. A fine house influenced the people who dwelt within its walls. The placement of a window, the color of a frieze, or the curve of a newel post—every element touched by eye or hand touched back, shaping the soul.

This grizzled warrior understood her work as no other patron ever had, yet there lay the irony. Such passion combined with such avarice and lust for power in one heart—it was like yoking a colt to an ox; they could not pull true.

It was an open secret that many of the artists and craftsmen whom the Emperor had patronized had not lived long to enjoy the glory. Every apprentice knew the legend of King Iregi, who'd put out his master builder's eyes after the completion of a magnificent temple, only to have the man dictate the plans for a greater one to a drafting scribe years later. Apparently the Emperor knew this tale, too, and meant to improve upon it. The great muralist Sartin had fallen from a scaffold the day his work at the Temple of the Solstice was completed. Mikos of Dardia, whom Myriel had loved like a son, had sickened and died within a moon's turning of his final chisel stroke on the Emperor's portrait statue. And there were others, so many others.

"Will you build me such a palace, Mistress?" the Emperor asked with disarming earnestness. He knew she could not be commanded to great work.

I am a very old woman, she thought, rising to her feet and bowing. *The gods honor me, placing such a commission in my path, even if it is to be my last.* "Most Exalted Majesty, I accept the commission."

"How long, Mistress Myriel? How long until I can walk the halls of my palace?" And there it was again, that spark of greed marring the fine soul.

"With your resources, August One, five years." Time enough to arrange her affairs, and to groom and safely disperse her disciples, who would carry on her methods far from this decadent court. "The creation is yours, August One. I am but the instrument which gives it form. I will accept no other commissions and oversee every detail myself. I promise you what you have asked. This shall be a palace like no other."

This pleased the Emperor very much indeed.

Myriel had never had such riches at her disposal, and the work began well. The site chosen was atop a rise just outside the capital. From here the Emperor could see for many miles on a clear day—south across the water to the island nation of Tyrime, whose capital he'd razed and salted after an uprising ten years earlier. Only sheep roamed that island now. To the west, just beyond the execution grounds, lay rolling acres of fine vineyards, tended by legions of slaves bearing the brand of the Emperor's Vintners on their thighs.

The ground was rocky and solid, offering a sure foundation. The lay of the land allowed exact east-west alignments that would ensure health and prosperity for future occupants. The building site was well watered, too, and Myriel and the Emperor spent many happy hours designing pools and waterfalls for the gardens.

The man's taste was impeccable; conservative of ornament, but lavish in materials. The first year he enslaved a small principality to the south, securing their famed quarries of pure white marble. The following year, after subduing the tiny kingdom of Irman, he crucified most of the male population but spared their exceptional craftsmen, transporting one hundred of the best tile glaziers to the workers' camp.

The capital prospered and poverty virtually disappeared, for anyone with a strong back soon found work at the new palace.

It took seventeen months to lay the sewers, drains, wells, and foundations. After that the walls seemed to sprout up like living things as the huge white blocks were laid in row upon row from dawn to dusk.

When the Emperor wasn't away making war, he strode about at Myriel's side like a senior disciple, with a sheaf of plans tucked beneath his arm. Indeed, except for her trusted old foreman, the Emperor was the only person allowed to see the plans. At night they sat in his study in chairs of equal height, laying out brilliant designs for paved floors and ventilated bathing chambers. The grand main entrance would face east over a large paved plaza for public gatherings. High above this, Myriel placed the Balcony of Victory, to be built in the exact shape and size of an imperial warship's prow. The sides would be carved with emblems of every nation the Emperor had brought beneath his sway, so that he might stand, literally and figuratively, on the backs of those he'd conquered. It would be a potent symbol, just the sort of imagery Myriel excelled in creating.

The gardens surrounding the palace would be miniature wildernesses, full of game, fish pools, and airy pleasure pavilions connected by underground passages to the rooms of his wives and concubines.

A consummate perfectionist in all things, the Emperor decreed that the inhabitants of his new home be chosen with equal care. As the fourth year of building came to an end, many servants, aging wives, and concubines who'd lost their savor were sold off or given away. Lovely fresh girls from every land were bought or captured and held in readiness for His August Majesty's new harems. Cadres of handsome little boys, the sons of peasants and merchants, were gathered up and held in readiness to be cut as eunuchs at the height of their youthful bloom.

Of course, some sacrifices had to be made. Fields went untilled when more laborers were pressed into service at the building site. Trade unrelated to the Emperor's project had been neglected, as were the courts and guilds.

There had been difficulties of other sorts, as well. A shipload of a particular clay Myriel required from distant Kolchi brought rats bearing a new and terrible sickness that had killed hundreds. Foreign slaves brought their false gods with them and cults had sprung up, luring many of the city's youth away from the gods of their fathers with fleshy rites and mysteries.

Despite the wondrous nature of the palace taking shape above the city, the people began to murmur at the excesses of the Emperor, and to speak openly against the foreign builder whose demands had brought such hardships.

These bitter mutterings eventually reached the Emperor's ears.

"Don't be troubled by such fleeting ills," his master builder counseled. "What are these things compared to the great work we are engaged in? A mere blink of the eye in the course of time. Soon the masses will understand what is being wrought here. This palace will stand for ages as a symbol of your rule."

By mutual agreement, Myriel laid some plans in secret. The hallmarks of her craft were the cunning tricks and eye-catching details she hid in abundance in each great house she created. In the final months of each project, she and her chief foreman would work long into the night, installing clever secret devices to be discovered later by the occupants of the house.

"Surprise me!" the Emperor had urged, delighted at the prospect.

"For you, August One, wonders without precedent," Myriel promised.

She never revealed to anyone where these lay, and it often took years before they were all discovered. The inadvertent pressure of a hand on a section of mural might reveal a clever bit of mechanical statuary. Sculptures burst to life as fountains months after construction was finished, a simple trick accomplished with hidden water pipes plugged with salt. She built whole scenes of figures that moved, seemingly on their own, when levers were manipulated by hidden weights or water wheels. Her singing mechanical birds were in such demand that she'd finally grown bored with them and refused to create any more.

Other effects were pleasing in their simplicity—magnifying lenses set into windowpanes of a tower room which allowed the occupant to view distant vistas more closely, or wind chimes hidden in air ducts that tinkled pleasantly only in certain weather. At the manor of Lord Oris, an astrologer of some repute, she positioned small round windows of colored glass in such a way that each was illuminated just once a year by a specific alignment of the sun or moon, much to the delight of her patron.

As a final touch, she gave each structure a secret name, which was only revealed by the discovery of one of the secret devices. In the water gardens of King Makir, mineral salts impregnated into the basin of the largest fountain reacted with the sulfurous water of that region so that the words "Flowing Haven" appeared in blue script a year to the day after the first water flowed in. In the case of the astrologer, Oris, the words "Celestial Eye" appeared the night after the house was completed when the moon struck a particular pane of glass, an alignment that would not reoccur for decades.

She was thought to be a wizard by some, and accused of witchcraft more than once by the ignorant. She smiled at this and made no answer for, in truth, engineering and imagination were all the magic she needed. With these she managed wonders which endured.

Construction proceeded on schedule, and Myriel was able to promise a dedication of the completed building on the occasion of the Emperor's fiftieth birthday. In honor of this, she had installed an equal number of secret delights throughout the palace, the most she had ever incorporated in a single structure.

"And have you decided the name for my house?" he asked.

"Ah, my dear Emperor!" she laughed, for so she called him now, after working so closely with him all these years. "That was decided the very day you engaged my services."

For weeks at a time Myriel was able to lose herself in the joy of creation, watching her masterwork rise and take shape under her direction. It was always like this—the excitement of the task at hand, to be followed by the inevitable bittersweet melancholy of its end. For her, the creation of a building was like the act of love—passionate, exciting, exhilarating while it lasted, but leaving one empty and dark inside when it was over.

This time, however, she knew there would be no afterward. Each block set in place shortened her life. Several of her principal artists had died already. Others had slipped away in the night, leaving apprentices to complete the final installations.

This spurred her on, especially in the final days as she and the foreman hurried to complete the last of their unique devices.

In the end, the Emperor was spared the unpleasant necessity of killing his master builder. Myriel was found dead in her bed with a peaceful smile on her lips, just a week before the dedication. Her old foreman lay on the floor beside her, apparently having killed himself out of grief at his mistress's passing.

The Emperor declared two whole days of mourning, an unprecedented honor for a mere craftswoman, and the people of the city grumbled even as they ate the funeral feast. This foreigner had broken their backs, brought disease and strangers to the very heart of the Empire. In their hearts some even grumbled against the Emperor himself, though none were fool enough to let such thoughts past their teeth.

The great day arrived at last. On the morning of his fiftieth birthday, the Emperor put on his finest new robes and led a formal procession up the hill to the new palace. Accompanied by the court, his two sons, his new favorite wives, and their new favorite eunuchs (a rather sullen company, if he'd chosen to notice), he set about exploring the pillared courts and dazzling chambers. There were 150 in all, not even counting the kitchens and servants' quarters.

Evidence of Mistress Myriel's genius was soon discovered. In the audience chamber, invisible bells tinkled softly as rain, but it was impossible to find where the sound came from. The elaborate throne was the last work of the famous wood carver, Delio, before his death. On the throne's velvet cushion lay a folded parchment. Inside, written in the builder's precise hand, the Emperor read, "Be seated, and behold." Grinning with anticipation, the Emperor sat down, and instantly stone gorgon heads on the walls to either side sprang to life as fountains. Water gushed from their eyes and drained away through into marble basins set into the floor.

Everyone gasped and applauded, then gasped again a moment later when a section of wall directly opposite the throne turned on hidden pivots to reveal an elegant mirror of polished silver. It was very large, and positioned so exactly that the Emperor was framed like a portrait. By some trick of the mirror grinder's art, he appeared twice the size of the people standing on either side of him.

"So many devices just in one room alone!" the Emperor exclaimed, admiring the cleverly distorted reflection. "She truly was a genius. What a loss her death is to us!"

Still, none of these devices had revealed what he most longed to know: the name of his great house. Gathering his robes in his hands, this conqueror of nations dashed on from room to room like an excited child on a treasure hunt.

He and his courtiers found more of Myriel's notes here and there. One at the house temple instructed the priest to light the little stack of wood laid ready on the altar. When this was done, the enameled doors of the sanctuary beyond it swung open by themselves to reveal magnificent golden statues of the Emperor's house gods. When the small fire died down, the doors closed again. No one had ever seen such a wonder, and the Emperor ordered that the mechanism be found and implemented in all his public temples to boost the revenues.

He was slightly disappointed to find no obvious devices in the imperial bedchamber, or any hint from the builder. But all agreed it was a magnificent room all the same. The floor, made of blood-red Mylilian marble, was so highly polished that it appeared wet. The vaulted ceiling was supported by graceful pillars of gilded black marble, and frescoed with a scene of the Emperor's first victory at the age of seventeen, over the king of Mylila.

"I remember that horse!" He craned his neck to take in the scene. His rearing black charger might have been rendered from life, right down to the white scar on its flank. Bound in golden chains, the vanquished king cowered on his knees under the beast's hooves as his wailing family looked on. Following popular convention, the painter had used many of the Emperor's friends and advisors as models for the secondary figures. They chattered and laughed aloud as they found themselves among the conquering soldiers.

"Why, look!" the Emperor said to his eldest son, a strong, bearded warrior. "There you are, carrying off one of the king's daughters."

"And there's me, pillaging a dead general," his younger son observed, delighted to find himself immortalized.

"And there's that builder of yours, too. I might have known she'd show up sooner or later," his Lord Chancellor chuckled. "I suppose it's not too arrogant a gesture, given the rendering."

It took the Emperor a moment to find Myriel, for the stupid artist had placed her among the prisoners. There she stood, a grave, ragged figure, watching the conquerors with accusing eyes. And wasn't that her foreman lying dead at her feet?

"How very odd," the Emperor murmured, frowning.

"A statement of modesty, perhaps?" his eldest son suggested.

"Ah, but that's no worthy legacy for her, not worthy at all. Make a note, scribe. We must have that fresco altered. I don't want to stare up at her looking like that year after year, poor woman!"

"The original artist is not longer available, August Majesty," the scribe murmured apologetically as he scribbled a note.

"My Emperor, the people have filled the plaza, awaiting your birthday address," his chamberlain reminded him.

"Ah yes!" The Emperor reluctantly let himself be led away; he'd rather hoped to find the secret name and announce it on this most auspicious of days.

The Balcony of Victory lay just down the corridor. It had been fitted with large double doors of oak and gold, matched in shape to the large windows on either side, and secured with a large lock of Myriel's own design. With a flourish, the Emperor took out the key she'd given him. Even this humble article was a work of art, made of polished steel damascened with gold, just like a fine sword. Inserting it into the lock, the Emperor imagined all his descendents doing the same, generation after generation, stepping out onto this place where only royal feet might tread, to survey their people. The key turned easily, and the great doors swung open to reveal yet another marvel. The Emperor's family and ministers gaped and clapped, and an expectant roar went up from the crowd below.

Just as Myriel had planned, the white marble balcony jutted gracefully out from the front of the palace in the shape of a warship's prow. Perfect in every detail, down to the ribs and planking in her sides, it seemed as if the Emperor's own flagship had been sculpted from snow and launched to sail the blue summer sky. Two stone steps had been set into the peak of the prow, so that he might be more visible to the crowds below.

The Emperor's heart swelled with gratitude for the dead builder. "Come," he said to his eldest son. "Let the people see you, their future emperor, standing beside me this happy day."

"Look, Father," his son said. "She's left you another message."

This parchment fluttered on the white marble deck a few feet from the doorway, secured under a lozenge of red jade carved with the builder's seal.

The Emperor forgot the crowd for a moment as a thrill of anticipation ran through him. "Come, let's see what it says!"

The prince retrieved the folded sheet and presented it to the Emperor. Inside, they read, "Behold the name, writ in gold."

"The name! But where?" The Emperor looked around again and

caught a glint of yellow light on the top step at the prow. "The secret name! She's set it there so that I can announce it today, just as I'd hoped. Wondrous woman!"

The two men hurried forward and bent to read the lettering.

Farewell

The Emperor just had time to frown over the puzzle before the cables that held the entire balcony in careful balance—cables much tested by the clever builder to be just strong enough to support the stonework, but not the additional and carefully directed weight of the Emperor himself, much less of that of his heir—snapped.

Builders who came to survey the wreckage later said it was a testament to Myriel's skill that the balcony came away so cleanly, arcing out just enough not to damage the impeccable facade. The balcony itself smashed to bits, of course, not to mention the Emperor and his son, and a number of his subjects who'd been standing just below. An expanse of costly paving stones was ruined as well, but an ample supply of replacements were discovered stacked in a storeroom soon after, making repairs a simple matter.

Before the crowd could recover from this catastrophe, the balcony doors crashed down onto the shattered marble. This released several large wooden plugs in the doorframe above, which fell out and in turn released two columns of sand. These leaked away, gently lowering a stone slab into place across the open doorway to seal the aperture. Made of the same shining white marble as the rest of the house, this glistening panel was inlaid with golden letters tall enough to be read as far away as the city market:

Perfection

Which proved in the long run to be an ironic and misleading name for this particular palace. Many people later shook their heads and sucked their teeth in grudging sympathy for the dead builder, who'd left such a misnamed legacy as her greatest work.

For in spite of all the care Mistress Myriel had put into its design, and her considerable personal oversight of each stage of construction, it was not long before a number of serious flaws were discovered, not the least of which was the faulty construction of the ceiling vaults in several rooms, including that of the Imperial bedchamber. While this did solve the problem of the displeasing ceiling mural, it also crushed the Emperor's only remaining heir in his bed.

Stranger still, the hidden passageways of the harems and eunuchs' quarters, which were supposed to lead to the garden pavilions, emerged instead far outside the palace walls, in the oddest and most obscure places.

The Compound

BY MICHAEL MARSHALL SMITH

Like Dr. Jekyll and Mr. Hyde, there is best-selling science fiction and horror author Michael Marshall Smith and his alter ego, best-selling psychological thriller author Michael Marshall. The former is responsible for the novels *Only Forward*, *Spares*, *One of Us*, *The Vaccinator*, and the short fiction collections *What You Make It* and *More Tomorrow and Other Stories*; the latter penned *The Straw Men*, *The Lonely Dead* (aka *The Upright Man*), and the recent *Blood of Angels*. He is a five-time winner of the British Fantasy Award and a three-time World Fantasy Award nominee. Smith has also worked extensively as a screenwriter, writing feature scripts for clients in LA and London. He is currently working as producer and script editor on a movie adaptation of one of his stories, cowriting a television series pilot, and starting a new novel.

" 'The Compound' is actually quite different to anything else I've ever written," said Smith, "a speculative kind-of-SF story of a type I've never attempted before or since. I wrote it because a series of images and atmospheres came into my head at the same time—and insisted they were relevant to each other. It turned out that they were, albeit in a strange way."

Michael Marshall Smith lives in North London, England. Find out more about Smith at his Web site: www.michaelmarshallsmith.com.

Daniel sat on his small chair by the bed and watched his mother sleeping. Enough light filtered through the drawn curtains for him to see the rise and fall of her chest beneath the bedclothes, and he counted the breaths as they came and went. As long as he could count the breaths she was still alive, and as long as they came, he would count them. He wished his mother had someone else to help her, someone who wasn't seven years old. But she hadn't, and so he had to do the best he could.

He looked at the glass on the bedside table and saw there was enough water there still. If she wanted more he could get some from the kitchen next door, but it was all right for now.

For now he would just sit, and count.

———

"The cold is within you," Dark thought, irritably. "You are not within the cold." He was trying to convince himself that it wasn't the snow around him which was making him feel numb, or the fact that it was twenty degrees below, or even that he just wasn't dressed for this kind of crap. It wasn't working. The cold was both within and without him, and getting colder. If he didn't get warm soon, he was going to die.

Getting out of the Compound was proving both less and more difficult than he'd expected.

When he'd woken to find himself laid out on the bed in the small cabin, he had at first no idea where he was. He realized he'd been there some time only when he tried to stand up. The weakness and confusion in his limbs made it clear that it must have been at least six months since he'd last been awake. The alarm this caused was soothed by the room he found himself in, which was cosy, its walls lined with dark pine. It reminded him of something, though he couldn't remember what.

For a week or so he'd been content to sit cross-legged on the bed, helping himself to the food which appeared in the fridge (cold cuts and mild cheese), his mind a content and comfortable blank. Then one day he tried the door to the cabin, and found it was unlocked. It opened onto a small balcony, and when he stepped out into the cold, Dark realized immediately where he was.

The balcony was about a hundred meters above ground level, and on a low mountain, and thus had a very good view. Good in the sense that you could see a great deal, at least. What you could see a great deal of, unfortunately, was snow. Snow and fir trees as far as the eye could see. Dotted over the landscape at irregular intervals, sometimes swaddled in a patch of deep emerald trees, sometimes stark against the ice, were other tall windowless buildings. The sky was black as night, but the scene was lit as if by a dim and hidden winter sun.

It could only be one place. The Compound.

Suddenly galvanized, Dark turned on his heel and walked back into his room. The Compound.

Bastards.

There had to be a way out, and as soon as he found it, he was gone. He made a perfunctory search of the cupboards and wall units first, looking for warm clothing. He didn't expect to find anything. He didn't. The room was plenty warm, and so far as They were concerned he was supposed to stay put. He took a look inside the fridge too, thinking it would be a good idea to take provisions, but for the first time it was empty. He suspected that was not a good sign, and immediately began looking for the door.

It was surprisingly easy to find, right where you would expect it to be. There was no handle, but he was able to get enough purchase on the edge of one of the panels to establish it wasn't locked. Five minutes' jiggling with the end of his knife worked the catch free, and the door popped open. Dark shook his head. Hardly maximum security.

Outside was a corridor, thickly carpeted in an orange kind of way. Unobtrusively banal music trickled down from small speakers in the ceiling. Dark closed his door carefully behind him and set off.

The walls of the corridor were studded with doors, each identical. He realized what his room had reminded him of. It was like a small suite in a dismal resort somewhere cold, a down-market ski village out of season. He considered opening one of the doors to see what was on the other side, but decided against it. It would probably only be someone lying on their bed or blankly munching salami. Also, it might set off an alarm, and in either event it was not germane to his purpose, which was getting out before anyone realized he was on the move. The last thing he needed was a passenger, especially one who hadn't the gumption to make their own way out of their room.

About fifty yards down the corridor he found a door that was rather larger than the others. It was split vertically across the middle, but didn't appear to have any handles. First casting a glance both ways down the corridor, Dark kicked it. Nothing happened. He tried slipping his knife between the two halves, but there was no give there either. Then he noticed that there was a panel on the wall by the door. He pushed it exper-

imentally and there was a pinging noise, followed by a sound from behind the door. The sound got louder, stopped, and then the two halves of
the door divided. Beyond them was a small room.

Dark stepped in to have a look. As soon as both of his feet were in the
room the doors shut behind him and the room started to fall. Dark was
deeply suspicious of this development, but it seemed to be dropping in a
controlled way, and there didn't appear to be anything he could do
about it. The room was paneled in the same wood as the suites, and full
of quiet music that went "Da dada da, da da dada da," but was in every
other way featureless.

After about a minute the room stopped falling, and the doors opened.
Dark cautiously poked his head out, and saw what seemed to be a large
foyer of some kind. Had it not been completely deserted it would have
looked like the lobby of a hotel. He stepped out into it. There was a *ping*
behind him and he whirled, knife at the ready, to see the doors of the
room shut again.

An elevator. That's what it was, an elevator.

Shaking his head, disturbed at having forgotten something so simple,
Dark put his knife back and walked quickly away toward the large doors
at the far end of the foyer. They were about fifty feet high and made entirely of glass, glass which looked six inches thick. Dark peered out into
the late winter afternoon for a moment, and then turned back to consider his position.

He didn't know much about the Compound. Nobody did. In all honesty, Dark hadn't really believed it existed. He'd first heard about it from
his mother, who'd told him it was where careless people went. His
mother had been off her head, though, and he'd felt safe in disregarding
pretty much everything she said. Then a long time later, but still a long
time ago, he'd heard people mention it when he was in the Corps. Some
of the Gillsans, worn out and stretched thin in the middle of a long campaign, had seemed to feel the Compound calling them. They didn't
know where it was, or what, but somehow they heard its voice. They appeared to both fear it and desire it, like some heroic kamikaze mission, a

type of suffering that was an end to other kinds. Some had disappeared as the campaign went on: perhaps they'd been brought here, were sitting behind the doors in some of the buildings. Someone else might have thought of launching a single-handed rescue mission, but Dark had left the Corps a long time ago. Other-directed heroics had never been his thing.

He turned back indecisively to the doors and gave one of them a push. Though heavy, it moved easily enough, allowing a stream of extremely cold air to curl into the lobby. He let it swing shut again.

He was going to have to go out there. That much was clear. Wherever an escape route lay, it was unlikely to be within the building. The problem was that he didn't really want to leave. It was going to be very cold, and he had no idea where to go once he got out. Even if he could find the edges of the Compound (assuming edges existed, and it wasn't infinite in its own terms), he had no conception of where it existed in relation to any world he knew.

He shook his head again. Such indecision was unlike him. He hadn't got to his position by being unable to stir himself when the need arose. True, his position was that of leader of the Spartan Bold, an increasingly marginalized group of mercenaries; and yes, they might all be dead by now, but the point still held. Perhaps the Compound wasn't a universal realm, as everyone assumed, applying equally to those from all sides. Perhaps it was under the control of the Goudy, and Gillsans fighters were brought here to take them out of the action. Maybe there was something in the air here that made you unsure, unwilling to go back and fight. If there was, it wasn't going to defeat him.

First pulling what there were of his robes around him, Dark shoved the door open and stepped out into the cold.

At four Daniel woke suddenly from a light doze. It took him a moment to remember where he was, and then to realize what had woken him. His mother's breathing was deeper, more labored, and the change in rhythm had alerted some still wakeful part of his brain. He sat forward quickly and looked at her face. It seemed relatively clear. Last time this had happened he'd phoned the doctor, sure that his mother was going to die. The doctor had told him not to worry, that the change in breathing didn't mean anything. Just before he'd put the phone down, Daniel had heard the sound of a woman's distant laugh at the other end, and wondered whether he'd caught the doctor at a time when patient care was not his foremost concern.

But the doctor had been right. His mother's breathing had returned to normal; and the same, he saw, was happening now.

Daniel made a tour of the bed, checking that the duvet wasn't rucked up anywhere or letting cold air in. It wasn't likely to be, as she hardly ever moved, but he checked it anyway, eyes running sightlessly over the pattern of faint interlocking rectangles. He'd spent too long looking at it to notice it anymore.

Sighing heavily, he picked up her glass and took it into the kitchen, walking quickly past the door to the cellar, which still made him nervous. He changed the water in the glass and put some ice in it, and then set about making a cup of tea for himself. A year ago he'd never drunk any tea, viewing it as a grown-up medicine. Now he drank it all the time. There were lots of tea bags, and his mother never seemed to want it anymore. He thought about looking in the fridge, but he knew what was in there because he'd put it there himself, and he wasn't hungry.

As he waited for the kettle to boil, he looked through one of the leaflets on the kitchen table. It was one of the ones his mother had designed, when she'd still been able to work. He could remember her being proud of it, explaining how she'd done it, why she'd chosen those particular typefaces. To him they'd just looked like words and letters.

They didn't anymore.

About three hours later, Dark was huddled up against the base of a tree in one of the clumps of firs. He had no way of telling how much time had elapsed since he'd left the building. The sky was still the same leaden late-afternoon gray, and he'd seen no one. He was telling himself that time had passed because he needed to feel that it had, and three hours seemed about right. He'd given up telling himself that the cold was within him, and had spent the last few minutes in amongst the trees to see if it was any warmer in there. It wasn't.

He realized now that getting out of the building had been too easy. It had been made easy because it achieved nothing at all. At first he'd followed a sort of path through the snow, hoping to find who'd made it. After a few hundred yards it ran out, and since then every pace had been a couple of feet deep. Occasional gusts of wind sent flurries into his already freezing face, and he'd tripped over a hidden branch once and gone sprawling. Twice he'd thought he'd seen more tracks in the snow, but as they appeared to start from nowhere and to just peter out after twenty yards, they couldn't have been real. Apart from those highlights, nothing had happened at all. Nothing except the tramping sound of his boots in freezing snow, and the constant curtain of yet more fucking snow falling against the velvet sky. His legs ached, but aside from that Dark had lost most of the feeling in his body.

What's more, there was something wrong. When he'd looked over the surrounding area from his balcony he'd been able to see several other buildings. They should have been in easy walking distance. They weren't. They had disappeared. He'd slogged across fields and clambered up and down huge steplike levels, but there were no buildings. At all. And no people, and no animals. Just clumps of unhelpful trees. He'd changed direction several times, hoping to find a more profitable tack, and now had very little idea of where he was in relation to his starting point.

It was all going very badly.

After flapping his hands against his sides vigorously to get the ice off, Dark put his head down and tramped away from the trees and up the hill in front of him. He hadn't liked being amongst the trees. The whole of the Compound had a forlorn atmosphere, but it had been worse in there, darker and older. He made a grimace with his face to see if he could move it. He could, but it was hard work. If he didn't find some shelter soon, he was in trouble.

The thought of death, he found, was still unappealing. So the Compound itself clearly wasn't death, unless his mind was just taking a long time to catch up with events. Maybe his mother had been right. Maybe this *was* where careless people went. The problem was working out what the hell that might mean. Maybe it was some kind of Symbolism: the Goudy had always been very keen on such weapons, had started to use them in earnest during the last few offensives. The Gillsans had never really understood Symbolism, and there had been great losses. That was why they had been prepared to use the services of outfits like the Spartan Bold, who were immune.

As he got farther up the hill he realized that it seemed to stop at the top, as if the drop was much steeper on the other side. This was confirmed when he reached the summit. In front of him the hill shaded away quickly, into several hundred feet of stepped fields. At the bottom was a valley, which was largely filled with trees. Squinting against the snow, however, Dark thought he could make out something else. Nestling into the edge of one of the clumps was a building. Hardly noticing he was cackling to himself, Dark rubbed his hands over his lips to thaw them and then set off carefully down the slope.

Carefully wasn't careful enough, and in the end he covered a third of the downward distance in one ungraceful slide, tumbling over and over through the snow. He fetched up in a painful heap at the base of a tree, but nothing was broken and as a means of descent it had been a lot quicker than walking. He picked himself up and hurried toward the bottom of the slope, not bothering to brush the snow off.

As he approached the building, it became clearer that it exactly resembled the one he had left, now at least four hours ago. It could have been one of the ones he'd seen from the balcony, were it not for the fact that it had taken far too long to get to, and had involved walking several miles. It was about thirty stories high and built of the same dark brown, almost black, stone. A dim glow showed behind the glass doors. Dark fell against them, expecting at the last moment for them to be locked, but they parted and he stumbled into the lobby.

It too was exactly the same as the one he'd left, deserted but warm. As the water began to drip out of his clothes and hair, Dark paced round the foyer, luxuriating in the warmth and considering what to do next. Striking out for the edges of the Compound was clearly not a viable course of action. Things didn't work properly out there, and it was just too fucking cold.

When he was perspiring lightly Dark stopped pacing, shook himself like a dog to get rid of the bulk of the excess water, and took stock. He felt much more together now, more alive. Nearly freezing to death had done that much for him, at least. It had also made him irritable. He was fed up with being in a cold no-man's-land. He wanted to get back to the fight. But how?

It was impossible to tell whether this was actually the building he had left before going out into the cold. It shouldn't have been by any logical means, but it might be. It was so identical that it could be either the same one, or a different one that was exactly the same. Dark decided that his first step should be finding out which was the case. If this was the building he'd left, which was clearly impossible, then there was definitely Symbolism at work; and in that case the Compound was almost certainly Goudy territory. If so, then he'd know what to do. Liberate any imprisoned Gillsans sleepers he could find and try to discover the way out, killing any attendants who showed up.

If it wasn't, he still had to find a way out, but he'd be doing it by himself. Loosening his robes he strode toward the elevator.

The elevator looked the same, and the music was the same, but that didn't really prove anything. Elevators were always the same. As the doors shut behind him, Dark realized he didn't know what floor his suite had been on. Looking round the room he saw it wouldn't have made any difference. There were no buttons to press. It would either take him there, or it wouldn't.

It didn't. The elevator flowed smoothly upward, and after about three minutes Dark was forced to concede that it wasn't going to stop anywhere near the floor he'd found himself on earlier. After about twenty minutes he began to wonder if it was going to stop at all, and after an hour he lay down on the floor and went to sleep.

When he woke the elevator was still climbing at the same steady rate. Dark dedicated a desultory couple of minutes to checking once more that there really was no way of influencing the elevator's progress, but soon gave up. He used up some time looking at the carpet, trying to work out where the bland, almost indiscernible pattern might have come from. Its regular overlapping rectangles looked a little like Goudy workmanship, but not enough to make anything of.

Just when Dark was becoming convinced that the elevator was destined to climb calmly forever, the sound of ascent dropped rapidly in pitch and the room juddered to a halt. The doors took a moment to open and Dark readied himself in front of them. His bet was that they would open on the foyer, proving that there was Symbolism afoot. If so, he'd just have to find some other way upstairs. He took his knife out and held it lightly behind him, just in case.

When the doors did open, however, it wasn't onto the lobby. It wasn't clear what it was, in fact. All Dark could see was a faint dark green tinge, accompanied by distant dripping sounds. He stepped carefully up to the door.

It took him a second or two to make sense of what he was seeing. The elevator opened out of a wall, a wall of mossy concrete that seemed to stretched indefinitely in all directions. The only light was a faint glow, probably some kind of phosphorescence. Just below the elevator door was a narrow staircase made of wrought iron. About two feet wide with a low handrail, it climbed at an angle of forty-five degrees up the wall into the darkness. About thirty yards away, directly in front, was a similar wall. That was all he could see, though as he listened carefully he

could hear occasional dripping sounds, and, very far below, the suggestion of a larger body of water.

Sighing irritably, Dark stepped onto the staircase. The elevator pinged
and the doors shut behind him, removing some of the light. It was much
warmer here than it had been in the building, and he loosened his robes
before setting off up the steps.

At six Daniel returned to the kitchen, and made himself some dinner. It
was bologna and cheese again, which he was heartily sick of, but until
Mrs. Johns called by tomorrow morning with more groceries, that was
all there was. He might try asking Mrs. Johns if she could bring him
something different this time, but she was old and didn't seem to hear. It
was more important that he kept her from realizing that his dad had
gone away, leaving them alone. For two weeks he'd kept up the pretense
that he'd just popped out for an hour. If people found out, they'd come
and take his mother away and he knew she didn't want that. He finished
his food and then warmed a little chicken noodle soup and put it into a
cup for his mother.

His mother didn't eat again, though, didn't take even a little. He tried
to prop her head up and pour some into her mouth, but it wouldn't stay
open for long enough. The skin stretched thin on her forehead was very
hot, her hair matted on her neck. She seemed hotter than she had yesterday, and he wondered again how she could stand the duvet on top of her.

Daniel turned the bedside light on, thankful for the glow it pooled
onto the little table. Of all the watching times, the evenings were the
worst. It was very quiet in the house, quiet upstairs, quiet in the kitchen.
He could have turned the television on, but somehow that made things
even worse. When you went into the kitchen it sounded as if you were
outside the house.

When he'd washed up, Daniel made himself another cup of tea,
changed the water in his mother's glass, checked for the fourth time that
the door to the cellar was firmly shut, and settled back down to count.

He walked up steps, he walked down steps. Dark was reconciled to the fact that he had to tramp up the damn things, but it was galling to find yourself suddenly sent down again, undoing all of the previous hour's tramping.

There didn't seem to be an alternative. The metal staircases hugged the walls, going around the corners of the huge blocks, sometimes up, sometimes down. At one point it dropped for hundreds and hundreds of steps, and Dark got close enough to the water to see its slow lapping against the walls. The water looked very deep and viscous, but he didn't think anything lived in it.

The overall trend was now upward, which was both good and bad. It was good because it meant he was closer to wherever the staircase led, and bad because it kept getting hotter and hotter. Several times he had considered jettisoning his robes, but he didn't know if he'd need them later. He was presumably going to have to face someone at some point, either the Goudy or whoever the hell else ran this place. He'd rather not do that clad only in a grubby loincloth: it was difficult to exude the necessary violent authority while informally clad.

The higher he got, the lighter it became. Visibility was still no more than fifty yards and still showed nothing but walls, sometimes nearer, sometimes farther, but it seemed to prove he was getting somewhere. It was getting lighter because the moss that covered the walls was getting thicker. Dark didn't like the moss. He suspected it was alive in some unusual way, and he knew it was where the heat was coming from. As time went on he began to think he could hear a rustling sound, a damp scratching. The moss was twisting, reproducing, dividing, and swelling. Where before it had been patchy, now it was universal, and six inches thick in places. It was taking over the walls, and it didn't look like it would be very long before it clogged the spaces in between them, choking them. It was like the Goudy themselves had been, insinuating themselves slowly, unnoticeably, and then suddenly striking; blossoming blackly and taking over their hosts.

Suddenly afraid as well as angry, Dark plunged his hand into the moss and ripped out a lump. It was hot and fleshlike and seemed to pulse in his hand, and he flicked it away with distaste. He was now too high above the water to hear the splash. A sensation was left in his hand, a feeling of disease, and he realized that all this was not Goudy at all. In some way he didn't understand, it was Gillsans, and it was a weapon.

Confused, Dark continued to climb, getting hotter and hotter. The steps led always upward now, and the higher he got the odder he felt. It was partly the heat, and partly the moss, which was now over a foot deep and exuding an unpleasant decaying odor as he pushed through it. But it wasn't just that. His mind was becoming unclear, watery, as if it was boiling with fever. A couple of times he stumbled hard against the railing, and it was only years of dedicated self-preservation that enabled his hands to instinctively grip it in time. He climbed for a while with his eyes shut, but that didn't make it any better. It felt as if he was pushing upward through the revolting moss, cutting a channel through its black and glistening warmth.

The opposite wall was getting closer, too. At times it had been as far as a hundred yards away, but now it was only a matter of six or seven feet. The moss was pushing out from there too.

Dark jerked his neck back as he tried to roll the ache out of his shoulders, and saw that far above, there was a roof. The stairs led up to a door set in the wall where it met its opposite. He stumbled and fell hard onto one knee on the stairs, making them vibrate. Shaking his head made no difference. His mind was running as if stirred with a warm finger. He pulled himself to his feet again and hauled himself up the steps.

Hand on the phone, Daniel watched his mother. Something was wrong, much more wrong than usual. Her breathing had deepened again and was very uneven. She seemed to be even hotter; from where he stood Daniel believed he could feel the waves of heat coming off her. She gasped suddenly, a wet choking sound, her mouth gaping open.

Daniel turned. He'd heard something else. His mother was still breathing loudly through the black clogging mass in her lungs, but that wasn't it. It was the sound he'd heard before. Fifteen minutes ago, when his mother was still quiet, he'd thought he'd heard something from behind the cellar door. It had been very faint, a distant muffled clang, as if something was approaching from below. This sound was similar, but different. It sounded closer.

Dark picked himself up again, oblivious to the fact that his knee was pouring blood. It wasn't surprising he'd tripped. It was too hot, too hot to live. The moss was squirming around him like meat full of struggling worms. The brightness was too intense to see by, and all he could do was fall forward step by step. It was only a matter of yards now.

Daniel's mother let out a soft sound, a kind of gurgle, but Daniel didn't even hear it. He was staring in the other direction, toward the door to the cellar. There was something down there. The room was full of heat and there was a smell. Daniel looked back at his mother, and realized it was coming from her.

Dark fell against the door and it gave way before him. Daniel stared at the cellar door as it creaked slowly open, revealing the darkness of the stairs that led down into the gloom beneath the house. Suddenly his mother's chest rose up, and her breaths lost all rhythm, stopped being many and became just single spasms, part of no sequence, no longer a necessary condition. Dark felt the heat reach a peak, felt himself lost in it, lost in this room of churning, dying flesh. He felt it contract harder and tighter, and knew that it couldn't last, that this would have to end.

Daniel tore his eyes away from the cellar door and knelt by his mother, gripping her hand. He didn't need the doctor to tell him this was the end, that this was the final minute, that time stopped here. His mother let out a moan that escalated into a rasping gasp, and Dark felt himself spiralling upward faster and faster, losing his sense of himself, propelled upward until there was just a blur.

Her chest hitched again, and as Daniel glared through his tears at her face, his mother's eyes suddenly opened. She saw him, he knew, saw him and knew who he was, and then she died.

For a moment Daniel thought he saw something coming out of her mouth, the faintest of shapes escaping in the air, and then there was just afterward, and tomorrow, and the cooling huddle of his life up till then.

Sea Child

A Tale of Dune

BY BRIAN HERBERT AND KEVIN J. ANDERSON

Best-selling authors Brian Herbert and Kevin J. Anderson have previously collabo-
rated on the Prelude to Dune trilogy (*House Atreides, House Harkonnen,* and *House
Corrino*), the Legends of Dune trilogy (*The Butlerian Jihad, The Machine Crusade,
The Battle of Corrin*), and *The Road to Dune.*

When Frank Herbert wrote his original six Dune novels, the last two—*Heretics of
Dune* and *Chapterhouse Dune*—were the first parts of the grand climax to the epic
saga. Frank Herbert died before completing the story, leaving only a detailed outline
for "Dune 7." Using that outline, the Herbert and Anderson team are currently writing *Hunters of Dune* and *Sandworms of Dune,* the chronological finale to the story.

"Sea Child" introduces part of that story arc, with the beleaguered Bene Gesserit
Sisterhood facing their destructive dark counterparts, the Honored Matres, who have
destroyed the planet Dune. "Sea Child" takes place during the events of *Chapterhouse Dune,* and should be enjoyed by any fans of the Dune series.

Brian Herbert lives on an island off the coast of Washington State; Kevin J. Anderson lives in Monument, Colorado, with his wife, author Rebecca Moesta.

---

*Bene Gesserit punishments must carry an inescapable
lesson, one which extends far beyond the pain.*
—Mother Superior Taraza, Chapterhouse Archives

As she had done since the brutal Honored Matres had conquered
Buzzell, Sister Corysta struggled to get through the day without attract-
ing undue notice. Most of the Bene Gesserit like herself had already been
slaughtered, and passive cooperation was the only way she could survive.

Even for a disgraced Reverend Mother such as herself, submission to
a powerful though morally inferior adversary galled her. But the handful
of surviving Sisters here on the isolated ocean world—all of whom had

been sent here to face years of penance—could not hope to resist the "whores" that arrived unexpectedly, in such overwhelming force.

At first, the Honored Matre conquerors had resorted to primal techniques of coercion and manipulation. They killed most of the Reverend Mothers during interrogation, trying unsuccessfully to learn the location of Chapterhouse, the hidden homeworld of the Bene Gesserits. Thus far, Corysta was one of twenty Sisters who had avoided death, but she knew their odds of continued survival were not good.

Back in the terrible Famine Times after the death of Leto II, the God Emperor of Dune, much of humanity had scattered into the wilderness of star systems and struggled to survive. Left behind in the core of the old Imperium, only a few remnants had clung to the tattered civilization and rebuilt it under Bene Gesserit rule. Now, after fifteen hundred years, many of the Scattered Ones were coming back, bringing destruction with them. At the head of the unruly hordes, Honored Matres swept across planets like a raging spacestorm, returning with stolen technology and grossly altered attitudes. In appearance, the whores bore superficial similarities to the black-robed Bene Gesserits, but in reality they were unimaginably different, with different fighting skills and no apparent moral code—as they had proved many times with their captives on Buzzell.

As dawn gathered light across the water, Corysta went to the edge of a jagged inlet, her bare feet finding precarious balance on slippery rocks as she made her way down to the ocean's edge. The Honored Matres kept the bulk of the food supplies for themselves, offering little to the surviving inhabitants of Buzzell. Thus, if Corysta failed to find her own food, she would starve. It would amuse the whores to find out that one of the hated Bene Gesserits could not care for herself; the Sisterhood had always taught the importance of human adaptation for survival in challenging environments.

The young Sister had a knot in her stomach, pangs of hunger similar to the pains of grief and emptiness. Corysta could never forget the crime that had sent her to Buzzell, a foolish and failed effort to keep her baby secret from the Sisterhood and their interminable breeding program.

In moments of despair, Corysta felt she had two sets of enemies, her own Sisters and the Honored Matres who sought supremacy over everything in the old Imperium. If the Bene Gesserits did not find a way to fight back—here and on other planets—their days would be numbered. With superior weaponry and vast armies, the Honored Matres would exterminate the Sisterhood. From her own position of disadvantage, Corysta could only hope that her Mother Superior was developing a plan on Chapterhouse that would enable the ancient organization to survive. The Sisterhood faced an immense challenge against an irrational enemy.

In a fit of violence, the Honored Matres had been provoked into unleashing incredible weapons from the Scattering against Rakis, the desert world better known as Dune. Now, the legendary planet was nothing more than a charred ball, with all sandworms dead and the source of spice obliterated. Only the Bene Gesserits, on faraway Chapterhouse, had any stockpiles left. The whores from the Scattering had destroyed tremendous wealth simply to vent their rage. It made no sense. Or did it?

Soostones were also a source of wealth in the Known Universe, and were found only on Buzzell. Therefore, Honored Matres had conquered this planet with its handful of punished Bene Gesserit Sisters. And now they meant to exploit it. . . .

At the water's edge, Corysta reached into the lapping surf, withdrawing her hand-woven traps that gathered night-scurrying crustaceans. Lifting her dark skirt, she waded deeper to retrieve the nets. Her special little cove had always provided a bounty for her, vital food that she shared with her few remaining Sisters.

She found footing on the slick, rounded surface of a submerged rock. The moving currents stirred up silt, making the water murky. The sky was steel gray with clouds, but she hardly noticed them. Since the arrival of the Honored Matres, Corysta spent most of her time with her gaze lowered, seeing only the ground. She'd had enough punishment from the Bene Gesserit. As unfair as it was in the first place, her suffering had been exacerbated by the whores.

As she pulled in the net, Corysta was pleased to feel its heaviness, an indicator of a good catch. *Another day without starvation.* With difficulty she pulled the net to the surface and rested it on the rocks, where she discovered that its tangled strands did not hold a clatter of shellfish but, instead, contained a weak and greenish creature. To her surprise, she saw a small humanoid baby with smooth skin, large round eyes, a wide mouth, and gill slits. She immediately recognized the creature as one of the genetically modified "phibian" slaves the whores had brought to Buzzell to harvest soostones. But it was just an infant, floating alone and helpless.

Catching her breath, Corysta splashed back to the shore rocks behind her. Phibians were cruel and monstrous—no surprise, considering the vicious whores who had created them—and she was afraid she would be beaten for interfering with this abandoned child. Adult phibians would claim the infant had been caught in her nets, that *she* had killed it. She had to be very careful.

Then Corysta saw the baby's eyes flutter open, its gills and mouth gasping for oxygen. A bloody gash marred the infant's forehead; it looked like an intentional mark drawn by the single claw of a larger phibian. This child was weak and sickly, with a large discoloration on its back and side, a glaring birthmark like ink spilled on a quarter of its small body.

An outcast.

She had heard of this before. Among the phibians, the claw wound was a mark of rejection. Some aquatic parent had scarred its own frail child in disgust because of the birthmark, and then cast the baby away to perish in the seas. Stray currents had brought it to Corysta's nets.

Gently, she untangled the creature from the strands and washed the small, weak body in the calm waters. It was male. Responding to her ministrations, the sickly little phibian stirred and opened its alien, membranous eyes to look at her. Despite the monstrous appearance, Corysta thought she saw humanity behind the strange eyes, a child from the sea who had done nothing to deserve the punishment inflicted upon it.

She gathered the baby in her arms, folding him in her black robe to hide him from view. Looking around, Corysta quickly ran home.

On Buzzell, deep, plankton-rich oceans swallowed all but a few patches of rough land. It was as if the cosmic creator had accidentally left a water tap running and filled the planet to overflowing.

On the only patch of dry land suitable for use as a spaceport, Corysta worked with several other beaten Bene Gesserit Sisters. The women carried heavy sealed boxes of the milky gems called soostones. After all their specialized training, including a remarkable ability to control their bodily chemistry, Corysta and these defeated Sisters were nothing more than menial laborers forced to work while the brutal Honored Matres flaunted their dominance.

Two Bene Gesserit women walked beside Corysta with their eyes cast down, each one carrying a heavy satchel full of the harvested gems. The Honored Matres enjoyed grinding the disgraced Reverent Mothers under their heels. During their exile here, Corysta and her fellow Sisters had all known one another's crimes and supported one another. But in their current situation, such minor infractions and the irrelevant penance and retribution meant nothing. She and her companions knew the impatient whores were sure to kill them soon, rendering their life histories meaningless. Now that the phibians had arrived as a specialized workforce, the Sisters were no longer necessary for the economic processes of Buzzell.

On Corysta's left, five adult phibians rose out of the water, lean and powerful forms with frightening countenances. Their unscaled skins shone with oily iridescence; their heads were bullet-shaped, streamlined for swimming. The Honored Matres had apparently bred the creatures using technology and knowledge brought by Tleilaxu gene masters who had also fled in the Scattering. Experimenting with human raw materials, had those Tleilaxu outcasts cooperated willingly, or had they been forced by the whores? The sleek and glistening phibians had been well designed for their underwater work.

The humanoids stood dripping on the land, carrying nets full of gleaming soostones. Corysta no longer found the jewels appealing. To her, they had the look and smell of the blood that had been spilled to get them. Thousands of Buzzell inhabitants—exiled Sisters, support personnel, even smugglers and traders—had been slaughtered by the Honored Matres in their takeover.

The whores in charge of the work crew snapped orders, and Corysta took a webbed net from the first phibian. On the creature she smelled salty moisture, an iodine-laced body odor, and an undertone of fish. The slitted eyes were covered by a moist nictitating membrane.

Looking at the repugnant face, she sensed coldness, and wondered if this might be the father of her sea child, who was now secretly recovering in her hut. As that thought crossed her mind, the adult phibian struck a blow that knocked her backward. In a bubbly voice, the creature said, "Too slow. Go work."

She grabbed the satchel of soostones and scurried away. She did not want the Honored Matres to focus on her. Her instinct for survival was ever-present.

No one would be coming to rescue them. Since the devastation of Rakis, the Bene Gesserit leadership had holed up on Chapterhouse to hide from the unrelenting hunters. She wondered if Taraza was still Mother Superior of the order, or if—as rumor suggested—the Honored Matres had killed her on Rakis.

On this backwater world, Corysta and her companions would never know.

That evening, in her hut lit by a glowing fish-oil lamp, Corysta cradled the phibian baby in her arms and fed it broth with a spoon. How ironic that her own child had been taken from her by the Breeding Mistresses, and now in a strange cosmic turnabout she had been given this . . . creature. It seemed a cruel joke played by Fate, a monster in exchange for her beautiful baby.

Immediately she chastised herself for thinking that way. This poor subhuman child had no control over its surroundings, its parentage, or the fate that had befallen it.

She held the moist, cool baby close in the dim light and could feel the strange humming energy of its body next to hers, almost a purring sensation that made no detectable sound. At first the baby had fussed about the spoon, refusing to eat from it, but gradually, patiently, Corysta had coaxed it to accept the thin broth boiled with crustaceans and seaweed. The baby hardly ever whimpered, though it looked at her with the saddest expression she'd ever seen.

Life was so unpredictable, moment by moment and year by year, and so chaotic within the much larger chaos of the entire universe. People were anxious to do this and that, to go in directions they imagined were important.

As Corysta gazed down at the phibian and made gentle eye contact with it, she had the sensation of supreme balance, that the time they were spending together had a healing influence on the frenzied cosmos . . . that all of the chaos wasn't really what it appeared to be, that her actions and experiences had a larger, significant purpose. Each mother and child extended far beyond their own parochial circumstances, far beyond the horizons they could see or even begin to imagine.

In the distant past, the Bene Gesserit breeding program had focused on creating a genetic foundation that would result in the Kwisatz Haderach, supposedly a powerful unifying force. For thousands of years the Sisterhood had sought that goal, and there had been many failures, many disappointments. Worse, when they finally achieved success with Paul Atreides, Muad'dib, the Kwisatz Haderach had turned against them and torn apart their plan. And then his son, Leto II, the Tyrant—

"Never again!" the Bene Gesserit had vowed. They would never try to breed another Kwisatz Haderach, and yet their careful sifting and twining of bloodlines had continued for millennia. They must be trying for something. There must have been some reason her own baby had been torn from her.

Corysta had been ordered by Breeding Mistress Monaya to obtain specific genetic lines that the Sisterhood claimed it needed. She had not been told where she fit into the larger picture; that was an unnecessary complication in the eyes of her superiors. Complete information was known only to a select few, and orders were passed on down the ranks to the front-line soldiers.

I was one of those soldiers. Corysta had been commanded to seduce a nobleman and bear his child; she was instructed to feel no love for him or for the baby. Against her natural, inborn instincts she was supposed to shut off her emotions and perform the task. She was no more than a vessel carrying genetic material forward, eventually turning over the contents to the Sisterhood. Just a container of sperm and ovum, germinating something her superiors needed.

Inadvertently she had won half the battle; she hadn't cared at all about the man. Oh, he'd been handsome enough, but his spoiled and petulant personality had soured her even as she seduced him. She had gone away without ever telling him that she carried his child.

But the other half of the battle that came later was far more difficult. After carrying the baby for nine months, nourishing it from her own body, Corysta knew she would be unable to turn it over to Monaya. Shortly before her due date, she had sneaked away into seclusion, where all alone she gave birth to a daughter.

Only hours into the baby's life, before Corysta had time to know her own child, Sisters stormed in like a flock of angry black crows. Stern-faced Monaya took the newborn herself and spirited her away to be used for their own secret purposes. Still weak from giving birth, Corysta knew she would never see her daughter again, that she could never call it her own. Despite all she tried to feel for the girl child, the baby daughter had never belonged to her, and she'd only been able to steal moments with it. Even her womb was not her own.

Of course Corysta had been foolish in running, in trying to keep the baby for herself. Her punishment, as expected, had been severe. She'd been exiled to Buzzell, where other Sisters in her situation were sent, all of them guilty of crimes of love the Sisterhood could not tolerate . . . "crimes of humanity."

How peculiar to label love a crime. The universe would have disintegrated long ago without love, shattered by immense wars. To Corysta, it seemed inhuman for Bene Gesserit leadership to take such a position. The Sisters were, in their own way, compassionate, caring people, but Reverend Mothers and Breeding Mistresses spoke of "love" only in derogatory or clinical terms.

The Sisterhood reveled in defying compartmentalization, in espousing an odd juxtaposition of beliefs. Despite their apparent inhumanity in running roughshod over desires of the heart, the Sisters considered themselves expert at key aspects of being human. Similarly, the indoctrinated women professed to have no religion, but behaved as if they did anyway, adopting a strong moral and ethical base and rituals that could only be classified as religious.

Thus the complex, enigmatic Sisters were simultaneously human and inhuman, loving and unloving, secular and religious . . . an ancient society that operated within its narrow rules and belief systems, walking tightropes they had suspended over deep chasms.

To her misfortune, Corysta had fallen off one of the tightropes, plunging her into darkness.

And in her punishment, she had been sent here to Buzzell. To this strange sea child. . . .

As a storm whipped across the waters, ruffling the sea into whitecaps, Honored Matres dragged the surviving Bene Gesserits in front of the commandeered administrative buildings. The damp wind felt bitter on Corysta's face as she stood on an expanse of grass that was growing too long, since no one tended it. She dared to lift her chin, her own small act of defiance.

The Honored Matres were lean and wolfish, their faces sharp, their eyes feral orange from the adrenaline-based spice substitute they consumed. Their bodies were all sinew and reflexes, their hands and feet edged with hard calluses that could be as deadly as any weapon. The whores wore clinging garments over their figures, bright leotards and capes adorned with fine stitching. They flaunted themselves like peacocks, used sex to dominate and enslave the male populations on worlds they conquered.

"So few of you witches remain," said Matre Skira as she stood before the assembled Sisters. "So few. . . ." The sharp-featured leader of the whores on Buzzell, she had long nails, compact breasts like clenched fists, and knotted limbs with all the softness of petrified wood. She was of an indeterminate age; Corysta detected subtle behavioral hints that Skira assumed everyone believed she was much younger than she actually was. "How many more of you must we torture before someone reveals what we need to know?" Her voice bore an artificial undertone of honey, yet it burned like acid.

Jaena, the Sister standing next to Corysta, blurted, "All of us. No Bene Gesserit will ever tell you where Chapterhouse is."

Without warning, the Honored Matre struck out with a powerful kick of her leg, flashing like a whip. Before Jaena could even draw back, the hard side of Skira's bare foot danced across the outspoken Sister's forehead with a blur of speed.

"Trying to provoke me into killing you?" Skira asked in a surprisingly calm voice, landing back with the perfect balance and grace of a ballerina.

Skira had displayed precise control, delivering a blow just sufficient to cut the skin on Jaena's forehead. She left a bloody gash that looked remarkably similar to the mark of rejection on Corysta's sea child.

The injured Sister dropped, clutching her forehead. Blood streamed between her fingers, while her attacker chuckled. "Your stubbornness amuses us. Even if you don't provide us with the information we desire, you are at least a source of entertainment." Other Honored Matres laughed with her.

After returning from the Scattering, legions of whores used economics, military weapons, and sexual bondage against the human populations they encountered. They hunted the Bene Gesserits like prey, taking advantage of the Sisterhood's lack of strong political leadership or effective military forces. But still the Honored Matres feared them, knowing the Bene Gesserits remained capable of real resistance as long as their leadership remained in hiding.

As the storm continued to build out on the ocean, whipping chilly winds and rain across the narrow strip of land where the women stood, Matre Skira proceeded to question Jaena and two other Sisters, screaming at them and beating them . . . but letting them live.

Thus far, Corysta—ever quiet and alert as she shivered in the cold—had avoided the brunt of her captors' anger. In the past she'd been interrogated like the others, but not with the severity she had feared. Now the regular proceedings had evolved into light entertainment for the whores, who conducted them more out of habit than from any realistic hope of acquiring vital knowledge. But violence always simmered just beneath the surface, and the young Sister knew a massacre could occur at any moment.

The rain let up, and Corysta wiped moisture from her face. Despite the punishment and exile the Bene Gesserit had imposed, she remained loyal to the Sisterhood. She would kill herself before revealing the location of Chapterhouse.

Finally Skira and the other Honored Matres returned to the comfort and warmth of their administrative buildings. With a swirl of patterned capes over damp leotards, the whores left Corysta and her companions to make their way back through the rain to their squalid daily lives, supporting their wounded Sisters.

Hurrying along a cliffside trail that led to her hut after she had left the others, Corysta watched the surf crashing against rocks below and wondered if the phibians were looking up at her through the stippled surface of waves. Did the amphibious creatures even think about the child they had marked and then abandoned to the sea? They must assume it to be dead.

Glad to have survived another interrogation, she ran home and slipped into her primitive dwelling where the baby waited, now healthier and stronger.

Corysta knew she could not keep the phibian child forever.

Her moments of happiness were often ephemeral, like fleeting flashes of light in the gloom of a dark chamber. She had learned to accept the precious moments for what they were—just moments.

Though she wanted to clutch the sea child to her breast and keep it safe, she knew that was not possible. Corysta wasn't safe herself—how could she hope to keep a child safe? She could only protect the baby temporarily, giving him shelter until he grew strong enough to go off on his own. She would have to release him back into the sea. From the phibian child's rapid rate of growth, she felt certain that he would become self-sufficient faster than a human could.

One evening, Corysta did something she'd been dreading. As darkness set in, she made her way down to her hidden cove along the familiar path, taking the child with her. Though she could not always see the way in the gloom, she was surprised at how surefooted she was.

Wading out into the cold water, she cradled the child securely in her arms, and heard him whimper as the water touched his legs and lower body. She'd hidden and cared for her sea child for almost two months now, and already he was the size of a human toddler. His blotchy, prominent birthmark bothered her not at all, but she knew his own people had cast him out because of it. The terrifying prospect of this evening had been on her mind for weeks, and she'd feared that the phibian would just swim away and never look back at her. Corysta knew his connection with the ocean was inevitable.

"I'm here," she said in a gentle voice. "Do not be afraid."

With its webbed hands, the child clung to her arms, refusing to let go. The rapidly humming pulse of his skin against hers revealed the baby's silent terror.

Corysta waded back to the shallows, where the water was only a few inches deep, and sat there on the sand, letting the waves wash over her legs and the baby's. The water was warmer than the cool evening air, and felt good as it touched her. Out to sea, the water glowed faintly phosphorescent, so that the bullet-shaped head was profiled against the horizon. The darkness of the small shape reminded her of the mysteries contained within him, and in the ocean beyond. . . .

Each evening thereafter, Corysta developed a routine. As darkness set in, she would go to her hidden cove and dip into the water, taking the tiny phibian along. Soon the creature she called Sea Child was walking alongside her and swimming in shallow water on his own.

Corysta wished she could be a phibian herself and swim out there, to the farthest reaches of this ocean world, escaping the brutal Honored Matres and taking her sea child with her. She wondered what it would be like to dive deep into the ocean, even if she did so on an unseen tether. At least there she might experience a familial bond that was stronger than anything she felt toward her Bene Gesserit Sisters.

Corysta prodded Sea Child to speak, but the phibian succeeded only in making primitive and unformed sounds from an undeveloped larynx.

"I'm sorry I can't teach you properly," she said, looking down at the toddler as he played on the stone floor of her hut, moving on his webbed hands and feet. She was about to prepare breakfast, combining crustaceans with native herbs she had collected from between the rocks.

The child looked at her without apparent comprehension. He was surrounded by crude toys she had made for him, shells and woody kelp knobs on which she had marked smiling faces. Some of the faces were human, while others she'd made to look like Sea Child's own people. Curiously, he showed more interest in the ones that least resembled him.

The toddler stared into the carved human face on the largest piece of wood, picking it up with clumsy fingers. Then he looked up in sudden alarm, toward the door of the hut, peeling back his thick lips to expose tiny sharp teeth.

Corysta became aware of sounds outside and felt a bitter, sinking sensation. She barely had time to gather up the child and hold him against her before the door burst open in a hail of splinters.

Matre Skira loomed in the doorway. "What sort of witchery is this?"

"Stay away from us! Please."

Sinewy women in tight leotards and black capes surrounded her. One of them tore the phibian child from her grasp; another beat her to the floor in a flurry of fists and sharp kicks. At first Corysta tried to fight back, but her efforts were hopeless, and she covered her face. The blows still got through. One broke her nose, and another shattered her arm. She cried out in pain, knowing that was what the whores wanted, but her physical discomfort didn't compare with the terrible anguish she felt over losing a child. *Another* child.

Sea Child was hidden from her view, but she heard the baby phibian make his own terrible sounds, high-pitched squeals that chilled her to the bone. Were the Honored Matres hurting him? Anger surged through her, but she could not fight back against their numbers.

These whores from the Scattering—were they offshoots of the Bene Gesserit, descendants of Reverend Mothers who had fled into space centuries ago? They returned to the old Imperium like evil doppelgängers. And now, despite the dramatic differences between Honored Matres and Bene Gesserit, both groups had taken a child from Corysta.

She screamed in frustration and rage. "Don't hurt him! Please. I'll do anything, just let me keep him."

"How touching." Matre Skira rounded on her, feral eyes narrowing. "But do you mean it? You'll do anything? Very well, tell us the location of Chapterhouse, and we will let you keep the brat."

Corysta froze, and nausea welled up inside her. "I can't."

Sea Child let out a very human-sounding cry.

The Honored Matres scowled viciously. "Choose—Chapterhouse, or the child."

She couldn't! Or could she? She'd been trained as a Bene Gesserit, sworn her loyalty to the Sisterhood . . . which had, in turn, punished her for a simple human emotion. They had exiled her here because she dared to feel love for a child, for her own child.

Sea Child was not like her, but he did not care about Corysta's shame, nor did she care about a patch of discoloration on his skin. He had clung to her, the only mother he had ever known.

But she was a Bene Gesserit. The Sisterhood ran through every cell of her body, through a succession of Other Lives descending through the endless chain of ancestors whom she had discovered upon becoming a Reverend Mother. Once a Bene Gesserit, always a Bene Gesserit . . . even after what the Sisterhood had done to her. They had already taught her what to do with her emotions.

"I can't," she said again.

Skira sneered. "I knew you were too weak." She delivered a kick to the side of Corysta's head.

A black wave of darkness approached, but Corysta used her Bene Gesserit bodily control to maintain her consciousness. Abruptly, she was jerked to her feet and dragged down to the cove, where the women threw her onto the spray-slick rocks.

Struggling to her knees, Corysta fought the pain of her injuries. To her horror she saw Skira wade into shallow water with Sea Child. The little phibian struggled against her and kept looking toward Corysta, crying out eerily for mother.

Her own baby had not known her so well, snatched from her arms only hours after birth. Corysta had never gotten to know her own little daughter, never learned how her life had been, what she had accomplished. Corysta had known this poor, inhuman baby much more closely. She had been a real mother, for just a little while.

Restrained by two strong women, Corysta saw froth in the sea just offshore, and presently she made out hundreds of swimming shapes in the water. *Phibians.* Half a dozen adults emerged from the ocean and approached Matre Skira, dripping water from their unclothed bodies.

Sea Child cried out again, and reached back toward Corysta, but Skira held his arms and blocked his view with her own body.

Corysta watched helplessly as the adult phibians studied the mark of rejection on the struggling child's forehead. Would they just kill him now? Trying to remain strong, Corysta wailed when the phibians took her child with them and swam out to sea.

Would they try to kill him again, cast him out like a tainted chick from a nest, pecked to death and cast out? Corysta already longed to see him—if the phibians were going to kill him, and if the whores were going to murder her, she wanted at least to cling to him. Her Sea Child!

Instead, she saw a remarkable thing. The phibians who had originally rejected the child, who had made their bloody mark on the baby's forehead, were now clearly helping him to swim. Supporting him, taking him with them. They did not reject him!

Her vision hampered by tears, she saw the phibians disappear beneath the waves. "Good-bye, my darling," she said, with a final wave. She wondered if she would ever see him again . . . or if the whores would just break her neck with a swift blow now, leaving her body on the shore.

Matre Skira made a gesture, and the other Honored Matres released their hold, letting Corysta drop to the ground. The evil women looked at one another, thoroughly amused by her misery. They turned about and left her there.

She and Sea Child were still prisoners of the Honored Matres, but at least she had made the phibian stronger, and his people would raise him. He would prove the phibians wrong for ever marking him.

She had given him life after all, the true maternal gift. With a mother's love, Corysta hoped her little one would thrive in deep and uncertain waters.

Moebius Trip

BY JANNY WURTS

Janny Wurts is the author of more than fourteen novels and a short story collection, as well as the internationally best-selling Empire trilogy (*Daughter of the Empire*, *Servant of the Empire*, and *Mistress of the Empire*), coauthored with Raymond E. Feist. Her most recent title in the Wars of Light and Shadow series, *Traitor's Knot* (2005), culminates more than twenty years of carefully evolved ideas. The cover images on the books, both in the U.S. and abroad, are her own paintings, depicting her vision of characters and setting.

"I tend to take the amalgamate bit approach to short fiction," said Wurts. "If I hated mathematics, I had a love affair with geometry and a rapt fascination with the concept of a Moebius loop. The sculpture in front of the Smithsonian's Air and Space Museum still haunts me for its beauty. As a teen, I had a young thoroughbred I trained to saddle and a reflector telescope for stargazing—I devoured everything in *Sky and Telescope* magazine. My intent to major in astronomy foundered because, actually, I couldn't stop writing. Try growing roses in Florida, throw a character into the mix, and you get a field day for the imagination."

Janny Wurts lives in Florida with her husband, fantasy artist Don Maitz. Visit Wurts at her Web page: www.paravia.com/JannyWurts.

The weather was finicky that afternoon. Mark Haskell squinted up at the clouds as his shortened steps moved from the pink rose bed to the red one. Though the calendar read June it was August-hot, under sky banked with crowding cumulous. Thunderstorm later, Haskell thought. He trimmed a diseased shoot from a bush with an equally desiccated, age-flecked hand. He hoped the pending rain would hold off. Downpours bruised the new growth and battered off tender petals. The sultry heat was scarcely a benefit; the damage inflicted by blight and fungus was never so sudden or violent.

From a retirement well-pickled by the vinegar of past mistakes, Haskell's view held little to offer a perspective that aged beyond seventy. A decade ago he had been still full of himself, impetuous, even reckless.

His pert wife had wept for the gambling money he'd bet and lost on the ponies. But Ellen had passed on five years ago. Without her winsome smile and her nagging, few things of interest remained. Haskell tended his roses and grew quietly older, one unremarkable day at a time.

Haskell plucked a Japanese beetle off a green leaf and crushed the carapace with his thumbnail. "Pest," he muttered. The thought crossed his mind that only senile people talked to themselves. He glanced self-consciously over his shoulder before flicking the mangled insect into the grass.

That was the moment he noticed the woman.

She walked into his garden as though she belonged there, a bright figure clad in rippling silk with loud patterns that hurt in the sunlight. She was drastically slender. Either anorexic or a fashion model; most likely the latter, Haskell decided. She moved toward him with an effortless grace, too fluidly dignified to belong to a person lost and in need of directions. Young she was not, though her fathomless, dark eyes and porcelain features could have stopped a man's pulse between heartbeats.

Haskell squinted. He ransacked his memory to be certain she wasn't someone he'd met and forgotten. But no recollection matched her poised step, or those ethereal, long-fingered hands.

"Mr. Haskell," she addressed as she swept to a stop, self-assured as her brazen entry.

Haskell groped for a name that failed to materialize. Surely he had never encountered her like, despite her confident greeting. Confused, self-conscious, he kept his tight silence.

"Mark Wellings Haskell," the stranger enumerated, then extended an expectant palm for his handshake.

When her host hesitated, the odd visitor laughed. Amusement crinkled the flawless skin at the corners of exotic, sloe eyes. From her clothing, to her bobbed, onyx hair, she seemed untouched by the oppressive heat.

"We haven't met," she confessed, a concession that did little to ease Haskell's sweating embarrassment. "My name is Tanya. Moriah Tanya.

, I've been looking for one with your skills, as it happens, for quite a long time. Please forgive the fact I may have startled you."

Haskell cleared his throat. Blotting the juice from the squashed beetle against his pant leg, he accepted the offered, cool hand.

"No bother," he said, more than grateful to learn that his memory had not betrayed him.

"I understand you once pursued an amateur hobby of creating first-surface mirrors," the woman continued. If her name sounded foreign, her speech pattern carried no discernable accent. Her smile seemed a shade too ingratiating, and her knowledge of him was a shock.

Too aged for flattery, Haskell flushed red. His mirrors were nothing if not an anachronism. The old methods he used had been superseded by new technology and advanced equipment. The odd crank who collected telescopes might recall his work. Few others knew of his existence. Commercial demand had been too small for a home-grown engineer to bother to try for a patent. Haskell's tinkering had gone no further afield than the local sky gazers' gazette. The stored mimeographs he once compiled as handouts had faded, tossed out as illegible by his late wife.

The enigmatic visitor who had arrived in the yard scarcely could have been born when his ideas had been fresh.

Or had she? Haskell studied his visitor again. No mark or mannerism held any a clue to suggest the woman's origin. The disturbing fact surfaced that the back garden gate had rusted shut the past winter. Haskell had yet to free the stuck latch. Moriah Tanya's fine dress and immaculate grooming did not suggest she had made her way in by hopping over the picket fence.

"You *are* Mark Haskell," she repeated, clipped to suppressed impatience.

Haskell acknowledged with a gruff nod. He found people who patronized old folks annoying. Dismissed those who robbed him of dignity. "Ms. Tanya, who invited you into my garden unsolicited and unannounced?"

The woman's lips turned, not quite a smile. "I'm here to discuss your mirrors, dear man. Not to argue semantics or puzzle over the frozen latch on your gate."

Worse than youthful arrogance, Haskell disliked confrontation with obstinate females. He retrieved the clippers from the pocket of his baggy trousers and single-mindedly began to prune rose hips. He refused to cater to petty rudeness, or cosset the young with their faddish interests. "Elltron Glass makes the best first surface mirrors in the country," he said in pointed dismissal. "They have a trained staff for public relations, and a crew of research engineers with doctorates. Talk to them. I can't be bothered."

Moriah Tanya chuckled. Silk rustled like water as, without effort, her lithe stride adjusted to match Haskell's tromp toward the compost heap. "I have no use for Elltron. My commission's too sensitive. Is your equipment still operational?"

Haskell frowned. No one had mentioned his mirrors for years, except to amuse the nephews of his in-laws. He dumped his clippings. As he changed course and shuffled toward the garage, the adamant woman still flanked him.

"Why should you care?" Did it matter that he sounded like what he'd become—a lonely widower whose passionate interests had been plowed under by progress?

Moriah Tanya's smile stayed fixed. "I wish to purchase a mirror," she said. "No other maker will serve."

Haskell stifled his outright relief, no longer concerned that she might corner him into a demonstration. If his lab remained tidy: he had not surfaced a glass blank for too many years. What if he was incapable? His hands were arthritic. Mild cataracts clouded his eyesight. The aged rubber gaskets on the vacuum seal might not be trusted to withstand the force of high pressure. He had finished mirrors, several dozen, all new, packed away in the study. His unwanted visitor could take her pick, and his workroom could stay safely locked.

Haskell crossed the garage, feeling vaguely foolish as he motioned toward the side entrance the woman had surely barged through upon her arrival. He hung his clippers on a bent nail, wheezed up the cement steps, and shooed off the tabby cat crouched on the stoop. Moriah Tanya followed him into the house. The cat streaked ahead of them, across Ellen's neat, airy kitchen, and through the shut door into Haskell's domain, a bachelor's cluttered but air-conditioned living room. There, the pet settled into a well-used hollow on the couch, while Haskell shoveled the unopened mail on the love seat into a stuffed magazine bin.

"Sit," he relented. "Make yourself comfortable. I'll fetch out the boxes of mirrors."

Moriah Tanya folded her elegant form onto the sagged, quilted cushions that once had been Ellen's pride, for the needlework. "I'm sorry," she rebutted, "but the mirror I want needs to be custom done."

Haskell's stomach tightened. "I have all the unusual shapes, ready made. Surely we'll find one to suit you."

The woman's glance showed a contentious edge. "I have traveled a great distance to see you, Mr. Haskell. If a personal commission is impossible, then I regret. Because no other mirror will suit me."

"No bother, then," Haskell fibbed, all but flinching. Although Ellen was not there to berate his hypocrisy, his mouth turned dry. He dared not excuse himself now without admitting to fear for his shortfalls. Failure in the lab seemed preferable to the meek admission that he was too old to be useful. Haskell dug into the drawer in the side table until his fingers closed over his key ring.

"You might have to wait while I dust," he warned, a last effort to derail her interest. "Dirt, particles of any kind, will spoil the finish on a first-surface mirror."

"Time poses no problem," said Moriah Tanya. Her strange, worldly smile seemed satisfied, even as Haskell drew a shaky breath in a transparent effort to steady himself.

———

The lab was exactly as he had left it, neat and spotlessly gleaming. The temperature, humidity, and the purity of the air were always kept rigidly constant. The recirculating filtration system ensured there would be no stray speck of dust.

Haskell directed his guest to select a glass blank from the sizes and shapes of the samples displayed on a wall mount. Then he turned his back and busied himself. His clouded eyesight scarcely signified, since he measured the chemicals from memory. His hands were more worrisome. He could not still their trembling.

"Ah!" his visitor exclaimed in sparkling delight. "This round piece here should be perfect."

Haskell noted her choice with relief. Her interest was not meant to fit out a microscope or a telescope. He could be grateful the selection was flat, and not convex or parabolic for the purpose of altering magnification. The reflection she sought would be a direct facsimile of whatever lay inside the field of view. That at least spared him the additional worry over the critical focal point an optical mirror demanded.

He slipped surgical gloves over his palsied fingers, pulled the match from a bin, and peeled the protective covering. He peered at the blank and held it under the light, inspecting for flaws or stray fingerprints. The maneuver was done for showman's effect. Since clouded vision could scarcely determine whether the glass had been marred, Haskell proceeded and sprayed on the delicate layer of adhesive.

Inexplicably, his uneasiness climbed throughout the familiar preparations to vaporize the solution readied for silvering. He paused more than once to mop rolling sweat. If the heat had been left outside with his roses, the uncanny stance of the woman behind him played merry hell with his nerves. She might not actually breathe down his neck. Nonetheless, he twitched as her vampire's attention tracked each detail of his work.

The silvering process had to be finished under near-vacuum conditions. Haskell placed the coated glass blank in the chamber, dogged down the seal, and flicked on the switch that powered the pump. His state of uneasiness did not abate. Almost, he wished for an O-ring gone bad; any excuse to back away from the folly of his commitment.

Yet the motor purred steadily, expelling the air. Haskell was not deaf, yet. He could tell by the sound that the old-fashioned gauges read within normal. In contrast, his state of butterflies worsened with every passing moment. The air seemed too thick. Even the filtered light through the blinds seemed to shimmer with phosphorescence.

Haskell rubbed his strained eyes. A fine mess, if a spell of anxiety dropped him into a faint. Thoughts of a strange woman peeling him off the floor, or phoning the paramedics for an ambulance clenched his jaw. While he spat a muffled oath through his teeth and forced back his lagged concentration, his guest's polite poise stayed withdrawn. Her manner suggested nothing amiss, though his stressed senses insisted the shadows beneath the fluorescents seemed to have altered. The countertop danced with the ephemeral rainbows thrown off of a moiré pattern.

Haskell clamped down on his sweating distress. It would be too humiliating if he had a health crisis now. As the pressure neared zero, he twisted the tap and released the phial of gaseous chemicals to complete the silvering process.

The room blanked around him. His feet seemed to be drifting. The countertop under his hand buzzed with sound, and his eyesight went queer beyond reason. His surroundings turned a dusty, celluloid non-color, as though his perception had twisted and emptied. Haskell choked with panic. What if he succumbed to some sort of attack? His Ellen had collapsed on the couch from an aneurysm, with never an outcry of pain.

Though Haskell could hear the expected sharp hiss as the silvering mixture became sucked into the chamber, the pearlescent mist looked unnaturally opaque through the pane of the observation port. The jolt in his gut spoke of something *far wrong*. Only the woman's firm touch on his arm strangled Haskell's panic-struck outcry.

Whatever the fit that upended his mind, the room was quite suddenly normal. The white wall of the lab, the sliced sun through the blinds, the equipment and counter, every surrounding object regained its proper shape and perspective. The floor tiles beneath him felt solid as if no anomaly had ever happened.

Shaken, Haskell reviewed his equipment. Everything appeared stable. After several deep breaths, he made certain that the silvering process was finished. By habit, he released the check valve. Air whistled into the chamber. When the gauges had stabilized to atmospheric pressure, he uncramped his trembling, gloved fingers and loosened the wingnuts that fastened the hatch. The completed glass was nested inside. Haskell reached within and lifted what should be: a silver first surface mirror of glittering brilliance and clarity.

Yet something, *somewhere*, had gone drastically awry. Haskell gaped with stopped breath. Instead of a light-filled, reflective finish, this glass was dark. Polished, it gleamed like a lustrous, black pearl, or a crystal of smoky quartz; except that the flawless, shimmering piece cast no trace of a fixed reflection. *No image at all;* Haskell shuddered. Was he losing his grip? Not even the lit tubes of the neon fixtures impressed the jet surface before him.

Haskell swayed in confounded shock. He was a scientist who reveled in logic and a certified engineer. Unless he was touched, or slipping into insanity, he could not believe the queer seizure he had experienced could have blighted the finish on one of his mirrors.

He examined the strange glass. Frantic, he searched for a flaw in the procedure to explain the bizarre aberration. No theory passed muster. The surface in front of his eyes stayed inert. Past question, his age drove him toward mental breakdown. Too soon, he'd be locked in an "assisted living" facility, like the hospice where Ellen had lain through her failing, last days in a coma.

Haskell spun, snapped to frustrated rage. Before he could smash the confounding failure, a flutter of silk intervened. The strange woman whose presence had been forgotten snatched the offending glass out of his grasp.

"My good man!" she exclaimed. "Would you destroy what may be the most unusual mirror ever created?"

Haskell blinked. He balled his quivering hands into fists at his sides. "That's no mirror!" he shouted, near to hysterics. "It reflects no image. None at all."

"Bless you!" The woman's exotic glance flashed with reassurance. An unearthly vision amid the lab's sterile setting, she flourished her treasure with the poise of a Chinese porcelain. "Your work casts no reflection in *this* dimension. Which is well, since I've no use for a linear mirror at all."

"Jargon!" snapped Haskell. "Or else head-tripping nonsense."

Moriah Tanya tipped him her provocative smile. "See for yourself." She tilted the glass. In her grasp, the unsettling thing flared to life, un-reeling a sequence of buildings and landscapes, with people in stunning, cinematic detail.

Haskell swallowed. His unease increased. Never had he seen *anything* like the bizarre scenes displayed by the mirror before him. Worse, his head pounded. After all this, he had missed his light lunch. His thoughtless guest had also encroached on the hour he preferred for his nap.

"You are viewing from an altered perspective, downward into a lat-eral reflection of time," the woman ran on in cool explanation. "The same way that one dimension can be run through two, by the twist in a Moebius loop, I warped the time track of your perceived reality during the moment you silvered the mirror."

"Whoever you are, whatever your game, I don't care to be gulled by new-age gimmicks or parlor tricks!" Rattled to fury, Haskell snapped off his gloves. He blotted his drenched palms on his trousers. He needed a chair, in fact, he ached to sit down. Too shaken and flustered to tidy the lab, he left the door unlocked and gaping, and beat an unsteady re-treat.

". . . deserve compensation," Moriah Tanya was saying as she dogged his gimping flight up the stairway. "You've fashioned me a supe-rior tool, one I intend to use often."

"No bother!" grumped Haskell, wishing her gone. "Excuse my dull manners and let yourself out." He reeled across his untidy living room, managed to reach the worn haven of his armchair before his quaking knees failed him.

"What trip would you wish to serve as your reward?" his annoying, crank visitor persisted. She draped herself next to him, clouding his mind with the dizzying scent of perfume. "I can promise that the thrill of your favorite pastime could become an experience unforgettably different."

Before Haskell could rally his wits, her narrow fingers clamped over his nape with an alarming, tensile strength.

The old man was forced to stare into the mirror. When she tilted the sheet of obsidian glass, he was raked dizzy by vertigo. His whirling sight became barraged by a sequence of surreal images. Racetracks, he realized, despite himself wistful for one last chance to place a long-odds bet on the ponies . . .

As though his musing thought triggered change, his awareness spun and upended. Living room, armchair, and wallpapered surrounds were replaced by that eerie, no-color state that Moriah Tanya had claimed was some sort of altered perspective.

"Not again!" Haskell whispered.

He squeezed his eyes shut, gripped his hands onto *nothing*—then cried out as his ears were assaulted with noise. Aware of a seat supporting his body, he found himself buffeted amid the cheering tumult of a crowd.

He sat in a grandstand, packed to bursting capacity. The spectators about him were curiously strange, clad in jarring colors and outlandish styles of dress.

"No!" shouted Haskell.

Heads next to him turned. Fixed him with stares of astonished interest, or greeted him, smiling, with features not even remotely human. On a fenced track below, other six-legged creatures with scales were scuttling to the crowd's roar of delight. They had crab-like jockeys riding their backs in a nightmarish parody of a race course.

"My God, no!" Haskell cried. He clapped his hands over his eyes, feeling nauseated. He had gone crazy! Some poking doctor would declare him unfit and pack him off to an asylum. Any moment . . .

Tightness clamped Haskell's chest. He could not breathe. Then his mind blanked, and he fainted. . . .

Haskell awoke to the guttural roll of a thunderclap. Startled, he sat up in his own chair in the confines of his empty living room. The tabby that had just fled his lap stalked away, twitching her tail in offense.

Senile! thought Haskell. Hallucinations! Never had he believed he would experience the downward slide toward dementia. To die would be better, he had firmly insisted, than to suffer the demeaning indignity.

Thunder rumbled again. Rising wind battered a barrage of raindrops against the picture window. The kitchen casement was still open, Haskell realized. Failing or not he would have to get up, or Ellen's domain would be doused by the storm. Haskell pushed himself onto his feet, determined to handle the problem.

As he leaned past the sink to lower the sash, he stopped cold. An unfamiliar pot stood inside his fenced yard. The glazed vessel contained a rose bush like none he had ever encountered, not in any botanical flower show, or any of his leisurely excursions through the exotic seed catalogs.

Haskell forgot the unsecured window. He barged through the side door, overwhelmed by excitement and the need to protect the curious plant from the downpour.

And the find was a beauty! Sheltered in the garage, while the thunderstorm hammered his flowerbeds, Haskell fingered leaves that were vibrantly striped and bearing barbs that were something like holly. The luminous blooms made their vicious defenses worthwhile, a velvety rose with petals of deep, royal purple. The yellow centers gave off a heady perfume that livened his nerves like a tonic. Haskell caressed a bud, despite himself entranced.

Then he noticed the white paper that circled the stem: a fragment pasted into a moebius strip, inscribed in a woman's hand.

*To Mark Haskell, from Moriah Tanya, made in payment for a
most remarkable first surface mirror*

Haskell laughed out loud. If pending senility brought such rewards,
he might learn to enjoy the affliction. This "imported exotic" would
look well in his garden. He'd just have to take care not to mention the
outlandish experience that had brought him this alien plant.

That moment, behind him, the side door clicked open. Ellen's voice
emerged from the kitchen, chiding over the drum of the downpour.
"Mark Haskell! Will you *ever* be blessed with the plain common sense
to leave your gardening and shut the window?"

The Run to Hardscrabble Station

BY WILLIAM C. DIETZ

William C. Dietz is the best-selling author of more than twenty-five science fiction novels, the most recent of which is *Runner* (Ace, 2005). He grew up in the Seattle area, spent time with the Navy and Marine Corps as a medic, graduated from the University of Washington, lived in Africa for half a year, and has traveled to six continents. Dietz has been variously employed as a surgical technician, college instructor, news writer, television producer, and director of public relations and marketing for an international telephone company. For more information about William C. Dietz and his work visit www.williamcdietz.com.

"The Run to Hardscrabble Station" is set in Dietz's Legion of the Damned universe, which began with the full-length novel *Legion of the Damned*, and continued with *The Final Battle*, *By Blood Alone*, *By Force of Arms*, *For More Than Glory*, and most recently, *For Those Who Fell*. "The story was inspired by my youngest daughter," said Dietz, "who was working her way through the Naval Officer Candidate School in Pensacola, Florida. And yes, she wanted Intelligence, and wound up with Supply. I sent her the story in installments. The DIs sometimes make the candidates do push-ups as punishment for receiving mail—so who knows what it cost her." Ensign Dietz graduated from Naval Officer Candidate School in June 2005.

William C. Dietz lives in Washington State.

"One cart load of the enemy's provisions is equivalent to twenty of one's own . . ."
—*The Art of War*, by Sun Tzu, 500 B.C.

RIM PLANET CR-7201, HARDSCRABBLE STATION

The syndicate LST [landing ship transport] shuddered as a particularly strong gust of wind slammed into the port side. But the pilot had dealt with worse, *much* worse, and fired a steering jet as the boxy vessel continued its descent through Hardscrabble's stormy atmosphere.

Meanwhile, back in the vessel's otherwise empty cargo compartment, twenty heavily armed men and women waited nervously as the seconds ticked by. Some had been part of the attempt to usurp Earth's government many years before, while others had been recruited since. But the rebellion had been put down, forcing the mutineers to live out on the rim. Now, as the ship bucked, wobbled, and shook, all of the raiders were conscious of the fact that rather than attack an isolated colony, they were about to tackle the Confederacy of Sentient Beings. An interstellar government that included more than a dozen intelligent species. And while there weren't very many troops on the surface the assault team knew that Hardscrabble Station was protected by a ring of weapons emplacements that could blow their transport out of the air.

However, thanks to the security codes provided by a navy turncoat, they intended to land unopposed. That's what ex-lieutenant commander Beth Halby was thinking as the LST shook like a thing possessed, the trooper across from her mouthed a prayer, and the person next to him threw up. Halby wrinkled her nose in disgust, a veteran laughed, and gravity tugged the globules of vomit down toward the deck.

Such was Lieutenant Rik Kavar's eagerness to greet not only the incoming LST, but the replacement officer who was presumably aboard it, that the marine had ridden the all-purpose lift up to ground level where the huge Class III shelter clung limpetlike to Hardscrabble's stormy surface. Now, having stepped out onto the loading dock, the officer felt tiny bits of wind-driven silicone sand blast his hard suit as the massive storm doors hit their stops and an LST materialized between them. Lights strobed, and dust blew in every direction as the supply vessel rode her repellers into the sand-strewn shelter and settled onto massive skids. Kavar couldn't hear anything else because of his helmet, but Corporal Wamby's voice was crystal clear. "The security codes match . . . Engine shut down confirmed. Shall I close the doors, sir?"

"That's affirmative," Kavar replied, and watched the dim outside light start to narrow as air jets blew sand out of the durasteel tracks and amber beacons continued to flash. Soon, within a matter of twelve hours or so, the marine planned to board the ship in front of him and leave Hardscrabble for the last time. Then, having served a full year on the godforsaken turd ball, Kavar would go home on leave. His wife had been six months pregnant the last time he'd seen her, which meant his daughter was about nine months old, and a real handful according to a batch of letters received two months earlier. Kavar couldn't wait to hug them, eat some *real* food, and go swimming in the Pacific Ocean.

The marine's thoughts were interrupted as the doors met, the previously swirling sand settled to the floor, and the short-timer was free to remove his helmet as he made his way down off the loading dock onto the surface below. The ship's metal hull made loud *pinging* noises as it began to cool. Though no expert on navy ships, something about the LST bothered Kavar. It looked wrong somehow—like the transports in old war vids. Of course that could be explained by the fact that the war had forced the Confederacy to bring a lot of old equipment out of mothballs.

Less understandable, however, was the fact that both he and the rest of his tiny command had been told to expect *LST-041*, and while the ship in front of him had hull numbers, they were too faded to be legible. Added to that was the fact that the transport was five standard days *early*, an unheard-of occurrence given wartime conditions, and therefore strange . . . Still, the incoming ship had the correct codes, so why worry?

There was a steady *beep, beep, beep* as the stern ramp began to deploy. Cautious now, Kavar triggered his belt com. "Hey, Wamby . . . It's probably okay—but this ship looks a little strange to me. Hit the alarm. Tell the gunny that I want her and the rest of the platoon topside ASAP. Full combat load."

Wamby, who could see most of the shelter's artificially lit interior via the screen in front of him, said, "Yes, sir," but wondered if the loot was a bit rock-happy. Hell, the swabbies had the correct codes, didn't they? So why scramble the troops? But an order is an order, so the Marine slapped the big red button and heard the nearest klaxon start to bleat.

The noncom glanced at the weapons tech seated to his right and offered a characteristic grin. "Are we having fun yet?"

"The gunny's going to be pissed!" the other soldier predicted cheerfully.

But Beth Halby and the lead elements of her strike team were already halfway down the LST's stern ramp by that time. Kavar saw them, and was about to draw his sidearm when the renegade shot him in the face.

Wamby saw the lieutenant's head jerk backwards, swore as he came to his feet, and spun toward the weapons rack behind him. "Look for incoming targets!" the noncom shouted as he grabbed an assault rifle. "Kill anything you see!" The weapons tech did as she was told, but the screens were clear.

Wamby ducked into the main corridor and was running for the lift when he heard a muffled explosion and felt the resulting vibration through the soles of his combat boots. The corporal was no genius, but it didn't take one to know that the main lock had been blown, and that the same people who had murdered Lieutenant Kavar were inside Hardscrabble Station.

ABOARD THE *EPSILON INDI*, OFF RIM WORLD CR-8612

The CS [Combat Supply] vessel *Epsilon Indi* was more than three miles long, could carry five million tons of cargo, a fleet of 125 armored transports, and the 2,000-plus men, women, and robots that were required to run the ship, defend it if necessary, and crew the boxy LSTs that continually arrived and departed from the *Indi*'s cavernous launching bay. The corridor that ran down the length of the ship's spine was crowded with people as the watch changed. Deck officers, weapons officers, engineering officers, flight officers, supply officers, ratings representing dozens of specialties, camo-clad marines, civilian contractors, and a variety of robots all rubbed shoulders with each other while they talked, laughed, complained, argued, bragged, and in one unfortunate case attempted to sing.

Glow panels marked off regular six-foot intervals, the conduit-lined bulkheads were navy gray, and multicolored decals identified where first-aid kits, damage control stations, escape pods, weapons blisters, node points, and access panels could be found. The deck was spotless, thanks to the efforts of the tireless maintenance bots, and a constant stream of routine announcements could be heard as Ensign Tarla Tevo attempted to spot passageway B-12 before the moving walkway carried her past it. Something that was second nature for old hands but still represented a challenge for the ensign, who had been on the ship for less than a week.

Tevo saw the neatly printed sign, took a turn to starboard, and returned a med tech's salute. Then, heels clicking on the metal deck, she made her way down a smaller passageway toward the ship's C & C [command and control] Center and the warren of offices that surrounded it. She was looking for the compartment that belonged to Commander Tig Owani, the ship's XO [executive officer], and the man that could rescue the ensign from supply hell. Assuming that her father had been able to pull all of the necessary strings, Commander Owani would congratulate Tevo on being selected for the intel school on Terra and send her down to personnel. A few days later she would board a high-speed packet ship that would whisk her away to the glamorous universe of plot and counter plot.

Buoyed by that thought, and eager to begin her new career, Tevo came to a halt in front of the XO's compartment. The hatch was open and the officer was clearly at his desk, so the young woman rapped on the wooden "knock" panel. Owani's voice was a deep baritone. "Enter."

Having completed OCS [Officer Candidate School] seven months earlier, Tevo was well aware of the correct protocol. She took three steps forward and came to attention. Her eyes were focused on a point six inches above the XO's closely cropped head. "Ensign Tevo reporting as ordered, *sir!*"

The only light was that provided by the flat panel displays ranked in front of Owani and a single swing-arm lamp. The XO's chair *sighed* as the officer leaned back and rubbed his eyes. The deep lines that creased

Owani's brown skin and the black stubble on his cheeks suggested that he had been on duty for a long time. The XO blinked his eyes to clear them and looked up. The woman in front of him had brown hair, worn flat top style, and a pretty face. She wore a dark blue jumpsuit that had been tailored to fit her slim body. Gold bars rode her collars. He frowned. "Ensign *who?*"

Tevo kept her eyes up where they belonged. "Tevo, sir."

"Oh, yeah," the XO replied wearily. "Tevo, as in Secretary Tevo's daughter . . . Let's see, I have your request here somewhere . . ."

The mention of her father, and the use of his title, served to lift the young woman's spirits.

"So," Owani said as he scanned the screen in front of him. "Having just graduated from supply school, and having been ranked near the *bottom* of her class, Ensign Tevo 'respectfully requests a transfer to the Fleet Intelligence School, where, thanks to her considerable analytical, linguistic, and technical skills, she believes that she will be able to gain all of the knowledge necessary to successfully fill an NIO [Naval Intelligence Officer] slot on board one of the Confederacy's destroyers.' "

Owani lowered the hard copy and shook his head in mock astonishment. "What? Only a destroyer? Surely Ensign Tevo, daughter of *Secretary* Tevo, would prefer a battleship?"

Tevo knew she was in trouble by that time and felt a full range of emotions that included fear, anger, and resentment. There was nothing she could say, not unless invited to do so, and that was unlikely. "Yes, sir, I mean *no*, sir," Tevo stuttered, and knew that her chin was trembling.

When Owani stood it put his eyes on a level with hers. They were space black and equally cold. "Hear me, and hear me good, Ensign . . . First, I don't give a shit who your father is, unless he can provide me with the 200 tons of field rations that this vessel is supposed to have but doesn't.

"Secondly, I took a tour through your P-1, and there are good reasons why the folks at BuPers denied your request for Intel school. You can't speak Thrakie half as well as you think you can, you lack the psych profile required to work with XTs [extra-terrestrials], and the spooks are hot for techies right now.

"Thirdly, you may have heard that the Confederacy of Sentient Beings is currently at war with the Ramanthians. That means that while you were sitting on your ass, damned near flunking out of supply school, thousands of good men, women, and cyborgs were out there dying for you."

Owani put his weight on his fingertips. "Some of them died because they were outnumbered, outmaneuvered, or outsmarted. That's how war is . . . But some of those poor bastards died because they didn't have what it takes to win. Can you tell me what *this* is?"

The shell had been sitting on the corner of Owani's desk, half hidden by all the clutter. But when the naval officer grabbed the piece of ordinance and held it up for her to examine, Tevo recognized the object for what it was. "Sir, that's a .50 caliber round, *sir.*"

"That's right," Owani agreed soberly. "But this isn't just *any* .50 caliber round . . . It's special—and I'll tell you why. Back during the second Hudathan war, *before* the ridgeheads came over to our side, a little-known skirmish was fought on the surface of a planet called Devo-Dor. The battle took place between a company of legionnaires and a battalion-sized force of Hudathans. Well, the ridgeheads won, but only after losing sixty-eight percent of their troops. Not because they outfought the Legion, but because the poor misbegotten box heads [cyborgs] ran out of ammo and were slaughtered.

"A brigade of marines hit dirt one rotation later, the Hudathans were forced to pull out, and Devo-Dor was ours once again. Later, when my recovery team put down on the battlefield, we had to clear each legionnaire's weapon before we could crate them. And guess what? The legionnaires had only one round of ammunition left between them when they were wiped out—and *this* was it."

Light glinted off the brass casing and Tevo discovered that she couldn't take her eyes off of the shell. "*Sir*, yes, sir."

"So," Owani concluded as he put the round back on his desk, "the point is *this* . . . Supply is the most important function in the whole goddamned navy—and anyone who tells you different is an idiot. Therefore, given the importance of your existing specialty, your request for Intel school is hereby denied.

"Now, having agreed on what you *aren't* going to do, let's talk about what you *are* going to do. It seems that the bugs [Ramanthians] are extremely good at killing Lieutenants. That being the case I have no choice but to send ensigns like yourself to planets like Hardscrabble. I hear the planet is a paradise . . . You'll love it."

Tevo, who was still at rigid attention, fought to keep the disappointment off her face. "Sir, yes, sir."

Owani nodded. "Dismissed."

Tevo did a neat about-face, took two steps, and was about to complete her escape when the XO spoke again. "And one more thing . . ."

"Sir?"

"Don't screw up."

RIM PLANET CR-7201, HARDSCRABBLE STATION

The station's interior had been immaculate prior to the battle that had taken place within its passageways, and it was once more, thanks to exlieutenant commander Halby and her troops. As the officer made her way down the main corridor she could see where a section of bulkhead had been repainted, blood had been scrubbed off the deck, and the C & C Center's blast-damaged durasteel door had been removed. The strike team's com tech turned as the officer entered the compartment. She was seated at what had been Corporal Wamby's console—and was wearing *his* camos. They were slightly too large, but there weren't all that many choices, so Chow had to make do. She sported a page boy hair cut, almond shaped eyes, and wore a skull and crossbones tattoo on her left cheek. "Hey, boss . . . Look at this."

Even though most of the syndicate's members had military backgrounds and the organization was structured much as the confed navy was, an element of pirate-style democracy had crept in over the years. Traditional military courtesies were a thing of the past; commanding officers could be voted out if they failed to perform adequately, and everyone was entitled to a share of the loot. All of which meant that while "Hey, boss," was a perfectly acceptable form of address under normal circumstances, it was out of place within what was supposed to be a platoon of marines. "Watch it," Halby cautioned mildly. "I'm a gunnery sergeant . . . Remember?"

"Oops! Sorry about that," Chow responded wryly. "You look good in camos!"

"Yeah, sure I do," Halby replied skeptically. "Okay, what have you got?"

"Well, it looks like the stuff the informant provided was accurate . . . Not only are we standing on top of an SFR [strategic fuel reserve] containing 250 million barrels of A-5 [military grade aerospace fuel], there's a nice subsurface ammo dump buried about five miles east of here, all of which should add up to a nice payday."

"Yes, it should," Halby said gloomily. "Assuming that the tankers enter orbit on time—and we can boost all that A-5 into space."

"That's the part I don't understand," the com tech put in. "Why place an SFR on the surface of a planet? Why not put it on a moon? It would be a helluva lot easier, not to mention cheaper, to transfer fuel under zero-gee conditions."

"And you can be sure that the Confederacy has zero-gee SFRs," Halby answered confidently. "Lots of them. But some, like this one, are positioned to support FCBs [Forward Combat Bases]. Let's say the bugs take a run at this sector . . . All the feddies have to do is route a combat supply vessel to Hardscrabble, drop a few hundred thousand tons of material onto the surface, and presto! They're ready to construct a base on top of the SFR . . . Then, about two weeks later, they'd be ready to fight."

Chow nodded. "That makes sense . . . So what's next?"

Halby glanced at her wrist comp. The LST had cleared the atmosphere twelve hours earlier. So, assuming that all went well, the transport would rendezvous with the tankers and escort them back. In the meantime, a *real* Confed supply ship was scheduled to land on Hardscrabble with mail, fresh food, and other supplies. Assuming that Halby and her strike team were able to successfully fool the people aboard the LST, the feddies would depart the planet none the wiser and thereby extend the amount of time available to suck the SFR dry.

Or, if that strategy failed, they would kill the transport's crew and upload as much A-5 as they could before the navy came looking for their LST. The renegade had her doubts about that, but it wouldn't do to share them, so she grinned instead. "Well, I don't know about *you*, marine . . . But *I* could use some shut-eye."

ABOARD LST-041, *MAMA'S GIRL*

Even the transport was relatively small; she was large enough to mount a hyperdrive and carry a four-person crew, plus a six-person security detail and a passenger. All of whom were temporarily under the command of Ensign Tarla Tevo, who had sequestered herself within the tiny cabin set aside for use by the ship's CO [commanding officer]. It consisted of a locker, a narrow bunk, and a fold-down desk.

Now, as Tevo stared at the display in front of her, the challenge was to bring herself up to speed regarding the ship, its mission, and the people she had suddenly become responsible for. Tevo had left Owani's office only to discover that she had been placed in temporary command of *LST-041*, and the ship was departing for Hardscrabble Station in less than six hours. So while there was every reason to feel sorry for herself, there had been no time in which to actually do so. And now, in a desperate attempt to live up to her new responsibilities, Tevo was scrolling through her crew's personnel files.

The LST's pilot was a warrant officer named Lars Womack, who, in addition to successfully working his way up through the enlisted ranks, had numerous commendations to his credit.

The copilot, a chief petty officer named Liz Yanty, was not so distinguished. Not only had she been busted back to first class prior to making chief again, it appeared that the noncom had an on-again off-again drinking problem.

A first class petty officer named Omada was the ship's power tech, and a first class named Richy was the load master. Both had been in the service for quite awhile, had received good ratings over the years, and appeared to be reliable.

Tevo didn't have access to the P-1's for Staff Sergeant Pepe Mendoza and the six marines under his command, but took comfort from the fact that the jarheads certainly *looked* sharp. As for Marine Lieutenant Tony Pasco, who had orders to assume command of the marine detachment on Hardscrabble, he was along for the ride.

Confident that she had a handle on the human part of the equation, Tevo turned her attention to reviewing the many processes and procedures related to delivering, and accounting for twenty tons of valuable supplies. A task made all the more difficult by her failure to pay attention at supply school. Something she had already come to regret.

Two hours later Tevo emerged from the tiny cabin, nodded to Mendoza as the marine squeezed past her, and made her way forward. Omada was seated in the tiny C & C Center with his back to the corridor. He had black hair, Eurasian features, and the broad shoulders of a gymnast. As with most of the crew, the power tech knew the ensign was green as grass, but he was willing to cut the pork chop [supply officer] some slack so long as she didn't come on too strong. He raised his ever-present coffee mug by way of a greeting and was pleased when she took a moment to chat with him.

Then, confident that Omada knew what he was doing, Tevo stuck her head into the control room. It, like everything else on the ship, was small. There were two passenger seats, one of which belonged to Tevo, fronted by positions for the pilots, only one of which was occupied. Chief Yanty had the watch, and because the ship was in hyperspace, she didn't have a whole lot to do. She turned to see who had entered the compartment. She had frizzy red hair, broad cheekbones, and lots of freckles. Her eyes were small and bright. "So," Yanty began, "how was your nap?"

Tevo took note of both the petty officer's tone and what could only be described as a lack of military courtesy. The officer chose to ignore the petty officer's question and settled into the pilot's chair. "I took a look at your flight log, Chief," Tevo said evenly, "and I noticed that you and Womack have been to Hardscrabble before. That makes you an expert . . . So, tell me everything there is to know about Hardscrabble, starting with those nasty storms. Then I'd like to hear what the Confederation has on the surface—followed by whatever you can tell me about the poor bastards who are stationed there."

"Yeah, I'd like to hear that stuff too," a male voice put in, and Tevo turned to find that Lieutenant Pasco had entered the compartment. He had a wolfish countenance, hollow cheeks, and thin, nearly nonexistent lips. Not a pretty man, but the sort who looked as if he could think his way through most problems, and kill the rest.

Tevo nodded. "Welcome to the class, Lieutenant. Have a seat."

Within a matter of seconds, Yanty had been put in her place *and* elevated to the status of a subject matter expert. And, because she'd been dealing with officers for more than fifteen years, the petty officer couldn't help admiring the skill with which the feat had been accomplished. The result was a subtle change of expression and a grudging sense of respect for the young ensign, as she began what turned into a one-hour seminar on the planet Hardscrabble.

Eventually, after both officers had exited the cockpit, Womack came to relieve Yanty. He had a long, sorrowful face, a pilot's passion for detail, and a penchant for games of chance. Though not the sort of friends who go on liberty together, the twosome had a good working relationship and shared a common skepticism where regular officers were concerned. "So, how's the princess?" Womack inquired as he settled into the prewarmed seat. "Omada told me that she spent more than an hour up here."

"The ensign has a lot to learn," Yanty commented as she got up to leave. "But she knows that—and is willing to listen."

Womack's bushy eyebrows rose slightly. "That's high praise coming from you."

Yanty paused in order to look back over her shoulder. "Screw you, sir. No disrespect intended." Both of the pilots laughed.

RIM PLANET CR-7201, HARDSCRABBLE STATION

The tension within the underground C & C Center was so thick that Halby could have cut it with a knife as Chow's right index finger made contact with the screen before her. "Here they are," the com tech announced. "Right on time."

"Excellent," the officer replied grimly. "Challenge the bastards . . . and make it sound good."

So Chow demanded codes, a chief petty officer named Yanty provided the proper responses, and the incoming LST was cleared to land. Halby took advantage of the intervening time to hold a last-minute team meeting. "Remember," she concluded, "fool them if you can . . . But if it looks like one of them is onto you, kill them and put out the word. It would be nice to have the extra time, but we can lift a lot of A-5 without it, so don't hesitate to pull the plug. Questions?"

There weren't any questions, so the renegades dispersed. Some remained in the C & C Center, others sat down to eat, and some went to bed. Each team member knew which feddie they were pretending to be, had memorized that individual's P-1, and was at least passingly familiar with the dead person's specialty. Time seemed to crawl as the pirates waited for the LST to make its descent, people spoke in terse sentences, and the trap was ready.

The dome-shaped shelter was well camouflaged, and if it hadn't been for the rows of pole-mounted landing beacons that funneled the ship toward it, the blister would have been nearly impossible to see. It was a nice day by local standards, or so Womack thought to himself as he fired the ship's repellers, countered some moderate wind drift, and goosed the in-system drive.

Chief Yanty eyed the instrument panel as the ship closed with the dome—ready to warn Womack if any of the LST's systems fell below minimums. But the readouts remained in the green as the boxy transport passed between the huge metal doors, slowed as Womack fired the bow thrusters, and coasted to a stop. There was a noticeable *thump* as the skids touched down, followed by a marked increase in visibility as the big doors cycled closed.

Both Tevo and Pasco had left the cockpit, and the pilot was still in the process of shutting the propulsion system down when Yanty peered out through the view screen. Two people had turned out to greet the ship— but both were strangers. A virtual impossibility, since the petty officer had been on the *last* ship to land on Hardscrabble. She turned to look at Womack. "Hey, Wo, who *are* those people?"

The pilot had anticipated such a moment and was ready. The spring-loaded blade shot down into his right hand, and Yanty felt something slam into her chest as Womack's arm whipped around. She looked down, saw the metal handle, and felt something give way deep inside her body. The petty officer looked puzzled as she turned to confront the man beside her. "Why, Wo? *Why?*"

"I'm sorry," the warrant officer replied sincerely. "But I lost a lot of money when I was on leave, and the syndicate purchased the debt . . . It wasn't personal."

Yanty wanted to reply, wanted to tell Womack what an asshole he was, but the copilot lost consciousness before she could speak. There was a soft *thump* as her forehead made contact with the padded instrument panel, and a pool of blood began to collect in her lap.

The warrant officer hit the release on his flight harness and came to his feet. Then, having made his way back to the hatch, he slapped a button. Servos *whined* as the door closed, and there was a discernable *click* as Womack triggered the lock. The run to Hardscrabble Station was over.

Dust was still swirling around the ship, and the tang of ozone hung heavy in the air as Tevo made her way down the LST's ramp. Pasco was right behind her with a T-2 bag hanging from each fist. A man who identified himself as Lieutenant Kavar and a woman whom he introduced as Gunnery Sergeant Raster were there to greet the newcomers. Both wore hard suits and clutched helmets to their chests. "It's good to see you!" Kavar proclaimed enthusiastically. "Especially *you*, Lieutenant Pasco . . . Hardscrabble has been fun—but I'm ready to rotate out."

"Fun?" Pasco asked doubtfully as he shook the other man's hand. "It isn't nice to lie to a fellow officer." The man playing the part of Kavar laughed dutifully and offered to help with Pasco's bags.

In the meantime, each having performed a visual reconnaissance on the other, the women arrived at vastly different conclusions. Halby, in her role as a gunnery sergeant, liked what she saw. Ensign Tevo was young and, judging from the way she handled herself, barely out of supply school. Which meant the newbie would be that much easier to fool.

For her part Tevo felt somewhat intimidated by the marine noncom, who not only projected an aura of authority greater than that inherent in her rank, but looked to be tough as nails. Although it was unlined, Raster's face had a hard, almost mannish quality, and her eyes were like blue lasers. "Welcome to Hardscrabble, ma'am," the gunnery sergeant said, offering Tevo a very precise salute.

"Thank you," the ensign replied as she saluted in return. "Our loadmaster is getting ready to push the cargo modules off . . . Can your people lend a hand?"

"Yes, ma'am," Halby replied. "We were starting to run short of food—so you can count on some enthusiastic participation! I'll get a couple of exoskeletons up here and we'll empty that ship in no time."

"Good," Tevo replied. "We're supposed to clear the atmosphere by 0800 local tomorrow morning."

The sooner, the better, Halby thought to herself, and activated her suit com.

Tevo allowed herself to be given a tour of the underground complex after that, and had just returned to the hangar when she ran into Womack. The warrant officer looked concerned. "Have you seen the Chief?" he inquired.

"No," Tevo replied. "I thought she was with you."

"No, ma'am," the pilot responded. "She left the ship shortly after you went below. I haven't seen her since."

"I'll keep an eye peeled," Tevo assured him, and watched Womack walk away. *Should I be worried?* she wondered. *Or was the Chief simply goofing off somewhere?* And what about what she had observed in the complex below? Small things really, like the nonreg tattoo on the com tech's cheek, or the fact that a completely different man could be seen standing next to Kavar's wife in the holo cube on his desk. All of which could mean something—or absolutely nothing.

Servos whined loudly as a marine clad in a twelve-foot-tall exoskeleton stalked past. The framework was yellow with black stripes. Beacons flashed on durasteel shoulders. As Tevo followed the machine toward the ship, she noticed that a security camera was tracking along with her. That added to the sense of unease as the supply officer followed the exoskeleton up into the LST's cargo compartment, where she waved at the loadmaster on her way to the main lock and the compartments beyond. She was looking for Sergeant Mendoza, but was pleased to find both the noncom and Lieutenant Pasco in the tiny wardroom. They looked up as she entered. "Just the person we wanted to see," Pasco said as he came to his feet. "Would you like some coffee?"

Tevo shook her head. "No, thanks . . . What's up?"

"Well," Mendoza began, glancing at Pasco as if for reassurance. "I think something's wrong here."

Tevo's eyebrows shot up. "Really? Well, so do I . . . Tell me what you've got."

It turned out that the marine had noticed three incongruities. The first, and most glaring, item was that all of the station's marines were wearing sidearms, even though there was no reason to do so. Equally strange, from his perspective at least, was the fact that one of the privates was at least forty years old. And another, a teenaged kid, kept referring to Mendoza as "sir," rather than Sarge, or Sergeant.

Once Mendoza was finished, Tevo shared *her* observations, and the marines listened intently. Finally, when she was finished, it was Pasco who gave voice to what all three were already thinking. "I don't know how, or why, but I think these people either killed the marines who were stationed here or took them prisoner. That leaves us with very little choice but to take the place back."

Mendoza looked concerned. "Yes, sir, but what if we're wrong?"

"Then I'm going to have a job transforming large rocks into small ones," Tevo said grimly. "But the alternative, which is to do nothing, is even worse. Especially if they're after all the A-5 stored in the salt domes under the base. So, here's what I want you to do . . . The key is to communicate with our people one-on-one in a way that won't tip the bad guys off. Then, when everyone is ready, we'll make our move. Lieutenant, you're more qualified to handle that part of the operation, so let me know what I can do to support you."

Pasco had been hoping that the naval officer would delegate the actual assault to him and nodded wolfishly. "No problem, Ensign . . . The sergeant and I will prepare a plan."

"Good," Tevo said soberly. "But be careful . . . If we're wrong, and these people are legit, then I'd never forgive myself if somebody got killed."

"Roger that," Pasco acknowledged fervently. "By the way, we're outgunned, so can I include your people in the assault team?"

"Go for it," Tevo replied. "And while you're doing that—I'll locate Womack. Perhaps the two of us can find Chief Yanty."

The impromptu meeting broke up after that—and it was ten minutes later when Tevo entered the cockpit. Womack was there, seated in the pilot's position, where he was updating the ship's log. Yanty was nowhere to be seen. The warrant officer looked up as Tevo entered. He could see that something was wrong from the expression on her face. "Hey, Ensign . . . What's up?"

As Tevo dropped into the cramped copilot's seat, she noticed that it was damp, as if it had just been cleaned. Then, as she went to move one of her boots, it made a *scritching* sound. That seemed odd, but the naval officer had a lot on her mind, and was in a hurry to brief Womack. "So," she said, once the sitrep had been delivered, "all hell's going to break loose . . . But we need the chief. Did you locate her?"

With assistance from two of Halby's fake marines, Womack had been able to carry the dead petty officer into the cargo compartment, where they dumped the body into a half-empty cargo module. Loadmaster Richy had been standing no more than thirty feet away at the time— checking cargo off his manifest. But now, having learned that Tevo and Pasco were onto the deception, the warrant officer needed to speak with Halby as quickly as possible. He started to rise. "No, ma'am. But I'll take another look. If you're right, and these people are posing as marines, we need to find the chief pronto."

And it was then, as Womack began to get up out of his seat, that Tevo realized the truth. Like Yanty, the warrant officer had been to Hardscrabble *before*. So, if the people currently in control of the base were imposters, then Womack should have realized that and warned her. Unless the pilot was in on it—and part of a conspiracy.

That was the moment when Tevo knew that the sticky stuff under her boots was blood, that Womack had murdered Yanty, and that she was in trouble. Because just as some of the ensign's thoughts registered on her face, Womack's registered on *his*, and the pilot made his move. Being trapped within a tight space, and confronted with a much larger opponent, there wasn't much the supply officer could do but grab hold of Womack's wrists as his fingers wrapped themselves around her throat. The male was stronger than Tevo, however, so it wasn't long before the naval officer's vision began to blur. Knowing she was about to lose consciousness, Tevo let go of her assailant's wrists and scrabbled at the instrument panel. She wasn't a pilot, but she could read and knew where the intercom switch was. The officer's right thumb made contact, and as Womack was forced to momentarily release his grip, Tevo uttered a garbled cry.

Womack hit the supply officer with his fist. The blow hurt, but gave Tevo a chance to breathe, and that was good. Tevo brought a knee up into Womack's crotch, heard the pilot grunt, and stuck her right index finger into his left eye. That produced a cry of pain—and the pilot pulled back to clutch at his face.

Pasco arrived five seconds later, pistol-whipped Womack, and dragged the pilot back to the point where he could be strapped into a seat. Tevo followed, speaking as succinctly as she could, conscious of the need to take swift action.

"All right," Pasco said once the report was over. "The gloves are off! Womack did us a favor . . . Now that we know the score, some scumbags are going to die. Here, can you fire one of these?"

The pistol, which Mendoza had removed from the ship's arms locker, felt heavy in Tevo's hand. "I'm no expert," the supply officer confessed. "But I fired one in OCS."

"Terrific," the marine replied dryly. "Try not to shoot any of our people . . . And hide it. We're going to a party."

By the time the LST's full complement of marines and sailors left the ship carrying a large case of what Second Lieutenant Pasco promised were "liquid refreshments" and made their way toward the all-purpose lift, Halby had begun to feel pretty good about the way things were going. Chief Yanty's body had been disposed of by then and, given the petty officer's past problems with alcohol, Womack felt confident that Ensign Tevo would accept the story that the tipsy noncom had wandered out onto Hardscrabble's stormy surface and died of exposure.

So when Pasco, Tevo, and most of the men and women under the command entered the combination chow hall and rec room, neither Halby nor the members of her strike team were ready for what happened next. Just as the syndicate officer had begun to wonder why Womack wasn't present, Mendoza opened what was supposed to be a cooler full of beer and removed a 12-gauge shotgun, which he tossed to Pasco. Then, seizing a submachine gun for himself, the noncom turned to cover the room.

Tevo had been hopeful that the element of surprise, combined with overwhelming firepower, would cause the imposters to surrender without a fight, but, thanks to her role in the great mutiny, Halby had been sentenced to death in absentia. If captured, the people in her assault team were unlikely to fare much better. They knew that, and immediately went for their weapons as Pasco ordered them to "Freeze!"

What followed consumed less than sixty seconds, but it seemed to last for an eternity. The 12-gauge made a loud *boom* as a pirate drew his handgun, only to be snatched off his feet and slammed into the wall behind him.

Mendoza had the automatic weapon in position by then, and was just about to squeeze the trigger when Halby tossed a cup of hot coffee into the noncom's face. The marine swore and dropped the submachine gun to claw at his scalded skin. Halby's sidearm cleared the regulation shoulder holster a moment later and Tevo, who was still in the process of wrestling her weapon out into the open, saw that the woman she knew as Gunnery Sergeant Raster was going to shoot Pasco in the back. The shotgun went off again, Tevo's pistol finally cleared her clothes, and Halby fired. The slug hit Pasco high on his left shoulder and spun the marine around even as the rest of the LST's crew and security team entered the fray.

Tevo ignored everything else to focus on the woman who was about to shoot Pasco again. Having traveled for what seemed like forever, her handgun finally came into alignment; the naval officer pulled the trigger, and kept pulling the trigger, until all fifteen rounds had been fired. Halby jerked like a marionette on a string, and was already dead by the time the last nine bullets smashed into her broken body.

Tevo was still standing there, dry firing into the bloody corpse when Pasco closed a hand over her empty weapon. "That's what I like about you," the marine observed. "When you do something—you go all out."

Tevo came back to her senses, turned to see how the rest of battle had progressed, and was pleased to find that it was over. Roughly half of the imposters were dead or wounded. The rest stood with hands behind their heads as the marines patted them down. Satisfied that everything was under control, Tevo turned back to Pasco and yelled at Omada. "The Lieutenant's been hit! We need a first aid kit over here. . . ."

The next two hours were spent tracking the rest of the pirates to their various hidey-holes, where most were killed, although a few surrendered. Then, having been thoroughly searched, the surviving members of Halby's team were locked into an empty storage room. Rather than trust Womack to pilot the LST, Tevo instructed Omada to program one of the message torps that orbited the planet and send for help.

Tevo would have been happy to rest on her laurels at that point, but it wasn't to be. A scant twenty hours had passed before three syndicate tankers dropped into orbit and one of the commanding officers demanded to speak with Halby.

But it was Tevo who appeared on the com screen, demanded that the tankers surrender, and ordered Omada to launch surface to orbit missiles as all of the pirate vessels attempted to flee. One of the tankers escaped in time, but two were transformed into thousands of pieces of debris, which were still in orbit around Hardscrabble when the Confed relief force arrived a week later. Tevo was relieved of her temporary command at that point; Pasco and the rest of the crew were taken aboard a cruiser along with the surviving prisoners.

Two weeks later, Tevo found herself aboard the *Epsilon Indi*, in Commander Owani's office, standing at rigid attention. "So," the XO said as he eyed the ensign through steepled fingers. "You countered an attempt to hijack one of our SFRs and destroyed *two* syndicate ships, all on your first run. Not bad . . . So, now that you know what it's like to be a real honest-to-god supply officer, do you still want that transfer to Intel?"

Tevo felt her heart race but kept her eyes focused on a spot over Owani's head. "Sir! *Yes,* sir!"

Owani shook his head in mock disappointment. "Request denied. But, if it's any consolation, I put you in for a medal . . . Of course there's a war on, and the bureaucracy grinds slowly, so as much as a year may pass before you have an opportunity to wear it. In the meantime I want you to have *this.*"

Light glinted off polished brass as the .50 caliber shell cart wheeled through the air and Tevo reached out to grab it. The metal was cool to the touch—but the officer felt an inner warmth as her fingers closed around it. "Thank you, sir."

"You're welcome," Owani replied sincerely. "Now get the hell out of my office . . . I have work to do."

Tevo did a neat about-face, marched out into the corridor, and paused to examine the projectile that gleamed in the palm of her hand. Now, having been to Hardscrabble Station, she knew what the object was worth.

The Last Mortal Man

BY SYNE MITCHELL

Syne Mitchell is an award-winning author who lives in the rain-drenched mountains east of Seattle with her husband, Eric Nylund. She is the author of the books *Murphy's Gambit* (2000), *Technogenesis* (2002), *The Changeling Plague* (2003), and *End in Fire* (2005). Her short fiction has appeared in such publications as *Writers of the Future*, *Marion Zimmer Bradley's Fantasy Magazine*, and *Talebones*. "The Last Mortal Man" is set in the world of a soon-to-be-published novel of the same title. Whereas the novel paints a broad picture of a world where immortality is commonplace, the short story provides an intimate view of the personal consequences.

"The Last Mortal Man" was inspired by Mitchell's dissatisfaction with mortality. "I resent the fact that death is a 'when,' not an 'if,'" she said. "Being a writer, I get to invent my own worlds, so I created one which offered the possibility of immortality. Then, of course, being a writer, I set about figuring out why and how that would be a bad thing."

Visit her Web site at www.sff.net/people/syne.

HB: This is Hugh Billingsworth of KUKWY news, here at Cedars-Sinai standing beside what might possibly be the last deathbed in human history. Those of you who've followed Lysander Sterling's epic life know of his eccentricity regarding nanology, and his refusal—despite pleas from family, friends, and fans—to accept conversion to Deathless. Without treatment, doctors say Lysander has less than an hour to live. The question on everyone's mind is: in this, his potentially final minutes, will he break with his public stance of refusing conversion and accept eternal life?

HB: As we wait to see how this latest health crisis resolves, we'll interview those closest to Lysander, review his brilliant and innovative career as a digital artist and animator, interspersed with brain captures of Lysander's own memories—never before has the artist been this open with his public. Only KUKWY brings you this exclusive, live coverage of this emerging drama.

HB: To understand Lysander, the man, and his remarkable life, we have to go back to its beginning. Earlier today, Lysander allowed KUKWY technicians to record memories from critical points in his life. Those of you with full immersion units, get ready to experience how it all began:

She's there, trembling and pale in your arms, smelling of dandelions and cut grass. The wind riffles through her hair and trails golden strands across your cheek. The hammock cradling you both sways. Sunlight pierces the shifting leaves of aspen overhead.

You hold her gently, shocked at how thin she's become, how delicate the skin stretched over her bones.

"Please, Maria." You fight to keep your voice strong; tears would distract from your plea. "Let me help you. It's a simple procedure—everyone does it, eventually. I'll pay—"

She covers your lips with a thin, feverish finger. "No," she whispers, and replaces her finger with a kiss.

You grab her shoulders and push her up. She sits astride you now, legs dangling over the sides of the hammock.

"But why?" It's all you can do to keep from howling the words, from shaking her until she agrees. "You don't have to go through this pain, the vomiting, the fevers. You don't have to . . ." the last word—despite your resolution—is a choked whisper, ". . . die. Don't leave me."

Maria smiles very sadly. "I want to live." She strokes your cheek with hot, dry fingers. "I want to spend as much time with you as possible—that's why I can't convert."

You slide your hands down her back, pained to feel the ridges of her ribs, the knobs of her spine—so fragile. "Nanology can *cure* you, replace your cells with perfect replication and error checking. You won't die, you won't age. We can be together—forever."

Maria dips her hand below the hammock to capture a dandelion. She holds it like a wineglass. "If I pull a petal from this flower," she plucks one yellow tab away, "and replace it with a petal from another flower, is it still the original dandelion?"

You frown. You know where this argument is going. You've fought it a hundred different ways. "Of course it is."

"And if I replace them all." She continues plucking until the green center lies exposed.

"Biology," you tell her in a warning tone.

She continues as if you hadn't spoken, "And if I replace the center." She picks it and tosses it aside. "And if I replace the stem." She holds up empty, juice-stained hands. "Is it the same flower then?"

You catch her hands between yours and hold them tight, so she has to listen. "Every cell you were born with has died and been replaced thousands of times over. We're all constantly born anew. This is no different."

Maria shakes her head, a few more strands of golden hair float away on the breeze. Treasure for the robins in the morning. "I'm sorry. I just don't see it that way. Aging replaces me with me; nanology replaces me with nanoscale machines, pretending to be me."

You argue on, knowing it's hopeless. Maria's self-reliance and courage first drew you to her. Now those same traits may kill her. But you have to try. If by some logical legerdemain you could change her mind—just long enough for the procedure—

"Nature *is* nanoscale machines: proteins, ribosomes, viruses. Slightly different chemistry; a few less nucleotides, but it's all the same thing."

"No." Her lower lip trembles. "It's not. People change."

She's talking about Louis again. You want to search him out and beat him to death—now an impossible exercise—with your fists. Stupid, idiotic, thoughtless man. Maria's first love, converted the year before you met her. He'd had her for ten, illness-free years, and squandered every second.

Maria squirms her hands free—she has to talk with her hands—has to—holding them still is almost as effective as gagging her. "If it were just my heart, or my lungs, that would be one thing." She encircles the top of her head with her fingers. "But this is *me*. The seat of all I am. If this changes—I change." A tear breaks free from her lower eyelashes and rolls down her cheek. "I don't want to stop loving you."

You rise up from the hammock and cradle her against your chest, as hard as you dare. "You won't, love. You won't."

"Promise me," she snuffles against your chest. "Promise me you'll never be converted. I don't want you to stop loving me."

Her tearful voice is a lance through your soul. Right then, you'd promise her anything, even your life. "Never," you agree, raining kisses to blot out her tears. "I'll never convert."

HB: What a touching scene. There you have it. The moment that put Lysander on his life's path to become the last mortal man. It made him unique, it made him a living legend, and tonight it just might kill him. This is Hugh Billingsworth of KUKWY news, at Cedars-Sinai, standing deathwatch for Lysander Sterling. All night long, we'll intersperse never-before-recorded memories from Lysander himself with interviews from family, friends, and nanology specialists. With us now is Lucius Sterling, Lysander's great-great-grandfather and the pioneering venture capitalist whose company, Sterling Nanology, brought immortality to the world. He joins us via Gaia-Net, from his family compound in Maui.

HB: Mr. Sterling, as one of the founders of modern nanology, it's ironic that one of your descendents should become an icon because he refuses conversion. What do you think about Lysander's anti-nanology stance?

LS: The boy's an idiot. Nanology is, was, and always will be safe. Maria Ables died forty years ago. Ly should be converted, and get on with life.

HB: Lysander's fans would certainly agree with you, but there are those who say his amazing productivity, the depth of emotion in his work—that those are products of Lysander's knowing his life was finite. Without which, his life's work would have lacked focus.

LS: Fine. So his morbid fascination gave him focus in the past. That's no reason to prevent him from converting now. He's not going to be very productive dead, is he?

HB: It must be frustrating for a man of your position—used to being able to make things happen—to be so utterly helpless now. What was your reaction to the court's injunction against your having Lysander forcibly converted?

LS: The judge made a bad call. The Body-modification-freedom Act was intended to stop prejudice against nonhumanoid mods. It was never intended to make medical decisions. I've got a team in Washington. We'll get the law clarified on appeal, but . . .

HB: Too late to help Lysander.

LS: <sighs> Yeah.

Maria's breath is so slight, the sheet covering her barely moves. You hold your breath each time—until her chest rises. Her hand lies limp in yours. It won't be long now.

Please convert, you want to whisper. Even now, it might save her. But that would be a betrayal of the last few weeks. She's been so happy since you promised to refuse the change.

"I can go to heaven now," she'd whispered minutes ago, before her eyes fluttered closed in what would probably be her final sleep, "knowing that the man I love will go on. We'll meet again. Up there."

It finally clicks for you, sitting by her hospital bed, watching her chest rise and fall. She is Catholic. If she truly believes that conversion kills the original person—then choosing to become Deathless would be suicide, a mortal sin.

"Maria," you whisper and lift her hand to your lips. The skin on the back of her hand is so dry, so hot. She's burning up from the inside out, like a votive candle.

Could her unreasoning faith in an antique religion be classified as mental illness? The thought fills you with a short-lived hope . . . then shame. You won't betray her—not even to save her life.

To die naturally is Maria's decision.

It guts you. You will lose her.

Her chest falls. And for all your willing it, does not rise again.

The machines monitoring Maria flat-line and play a plaintive tone.

You sob and pull Maria's palm to your forehead. You rock with grief, knowing your life is over.

You will keep your promise, because you can't imagine eternity without her.

HB: Hugh Billingsworth of KUKWY news, with exclusive coverage of the ongoing Lysander Sterling drama. With us here at Cedars-Sinai is the genius who invented the nanology that keeps us all going: Dr. Leonardo Fontesca. He's standing by to perform the process personally, should Lysander change his mind.

HB: Dr. Fontesca, what's your take on all this? Should Lysander accept conversion?

LF: The point of nanology is to make the impossible possible. Not to impose an ideology. If Mr. Sterling wants the change, he should have it. But it should not be imposed on him against his will.

HB: So you disagree with Lucius Sterling?

LF: Lucius and I start from different places on this issue; it is to be expected we would reach different conclusions.

HB: But you, yourself, are converted. Surely you must feel it's safe. That Lysander's claim it represents a death of the original person is unfounded.

LF: The truth is, we don't know. Science does not concern itself with metaphysics. We know that we can take a person and, cell-by-cell, recreate them into a nearly indestructible form, with the same memories. Is that the same person? Or only a clever copy?

HB: That's a very scary thought, Dr. Fontesca. Are you saying each of us that's been converted might not be the same person we were?

LF: The same thing happens in biology, at a slower pace. Cells die and are replaced. A continual process of mitosis and apotheosis. Whether we are converted or remain natural humans, none of us are who we were born.

You work at your computer until your eyes dry and your hands cramp around the digital paintbrush.

The video walls of your studio flicker with previous work. The left wall displays your early images. Maria before her illness: porcelain skin, sparkling eyes, a full, teasing mouth. The right wall shows Maria as she might have been: glowing in her second trimester, smiling with crow's feet bracketing her mouth and eyes, a cascade of silver hair flowing over age-spotted shoulders.

These days, your work is more symbolic. You put the paintbrush in its cradle and flex your hands. The screen in front of you displays two dandelions: one yellow and bursting with captured sunshine, the other gone to seed—seconds away from dissolution, but all the more beautiful for its frailty.

It's good. But not good enough. The relative proportion between the two flowers is a hair off, and the light angle isn't quite right. If you had centuries, you could perfect it. But you don't. You save the image, freezing it and all its flaws for eternity.

You have to move on. No matter how hard you push yourself, there isn't time to do a tenth of the things you imagine.

You head to the kitchen. There's pizza in the fridge from last night. Or was it the night before? When you're close to finishing a piece, you lose track of time.

Your foot catches on something as you pass the front door. Your assistant has delivered more packages. The address on a gold mailing label on one catches your eye: The Academy of Motion Picture Arts and Sciences. This must be the statuette you won for your actress-design work on the digital film, *Mesopotamia*. You place the box, unopened, in the coat closet, with half a dozen others.

In the kitchen, you eat cold pizza and stare at the recorded messages on your video phone. The Guggenheim has acquired your *Maria in Absentia* triptych. The ad agency that bought your *The Time Is Now* series needs the new routing numbers to deposit your latest royalty checks. Interspersed among the business messages, like background noise, are pleas of reporters for interviews, and the adoration of fans.

It's been like that since the story of your refusal to convert—and the reason—became public knowledge. You've become a tragic romantic figure.

Women hound you with offers of love, to help you "get over" Maria. Men too, though less persistently.

They miss the point.

You don't want to forget Maria. It'd be like forgetting air. Impossible.

HB: Hugh Billingsworth at Cedars-Sinai, reporting on Lysander Sterling's condition for KUKWY news. With me via Gaia-Net is Dante Aldo, director of the Museum of Modern Art.

HB: Mr. Aldo, Lysander Sterling is an icon in the art and entertainment industries. What is it about his work that makes it so compelling?

DA: What resonates most for me in Lysander's work is the passion; each of his pieces *vibrates* energy. The technical flaws he deliberately leaves in give each piece a tension rarely found in the work of modern artists. They're like the skewed proportions of Michelangelo's sculptures, lifting the work beyond the representational, into the sublime.

HB: What's your position on today's dilemma? Should he accept conversion?

DA: As an art aficionado, of course I want Lysander to continue his marvelous work. But I have to wonder, if he changed his core beliefs—accepted the conversion he's rejected all these years—wouldn't his work change as well?

HB: But surely, having centuries to work on his craft, to explore every nuance, would make Lysander's video paintings even better.

DA: I don't know . . . It's been said that Michelangelo's genius was the ability to pull images out of stone, an unforgiving, limiting media. Perhaps the vitality of Lysander's work comes from a similar source: He pulls his art out of time.

You're used to the stares when you go out in public. With your thin, white hair, and soft wrinkled skin, you're an oddity. You pass people on the street whose bodies have been modified into fanciful shapes: swirling pigmentation, knees that bend backwards, scaled torsos in colorful patterns, claws, wings, nictating eyelids.

But it's you everyone stares at; they've never seen anyone old. You, the last human in Faerie.

The youngest sometimes congratulate you on your radical mods. Others puzzle out who you are and follow you with wide, amazed eyes.

You balance the silver-wrapped gift on your lap as the sub-Pacific bullet train accelerates. Lucius Sterling has commanded—by purchasing your studio's building and threatening eviction—that you attend his two hundredth birthday party. You hate the outrageous opulence and endless guest list of these events, but after two decades you owe him a visit. It was Lucius, after all, who funded the trust fund that kept you afloat in your early years. Ironic, that all your life you've benefited from the profits of the very technology you refuse.

You look out the porthole at the denizens of the deep. Glittering stars of bioluminescent plankton twinkle in the distance, broken only by the occasional spotlights of angler fish or the glowing bellies of eel-like snake dragonfish.

Your reflection stares back at you from the glass. It's no one you recognize. Every year it ages, but—aside from a growing of twinges and aches—you're still the man who courted Maria Ables on the college green.

The pressure creeps on you slowly. At first you think it's the deep, but the train compartment is kept at sea-level pressure. Numbness runs down your left arm, leaving your fingers weak and tingling. It's hard to draw breath. You gape like a fish, panicking.

You claw your chest, moan, and pitch forward. Facedown on the metal flooring, you fight for breath. Someone will notice you. Someone will help.

But it's been decades since anyone was ill. And social mores of accepted behavior have expanded.

No one comes.

Perhaps the other passengers think you're counting the rippled patterns on the floor. More likely they're all engrossed in Gaia-Net, passively entertained, or exploring endless fields of information.

It feels like a hand is crushing your chest. Each heartbeat hurts.

Right now, you'd give anything to be saved. Forget Maria, forget the promises. In this moment, isolated in pain, you want only to live.

You'd become a poster child for conversion if it would save you.

You don't want to die.

"Live." The word eases out of your lips on a sigh.

The pressure eases. You pull yourself back into your seat, sweating and weak. The present is still on the floor. It might as well be on the moon. Leave it there. You suck in breath after breath. Your chest feels as if it'd been kicked by a mule.

Relief floods you. Gratitude the attack is over. And shame.

You don't know if you'll be strong enough to keep your promise, when the time comes.

HB: KUKWY news, Hugh Billingsworth reporting on the unfolding drama at Cedars-Sinai. Only KUKWY brings you exclusive brain-captures of Lysander Sterling's memories. Only here can you *experience* his extraordinary life. We bring you the inside story no one else knows. Speaking of insiders, I'm outside Lysander's hospital room with Melissa Davies, Lysander's personal assistant for the past twenty years.

HB: Melissa, you've worked alongside Lysander for decades. You know him better than anyone. In these, his final moments, will he choose life?

MD: <sniffling> I don't know. I don't even know if I should be talking to you. Mr. Sterling insists on his privacy. So many people want things from him.

HB: I know this must be difficult. But remember, Lysander granted us license to broadcast his memories. He wants his story told.

MD: Mr. Sterling isn't like other people. He's known all his life that he was going to die. It gave him so much depth, perspective, you know? There's a wisdom in him. We never talked much, but sometimes we'd sit together. He'd drink coffee and I'd sort through his e-mail. Then he'd look up and say something like "Make the most of this moment, Melissa. It will never come again." Things like that. It really makes you think.

HB: Lysander Sterling lies dying inside the next room. In a tank next to him is the nanology that could save his life, make him immortal. He only has to say the word to be saved. The question on all our minds: Will he say it?

MD: I don't know. He always said he meant to go through it. But there were times—days he was really hurting and could barely get out of bed—and I'd see his face before he knew I'd entered the room. Oh jeez, I shouldn't be telling you this. But . . . he's afraid to die.

MD: <pounding on the closed door> Lysander! Don't die. Ask for help. Please! I can't live if you die. Please! Maria's been dead longer than she's been alive. It's stupid to die for an ideal!

HB: As you can see, passions are running high here at Cedars-Sinai. Lysander's long-time assistant Melissa Davies has just been escorted off the premises by hospital security.

HB: What's that? The doctors have just updated Lysander Sterling's status. His blood gases are falling. He has only a handful of minutes left to live—unless he chooses otherwise.

HB: Follow us inside Lysander's private hospital room for what may very well be his final moments. Those of you with immersion units, prepare for the experience of a lifetime, as we take you inside Lysander's current thoughts-live, from Cedars-Sinai.

You lie on the bed, an IV of saline dripping into your arm. It's the only measure you'd allow, and that only after they showed you the label.

The reporter comes in, camera gleaming like a diamond embedded in his right eye. He's got a too-hearty smile plastered to his face, and you take a petty pleasure knowing that, via live brain-capture, the whole world knows you think him a idiot. Vulture. He's come to feed on your impending death. They all have. The whole world crowds into your skull so they can know what it's like to grow old, to take that last step into death.

There would be reporters no matter what you did. By choosing one jackal, the others lost their meal. By dictating the terms of your cooperation, you can tell your story—not theirs.

The world will finally understand.

"Lysander," the reporter whispers, leaning close enough that you can smell the whiskey sour he had at lunch. He's either not getting the brain-capture feed, or he ignores your distaste. "Lysander Sterling, how does it feel to know your death is minutes away?"

It feels like hell—but you suppress that thought. It's too big a betrayal.

You try to answer, to ask if Melissa's safe, but the words won't bubble past your lips. It's too much effort. Why bother? It'll all be over soon.

You're too weak now to ask for help—even if you wanted to. And some part of you—some traitorous animal part of you—wishes to be saved.

Each breath feels like you're lifting the entire hospital with your ribs. There's not enough oxygen in the whole room to satisfy you. Your heart beats faintly, dispiritedly, in your chest. Eighty-six years of continual service, without maintenance. Not bad for unadulterated muscle.

"You could still choose," the reporter says. "Think the words and they'll be picked up on the brain-capture. The doctors could still save you." A bead of saliva hovers from his fleshy lower lip. He's drooling over the drama. You see ratings figures dance behind his eyes.

The door behind him bangs open. She stands there, hand still cupping the door, fallen angel in a black nano-fiber bodysuit. Five-foot-seven, slender build, heart-shaped face and pert nose. The most feared Deathless on the planet. Alexa DuBois: Lucius Sterling's enforcer.

She crosses the room with blinding speed, grabs the reporter and slams his face against the bedrail. Before he can recover, she tosses him out the door.

"I'm sorry, Ly," she says, withdrawing the IV from your arm. The tender look in her eyes holds centuries of regret. "Lucius never let a little thing like the law keep him from what he considers his. You're going to be converted." She lifts you from the bed as gently as a baby. "Whether you want it or not." Her small frame is deceptively strong.

Her lips are centimeters from your ear. "It's not so bad," she whispers.

She's so intent on being gentle with your delicate body, Alexa doesn't notice your fumbling fingers locate the brain-capture transmitter at the base of your skull. The producer carefully calibrated the setting for your failing body, and warned you that upping the gain would produce seizures.

The convulsions alone won't kill you—it wouldn't be suicide—tapping the control would only buy enough time to die naturally.

Alexa is a weapon of destruction, built in a time when it was still possible to kill. She doesn't have the skill to stop a fit. The doctors who could save you are too far away to intervene.

Be passive and live forever young and healthy. Or act now, and die as nature intended.

Your mind races. Alexa lowers you into the conversion tank beside the bed. You have only seconds to choose.

Seconds that might mean permanent obliteration of all thought and consciousness, the end to the unique point of view that was Lysander Sterling. Death eternal.

Maria would have chided you for your pride.

People died for eons. It's the natural order of things. It used to happen to everyone. One more death: no big deal.

What if Maria's religion is right, that something exists after death—

what if Maria is there now, hovering near, waiting to claim you? After a lifetime of living for her—without her. You might be reunited. Could you risk losing that?

And if she was wrong? Can you risk losing everything?

The viscous fluid swimming with nanology creeps up the side of your body, warm as blood. Already your skin itches as the nanoscale machines burrow in.

The slightest tap on the transmitter at the base of your skull, and you'll thrash free of the container.

Now is the moment you must decide. There's no time left.

You choose.

The Double-Edged Sword

BY SHARON SHINN

Sharon Shinn is the acclaimed author of *Archangel* and four additional novels in the world of Samaria (*Jovah's Angel, The Alleluia Files, Angelica,* and *Angel Seeker*), as well as seven other science fiction and fantasy novels, the latest of which is *The Thirteenth House.* She has also published two Young Adult novels, *The Safe-Keeper's Secret* and *The Truth-Teller's Tale*; her third Young Adult book, *The Dream-Maker's Magic,* will be released in 2006. She won the William C. Crawford Award for Outstanding New Fantasy Writer for her first book, *The Shape-Changer's Wife,* and was twice nominated for the John W. Campbell Award for Best New Writer. *Summers at Castle Auburn* and *The Safe-Keeper's Secret* have both been named to the ALA's list of Best Books for Young Adults.

" 'The Double-Edged Sword' takes place in a world I created for an unpublished fantasy novel," Shinn explains. "The fact that the whole world already existed in my head helped me give a certain richness to the details of the story. In particular, I already had designs and explanations for half the cards in the zafo deck. One of my Wiccan friends gave me a blank deck of cards so I could draw the zafo images that were described in the book. I've never actually finished the deck, but it was a lot of fun to come up with pictures and interpretations."

Sharon Shinn lives in St. Louis, Missouri.

I sat at the back of the dark tavern at the table that, in the past five years, had come to be known as mine. Even on the days when I did not bother to leave my house or leave my bed, no one sat in this booth except me. The townspeople knew better, and strangers who made the mistake of sitting in my place would be told politely by Samuel that the table was reserved. I was the only one who ever sat there, and Samuel was the only one who would approach me while I was in possession.

I idly shuffled my zafo cards and began laying out an unspecified fortune. It would be my own, of course; these days, I did not read for anyone except myself. And even then, I was rarely satisfied with the pictures I saw in the cards.

The swinging door to the back room swept open wide, admitting the appetizing smell of meat and onions as well as Samuel's tall, spare figure. Catching sight of me in the dim corner, he checked abruptly and came my way.

"Aesara. I didn't know you were here," he said. "What will you have to drink?"

"Wine, maybe. Do you have time to drink it with me?"

"In an hour or so I will."

"A glass of ale, then, until you are free," I said.

"Will you eat with me?" he asked.

I squinted up at him in the insufficient light. I had not been awake more than an hour and could not have said with any certainty what time it had been when I rose. "Is it almost dinnertime?" I asked.

"For you, it is," he said firmly. I laughed out loud. Samuel was convinced that I never ate unless he fed me. "Of course, I'm always hungry," he added with a smile.

This was meant to coax me to eat, for his sake. "I'll eat with you," I said. "It smells good."

"I'll get your ale, then."

He disappeared, returning in a minute with a glass of cold ale and a plate of bread. The bread made me laugh again. He grinned crookedly. He was sandy-haired and freckle-faced, with weathered skin and an unchanging ruddy coloring that made it hard to place his exact age. I knew it, though. He was fifty-eight, seven years older than I was, and he had been a widower for five years.

I had laid my zafo cards out in the standard grid—one card in the top row, four cards in each of the next two rows, and a single card in the bottom row—but I had not turned them face-up yet. Now, with the ale and bread arrived as a diversion, I did not feel like reading the cards after all. I swept them back into a pile, reshuffled the deck, and laid the cards aside.

The activity of the tavern went on quietly around me. I leaned back on my padded bench and watched. Although I talked to no one except Samuel, I knew all the employees and all the habitués by name. Sam's eldest son Groyce handled most of the up-front business: greeting customers, making sure everyone was attended, watching out for trouble. Groyce's wife, a small, pretty girl, waited on tables and flirted mildly with the local patrons. Two other young women served customers, and an old man cooked in the back.

At this early hour, there were only half a dozen people in the bar, talking quietly, playing board games, or teasing the young girls. I had lived in Salla City for five years now, and I could tell you the name of every man and woman who inhabited it, but I had yet to get closer to a single one of them than I was at this exact moment.

Except for Samuel, of course, and we were close only because of the bargain we had struck one night five years ago. At that, it was not true friendship. He felt grateful and I felt secure; and so he let me stay, and I stayed.

I sipped at my ale and watched with Samuel confer briefly with Groyce before disappearing again into the back room. This was the table I had taken that night five years ago, when I had just paused in Salla City to break my aimless journey for one night. Samuel had served me then, but absently, with clumsy, choppy motions that irritated me because some of the wine had spilled from his unsteady hands to the table. I was laying out the cards then too, and I had been afraid of staining one of them—although it didn't matter if the whole deck was ruined, if the whole deck was lost.

"Could you bring me a cloth, please," I had said coldly, "so I can wipe this up?"

He had immediately done so; but instead of handing me the linen, he had stood beside me wrapping the white napkin around and around his hands.

"You are a halana," he said, when I finally looked up with a scowl.

"Yes," I snapped. "What of it?"

"I have—my wife is next door. She is dying. That is—we have a halana in the city who has done what she can. She says my wife is dying."

Anger and fear had risen in me, for I knew what was coming next.

Knew, and did not want to deal with it. "She is probably right, then," I said.

"But you are a halana," he said almost stupidly.

Halana. Wise woman; healer. We have varied powers, we who are filled with the magical blood of Leith and Egeva. Some of us are very skilled and some of us are merely well taught, and I had no way of knowing just how good the local practitioner was.

"There is nothing I can do for you," I said.

He went on as if I had not spoken. "She is in such pain. Her head—her lungs—her whole body. She has begged me to take her life because she is in such terrible agony. But I can't do that."

I wanted to put my hands over my ears and shut out the sound of his voice; I also wanted to put them over my eyes to block out the sight of his face. I could not do both.

"There is nothing I can do for you," I said again. In the six years that I had been wandering through Sorretis—from the throne room of Verallis to the rocky hills of Limbeth—this was the response I had given to everyone who had asked a favor of me. There had not been many. I did not look, with my grim face and darkling expression, like a woman of kindly disposition.

"But she is dying," he said.

I opened my mouth to refuse him again, but somehow the words went unsaid. Perhaps it was the dazed grief in his gray eyes, or perhaps it was the dormant power in my own body that made me say what I had no intention of saying. "I will look at her," I said, rising. "But I make no guarantees. I doubt if there is anything I can do."

And so I accompanied him to the small house behind the big tavern, the house that, under other circumstances, would have been pervaded with a welcoming charm. But a woman lay dying inside, and so the house was filled with fear instead.

I knew as soon as I entered the sickroom that the woman was ill beyond my powers of healing. The chamber was shallowly lit by clusters of tapers shielded behind brightly painted screens. Someone had brought in fresh flowers in an attempt to cheer up the sick woman; everywhere were similar evidences of hopeful affection. But there were not enough flowers or candles in Sorretis to bring this woman back to life.

I did not say so, of course. She was conscious, but barely; she turned uneasily when I entered the room. "Sam?" she said faintly, and the lanky man crossed to her side. He took her hand so gently he could have been imprisoning butterflies. Nonetheless, she had to bite back a cry of pain. The look upon his face was sheer desolation.

"I've brought a halana to look at you, Mari," he said, in a low voice. I supposed her fever had made her ears sensitive to sound as well. "Can you say hello?"

"Halana?" she said drowsily and turned her eyes blindly my way. But I could see from the cloudy irises that she could not make out my features—nor, if it came to that, her husband's. I crossed the room quietly and held my hands on either side of her face. I did not quite touch her skin, and she did not moan aloud. Even without touching her, I could feel the heat from her cheeks burn against my palms.

I stayed in the room a few moments, trying to determine what her disease was, while Samuel talked nonsense to distract her. A few minutes was all I could stand; I left as soon as I could have been expected to make a diagnosis. Samuel followed me shortly. On his face was a look of fugitive hope.

"Well?" he said. "Do you think—what do you think?"

I was wont to be blunt at times like these, but he looked so vulnerable that I tried to temper my words. "There are some diseases that can be cured, and some that cannot," I said. "Hers is an illness for which there is no remedy."

He stared at me steadily, while all the light seemed to die slowly from his plain, good-natured face. I had not meant to add even this much, but his expression of despair moved me more than I wished. "I have something I can give her that will ease her pain," I said. "It will not make her well, but it will make her dying less terrible."

"You are sure she will die?"

"In less than a week. Yes, I am sure."

He had flinched when I named the time, but I saw no reason to spare him from the knowledge. "But you can lessen her suffering? With some potion?"

It was not a potion, exactly. I would speak a complex spell over a simple glass of water, and its very essence would change. But I did not explain this to him. Those who are not halani prefer to believe in philtres and potions. It makes them uneasy to rely upon incantations. "That is exactly it," I said. "Wait here, and I will return with the drug."

And so I had gone to the bar and requested water, and paused a moment to pour it into one of the small glass vials I always carried. Shortly thereafter, the medicine had been administered. I had not stayed to see the efficacy of my drug. I was hungry, and I had gone back to the tavern to eat my interrupted meal.

Sam had rejoined me in something less than an hour, his face transformed with wonder. Mari was lucid, she who had been raving before. She had allowed him to take her hand, to kiss her face, without crying out from the agony his lightest touch inflicted. He had told her that she was dying, that this blessed surcease was a gift but not the greatest gift, and even so she had laughed. "I feel so good," Mari had exclaimed. "Even the gift of my life could not make me so happy." Sam related this whole conversation to me.

"I am glad to hear it," I had said somewhat sourly, trying to finish my meal.

"How can I thank you?" he demanded. "Such a wondrous thing you've done—"

"I have not saved her," I warned him. "Don't be deceived. Her body is careening headlong toward death, and I can do nothing to arrest that journey."

He watched me steadily again with those gray eyes. I thought somewhat irrelevantly that this man was nobody's fool. "I understand that," he said almost patiently. "But *you* don't understand. She was in such pain and now she is at peace. There is nothing I would not do to thank you."

"Let me finish my dinner in solitude," I said. "And tell no one what I have done for you tonight."

"But—"

"No one," I interrupted. "If you want to thank me, leave me alone. I am not much interested in interfering in the lives of others. And I do not want them interfering in mine."

He had continued to watch me with that narrowed, intelligent gaze, and I had the sudden feeling that I had told him, in a few simple sentences, the whole story of my tangled life. But all he said was, "I understand. I will say nothing to anyone. You will be free from importunity as long as you stay."

Mari had died six nights later. I did not attend the funeral services; Samuel did not ask me to. He did not ask me how long I planned to stay in Salla City. He never asked me to intercede for the life or health of any other citizen, and I was relatively certain that he knew of others, over the years, who could have used my help. He did ask me, the day after Mari died, what my name was. *Aesara,* I said. If he recognized it, he gave no sign.

Samuel himself brought two steaming plates of food to the table about an hour later. Groyce's pretty wife followed with a bottle of wine and two glasses. She smiled at me shyly but said nothing, and fled as soon as she had set the pieces upon the table. Samuel decanted and poured.

"She's afraid of me," I observed.

He looked after his daughter-in-law. "Who, Lina? She thinks you're a crazy old woman. Everyone does."

"I'm not that old," I said.

"But crazy?"

I shrugged. "Who isn't?"

The food was delicious, as always. After Lina had cleared our dishes away, Sam leaned back and stretched his arms. Out of habit, I pulled out my zafo cards again and began shuffling. Sam and I never talked much during meals or after them, but our silences were filled with a wordless companionship.

Now he spoke, surprising me. "Do you ever look at them?" he said.

I glanced up. "What?"

He gestured to the cards that I had laid out again, absent-mindedly, in the standard grid. "Your cards. You always place them on the table this way, but you never turn them over and look at them."

I made a wry face. "Sometimes I do. I don't like the pictures I see."

"What pictures do you see?"

"What pictures does one ever see in a zafo deck?"

"I don't know. I've never seen one."

Now I was amused. "You've never had your fortune told? Not even once, just for fun?"

"No, never. I have too much respect for the powers of the halani to approach one lightly."

"Now you do, perhaps," I scoffed. "Since you have such high respect for me."

He grinned. "So do you want to read my fortune?"

I shook my head. "I never read for anyone but myself."

He motioned at the cards again. "Then read one for yourself. I would like to see the pictures."

I hesitated a moment. He caught my reluctance. "Then don't," he said swiftly.

I shrugged and smiled. "Why not? They can't tell me anything I don't know already. But if you have never seen this done, I will have to explain everything."

I turned over the top card, alone in the upper row. "This is called the primary significator," I told him. "It represents me as I am or as I was."

No surprise, the top card was the black queen. I was dark-eyed and dark-haired, but the card meant more than that; it spoke of a somber personality weighted with heavy cares. The brooding queen invariably turned up in my fortune, either as my present or my future.

"Now, most halani read the cards in the order in which they are laid out, but I like to skip around," I told him, reaching for the last card, the single one in the fourth row. "This card will tell us who I will become."

The image revealed was not one I was expecting. It was the hooded figure, a dark, faceless form with its hands outstretched.

"It looks somewhat threatening," Samuel observed.

"Indeed. This card means many things, most of them ominous. It stands for the shadowed future, the as-yet-to-be-revealed. Sometimes it is an intimation of death. At other times, it is a warning of a change to come." I gave Sam a twisted smile. "I told you I do not much care for the readings I do."

"You do not have to go on, then," he said seriously.

"No, now I am curious."

I indicated the four cards in the second row. "Fortune, home, heart, career," I recited. "The pictures of my past."

I turned over the cards in order. Fortune: the open box, everything the soul could desire. Home: the lord's castle, with its white stone walls and graceful gables. Heart . . . but here my own heart nearly stopped beating. The black king, reversed.

"What does it mean when a card is upside down?" Sam wanted to know.

"It means the opposite of whatever the card usually means," I said through a constricted throat. "Or that something has gone wrong with—that person or that thing—"

The last card in this row was scarcely any more comfort. Career: the spilled wine. Promise gone awry . . .

"None of this makes any sense to me," Sam said.

Perhaps it would not seem so terrible said aloud. "The cards say that at one time I lived a grand life, in a grand house, and my every wish was indulged," I said. "I cared for a dark-haired man but he—something happened to him. And my career from that point on became something of a waste."

He lifted his eyes to my face, his eyebrows raised, but he did not ask me if any of this was true. "And what about your future?"

I was more cautious this time, and turned the cards over one at a time. "Fortune," I murmured. "The double-edged sword. What I have is equally likely to be used for good or for evil. Home." I smiled. "The roadside tavern. Any place of well-being or cheer."

Sam was pleased. "My bar is in your cards?"

"It looks that way." I turned over the third card: the battling twins. "Interesting."

"What? What does that mean?"

"My heart is in conflict. My dreads and my desires pull me in two."

He was watching me again, as if trying to assess the truth of that. "I suppose you know whether or not any of this has any relevance to you," he remarked.

I laughed shortly. "I suppose I do." I turned over the last card. "Career," I named it. "The white queen. It seems a fair-haired woman, or a very good woman, is going to become my patron."

Now Sam was smiling. "That does not seem too likely, at least," he said.

"No," I replied.

Just then the front door opened, and a phalanx of uniformed guards strode in, their feet making a rhythmic tattoo on the wooden floor. It was late spring, and cold, and they wore fur-edged cloaks over their blue-and-gold livery. Behind them, her silk-white hair haloed by the low afternoon sun, entered a small blond woman with an unmistakably noble face. Everyone in the bar stared at her during the few minutes it took her eyes to adjust to the dimness inside. After my first quick look, I turned my eyes back to the table and pushed all my cards together. I knew even before I heard her hesitant footsteps crossing the floor that she had come to Salla City looking for me.

She wanted to speak to me privately, but I insisted that Sam stay to hear our conference. "Whatever you tell me, I will repeat to him," I said listlessly. "He may as well hear everything as you say it."

So Sam moved to my side of the table, and the stranger seated herself across from us, and her five guards arranged themselves as a screen between us and the rest of the tavern. Groyce brought a fresh bottle and a third glass, and Sam poured for us all.

She just touched her lips to the amber liquid and laid the glass aside. "I know who you are," she said.

I felt Sam physically restrain himself from looking at me. He thought I would ask him to leave now, but why should I? He had not betrayed me in the five years he had known me. No matter what was revealed now, it seemed unlikely he would repeat it to anyone.

"How did you find me?" I wanted to know.

She was not ready to drop the discussion of my identity. "Aesara Vega," she said, as if it was a challenge. "Halana rex."

The king's halana. I closed my eyes briefly. "Former halana rex," I corrected, looking at her again. She was very beautiful. She had pale skin over delicate bones; her eyes were a flawless blue. On every finger of her left hand she wore a ring that looked impossibly expensive. On her right hand she wore only two rings, but neither of them looked cheap, either. "How did you find me?" I asked again.

"Someone who had been in Verallis passed through here several months ago," the woman said. "She recognized you."

It had been eleven years since I had lived at the king's palace in Verallis, and I had changed since then. Whoever had recognized me must have had very sharp eyesight. "I can only suppose," I said quite dryly, "that you have come to me because you need a favor."

"It is a terrible favor to ask," she said. Her voice was low and sweet, and she pitched it most persuasively. The blue eyes looked dense with sadness. I braced myself for what she was going to say, because I knew what it would be, and I was right.

"I want you to kill a man," she said.

I heard Sam inhale sharply. I glanced over at him and smiled. He was trying hard to keep his face under control, but her words had undoubtedly shocked him. "She asks me this," I explained kindly, "because it is believed that I once killed a man in Verallis."

"The king," she said.

Her name, she told us, was Leonora Kessington. Her husband was Sir Errol Kessington, son of Sir Havan of Kessing, a wealthy territory not far from Salla City.

"Six months ago, Sir Havan was in a terrible hunting accident," she said. She could scarcely look at us while she told the story; instead, her eyes were fixed on her interlaced fingers. "Something frightened his horse, and the animal bolted. Sir Havan was thrown from the saddle, but his—his foot caught in the stirrup, and he was dragged along the ground . . ." When she resumed speaking her voice was even softer than before. "When they found him, his leg was broken, and his collar was broken, and his neck—was broken—"

Samuel gave her one of the linen napkins. She pressed it to her eyes and it came away damp. She still did not look at us.

"They did not think he would live," she continued. "But he did. His leg healed and all the cuts and bruises healed—but something else had broken, something in his neck. He cannot feel anything anywhere in his body—or, at least, they do not think he can. He does not react when his body is touched. But he cannot speak and tell us what he feels and what he does not feel—"

"He can't speak?" Samuel asked her. "Can he hear you? Can he think and see?"

"His eyes are open, and sometimes he moves them to follow activity. He can grunt and make noises, but they cannot be understood. We can't ever be sure he understands us, but Bella believes he can."

"Bella?"

"His wife. My husband's mother. She tends him night and day, she dribbles food down his throat and cleans him—" Leonora shuddered delicately. I took that to mean that caring for the invalid was no easy task. "She is devoted to him," she whispered.

"Who is looking after the affairs of Kessing?" Samuel wanted to know. It was a fair question. Kessing was a good-sized territory and its lord was absolute law for several thousand souls.

"Lady Bella and my husband divide much of the work between them," Leonora said. Once she had finished the harrowing tale of Sir Havan's accident, Leonora felt capable of facing us again. She lifted her drowned blue eyes and fixed them on Samuel. I wondered what sort of effect their limpid sweetness would have on him. "But at Kessing, we maintain the fiction that Sir Havan still rules."

"How is that done?" I asked.

She looked at me. "Sir Havan has always held a public audience twice a month at which any vassal or tenant could air a grievance or sue for a favor," she said. "He still holds these open meetings—we carry him out and set him upon a chair, and people recite their petitions. Bella and Errol actually decide the cases, but if they make a ruling with which he disagrees, he grunts and moans and twists in his chair. So they call back the petitioner and revise their original judgment."

"So he is able to communicate," Sam said thoughtfully.

"In a way."

"And he is able to understand what goes on around him."

"He seems to be."

"And yet his condition has not improved for six months?"

"It has not improved, it has not deteriorated. It has not changed at all."

"And what do your halani say? I assume you have consulted one or two."

A smile touched her sad lips. "Dozens. They have fed him no end of potions and chanted hundreds of spells over his head. Nothing has availed. His body remains broken and his spirit remains trapped."

"And so you want me to kill him," I said evenly.

She looked at me quickly, her blue eyes utterly serious. "I have always loved Sir Havan," she said. "He is a good man and he has done many good things. But I cannot bear to see him suffer so much, day after day, dependent on another's hand to feed him and bathe him and tend him. You don't understand—you never knew him—he was so alive, so active, so sure of himself. To see him like this . . . I would not want to live in such a way. I would not condemn anyone to such a life."

"And why should Aesara be the one to murder him?" Sam asked bluntly. "If you have dozens of halani already at your fortress—"

"It is a terrible thing to ask another human being to take a life," she said quietly. "And it is, as you say, murder. If one of the resident halani were to commit such an act, and be discovered, he or she would be put to death as well. I cannot ask them to do it."

"And Aesara? What if someone discovered *she* had poured the poison into the lord's drink?" Sam asked. "You've asked it of *her*."

"No one knows her at Kessing," Leonora replied quickly.

"One person has already recognized her," he pointed out.

"But Aesara could come in disguise. No one would ever know she had been the one to kill him."

I smiled at Sam again. He was such an innocent. All the years of intrigue that I had witnessed at Verallis would stand me in good stead now. "No, and no one would ever be certain if he had been murdered or if he had merely died at last," I told Sam. "That is the other reason the lady would like to hire my services."

Sam looked from me to Leonora and back at me. "I don't understand."

I kept my eyes on Leonora and my voice casual. "It has been eleven years, but surely you remember the scandal that attended King Raever's death?" I asked. "He had been unwell for a few days—everyone knew this, for there are no secrets at Verallis—and I had mixed him a batch of potions to restore him to good health. Shortly after taking one of them, one night, he died. Did I kill him? Was he much sicker than anyone had supposed? Did some prince or courtier, knowing I might be blamed, mix a deadly philter and administer it in place of mine? No one was ever completely certain—which is why, Samuel, my friend, I sit here with you today in Salla City instead of drifting over the scattered lands of Sorretis as smoke and ashes, having been burned at the stake for treason."

There was a short silence. Leonora did not say baldly that she was sure I had killed my king, although clearly she believed it. Sam offered no comment at all.

"I'm interested in knowing," I said, "what the lord's wife and son think about this idea of yours."

The blue eyes were utterly guileless; she met my gaze openly. "It was Bella's idea," she said softly. "She is the one who recognized you here a few months back."

My eyes narrowed. That could very well be the truth. I had seen the traveling coach bowl through Salla City and recognized the heraldry on the door, for all of Raever's vassals were known to me, at least by reputation. I had not gone to the trouble of ducking behind a doorway as the horses slowed and passed. I had not expected to be identified.

"And your husband?" I asked.

"He is not convinced. But he has said to me in private that it would be a blessing for his father if he should die."

"And who rules Kessing when Sir Havan is gone?"

"Errol. And if Errol should die without heirs, his sister."

"And what does she think of this scheme to dispatch her father?"

"She has not been informed."

I picked up my glass of wine, which, like Leonora's, was almost untouched. Even Sam had only taken one or two swallows. I sipped the sweet, heavy liquid meditatively and thought it over. Well, clearly this angelically fair woman would profit if the murder were carried out, but as the case was presented, it was hard to tell if that was her motive. Giving all the participants the benefit of the doubt, it could be that they truly planned a mercy killing for which the corpse itself would thank me. For which all of Kessing would thank me, no doubt. I knew how uneasy subjects and vassals could become when their leader fell ill or grew uncertain. But to coolly and with calculated forethought kill a man . . .

"When is the next public audience?" I asked her.

She tried to smother her hopeful look. "A week from today, halana," she said. "Will you come?"

I nodded slowly. "I think so. I want to see Sir Havan for myself. At that point I will decide whether I will help you or not."

"And if you decide to help me?"

"I will give you a potion to give to your lord."

It was nearly full dark by the time Leonora left. Sam escorted her out; when he returned to my table, he was carrying a fresh bottle of wine. We had drunk very little of the sweet, fruity stuff he had brought for his visitor, but this was a dry red wine Sam usually chose for his serious drinking. He had finished two glasses before either of us said a word.

"Why don't you go ahead and ask me?" I said finally. I had elected to stay with the sweeter vintage, and I was sipping it much more slowly.

He poured himself another glass. "Why did you agree to go to Kessing and look this lord over?"

I was surprised into a laugh. "That's not the question," I said.

"It's the question I'm interested in the answer to."

I raised my own glass and inhaled the heavy, honeyed aroma. I said, "The real question is: Did you kill King Raever, or did you not?"

"That's not something I would ask you," Sam said quietly.

"I have always wanted to know," I said, "if you recognized my name when I arrived here five years ago."

"I recognized it."

"And so you must have known the scandal that followed me across Sorretis?"

"I had heard it."

"And yet you never wondered whether or not you harbored a murderer in your establishment?"

"I did not care," he said deliberately. I had erased pain from his wife's body, and so he did not care what I had done to others. He added, "Then."

I pounced on the word. "Then? And now?"

He raised his eyes and regarded me steadily. It was a familiar look; he often studied me this way. I was never sure what he hoped to learn. "I have always thought that you probably know how to kill a man."

I swallowed some of my wine. "I do."

"And that you have probably, in fact, killed one or two in your life."

I took another swallow. "I have."

"And it has seemed to me that whatever reasons you would have had for such actions would satisfy me. So I didn't worry about it."

That easily. I had won a man's trust merely by keeping silence for five years. I leaned back against the bench and closed my eyes. "When I was first named halana rex," I said, "I was known more for healing than for killing. For I had quite extraordinary abilities. Some halani are born healers—they need only to lay their fingers upon a man to cure his disease or to knit together the severed fibers of his bones. I had such skills, in those days. I radiated power—my hands seemed to glow at night when I watched them in the dark."

I had consumed more of the wine than I had thought, for my head was beginning to ache and behind my closed eyes I felt the bar rock gently around me. "Five summers after I joined Raever's court," I said, "there was an epidemic. A plague. It swept through the villages on the roads leading to Verallis—it rampaged through the royal household—it laid low guards and servants and noble ladies and faithful vassals and visiting dignitaries. No one was safe. No one was spared.

"Except me. So strong were my healing powers that I never succumbed to illness. Naturally, I ran through the castle, wherever the sickness took root, laying my hands upon the afflicted ones and exorcising the plague. I went to the guardhouses and the guesthouses and the nearby inns and villas, to find felled bodies writhing on the beds and on the floors. On each hot cheek I laid my cool hands, and the disease was routed. I rode like a madwoman through the night to the nearest villages, and stretched my arms out so that twenty people at a time could crowd around me and scratch at my flesh and be healed just by touching me. So exhausted was I, after three days of riding, that I collapsed in the square of one of these villages, unconscious and unmoving. And still they brought the ill and the helpless to my side, and still they reached out to touch me, and still they were cured."

I was silent for a long moment. I had not noticed Sam finishing his last glass of wine, but now I heard him pour another one. "Yet it is not healing for which I am remembered," I said finally. "But for killing."

"You never answered my question," he said.

I opened my eyes and looked at him. The wine or the memories or the dim lighting of the bar made him look softer and younger than usual. "What question was that?"

"Why did you agree to go to Kessing and see the lord? You have not raised a hand to help a soul since the night you gave peace to my Mari."

I closed my eyes again. "Because Leonora was wrong," I said. "I did know Sir Havan of Kessing. Eleven years ago, when I lived at Verallis."

I had expected the public audience at Kessing to be gruesome, and it was. Like most of the major fortress holdings of Sorretis, Kessing was built of a heavy gray stone that even on sunny days seemed to enclose a gloomy chill. Inside was a huge chamber where all the supplicants gathered twice a month to make their requests of their lord. Such public audiences were often loud and boisterous affairs; but at Kessing, where the petitioners spoke to a pitiful shell of a man, the mood was sober and deeply depressing.

Sam had casually offered to accompany me on the journey, and I had casually accepted, but inwardly I had been extremely grateful for his escort. I was doubly grateful for his presence now, a solid bulk in this sea of strangers. We stood at the back of the enormous room, gazing over perhaps two hundred bodies, staring toward the dais at the far end where Sir Havan of Kessing had been installed.

Everything Leonora had said of him was true. His head lolled back on his unsupportive neck; his arms and legs hung uselessly down. He had been tied to a large, cushioned chair so that he seemed, at least, to be sitting up and facing us. But his slack mouth and unfocused eyes gave little evidence that his mind was engaged.

Beside him, Lady Bella knelt on an embroidered stool. Leonora stood behind him, gazing down at the inexpressive face. Sir Errol stood at the head of the stage, a herald beside him to call out names, and he gravely listened to each petition. It was not a cheery or inspiring scene.

"What do you think of the lord's wife?" I whispered in Sam's ear, as we watched the slow procession.

"She seems to genuinely love the man," he whispered back. "It's a hard thing to counterfeit under such conditions."

I nodded. "And his son?"

"He seems capable enough, but not a happy man."

"Does he want his father dead?"

"Wouldn't you," Sam said slowly, "if your father lived like this?"

"And the son's wife?"

Only once had Leonora lifted her head and surveyed the crowd. Within minutes, she had spotted us. I could see the color of her eyes even across the wide stone floor. She had not smiled or nodded, but merely dropped her gaze again to her father-in-law's face.

"She's ambitious, I think," Sam said slowly. "But she does not look cruel."

"Tell me," I said. "What would you choose, if you were Sir Havan of Kessing? Would you want to continue to live, imprisoned in such a wreck of a body? Or would you want some kind soul to mete out the poison that would let you die, quietly and in peace?"

"I would drink the poison, and gladly," Sam said.

"So would I."

For a few moments longer, I watched Sir Havana across the room. As I had told Sam, I had known Havan and Lady Bella, but not well, and that had been eleven years ago. He had been a laughing, virile, confrontational man who had had as many friends as enemies at Verallis. Raever had trusted him, though they had disagreed often enough, and spectacularly enough, to be considered wary allies. I had not dealt much with court politics, but of course I had met most of the personalities of the day, and Havan had been one of the brightest.

He had not been at Verallis when Raever died. He had not been one of those who accused me or defended me. I wondered what opinion he had, in fact, held of me—not that the knowledge would influence me one way or the other now.

We had been there maybe an hour when a strange commotion erupted on the dais. Sir Errol had just pronounced some sentence on a cowed-looking yokel, when the mangled body of Sir Havan made a violent reaction. Even from this distance, we could hear the formless grunts and whines. We could see the head shake and the shoulders twitch against the sides of the chair. Leonora's hands flew to her cheeks. Bella's fingers wrapped themselves around her husband's wrist. Errol crossed to his father's side and bent over the shivering body as if to try and understand the indecipherable sounds. He turned back to the man he had just dismissed.

"Wait!" he called out. "My father has reversed the judgment."

On the words, Sir Havan grew calm again. The dejected man straightened and made a field hand's salute toward the stage. "My lord," he said, and backed into the crowd. All around us the audience murmured in a muffled unease.

"I can't stand this," I said. I found that my fingers had clutched Samuel's arm in a grip that must have been painful; I dropped my hand.

"Do you want to leave?" he asked.

I shook my head. "I owe Havan the courtesy of staying long enough to be certain."

And so we stayed, through each grim petition, each inaudible argument. Havan did not again attempt to communicate. It was with indescribable relief that I saw the last petitioner make his case, hear his judgment, bow, and rejoin the assembly. Now what? Everyone appeared to be waiting for some cue, some gesture of release. I saw activity on the dais and realized that four footmen had lifted the lord's chair and now were carrying it carefully off the stage, down through the ranks of petitioners, and toward the exit. No one would leave the room before the lord. As the crowd divided, Sam and I found ourselves along the aisle that opened between the dais and the door. Wordlessly, we watched as Havan was carried toward us, his arms flopping against the sides of the chair, his gaze running wildly around the circle of watching faces.

He saw me and his eyes locked on mine.

It was as if he tried to lunge from the chair. His body spasmed and one of his feet kicked out, landing with considerable force against a footman's chin. The servant stumbled, lost his grip, and came to his knees, desperately trying to keep his hold. Bella screamed from the stage. The crowd loosed a collective gasp of dismay and stepped backward as if to avoid contamination.

The other footmen hastily settled the chair on the floor as Sam strode over to offer assistance. I trailed reluctantly behind. "Shall I call for help?" Sam asked. "Do you want me to carry one leg?"

"No, no, I just lost my balance," said the shaken servant.

I paid little attention to the conference between Sam and the footmen; I ignored the sound of Bella's footsteps hurrying across the hall. Havan was still staring at me, still trembling in his seat. His mouth worked as if he would speak the most urgent message. He recognized me, that was clear. He knew what I was capable of. Did he want to shriek at me to go away, to leave him alone, to take my sorcerous potions elsewhere?

Did he want to beg me to release him?

I knelt before him and took one nerveless hand in mine, feeling the fingers lax and chilly. As soon as I touched him, he grew still; he stopped his frantic jerking. Even his eyes seemed more serene, though they never wavered from my face. I could read that look, I thought. *Do what you can for me.* I squeezed his fingers, then dropped his hand as Bella came skidding to a halt beside him. I did not want her to see me again, to guess why I had come. I stepped back into the silent crowd and turned my face away until Havan had finally been carried out the door.

We had agreed to meet Leonora at a small inn just outside the fortress gates. She came to us that evening with another cadre of guards in the blue-and-gold livery of Kessing.

"Well?" she asked the instant she was shown into our room. "Do you believe now that I told you the truth?"

"I believe you," I said wearily. I had mixed up a potion as soon as we entered the inn. I had sworn to never again interfere in the lives of others, but it is easier to break a promise to yourself than to break a promise to someone else. "No one should have to live like that."

I handed her the vial, wrapped in blue silk, the color of her eyes. She took it from me with those eyes at their widest. "This is it? Already? This is the potion?" she asked, almost stammering. "What must be done?"

"He must drink all of it," I said. "There is not much and it has no flavor. It can be mixed in wine or water. He will not know what he is taking."

She unwrapped the vial and stared at the clear liquid through the glass. "And it will not hurt him?" she whispered. "He will feel no pain?"

"None, I swear to you," I said.

Quickly she rewrapped the philter and tucked it inside her reticule. I wondered exactly how she planned to administer this to him, but decided not to ask. She seemed quite resourceful. "What do I owe you?" she wanted to know.

I shook my head. "I want nothing from you."

"But—surely—I have brought gold with me, and jewels—"

"This is not a service for which I wish to be paid," I said quietly.

She hesitated a moment, then nodded. "Very well," she said. "On behalf of Sir Havan and his family, I thank you."

"I don't want thanks, either," I said.

She could see that I would not take her hand, but she required something more of a leavetaking, so she offered her hand to Sam. He took it gravely, shook it, and released her. "Good-bye, my lady," he said, and ushered her toward the door.

I was staring out the single small window, but I knew he had turned back to watch me once he locked Leonora out. "Do you want to leave for Salla City first thing in the morning?" he asked.

It was not quite dusk, and the trek would take us several hours. "No," I said, "I want to leave tonight. Now."

We did not push the horses, and in fact the cool, starlit journey was almost pleasant. In the night air, sounds seemed to be invested with a strange significance; each hoofbeat, each jingle of the bridle sounded distinct and mysterious in the plush silence. We encountered no other travelers on the way.

We had been riding for nearly two hours when I began, without prompting, to tell my story. "Raever was dying," I said. "I was the only one who knew it. He had contracted a disease of the blood for which I did not have the remedy. I tried—Leith and Egeva, how I tried—to produce an antidote that would save him, but there are some diseases, I have learned, for which there are no cures. He was not in great pain—that much, as you know, I could do for him—but his body was growing frail and his memory had become unreliable. As I said, no one but me knew just how sick he was, and me he had sworn to secrecy.

"Raever did not fear many things, but he had an absolute abhorrence of weakness, of dependency. He hated to see someone beg—he did not even care much for humility. The idea of a gradual, wasting illness, which would leave him utterly at the mercy of others, was terrible to him. And so he asked me for a philter that would release him early into death."

I fell silent a moment. Samuel made no comment. Had I not seen his fingers shift upon the reins, I would have thought he was asleep. "At first, I refused, for he was my king and I did not want him to die. Also, I had not yet despaired of finding a cure. But no more than he could, could I bear to see him fall into faintness and delirium, and we agreed that if he were to die by his own hand, it should be while he was still able to rationally choose such a death.

"It was Raever who came up with the plan. He had me mix up a month's supply of potions, all in separate, identical bottles. Twenty-nine of them would be filled with a few harmless ounces of water—only one would carry the death dosage inside. He would drink one every night before he went to bed, destroying the bottle before he slept so that no one would find it and later suspect that I had given him poison. He chose this method," I added, "because he said that no man, even one who wanted to die, should know with certainty the hour of his death."

"And did you in fact present him with the thirty bottles?" Samuel asked at last.

"I did."

"And upon which night did he die?"

I whispered, "The twenty-third."

"It seems to me," Sam said, his voice slow and comforting in the dark, "that a king as clever as Raever was said to be would know that suspicion would fall on you, no matter how careful he was with these bottles."

"Oh, he knew it. I knew it. He wanted me to leave Verallis a few days before he began taking his nightly potions, so I would not be there for any inquisition. But I could not bear to leave him while he was still alive, while there still might be something I could do for him, however small. I was prepared for the maelstrom that followed. At that, I did not greatly care if they condemned me to death or allowed me to live. Not much really mattered to me once Raever was dead."

"You loved him," Sam said.

"He had a wife and three daughters, and he was twenty years older than I was."

"Yet you loved him," Sam repeated stubbornly.

"I *believed* in him," I said. "He was an autocratic and domineering man, but he had such vision and strength of purpose. There was nothing he could have asked me to do that I would not have done, for it seemed to me that this man, more clearly than anyone I had ever met, understood right and wrong in the largest sense. I am not the only one from whom he commanded great devotion. We were a court of disciples, and we fell apart when our leader died."

"And yet I hear good things about his daughter, who is now the queen."

"Yes," I said wearily. "She is an intelligent woman, and she rules well. But she is not Raever. Something went out of the world when Raever died."

"Something went out of you," he said.

I looked over at him, but I could not see much in the dark. "What do you mean?"

"You're the healer," he said. "Mend your own broken heart."

"*Your* heart has been broken," I said swiftly. "Do you think it is an easy thing to fix?"

"I think," he replied carefully, "that someone with the right skills could heal me."

I faced forward again. The road ahead looked endless. "There are some things for which there are no cures," I said.

It might have been my imagination, but I thought I heard him sigh. We rode on into the unchanging darkness.

Naturally, I slept late the next day. It had only been a few hours before dawn when Sam and I arrived in Salla City. He had accompanied me to the cottage I had rented on the edge of town, watched me dismount, and taken the reins of my horse. It was, after all, his horse. He did not say good-bye as he rode away, and I did not look back at him as I let myself into my unlit house.

Now it was late afternoon, and I was, surprisingly, hungry. I had not eaten for nearly twenty-four hours, but still, hunger was a sensation I rarely experienced. I rose and moved aimlessly about my cottage, but there was very little in the cupboards that could be turned into a meal. I felt a curious reluctance to go to Sam's for dinner, certain as I was that he would join me for the meal. I knew better than to rely on the gentleness and seeming strength of any man. I had gone so long without yielding my burdens to anyone. What made me long now to take my comfort from somebody else's heart?

I shook my head and concentrated on putting together a makeshift meal from some moldy biscuits and a vinegary jug of wine. Out of habit, I pulled out my zafo cards and shuffled them. Mostly to distract myself, I laid out a standard grid and turned the cards over in my own unconventional order.

The primary significator: the hooded figure. The final outcome: the black queen. I smiled faintly. These same two cards had appeared in the last reading I had done, only then their positions had been reversed. Now the shadowy, unformed image was in my past, and in my future was the assured, powerful, dark-haired woman. What had I left behind, then, and what was I to become?

The four cards in the second row, the pictures of my past, showed more hazy and undefined images. There, the secretive moon that refused to answer questions; there, the locked box, showing that treasures had been denied. Again, the black king reversed. Beside him, the roan stallion, who bespoke restlessness, travel, and change.

In the third row, all was altered. A stack of twelve coins indicated the richness of my fortune, and a blazing sun shone upon my home. The white king appeared to answer the questions of my heart, and in the position that indicated career, the winged horse spread its alabaster wings. This last card was the elemental symbol for air and had been taken by the halani to mean magical ability. A rebirth of my power; a professional renaissance.

I chewed on another stale biscuit and thought for a moment. Clearly, it was going to be impossible to keep the events of Kessing a secret. I had known that before I undertook the journey. Bella had recognized me on the street and had spoken my name at least once. She would be even more likely to mention it again after all this. If I stayed in Salla City, I would be found. If I was found, there were others who would bring requests to me of a dangerous and highly emotional nature. I had sworn never to interfere again in the lives of others, but Raever had made me take another vow.

"Promise me you will not kill yourself after I am dead," he had said. I had been amazed. How had he known about the second vial I had mixed up, giving one to him and keeping one for myself? "Promise me this disease will only take one life."

And because I had been unable to refuse him anything, I had promised, but I had only in the most rudimentary way kept my vow. You could not say I had really lived in the past eleven years.

Except for the last couple of days, when once again I had held life and death in my hands, and shuddered at the responsibility.

I picked up the white king and studied it a moment. A fair-haired man, or a good man, or an old man; the card meant all of these things. I had not looked for such a card in such a position at such a time in my life.

Outside, I heard the gate squeal on the unoiled hinges, and running footsteps crossed the gravel walk. I did not have much time to debate whether or not I would answer the door before it was flung open and Sam strode into the room. He had never before entered my house, for he had never been invited in, and I stared at him in astonishment.

He was laughing. Before I could move toward him or away, he was upon me. He grabbed me around the waist and lifted me in the air. I clutched at his shoulders to keep my balance, staring down at him in excitement and alarm.

"Samuel Berris!" I cried out. "What are you doing?"

He actually tossed me in the air once before setting me on my feet. Then he hugged me and finally let me go.

"The news from Kessing arrived this morning," he said.

I made a big show of smoothing my hair down after the unexpected, rough treatment. "It did?" I said coldly.

"It was a miracle, they say. None of the halani can explain it. Sir

Havan of Kessing awoke this morning a whole man, with all his limbs answering the call of his will and his mind completely sharp. He is weak, of course, and they think it will be some time before he walks again under his own power, but he is well; he is healed. There has been a general rejoicing throughout Kessing."

"I'm sure there has been," I said. "Who brought the news to Salla City?"

"Some peddler. Not the Lady Leonora."

"I wonder how she reacted to the news this morning," I said.

Sam grinned. "She is a most dutiful and loving daughter-in-law," he said. "I'm sure she fell to her knees in gratitude."

"I doubt she will ever thank me personally," I said.

Sam was watching me, some of his elation tempered now with speculation. "Lady Bella will, though," he said. "Or the lord himself. You cannot expect this secret to be kept."

"No," I said. "I can't."

"And will you be here when they come?" he asked. "And when the others come, with terrible stories of dying lords and sick children and beloved mothers wracked with pain? Will you be here when travelers come to Salla City, looking for you?"

I glanced around the rented cottage. Perhaps I could have done more with it, changed the curtains or stocked the larder. "I don't care much for this place," I said. "That's why I spent so much time in your tavern."

"I have a house that is too big for one," he said. "And it's very close to the tavern."

I looked at him. "I thought your heart was broken," I said.

"I know a healer," he replied.

"I will be traveling a lot," I said. "None of these sick mothers and crying babies will be able to journey to Salla City."

"I like to travel," he said. "Groyce can mind the bar."

"Then I suppose I will stay in Salla City," I said.

"Good," he said, "I'll help you pack."

Not that there was much to transfer to the small, welcoming house behind the tavern. Groyce and Sam carried the heavier items I elected to keep. Lina helped me organize my clothes. She smiled at me shyly, and for the first time in the five years that I had known her, I attempted to make conversation.

"I'm glad you're staying," she told me when I asked her how she was. "I'm going to have a baby."

It was not quite dark yet, and we had just moved the last of my things into Sam's house when one of the girls from the tavern ran over with more news. A delegation had been spotted on the road, led by a virtual army of blue-and-gold-clad guards.

"So soon?" I murmured, wiping dust from my face.

"They're late," Sam said. "They should have been here by noon."

"Who are they?" Groyce asked. "Friends of the noblewoman who was here?"

"Friends of Aesara's," Sam said. He took my hand, and we went outside together to greet the travelers.

Night of the Dolls

BY SEAN WILLIAMS AND SHANE DIX

Adelaide author and occasional DJ, Sean Williams has published nineteen novels and more than sixty short stories. Multiple winner of Australia's speculative fiction awards, recipient of the "SA Great" Literature Award, and *New York Times* bestseller, he has also written a sci-fi musical and the odd piece of bad haiku. You can find out more about Williams and his writing at his excellent Web site: www.seanwilliams.com. In collaboration with author Shane Dix, he has produced the Evergence and Orphans trilogies and cowritten three books in the *Star Wars: New Jedi Order* series.

"Night of the Dolls" is set in their Geodesica world. Forthcoming in 2006, *Geodesica: Descent* is the concluding volume of a diptych begun with *Geodesica: Ascent* in 2005. As much about grief as the alien artifact after which it's named, the series explores the ramifications of a single, localized catastrophe on the million-year future history of humanity, as witnessed by Isaac Forge Deangelis during his long, posthuman life. "While it's doubtful he would seem very human to someone from the twenty-first century," said Williams, "he would recognize us perfectly well and, I honestly believe, approve without reservation of the outpouring of generosity following the December 26 Indian Ocean earthquake."

Williams and Dix both live in Adelaide, South Australia.

August 15, 2381, on a sumptuous Southern Hemisphere spring evening in a region that had once been the birthplace of humanity, Isaac Forge Deangelis—barely seven years alive and still finding his feet in the mind-rich environment of Sol System—accepted the invitation to attend the Annual Graduate's Ball. He did so on the advice of the Archon, whose encouragement that it would be an educational experience had been enough to convince him. Deangelis knew before stepping through the front door that it would be a challenge, and used the decadently quaint cover of "fashionably late" to dawdle along the way. It fit the theme of the evening, anyway.

The magnificent glass ballroom, constructed in the middle of nowhere on the boundary of old Richtersveld National Park, stood out against a backdrop of jagged mountains that bore the scars of their volcanic origins. The sun had already set, but the sky still glowed a deep, diamond-sparkled purple, fading to black in the east. A stand of immature quiver trees made him think of alien soldiers from a B-grade, twentieth-century movie as he walked up the long, sweeping drive, feeling like a complete fool in his black tuxedo with a silk tie choking his Adam's apple. The rest of him, scattered across the system, watched with a mixture of fascination and amusement at the anachronistic getup. No matter how hard he tried to distract himself, his attention kept returning to Earth.

His feet crunched on gravel with a raw, startling sound. A butler met him at the top of the marble stairs and offered to take his coat. The sound of voices grew louder as he trod thick red carpet through an arched doorway and entered the ballroom.

It was an odd experience, being in the company of so many people at once. Like the other guests, he freely roamed the Earth in both corporeal and virtual forms, interacting and communicating with his peers and himself via all manner of media, not needing to be face-to-face for any conceivable reason. The presence of his body on that particular evening, he had assumed, was a mere formality, no more or less anachronistic than the suit he had been asked to wear. Both could have been assembled at will in a moment, as could have a belly dancer's outfit and a body to match. That he hadn't yet decided what his physique would be when he finished his training wasn't an issue he spent much time considering; while he waited, he wore a physical form of indeterminate age, with blond hair and broad shoulders generated by the genes the Archon had bestowed upon him. It fitted.

The ballroom was expansive and gleaming and full of music. That was his first impression. His second was of the crowd, all beautiful and familiar and garbed in clothes no less outlandish than his own. Out of a thousand, two dozen pairs of eyes looked up when he crossed the threshold—recognizing him, he assumed, just as he recognized them in turn. He went to wave.

Their true reason for looking at him became apparent when his body lost all connection to the rest of *him*, scattered across the system, and collapsed down to a mere individual. He stumbled, as disoriented as if he had lost his sense of sight or balance. His perception of the world, and of himself, suddenly crashed to *just him* in *just one room.* Mentally reeling, he struggled to work out what could possibly have gone wrong. Since his awakening in many bodies scattered all across Sol System and experiencing the wondrous union that had risen out of his disparate thoughts, he had never been alone. The experience was jarringly dysfunctional, even frightening.

"Fear not, old boy," said a familiar voice. A hand clapped down on his shoulder. Lazarus Hails was all grin and gloat as he came round to confront his fellow student. He too hadn't fixed his final form, but his nose bore a patriarchal prominence that would remain later. "All part of the experience. You'll find our bodies don't quite work the same way anymore, just like our minds."

Deangelis watched Hails with some puzzlement. His balance centers seemed dangerously out of whack, and his speech patterns were different. He had clearly suffered the same mental impairment Deangelis had on entering the ballroom. Were they under attack? Could their brain damage possibly be *permanent?*

A laugh as sharp as a cut diamond drew Hails's attention away from Deangelis. Lan Cochrane, dressed in a lime green flapper's outfit, was puffing on a cigar—the genuine, burning article—and blowing rings of smoke at Frederica Cazneaux. Dark-skinned and wonderful in a black suit of her own, Cazneaux batted the smoke away and turned down a chance to try a drag for herself, despite her friend's insistence. Cazneaux held a cocktail glass containing an electric blue liquid balanced between two fingers; she raised a perfectly shaped eyebrow at Hails as he took Cochrane's cigar and blew a messy cloud between them. Deangelis looked around in disoriented wonder. Across the shimmering expanse of the ballroom, the vast majority of the Exarchate's future leaders were engaged in similar physical debaucheries:

dancing, drinking, snacking, smoking, and singing as though 350 years had rolled back and plunged them all into some upper class Light Ages.

"I think it's an experiment," said Jane Elderton, appearing at Deangelis's side with a thin, white-papered cigarette in a long filter pinned between gloved thumb and forefinger. She smelled of perfume and smoke. "A test, perhaps."

"Not a graduation party?"

"We're beyond that," she said, pale lips pursing in faint amusement. Her skin was porcelain-pale and her gaze a startling blue. Blond hair—longer than he'd ever seen on her before—curled exquisitely tight around her skull and ears. The color of her silk dress matched her eyes. Deangelis took in her silver necklace, her cleavage, the delicate bracelet on her left wrist, and her thin-strapped shoes with one sweep.

"We don't need rites of passage," she went on, taking a sip of smoke and inhaling it as though she had done so every day of her life. Wisps emerged from her mouth and nostrils as she spoke. "Growing up is something anyone can do. Even animals, and we don't throw them parties."

"Bonding, then, before we all go our separate ways?"

"Wrong again, Ike. Why join something destined to be shattered? We're designed to be loners. It goes with the territory."

He looked around. Something thrilled in the air. He could guess what from the way his flesh responded to it. His heart rate was rapid, along with his respiration. His pupils dilated and his skin tingled. He felt his body in a new way, or a very old way—primal and not entirely unpleasant.

"You need a drink," Jane said. "Is there something you've always wanted to try? Gin and tonic? Sea breeze? Gimlet?"

"Gimlet. How do I—?"

A waiter—artfully humaniform like the butler outside but obviously no more than that—appeared beside him holding a silver tray. His drink rested on it, gleaming with condensation. Deangelis took the glass and sipped carefully. Volatile alcohol made his tongue and throat sing. He laughed at the play of chemicals on and in his suddenly unpredictable body. It was like reading an old novel in its original language, or listening to the first take of a famous jazz recording: full of unexpected nuances and subtleties that he had never anticipated. In the raw flesh, with nothing to distance himself from the play of molecules in his bloodstream, he was suddenly, vividly, nothing but a man. A gendered man in a room full of people, as men had been for tens of thousands of years before him.

He drank and danced and laughed with the rest of them, awash with hormones and pheromones and as utterly delighted as a child with a new toy.

Dinner came, an extended six-course feast with dishes from all over the old world. Some of the partygoers forwent the meal, preferring to keep dancing, but Deangelis took the opportunity to experience another lost art. He had been born with a complete range of culinary skills and knowledge, none of which he had ever expected to use; until now, it had been just one miniscule part of the enormous pool of human knowledge he had inherited. Dining came as naturally as play, and he wallowed in the succulence of meat, the richness of gravy, the texture of vegetables, the indulgence of pavlova. Crayfish, pigeon, artichoke, plum; caviar, sturgeon, puy lentils, bread.

The Archon had been absolutely right; the evening was an education he hadn't known he needed. He raised his glass to their absent creator, wondering what it made of the evening's activities from its lofty perspective.

An intoxicating rainbow of after-dinner drinks followed. Port. Sherry. Coffee. Brandy. His grip on proceedings began to slip. He knew he wasn't thinking properly, but that didn't stop him from attributing far too much weight to the thoughts he did have. There was no baseline profundity against which he could measure his drunken revelations. They seemed groundbreaking. Every emotion felt new and powerful. And why couldn't they be? He was content for the moment to be tugged along by alcohol's smooth, seductive currents.

The party spilled out into the night, onto a green glassy lawn he would have sworn hadn't been there before. The interference that separated them from the rest of their minds followed them, maintaining the illusion that they and they alone were the full extent of their beings. Among prickly green hedges and mazes they ran like fools, shouting and stumbling and willfully ignorant.

He gravitated naturally to those whose systems his would neighbor and basked in the broader ambience of merriment. Lazarus Hails's jokes and wickedly timed outrages had kept them all amused through dinner. In another age, he might have been a Byron or a Nicholson, genetically tailored for carousing. Deangelis was content to go with the flow, sipping Merlot or Shiraz on the fringes of the group, only interacting when Giorsal McGrath or Jane Elderton or one of the others drew him in.

He caught Frederica Cazneaux and Lan Cochrane whispering about him behind their hands. They actually blushed. "You're beautiful, darling," Cochrane said when he pressed her for an explanation. "Don't you know it? You really scored when the genetic dice tumbled. I wonder where your stock comes from."

Lan was a Vietnamese name meaning "orchid." She looked more Malaysian, Deangelis thought, full and high-cheeked, with hair subtly framing her face. Her brown eyes were wide and laughing. He felt the butt of a joke, and blushed in turn.

He became aware of other people looking at him. Some did more than look. In the torch-lit wonderland of the gardens, with shapes rushing by and laughter everywhere, hands touched him; lips pressed against his ear, whispering jokes or flirtations. Warm fingers laced with his and soft hair brushed his cheek. Dizzying stimuli prompted yet more novel sensations.

"Come with me," Frederica Cazneaux breathed in his ear, tugging him down a dead-end in a hedge maze. His free hand held a bottle of champagne he didn't remember picking up.

She pulled him to her in the darkness and kissed him. The smell and taste of her occupied his mind more completely than any training exercise. Her lips were full and warm. The touch of her moist tongue against his made his skin shimmer from head to toe. The feel of her body was unimaginable.

Where that kiss might have gone, he would never know. With a rustle and crack of vegetation, Lazarus Hails's head burst through the hedge.

"Enough of that, you two," he said. "Dalman's climbed onto the roof and says he's found a stash of dope!"

They pulled apart. Intrigued by the possibility of yet more sensory destabilization, Deangelis said that he would come. Satisfied, Hails's head retreated through the gap in the hedge. He followed Hails out of the maze and across the lawn, where a conga line had formed. Cazneaux trailed him at first, then fell behind to join the dance.

The sound of raised voices didn't alarm him, nor did the sight of someone vomiting into a flower bed. He was fully aware of the effects of alcohol poisoning, and had no doubt that he, too, would experience them at some point that night, especially in combination with other drugs. That concern seemed distant and unimportant. His entire being was focused like a poorly tuned laser on the now, with no thought for what had come before and what might follow. His body seemed to move of its own accord. He was little more than a passenger.

Later, he clearly remembered his first hit of marijuana and the rocketing sensation it gave him inside his head. The thick smoke burned his throat and made him cough, but he went back for more as the joint passed round his circle of friends. The notion of stoned Exarchs seemed the height of humor and set off a wave of giggling. The last sequential memory he possessed of that night was of snorting smoke though his nostrils and choking so hard he almost threw up. Flashes remained, like fragments of a smashed vase. He couldn't piece them together, but he could make out the rough shapes of those that were missing. More kissing followed an extended discussion with Giorsal McGrath over the long-term goals of humanity. What conclusion they came to, he couldn't remember, but it seemed deeply important. They had called out to the Archon, wanting to share their wisdom, but they had not received a reply.

A blur of faces. People everywhere. Women were soft to the touch, men hard and angular, their stubble rough against his lips. He stuck with women in the end, but wondered if he had made the right decision when a fight broke out between Lan Cochrane and Frederica Cazneaux over who had kissed him first, and what rights that gave them over him. Hails joined in, seeming upset that Cazneaux wasn't paying him enough attention. Deangelis felt removed from it all, wanting nothing but to touch and be touched. Rows flared over sexual partners, territory, imagined slights, nothing at all. He wandered off, feeling suddenly tired.

"Strike up the band," said Jane Elderton, who had appeared at his side again, her hair unpinned and her cheeks red. "We're apes dancing to tunes we didn't even know we knew."

"Is this all it takes?" he asked. "Are we so close to chaos, to savagery?"

"They're not the same thing, Ike—but yes, I think we are. You can fire clay and turn it into brick; you can lay a brick in a wall and make it part of a building; that building can be one of thousands in a city; but at the end of the day it's all still clay. And so are we, underneath. If we don't understand the clay, we don't understand the city."

"*That's* what this is all about, then?"

"I think so. Don't you?"

He shrugged. "I'm enjoying *not* thinking, for once."

Her smile warmed him. "I'm glad. Let's go."

The darkness awaited them. He wanted to run, to let muscles swing and push and carry him blindly across the ancient land, naked under the stars they claimed. The two of them might have run together a mile or ten, or not run at all; he didn't remember; but the night ended with his breath coming fast and hot from his lungs, and her moving against him with a feverish urgency of her own. All semblance of rational thought vanished in an explosion of nerve impulses. His spinal chord, electrified from base to brain, seemed to dissolve, and the night dissolved with it. Skin against skin, they reveled.

Everything was gone when he awoke the next morning: the ballroom, the gardens, his fellow Exarchs, the maze. If being human meant enduring a hangover, he resolved to do so for as little time as he could. Still, it took him almost an hour to flush out the last of the toxins—an eternity during which he railed at the quiver trees and the hills in lieu of the Archon and yearned for reconnection with the rest of himself.

Why hadn't the Archon warned them? If they'd known in advance, they could've been prepared. They would've behaved better. Unless behaving badly was the whole point Humans had once done so as a matter of course. If he'd gotten together with his peers for a lovely chat and maybe a nice game of bridge, what would he—this part of him, excised from the rest and brutally exposed to ancient impulses—have learned about humanity then?

It hadn't all been bad, he supposed. The night had actually started off perfectly well, even if it had degenerated with a terrible, inexorable momentum. He viewed the world anew as a result—unwilling to trust himself, wary of what lay just beneath the skin of civilization. He resolved to change his body—*all* his bodies, wherever they were—to appeal less to the suspect levels of his mind and those around him. It had all been so pointless: the squabbling, the fighting, the petty rivalries, the poisoning. He wanted no part of it.

"If we need to understand ordinary humanity in order to rule it," he yelled at the Archon as the rest of him rolled back into place and the solar system unfolded before him, "don't we need to experience it from above as well as below? Shouldn't we get a glimpse of the world through *your* eyes, so we can see a bigger picture still?"

Fifteen years later, when the complete Isaac Forge Deangelis went forth to govern his remote pocket of the Exarchate, he was still waiting for an invitation.

The Potter's Daughter

BY MARTHA WELLS

Martha Wells's first novel, *The Element of Fire* (Tor, 1993), introduced readers to the fantasy world of Ile-Rien. Wells returned to this world in 1998 for her Nebula-nominated *The Death of the Necromancer*, and again in 2003 when she launched the Fall of Ile-Rien trilogy (*The Wizard Hunters, The Ships of Air*, and *The Gate of Gods*). She has had short stories published in the magazine *Realms of Fantasy* and has an essay on the TV show *Farscape* in the nonfiction anthology *Farscape Forever* (BenBella Books, 2005).

The Ile-Rien of *The Element of Fire* is based on a seventeenth-century time period where magic exists and the world of Fairy is a very real threat to the human inhabitants. In the timeline of the series, "The Potter's Daughter" is a prequel to *The Element of Fire*, where Kade was one of the main characters. "One of the themes in *The Element of Fire* is Kade coming to terms with the fact that she's more human than fairy," Wells says. "'The Potter's Daughter' is about the thing that really made her start to confront those feelings."

Martha Wells lives in Texas. Find out more about her on her Web site: www.marthawells.com.

The potter's daughter sat in the late afternoon sun outside the stone cottage, making clay figures and setting them out to dry on the flat slate doorstep. A gentle summer breeze stirred the oak and ash leaves and the dirty gray kerchief around her dirty blond hair.

Someone was coming up the path.

She could hear that he was without horse, cart, or company, and as he came toward her through the trees she saw that he was tall, with dark curly hair and a beard, with a pack and a leather case slung over one shoulder. He was unarmed and dressed in a blue woolen doublet, faded and threadbare, brown breeches, and brown-top boots. The broad-brimmed hat he wore had seen better days, but the feathers in it were gaily colored. Brief disappointment colored her expression; she could tell already he wasn't her quarry.

Boots crunched on the pebbles in the yard, then his shadow fell over her and he said, "Good day. Is this the way to Riversee?"

She continued shaping the wet clay, not looking up at him. "Just follow this road to the ford."

"Thank you, my lady Kade."

Now she did look up at him, in astonishment. Part of the astonishment was at herself, that she could still be so taken by surprise. She dropped the clay and stood, drawing a spell from the air.

Watching her with delight, he said, "Some call you Kade Carrion, because that is the sort of name given to witches. But the truth of the matter is that you are the daughter of the dead King Fulstan and Moire, a woman said to be the Dame of Air and Darkness of the fayre." He was smiling at her. His eyes were blue and guileless, and he had a plain open face.

Kade stopped, hands lifted, spell poised to cast. Names could be power, depending on how much one knew. But he was making no move toward her. Intrigued, she folded her arms and asked, "Who soon to be in hell are you?"

"I know all the tales of your battle with the court, the tricks you play on them," he told her, his expression turning serious. "But the story I tell of you is the one about the young gentlewoman of Byre, who died of heartbreak in the Carmelite Convent's spring garden when the prince of a rival city took her maidenhead and mocked her for it afterwards."

Kade lifted an ironic brow. "I remember the occasion. I didn't realize how entertaining it was. Finding an untidy dead woman in my favorite garden was not the high point of my day." It was incredible that he had recognized her; no one in their right mind would expect a half-fay half-human witch to be barefoot and wearing a peasant's muddy dress. As a rule the fay were either grotesquely ugly or heartbreakingly beautiful. Kade was neither. Her eyes were merely gray, her skin tended to brown or redden rather than maintain an opalescent paleness, and her features were unfashionably sharp. She had never looked like anyone expected her to look, and this was why she had never expected anyone to recognize her when she didn't want to be recognized.

Oblivious, he continued. "You took on the appearance of the poor lady and waited there, and when the prince returned—"

"He found me instead, and we all know what happened to him then, don't we?"

"Yes," he agreed readily. "You found that the little idiot had consented, and that she had been as guilty of bad judgment and weak nature as he was guilty of being a rake. So instead of killing him you cursed him with a rather interesting facial deformity to teach him better manners."

Kade frowned, startled in spite of herself. She had never heard anyone tell the incident in that light. It was astonishingly close to her own point of view. "And what does that tell you?"

"That you have a sense of justice," he assured her, still serious. "I've told many stories of you, and it's one of the things about you that always impressed me."

Kade considered him carefully. He evidently knew his danger and didn't shrink from it, though he hadn't exactly dared her to be rid of him. It had been a long time since anyone had spoken to her this way, with a simple fearless acceptance. Kade found herself saying, "She didn't perish dramatically of heartbreak, you know. She killed herself."

He shifted the pack on his shoulder and shook his head regretfully. "It's all the same in the end." He looked up at her, his gaze sharp. "But I'm here now to tell the story of the potter of Riversee who was murdered, and how you avenged her. I'm Giles Verney, a balladeer."

The balladeer part she could have guessed, but she still wasn't sure what to make of this man. *Surely he can't be simply what he seems*, she thought. People were never what they seemed. "Very well, Giles Verney, how did you know me?"

"There's a portrait of you in the manor at Islanton. It's by Greanco, whom you must remember, as he was court artist when—"

"I remember," she interrupted him. The only other portrait of her had hung in the Royal Palace in Vienne, and was probably long destroyed. Greanco was a seventh son and had the unconscious ability to put a true representation of the soul of his subject into his work. Kade could weave glamour into an effective disguise, but hadn't bothered for the inhabitants of Riversee, who had never seen her before. "You came here for the story of the dead potter."

Giles looked toward the door of the cottage. "I was in Marbury and heard about it from the magistrate there." He shook his head, his mouth set in a grim line. "It's a shocking thing to happen."

Maybe if I show him exactly how shocking it is he'll go away, she thought. She said, "See for yourself."

He followed her into the cottage with less hesitation than she would have expected, but stopped in the doorway. It was dark and cool, and flies buzzed in the damp still air. The plaster walls were stained with dried blood and the rough plank floor littered with the glazed pieces of the potter's last work, mixed with smashed furniture and tumbled cooking pots. After a quiet moment he asked, "Do you know what did this?"

She hesitated, but his story of the gentlewoman of Byre alone had bought him this answer. "Yes."

Giles stepped forward, stooping to pick a piece of wooden comb out of the rubble. His face was deeply troubled. "Was it human?"

"I don't know. But you'd be surprised how often something like this is done by a man, despite the number of tales where giant hands come down chimneys." Kade rubbed the bridge of her nose. She was tired and the whole long day had apparently been for nothing. She made her voice sharp, wanting to frighten him. "Now why don't you go away? This isn't a game and I'm not known for my patience."

He looked up at her, the death in the poor little room reflected in his eyes. As if it was the most self-evident thing in the world, he said patiently, "There has to be an end to the story, my lady."

Stubborn idiot, if you are what you seem, Kade thought wearily. "There might be no end. I've waited all day here and all I caught was you, a human mayfly."

His expression turned quizzical. "You're pretending to be another potter?"

"Clever of you to notice." Kade regarded the thatched ceiling sourly. The inhabitants of Riversee knew her only as the potter's daughter, come from another village to see to her mother's body and continue her craft. But now Giles's recognition of her made her wonder. Had she fooled anyone? Did the whole village whisper of it behind her back?

"Do you know why it was done?" Giles dropped the comb and got to his feet, dusting his hand off on his doublet.

She wouldn't give him that answer. "No."

"She was killed because potters are sacred to the old faith, or you wouldn't be here." Giles glanced around the room again, frowning in thought. "Could it have been the Church?"

Kade shrugged, scratching her head under the kerchief. "The local priest is about as old as his god's grandfather. I'm not discounting misplaced religious fervor, but he hasn't the strength or the temperament." As for the rest of Riversee, they might be baptized in the Church and pay their tithes regularly, but they still left fruit and flowers for the nameless spirits of the water and the wood, as well as the fay. Then she glared at him, because he had drawn her in again and she had hardly noticed.

Giles nodded. "That's well, but as you say, it's best not to discount it altogether. What do you plan next?"

She stared at him incredulously. "Are you mad?"

He smiled, with the air of someone waiting for a joke to be explained so he could laugh too. "Why do you say that?"

Kade clapped a hand to her forehead in exasperation. "In all the stories you've supposedly told of me, did it ever occur to you that I'm easily angered and don't appreciate human company?"

Apparently this hadn't occurred to him. He was aghast. "Don't you want the truth told?"

"Not particularly, no." Kade waved her arms in frustration. She still couldn't believe she was having this conversation.

"Why?" he demanded.

"Because it's my concern," she said pointedly.

"My concern is to tell tales. This would make a very good tale," he assured her, all earnest persuasion.

Gritting her teeth in frustration, Kade pulled a bit of yarn off her belt and knotted it into a truthcharm. The strands held together and she knew he believed what he said, and she was enough of a judge of character to know that he wasn't merely overdramatizing himself. She took a deep breath, flicking the charm away, and tried to reason with him. "That's all well and good, Giles, but I've made this my battle, and I don't need interference."

"People will tell things to a balladeer they wouldn't think of saying to any other stranger," he persisted. "I could be a great help to you."

Apparently reason worked as well with him as it did with the birds in the trees. "I don't need help, either." Exasperated, she stepped out of the shadowed cottage into the bright sunlight of the dirt yard.

He followed, the leather case he carried bumping against the door-frame with a suspicious twang. Kade hesitated, her attention caught. "What's in there?" she asked warily.

He patted it fondly. "A viola d'amore."

Despite her best intentions, she found herself eyeing the case, torn between caution and greed. Like all her mother's people, she had a weakness for human music. She conquered it and shook her head, thinking, *if I wanted to trap myself, I would send just such a man. Inoffensive and kind, easy to speak to, with a legitimate purpose for being here.* "I want you to leave, on your own, or I'll make you."

"Is it trust? Wait, here's this." Giles set his pack on the ground, knelt to fish a small fruit knife out and used it to cut off a lock of his hair. He held it up to her. "There's trust on my part. This should be enough to show you that there can be trust on yours."

She took it from him mechanically. That was trust. For a man without any magical knowledge it was also the greatest foolishness. For someone who knew as much about her as he plainly did it bordered on insanity.

She sighed. He might have a touch of the sight; the best balladeers did. Whatever it was, she really couldn't see her way clear to killing him.

No need to tell him that immediately. She lifted a brow, regarding him thoughtfully. "Did you ever hear the story of the balladeer who spent the rest of his life as a tree?"

Kade led Giles through the crumbling town walls and into the cluster of cottages that surrounded Riversee's single inn. The small houses on either side of the rough cart track were made of piled stone with slate or thatched roofs, each in its own little yard with dilapidated outbuildings, dung heaps, and overgrown garden plots. The ground was deeply rutted by wagon wheels, dusty where it wasn't muddy with discarded slops. The nearby post road made Riversee more cosmopolitan than most villages, but the passersby still watched Giles narrowly. They had become used to Kade, and a few nodded greetings to her.

As they passed under the arched wagongate of the inn's walled yard, Kade said quietly, "Tell your stories of someone else, Giles. I can be dangerous when I'm embarrassed." She added ruefully, *And I've embarrassed myself enough, thank you, I don't need any help at it.*

He smiled at her good-naturedly, not as if he disbelieved her, but as if it was her perfect right to be dangerous whenever she chose.

The inn was two stories high, with a shaded second-story balcony overlooking outside tables where late afternoon drinkers gathered with the chickens, children, and dogs in the dusty yard. A group of travelers, their feathered hats and the elaborate lace of their collars and cuffs grimy with road dust, argued vehemently around one of the tables. To the alarm of bystanders, one of them was using the butt of his wheel lock to pound on the boards for emphasis. Kade recognized them as couriers, probably from royalist troops engaged in bringing down the walls of some noble family's ancestral home. Months ago the court had ordered the destruction of all private fortifications to prevent feuding and rebellious plots among the petty nobility. This didn't concern Kade, whose private fortifications rested on the bottom of a lake, and were invisible to all but the most talented eyes.

Kade took a seat on the edge of the big, square well to watch Giles approach the locals. The men seated at the long plank table eyed him with suspicion as the balladeer started to open the leather case he carried. The suspicion faded into keen interest as Giles took out the viola d'amore.

Traveling musicians were usually welcomed gladly, balladeers who could bring news of other towns and villages even more so. Within moments they would be fighting to tell him their only news—the grim story of the potter's death, or at least what little they knew of it. Kade stirred the mud near the well with her big toe. She was disgusted, mostly with herself. She knew why the potter had been killed well enough—to attract her attention.

In the old faith, the villages honored the fay in the hopes that the erratic and easily angered creatures would leave them alone. Riversee was dedicated to Moire, Kade's mother, and Kade could only see the death of the village's sacred potter as a direct challenge. A few years ago it might have pleased her, this invitation to battle, but now it only threatened to make her bored. She wasn't sure what had changed; perhaps she was growing tired of games altogether.

That night, seated atop one of the rough tables in the inn's common room, Giles picked out an instrumental treatment of a popular ballad, and watched Kade. She sat near the large cooking hearth in the center of the room, regarding the crowd with an amused eye as she tapped one bare foot to the music.

The inn was crowded with a mix of locals and travelers from the nearby post road. Both the magistrate and the elderly parish priest were in attendance; the first to count the number of wine jugs emptied for the

Vine-growers' Excise and the second to discourage the patrons from emptying the jugs at all. Smoke from clay pipes and tallow candles and the heat of the fire made the room close and muggy. The din of talk and shouted comments almost drowned the clear tone of the viola, but whenever Giles stopped playing enraged listeners hurled crockery at him.

If Giles hadn't known better he would've thought the dim flickering light kind to the rather plain woman who called herself the old potter's daughter. But when firelight glittered off a wisp of pale hair as she leaned forward to catch some farmer's joke, he saw something else instead. *The daughter of the spirit dame of air and darkness, and a brute of a king*, Giles thought, and added a restless undercurrent to the plaintive ballad. Smiling at his folly, he bent his head over the viola.

Over the noisy babble and the music there were voices in the entryway. Two men with a party of servants entered the common room. One was blond and slight, with sharp handsome features and a downy beard. His manner was offhand and easy as he said something with a laugh to one of the servants behind him. His companion could not have been a greater contrast if nature had deliberately intended it. He was tall, muscled like a bull, with dark, greasy hair and rough features. Both men were well turned out, though not in the latest city style, and Giles labeled them as hedge gentry.

He also had a good eye for his audience, and saw tension infect the room like a plague in the newcomers' wake. There was muttering and an uneasy shifting among the local people, though the travelers seemed oblivious to it. In Giles's experience the nobility of this province were little better than gentlemen farmers and usually got on quite well with their villages and tenants, except for the usual squabbles over dovecotes and rights to the mall. Obviously the relationship in Riversee was somewhat strained.

Seated at the table Giles was using as a stage were the grizzled knife grinder who worked in the innyard, a toothless grandmother who might have been a hundred years old, and a farmer in the village to sell pigs.

Giles nodded toward the new arrivals and asked softly, "And who is that?"

The knife grinder snorted into his tankard. "The big one is Hugh Warrender. Some distant kin of the Duke of Marais."

"Fifth cousin, twice removed," the piping voice of the old woman added.

The farmer said, "Fifth cousin . . . ? Quiet, you daft old—"

"The boy is Fortune Devereux," the knife grinder continued, oblivious to his companions' comments. "He's a brother from the wrong side of the bed, come up from Marleyton."

"From Banesford," the old woman put in, almost shouting over the farmer's attempts to keep her quiet.

"He first came here two years ago." The grinder shrugged. "Warrender's not well thought of, but Devereux's not so bad."

"Wrong!" The old woman glanced suspiciously around the room and lowered her voice to a shriek. "He's worse, far worse!"

Kade watched as a table was cleared for Warrender and his men near her seat beside the hearth, a process which involved a good deal of shouting, jostling, and imprecations. As the group argued with the landlord, her eyes fell on the blond Devereux. He was an attractive man, but she wasn't sure that was what had drawn her eye. There was something else about him, something in his eyes, the way he moved his hands as he made a placating gesture to the ruffled landlord. Whatever the something was, it made the back of her neck prickle in warning. She was so occupied by it that she was caught completely unawares when Warrender turned with a growl and backhanded a grubby potboy into the fire.

No time for thought or spell, her stool clattered as Kade launched herself forward. She landed hard on her knees, catching the boy around the waist before he stumbled into the flames.

Thwarted, Warrender snarled and lifted a hand to strike both of them. Kade knelt in the ashes, the fearful boy clutching a double handful of her hair. "Yes, it would hurt me," she said quietly to the madness in Warrender's face. "But it would also make me very, very angry."

Something in her face froze Warrender. He stared at her, breathing hard, but didn't drop his arm. The moment dragged on.

Then Fortune Devereux stepped forward, catching his brother by the shoulder. Past Warrender's bulky form Kade met the younger man's gaze. Though his expression was sober, his eyes danced with laughter. *Yes*, she thought, her grip on the boy unconsciously tightening, *Oh yes. And now I know.*

The tension held as Warrender hesitated, like a confused and angry bull, then he laughed abruptly and let Devereux lead him away.

Kade felt the potboy shiver in relief and released him. He scrambled up and darted away through the crowd. She was aware that across the room Giles was on his feet, that an older man had him by the wrist, trying to pry a heavy wooden stool out of his hand. As Warrender and the others moved away, Giles forced himself to relax and let the man take the makeshift club. He retrieved the viola from the table where he had dropped it and sat down heavily on the bench. She saw his hands were shaking as he rubbed at an imperfection on the instrument's smooth surface.

As the rest of his party took their seats, Devereux strolled over to the balladeer's table. He spoke, smiling, and tipped his hat. Giles looked up at him warily, gave him a grudging nod.

Kade looked away, to keep from betraying any uneasiness. Devereux had marked Giles's reaction, had seen him ready to leap to her defense. *That*, she thought, *cannot mean anything good.*

"What did he say to you?" Kade's voice floated down from the cavernous darkness of the stable's loft.

"Nothing." Giles had finished wrapping the viola d'amore in its oiled leather case. He was not sure when Kade had gotten into the loft or how.

The stable, the traditional sleeping place of itinerant musicians and entertainers, was warm and dark except for the faint glow of moonlight through the cracks in the boards. The horses and mules penned or stalled along the walls made a continuous soft undercurrent of quiet snorts and stamping as they jostled one another. Straw dust floated down from above and into Giles's hair. He stretched slowly, trying to ease the knots out of his aching back. This had not been one of his better nights.

He knew he was a fool, but he would rather no one else know it; when Warrender had been a breath away from knocking Kade into the fire, he had come dangerously close to exposing his feelings. *She's the most dangerous woman in Ile-Rien,* he told himself ruefully. *She doesn't need your defense.* Except in his songs maybe, that spoke the truth about her when others lied.

"I know he said something to you, I saw his lips move," she persisted impatiently.

"Nothing that meant anything. Only gloating, I think. He said he was sorry for the disturbance." Giles hesitated. "What would you have done?"

"When?"

Irritated, he replied more sharply than he meant to. "When that hulking bastard was about to push you into the fire, when do you think?"

"I wouldn't turn to dust at the first lick of flame, you know." There was a pause. "I did have in mind a certain charm for the spontaneous ignition of gunpowder. And considering where he carried his pistol—" She added, "Devereux made his brother do it, you know."

Giles turned to look up at the dark loft, startled. "What?"

"Warrender's under a binding spell. You could see it in his eyes."

"Devereux is a sorcerer?" Giles frowned.

Her voice was lightly ironic. "Since he can do a binding spell, it's the logical conclusion."

"But why would he do that? Did he kill the potter?"

"Assuredly."

Giles gestured helplessly. "But why?"

She sounded exasperated. "I'm only an evil fay, ballad-maker, I don't have all the answers to all the questions in the world."

Giles drew a deep breath, summoning patience. Then he smiled faintly to himself. "My lady Kade, the playwright Thario always said that it was how we behave in a moment of impulse that told the true tale of our souls. And you, in your moment of impulse, kept a boy from being pushed into a fire. What do you say to that?"

An apple sailed upward out of the loft, reached the peak of its ascent, then dropped to graze his left ear. There was a faint scrabble and a brief glint of moonlight from above as a trap door opened somewhere in the roof. "My mother was the queen of air and darkness, Giles," her voice floated down as if from a great height. "And darkness. . . ."

Giles rolled over, scratching sleepily at the fleas that had migrated from his straw-filled pallet. The stable had become uncomfortably warm, and the summer night was humid. The sound of a woman sobbing softly woke him immediately. Wiping sweat from his forehead, he sat up and listened. It was coming from the stableyard, the side away from the inn.

He pushed to his feet and pulled his shirt on. Moonlight flickered down through the cracks in the high roof. As he crossed the hay-strewn floor, a horse stretched a long neck over a stall and tried to bite him.

The sobbing was slightly louder. It seemed to blend with the whisper of the breeze outside, forming an ethereal lament. Giles stopped, one hand on the latch of the narrow portal next to the large wagon door, some instinct making him wary.

Even through tears, the voice was silvery, bell-like. Odd. If the woman was under attack by whatever had killed the potter, she wouldn't be merely crying quietly.

On the chance that this was some private lover's quarrel and that interruptions, no matter how well meant, would be unwelcome, he groped for the rickety ladder in the darkness and climbed to the loft. The window shutters were open to the breeze and the big space was awash in moonlight. The hay-strewn boards creaked softly as Giles crossed it and crouched in front of the window.

A woman was pacing on the hardpacked earth in front of the stable, apparently alone. Her hair was colorless in the moonlight, and she wore a long shapeless robe of green embroidered with metallic threads. She swayed as the wind touched her, like a willow, like tall grass. Behind her the empty field stretched out and down toward the trees shadowing the dark expanse of the river.

The woman tilted her head back and the tears streamed down her face, into her hair. Giles had one leg out the window when Kade caught the collar of his shirt and jerked him back. He sat down hard and looked up to see her standing over him.

He shook his head, dizzy and a little ill, suddenly aware his mind had not been his own for a moment. His gut turning cold, he looked out at the weeping woman again, but this time saw her gliding progress as strange and unnatural. "What is it?" he whispered, prickles creeping up his spine.

Kade knelt in the window, matter-of-factly knotting her hair behind her head and tucking it into her kerchief. "A glaistig. Under that dress it's more goat than human and it's overly fond of the taste of male blood. They usually frequent deep running water. Someone must have called her up from the river."

Giles looked down at the creature again, warily fascinated.

Kade said grimly, "Mark it well for your next ballad, that's your killer."

"Devereux controls it?" Giles guessed, thinking of the red ruin of the potter's house. "He made it kill the potter?"

"He must have. It wouldn't attack an old woman unless it was forced."

"But why send it here?"

Kade threw him an enigmatic look. "There's been too much happenstance already tonight. She's not trying to seduce a pack mule. She's after you."

"Me?" he said, startled, but Kade was already gone.

Kade closed her eyes and pulled glamour out of the night air and the dew, drawing it over herself. It was a hasty job, and it wouldn't have fooled anyone in daylight, but the creature below was not intelligent and the dark would lend its own magic.

She grabbed the tackle that hung from the loft and swung down, the heavy rope rough against her hands and bare feet.

The glaistig turned toward her, smiling and stretching out its arms. It would see a young man, in shirt and breeches, barefoot, details of feature and form hidden by the barn's shadow. Kade moved toward it, dragging her feet slightly, as if half-asleep. She was thinking through the rote words of a binding spell, to tie the glaistig to her and let her call it whenever she chose. The difficulty was that she had to touch the creature for the binding to take effect.

Within touching distance the glaistig hesitated, staring at her. Its eyes threw back the moonlight like the glassy surface of a pool, but Kade could read confusion and suspicion there.

Before it could flee, Kade leaped forward and grabbed its hands. It shrieked in surprise, the shrill piercing cry turning into a growl. It tried to jerk free and only succeeded in dragging Kade across the dusty yard.

Kade stumbled, the gravel tearing into her feet. The glaistig was a head taller than she and heavier. She dug her heels in and gasped, "Just tell me why he sent you after my new favorite musician and we'll call this done."

"Let go!" Far gone in rage, the creature's voice was less alluringly female, but far more human.

Straining to stay on her feet, Kade hoped it didn't get the idea to slam her up against the barn or the stone wall of the innyard, but the creature seemed just as bad at advance planning as she was. "I'm giving my word. Tell me why he sent you and I'll let you go!"

The glamour had dissolved in the struggle, and the residue of it lay glittering on the earth like solid dewdrops. The glaistig abruptly stopped struggling to peer at her, confused. "What are you?"

"I've power over all the fay and if you don't tell me what I want to know now I'll bind you to the bottom of the village well in a barrel with staves and lid of cold iron. Does that tell you who I am?" Kade snarled. She had no idea if that would tell the glaistig who she was or not. And with her spell trembling like sinew stretched to the breaking point she couldn't have bound a compass needle to true north.

The glaistig shivered. "He didn't tell me."

"Oh, come now, you can do better than that." Sweat was dripping into Kade's eyes.

"I don't know, I don't know," it wept, sounding like a human woman again. "I swear, he told me to come here after the music maker, he didn't tell me why. Do you think he would tell me why? Let me go."

Kade released the spell in relief and the glaistig flung away from her. It stumbled, then fled toward the river in an awkward loping run. Kade sat down heavily on the hard-packed earth. She realized Giles was standing beside her, that he had been outside watching nearly the entire time.

He said, "You could have been killed."

She got to her feet, legs trembling with strain. "No, only nibbled on a little." She shook the dust out of her hair. "I can call that glaistig back whenever I want it. Though I'm not sure why I would. This all started out in a very promising way, but Devereux hasn't tried to fight me, or set me any puzzles to solve."

There was a moment of silence, then Giles said, "What do you mean?"

Something in his voice made Kade reluctant to answer. She watched the glaistig disappear among the trees near the river. Beautiful as it was, it was still just as empty-headed and perverse as the rest of the fay. It might guide a child out of the forest or care for elderly fishermen, but it would certainly kill any young man it could catch.

Giles asked, "Did he have any reason at all to kill the potter?"

"No." She could all but hear him drawing that last conclusion. If Giles Verney, balladeer, knew enough about Kade Carrion to realize that killing the village potter would bring her here, than surely the local sorcerer would realize it as well.

"The potter did nothing to him, knew nothing about him?"

Kade looked at him, his face a white mask in the moonlight. "What did you think this was?" she asked quietly.

"I didn't think it was a game. I didn't think he did it just to get your attention." He didn't sound shocked, only resigned.

With a snort of irony, Kade said, "It's what we do, Giles." She drew the fallen, scattered glamour around her to cloak herself in moonlight and shadow, and walked away.

Later in the night, when the moon was dimmed by clouds, Kade walked up the cart track to the gates of the Warrender manor house. The walls were crumbling like those around the village, too low to attract royal attention and be torn down. The house was small by city standards, but it was better than anything anyone else in Riversee had. It was two stories, with high, narrow windows shuttered against the darkness.

It had never mattered before what anyone else thought of her. The fay disliked each other as a matter of course, and Kade had never regarded her relatives on either side of the family with anything but anger or contempt. Having Giles's idealistic vision of her shattered shouldn't twist in her heart. But she hadn't chosen this game, Devereux had; she would find out what he wanted and end it tonight, one way or another.

Two servants were sleeping in a shabby outbuilding that housed the dovecote; she heard one cough and stir sleepily as she passed the door but neither wakened.

As she had hoped, there was a doorway near the back of the house, open and spilling lamplight. A postern door here would make a convenient exit for someone who wanted to leave or enter late at night without drawing attention.

The dry grass caught at her skirt as she stepped up to the open door. The room inside was low-ceilinged and cluttered with the debris of sorcery. Two long tables held heavy books, clouded glass vessels, curiously shaped and colored rocks or fragments of crystal. Wax had collected at the bases of the candles, their wan light revealing bare stone walls and soot-stained rafters. Fortune Devereux stood at the far end of the room, his back to her, leaning over an open book.

Kade held out a hand, took a slow breath, tasting the aether carefully. There was nothing, no wards that would set off nasty spells if she touched the doorsill. She took the last step forward and leaned in the doorway, saying, "Now what do you need this mess for?"

Devereux turned, his smile slow and triumphant. His doublet and shirt were open across his chest and she saw again that he was a very attractive man. "I didn't think you'd come."

She added that smile to what she knew of sorcerers and thought *so this room is warded*. She tested the aether again and felt the tug of the spell this time. *Damn.* She hadn't felt it outside because it wasn't set to stop her from entering the room; it was set to stop her from leaving. *Idiot. Overconfidence and impatience will kill you without any help from Devereux.* She didn't like stepping into his trap, but she still thought her power was more than equal to this mortal sorcerer's. If he struck at her directly, he would find that out. She smiled back, making it look easy. "I've only just gotten here and you're lying already."

His expression stiffened.

"You bound a glaistig and killed an old potter in the village you know by tradition I consider my property. Simply to get my attention. But you expected me not to take the bait and appear? Really, that makes you something of a fool, doesn't it?"

Devereux lifted a brow. "I misspoke. I didn't think you would come tonight, since you were occupied with your musician."

"I see." She nodded mock-complacently. "Jealousy, and we've only just met. Did it ever occur to you that all I had to do was point you out to the villagers, explain how you used the glaistig to kill the old potter, and this house would be burning down around your ears now?"

He laughed. "And I thought your loyalty to these people was as fickle as that of the rest of the fay. I didn't realize you were so virtuous."

Kade lifted a cool brow, though for some reason the jibe about loyalty had hit home. "My loyalty is fickle, but at least they gave me fruit and flowers. What did you ever do for me?"

"I have an offer for you." Devereux took a step forward. "You could benefit from an alliance with me."

"Benefit?" She rolled her eyes. "I repeat, what did you ever do for me?"

"It's what I can do for you. I can give you revenge."

This was new. No one had ever offered that before. Kade watched his calm face carefully, intrigued. "Revenge on whom?"

"The court, the king. The tricks you play on them, however deadly, aren't worthy of you. With my help, and the help of others that I know—"

"You want to use me against my royal relatives," Kade shook her head, disappointed, and added honestly, "It's an audacious plan, I'll willingly give you that much. No man's had the courage to suggest such a thing to me before."

His face had hardened and she knew it had been a long time since anyone had refused him anything. "But it is not to your taste, I take it."

Kade shrugged. "If I really wanted to kill my mortal brother I could have done it before now. What I want to do is make him and his mother suffer, and I don't think you or your supporters would agree to that. And as soon as I wasn't useful to you anymore one of you would try to kill me, then I'd have to kill one or more of you, and the whole mess would fall apart." She hesitated, and for some reason, perhaps because he was so comely, said, "If you had approached me as a friend, it could have been different. Perhaps we could have worked something out to serve your end."

But from his angry expression he didn't recognize it as the offer it was, or he felt it was a lie or a trap. *Maybe it was,* Kade admitted to herself. Maybe what she really wanted was something else entirely, something Devereux simply hadn't the character to offer her.

"I suggest you reconsider," Devereux said, his voice harsh.

She said dryly, "I suggest you stick to sorcery and leave politics to those with the talent for it."

He stepped back, giving her a thin-lipped smile. "You can't leave. This room is warded with a curse. If you break the barrier, the creature that loves you most in the world will die."

Relieved, Kade laughed at him as she slipped out the door. Fay didn't love each other, and there was no mortal left from her childhood who didn't want to see her dead. He had chosen this spell badly. "Curse away. I've nothing to lose."

"I think you have!" Kade heard him call after her as she ran through the tall grass. As she came around the side of the house there was a shout. Ahead in the darkness she saw moving figures and the glow from the slow match of a musket. She swore and ducked.

The musket thundered and there was a sharp crack as the ball struck the stone wall behind her. *If they hit me with that thing,* Kade thought desperately, *we're all going to find out just how human I am.* The musket balls were cold iron, and her fay magic could do nothing to them.

But that protection didn't extend to the gunpowder inside the musket. She covered her head with her arms and muttered the spell she had considered using on Warrender in the inn.

There was an explosion and a scream as someone's wheel lock pistol went off, then a dozen little popping sounds as the scattered grains of powder from the musket's blast ignited.

Kade scrambled to her feet. The grass near the gate had caught fire and she was forgotten in the face of that immediate threat. She ran to the back wall with its loose bricks and crumbling mortar and climbed it easily. At the top she paused and looked back. In the glow of the grass fire she could see Devereux walking back and forth, shouting at the servants in angry frustration. Revenge against her royal relatives would have been sweet. *But it would never have worked, not with him, anyway*, she thought with a grimace. *Too bad.*

It was barely dawn when she reached the inn, and through the windows she could see that candles had been lit in the common room. From just outside the door she thought there was more noise than seemed normal at this hour, especially after last night's drinking bout.

When she stepped inside, she heard a woman say, "Must have died in his sleep, poor thing."

The morning was well advanced when Kade waited for the Glaistig beneath a bent aging willow in a stretch of forest near the river.

It dropped a lock of golden hair into Kade's palm.

"Did he notice?" Kade asked, looking up at the creature.

The glaistig's eyes were limpid, innocent. "I did it while he slept."

"Very good." She should have treated Devereux's curse with more caution, she had said that to herself a hundred times over the rest of the long night. *And you should have known.* All those brave stories Giles had told of her, his audacity in coming here to find her should have said it plainly enough. She had also said that she didn't care, but no amount of repetition could make a lie the truth. *Giles knew I was dangerous company to keep.* Yes, he knew, but he had kept it anyway. And that made it all the worse.

She added the hair to a small leather pouch prepared with apricot stones and the puss from a plague sore, then sat down on a fallen log to sew it up with the small neat stitches she had learned as a child.

"The sorcerer was lovely," the glaistig said regretfully, watching her.

"He was lovely," Kade agreed. "And cunning, like me. And I would trade a hundred of both of us to know that one unlovely ballad singer was still alive somewhere in the world."

Kade left Riversee after that. She had thought to stay to see the result of her handiwork but she had discovered that knowing was enough.

Gray clouds were building for a storm, and she might have summoned one of the many flighted creatures of fayre and ridden the wind with it, but she had also discovered that she preferred to walk the dusty road. Some things had lost their pleasure.

The Day of Glory

BY DAVID DRAKE

David Drake has written or cowritten more than fifty books and edited or coedited more than thirty. He is the author of the Isles series of fantasy novels (beginning with *Lord of the Isles*) and the science fiction RCN series (beginning with *With the Lightnings*), but he is most well known as the creator of the futuristic military unit Hammer's Slammers.

The Hammer's Slammers series began as a collection of short stories published in 1979, each with a sophisticated military background that drew heavily on Drake's own experiences while serving in the United States Army in Vietnam and Cambodia. The series has continued over the last twenty-seven years in the form of novels, novellas, and short stories. The pieces in the Hammer series are (with only a very few exceptions) self-standing and in no particular order. In addition, there are very few continuing characters. Drake feels this is a benefit. "A reader who never heard of me or the series should be able to read 'The Day of Glory' with understanding as complete as that of someone who's read every story I've written."

David Drake lives in North Carolina.

The locals had turned down the music from the sound truck while the bigwigs from the capital were talking to the crowd, but it was still playing. "I heard that song before," Trooper Lahti said, frowning. "But that was back on Icky Nose, two years ago. Three!"

"Right," said Platoon Sergeant Buntz, wishing he'd checked the fit of his dress uniform before he put it on for this bloody rally. He'd gained weight during the month he'd been on medical profile for tearing up his leg. "You hear it a lot at this kinda deal. *La Marseillaise.* It goes all the way back to Earth."

This time it was just brass instruments, but Buntz's memory could fill in, *"Arise, children of the fatherland! The day of glory has arrived. . . ."* Though some places they changed the words a bit.

"Look at the heroes you'll be joining!" boomed the amplified voice of the blond woman gesturing from the waist-high platform. She stood with other folks in uniform or dress clothes on what Buntz guessed in peacetime was the judges' stand at the county fair. "When you come back in a few months after crushing the rebels, the cowards who stayed behind will look at you the way you look at our allies, Hammer's Slammers!"

Buntz sucked in his gut by reflex, but he knew it didn't matter. For this recruitment rally he and his driver wore tailored uniforms with the seams edged in dark blue, but the yokels saw only the tank behind them. *Herod*, H42, was a veteran of three deployments and more firefights than Buntz could remember without checking the Fourth Platoon log.

The combat showed on *Herod*'s surface. The steel skirts enclosing her plenum chamber were not only scarred from brush-busting but patched in several places where projectiles or energy weapons had penetrated. A two-meter section had been replaced on Icononzo, the result of a fifty-kilo directional mine. Otherwise the steel was dull red except where the rust had worn off.

Herod's hull and turret had taken an even worse beating; the iridium armor there turned all the colors of the spectrum when heated. A line of rainbow dimples along the rear compartment showed where a flechette gun—also on Icononzo—had wasted ammo, but it was on Humboldt that a glancing 15-cm powergun bolt had flared a banner across the bow slope.

If the gunner from Greenwood's Archers had hit *Herod* squarely, the tank would've been for the salvage yard and Lahti's family back on Leminkainen would've been told that she'd been cremated and interred where she fell.

Actually Lahti'd have been in the salvage yard too, since there wouldn't be any way to separate what was left of the driver from the hull. You didn't tell families all the details. They wouldn't understand anyway.

"Look at our allies, my fellow citizens!" the woman called. She was a newsreader from the capital station, Buntz'd been told. The satellites were down now, broadcast as well as surveillance, but her face'd be familiar from before the war even here in the boonies. "Hammer's Slammers, the finest troops in the galaxy! And look at the mighty vehicle they've brought to drive the northern rebels to surrender or their graves. Join them! Join them or forever hang your head when a child asks you, 'Grampa, what did you do in the war?'"

"They're not *really* joining the Regiment, are they, Top?" Lahti said, frowning again. The stocky woman'd progressed from being a fair driver to being a bloody good soldier. Buntz planned to give her a tank of her own the next time he had an opening. She worried too much, though, and about the wrong things.

"Right now they're just tripwires," Buntz said. "Afterwards, sure, we'll probably take some of 'em, after we've run 'em through newbie school."

He paused, then added, "The Feds've hired the Holy Brotherhood. They're light dragoons mostly, but they've got tank destroyers with 9-cm main guns. I don't guess we'll mop them up without somebody buying the farm."

He wouldn't say it aloud, even with none of the locals close enough to hear him, but he had to agree with Lahti that Placidus farmers didn't look like the most hopeful material. Part of the trouble was that they were wearing their fanciest clothes today. The feathers, ribbons, and reflecting bangles that passed for high fashion here in Quinta County would've made the toughest troopers in the Slammers look like a bunch of dimwits. It didn't help that half of 'em were barefoot, either.

The county governor, the only local on the platform, took the wireless microphone. "Good friends and neighbors!" he said and stopped to wheeze. He was a fat man with a weather-beaten face, and his suit was even tighter than Buntz's dress uniform.

"I know we in Quinta County don't need to be bribed to do our duty," he resumed, "but our generous government is offering a lavish prepayment of wages to those of you who join the ranks of the militia today. And there's free drinks in the refreshment tents for all those who kiss the book!"

He made a broad gesture. Nearly too broad; he almost went off the edge of the crowded platform onto his nose. His friends and neighbors laughed. One young fellow in a three-cornered hat called, "Why don't *you* join, Jeppe? You can stop a bullet and save the life of somebody who's not bloody useless!"

"What do they mean, 'kiss the book'?" Lahti asked. Then, wistfully, she added, "I don't suppose we could get a drink ourself?"

"We're on duty, Lahti," Buntz said. "And I guess they kiss the book because they can't write their names, a lot of them. You see that in this sorta place."

"*March, march!*" the sound truck played. "*Let impure blood water our furrows!*"

It was hotter'n Hell's hinges, what with the white sun overhead and its reflection from the tank behind them. The iridium'd burn 'em if they touched it when they boarded to drive back to H Company's laager seventy klicks away. At least they didn't have to spend the night in this Godforsaken place. . . .

Buntz could use a drink too. There were booths all around the field. Besides them, boys circulated through the crowd with kegs on their backs and metal tumblers chained to their waists. It'd be rotgut, but he'd been in the Slammers thirteen years. He guessed he'd drunk worse and likely *much* worse than what was on offer in Quinta County.

But not a drop till he and Lahti stopped being a poster to recruit cannon fodder for the government paying for the Regiment's time. Being dry was just part of the job.

The Placidan regular officer with the microphone was talking about honor and what pushovers the rebels were going to be. Buntz didn't doubt that last part; if the Fed troops were anything like what he'd seen of the Government side, they were a joke for sure.

But the Holy Brotherhood was another thing entirely. Vehicle for vehicle they couldn't slug it out with the Slammers, but they were division-sized and bloody well trained.

Besides, they were all mounted on air cushion vehicles. The Slammers won more of their battles by mobility than by firepower, but this time their enemy would move even faster than they did.

"Suppose he's ever been shot at?" Lahti said, her lip curling at the guy who spoke. She snorted. "Maybe by his girlfriend, hey? Though dolled up like he is, he prob'ly has boyfriends."

Buntz grinned. "Don't let it get to you, Lahti," he said. "Listening to blowhards's a lot better business than having the Brotherhood shoot at us. Which is what we'll be doing in a couple weeks or I miss my bet."

While the Placidan officer was spouting off, a couple of men had edged to the side of the platform to talk to the blond newsreader. The blonde snatched the microphone back and cried, "Look here, my fellow citizens! Follow your patriotic neighbors Andreas and Adolpho deCastro as they kiss the book and drink deep to their glorious future!"

The officer yelped and tried to grab the microphone; the newsreader blocked him neatly with her hip, slamming him back. Buntz grinned; this was the blonde's court, but he guessed she'd also do better in a firefight than the officer would. Though he might beat her in a beauty contest. . . .

The blonde jumped from the platform, then put an arm around the waist of each local to waltz through the crowd to the table set up under *Herod*'s bow slope. The deCastros looked like brothers or anyway first cousins, big rangy lunks with red hair and moustaches that flared into their sideburns.

The newsreader must've switched off the microphone because none of her chatter to one man, then the other, was being broadcast. The folks on the platform weren't going to use the mike to upstage her, that was all.

"Rise and shine, Trooper Lahti," Buntz muttered out of the side of his mouth as he straightened. The Placidan clerk behind the table rose to his feet and twiddled the book before him. It was thick and bound in red leather, but what was inside was more than Buntz knew. Maybe it was blank.

"Who'll be the first?" the blonde said to the fellow on her right. She'd cut the mike on again. "Adolpho, you'll do it, won't you? You'll be the first to kiss the book, I know it!"

The presumed Adolpho stared at her like a bunny paralyzed in the headlights. His mouth opened slackly. *Bloody Hell!* Buntz thought. *All it'll take is for him to start drooling!*

Instead the other fellow, Andreas, lunged forward and grabbed the book in both hands. He lifted it and planted a kiss right in the middle of the pebble-grain leather. Lowering it he boomed, "There, Dolph, you pussy! There's one man in the deCastro family, and the whole county knows it ain't you!"

"Why you—" Adolpho said, cocking back a fist with his face a thundercloud, but the blonde had already lifted the book from Andreas. She held it out to Adolpho.

"Here you go, Dolph, you fine boy!" she said. "Andreas, turn and take the salute of Captain Buntz of Hammer's Slammers, a hero from beyond the stars greeting a Placidan patriot!"

"What's that?" Andreas said. He turned to look over his shoulder.

Buntz'd seen more intelligence in the eyes of a poodle, but it wasn't his business to worry about that. He and Lahti together threw the fellow sharp salutes. The Slammers didn't go in for saluting much—and to salute in the field was a court-martial offense since it fingered officers for any waiting sniper—but a lot of times you needed some ceremony when you're dealing with the locals. This was just one of those times.

"An honor to serve with you, Trooper deCastro!" said Lahti. That was laying it on pretty thick, but you really couldn't overdo it in a dog-and-pony show for the locals.

"You're a woman!" Andreas said. "They said they was taking women too, but I didn't believe it."

"That's right, Trooper," Buntz said briskly before his driver replied. He trusted Lahti—she wouldn't be driving *Herod* if he didn't—but there was no point in risking what might come out when she was hot and dry and pretty well pissed off generally.

"Now," he continued, "I see the paymaster—" another bored clerk, a little back from the recorder "—waiting with a stack of piasters for you. Hey, and *then* there's free drinks in the refreshment car just like they said."

The "refreshment car" was a cattle truck with slatted steel sides that weren't going to budge if a new recruit decided he wanted to be somewhere else. A lot of steers had come to that realization over the years and it hadn't done 'em a bit of good. Two husky attendants waited in the doorway with false smiles, and there were two more inside dispensing drinks: grain alcohol with a dash of sweet syrup and likely an opiate besides. The truck would hold them, but a bunch of repentant yokels crying and shaking the slats wouldn't help lure their neighbors into the same trap.

Buntz saluted the other deCastro. The poor lug tried to salute back, but his arm seemed to have an extra joint in it somewhere. Buntz managed not to laugh and even nodded in false approval. It was all part of the job, like he'd told Lahti; but the Lord's truth was that he'd be less uncomfortable in a firefight. These poor stupid bastards!

The newsreader had given the mike back to the county governor. It was funny to hear the crew from the capital go on about honor and patriotism while the local kept hitting the pay advance and free liquor. Buntz figured *he* knew his neighbors.

Though the blonde knew them too, or anyway she knew men. Instead of climbing back onto the platform, she was circulating through the crowd. As Buntz watched she corralled a tall, stooped fellow who looked pale—the locals were generally red-faced from exposure, though many women carried parasols for this event—and a stocky teenager who was already glassy-eyed. It wouldn't take much to drink in the truck to put him the rest of the way under.

The blonde led the sickly fellow by the hand and the young drunk by the shirt collar, but the drunk was really stumbling along quick as he could to grope her. She didn't seem to notice, though when she'd delivered him to the recorder, she raised the book to his lips with one hand

and used the other to straighten her blouse under a jumper that shone like polished silver.

They were starting to move, now, just like sheep in the chute to the slaughter yard. Buntz kept saluting, smiling, and saying things like, "Have a drink on me, soldier," and, "Say, that's a lot of money they pay you fellows, isn't it?"

Which it was in a way, especially since the inflation war'd bring—war *always* brought—to the Placidan piaster hadn't hit yet except in the capital. There was three months' pay in the stack.

By tomorrow, though, most of the recruits would've lost the whole wad to the trained dice of somebody else in the barracks. They'd have to send home for money then; that or starve, unless the Placidan government fed its soldiers better than most of these boondock worlds did. Out in the field they could loot, of course, but right now they'd be kept behind razor ribbon so they didn't run off when they sobered up.

The clerks were trying to move them through as quick as they could, but the recruits themselves wanted to talk: to the recorder, to the paymaster, and especially to Buntz and Lahti. "Bless you, buddy!" Buntz said brightly to the nine-fingered man who wanted to tell him about the best way to start tomatoes. "Look, you have a drink for me in the refreshment car and I'll come back and catch you up with a couple more as soon as I've done with these other fellows."

Holding the man's hand firmly in his left, Buntz patted him on the shoulders firmly enough to thrust him toward the clerk with the waiting stack of piasters. The advance was all in small bills to make it look like more. At the current exchange rate three months' pay would come to about seventeen Frisian thalers, but it wouldn't be half that in another couple weeks.

A pudgy little fellow with sad eyes joined the line. A woman followed him, shrieking, "Alberto, are you out of your mind? Alberto! Look at me!" She was no taller than the man but easily twice as broad.

The woman grabbed him by the arm with both hands. He kept his face turned away, his mouth in a vague smile and his eyes full of anguish. "Alberto!"

The county governor was still talking about liquor and money, but all the capital delegation except an elderly, badly overweight union leader had gotten down from the platform and were moving through the crowd. The girlishly pretty army officer touched the screaming woman's shoulder and murmured something Buntz couldn't catch in the racket around him.

The woman glanced up with a black expression, her right hand rising with the fingers clawed. When she saw the handsome face so close to hers, though, she looked stunned and let the officer back her away.

Alberto kissed the book and scooted past the recorder without a look behind him. He almost went by the pay table, but the clerk caught him by the elbow and thrust the wad of piasters into his hand. He kept on going to the cattle truck: to Alberto, those steel slats were a fortress, not a prison.

A fight broke out in the crowd, two big men roaring as they flailed at each other. They were both blind drunk, and they didn't know how to fight anyway. In the morning they'd wake up with nothing worse than hangovers from the booze that was the reason they were fighting to begin with.

"I could take 'em both together," Lahti muttered disdainfully. She fancied herself as an expert in some martial art or another.

"Right," said Buntz. "And you could drive *Herod* through a nursery, too, but they'd both be a stupid waste of time unless you had to. Leave the posing for the amateurs, right?"

Buntz doubted he *could* handle the drunks barehanded, but of course he wouldn't try. There was a knife in his boot and a pistol in his right cargo pocket; the Slammers had been told not to wear their sidearms openly to this rally. Inside the turret hatch was a submachine gun, and by throwing a single switch he had control of *Herod*'s tribarrel and 20-cm main gun.

He grinned. If he said that to the recruits passing through the line, they'd think he was joking.

The grin faded. Pretty soon they were going to be facing the Brotherhood, who wouldn't be joking any more than Buntz was. The poor dumb bastards.

The county governor had talked himself out. He was drinking from a demijohn, resting the heavy earthenware on the cocked arm that held it to his lips.

His eyes looked haunted when they momentarily met those of Buntz. Buntz guessed the governor knew pretty well what he was sending his neighbors into. He was doing it anyway, probably because bucking the capital would've cost him his job and maybe more than that.

Buntz looked away. He had things on his conscience too; things that didn't go away when he took another drink, just blurred a little. He wouldn't want to be in the county governor's head after the war, though, especially at about three in the morning.

"*Against tyrants we are all soldiers,*" caroled the tune in the background. "*If our young heroes fall, the fatherland will raise new ones!*"

The union leader was describing the way the army of the legitimate government would follow the Slammers to scour the continent north of the Spine clean of the patches of corruption and revolt now breeding there. Buntz didn't know what Colonel Hammer's strategy would be, but he didn't guess they'd be pushing into the forested highlands to fight a more numerous enemy. The Brotherhood'd hand 'em their heads if they tried.

On the broad plains here in the south, though. . . . Well, *Herod*'s main gun was lethal for as far as her optics reached, and that could be hundreds of kilometers if you picked your location.

The delegation from the capital kept trying, but not even the blond newsreader was making headway now. They'd trolled up thirty or so recruits, maybe thirty-five. Not a bad haul.

"Haven't saluted so much since I joined," Lahti grumbled, a backhanded way of describing their success. "Well, like you say, Top, that's the job today."

The boy kissing the book was maybe seventeen standard years old—or not quite that. Buntz hadn't been a lot older when he joined, but he'd had three cousins in the Regiment and he'd known he wasn't getting into more than he could handle. Maybe this kid was the same—the Army of Placidus wasn't going to work him like Hammer's Slammers—but Buntz doubted the boy was going to like however long it was he wore a uniform.

The last person in line was a woman: mid-30s, no taller than Lahti, and with a burn scar on the back of her left wrist. The recording clerk started to hand her the book, then recoiled when he took a look at her. "Madame!" he said.

"Hey, Hurtado!" a man said gleefully. "Look what your missus is doing!"

"Guess she don't get enough dick at home, is that it?" another man called from a liquor booth, his voice slurred.

"The proclamation said you were enlisting women too, didn't it?" the woman demanded. "Because of the emergency?"

"Sophia!" cried a man stumbling to his feet from a circle of dice players. He was almost bald, and his long, drooping moustaches were too black for the color to be natural. Then, with his voice rising, "Sophia, what are you doing?"

"Well, maybe in the capital," the recorder said nervously. "I don't think—"

Hurtado grabbed the woman's arm. She shook him off without looking at him.

"What don't you think, my man?" said the newsreader, slipping through what'd become a circle of spectators. "You don't think you should obey the directives of the Emergency Committee in a time of war, is that what you think?"

The handsome officer was just behind her. He'd opened his mouth to speak, but he shut it again as he heard the blonde's tone.

"Well, no," the clerk said. The paymaster watched with a grin, obviously glad that somebody else was making the call on this one. "I just—"

He swallowed whatever else he might've said and thrust the book into the woman's hands. She raised it; Hurtado grabbed her arm again and said, "Sophia, don't make a spectacle of yourself!"

The newsreader said, "Sir, you have no—"

Sophia bent to kiss the red cover, then turned and backhanded Hurtado across the mouth. He yelped and jumped back. Still holding the book down at her side, she advanced and slapped him again with a full swing of her free hand.

Buntz glanced at Lahti, just making sure she didn't take it into her head to get involved. She was relaxed, clearly enjoying the spectacle and unworried about where it was going to go next.

The Placidan officer stepped between the man and woman, looking uncomfortable. He probably felt pretty much the same as the recorder about women in the army, and maybe if the blonde hadn't been here he'd have said so. As it was, though—

"That will be enough, Señor Hurtado," he said. "Every family must do its part to eradicate the cancer of rebellion, you know."

Buntz grinned. The fellow ought to be glad that the blonde'd interfered, because otherwise there was a pretty fair chance that Lahti would've made the same points. Lahti wasn't one for words when she could *show* just how effective a woman could be in a fight.

"We about done here, Top?" she said, following Sophia with her eyes as she picked up her advance pay.

"We'll give it another fifteen minutes," Buntz said. "But yeah, I figure we're done."

"*Arise, children of the fatherland . . . ,*" played the sound truck.

"It's gonna be a hot one," Lahti said to the sky above *Herod*. The tank waited as silent as a great gray boulder where Lahti'd nestled it into a gully on the reverse slope of a hill. They weren't overlooked from any point on the surface of Placidus—particularly from the higher ground to the north which was in rebel hands. Everything but the fusion bottle was shut down, and thick iridium armor shielded that.

"It'll be hot for somebody," Buntz agreed. He sat on the turret hatch; Lahti was below him at the top of the bow slope. They could talk in normal voices this way instead of using their commo helmets. Only the most sophisticated devices could've picked up the low-power intercom channel, but he and Lahti didn't need it.

He and Lahti didn't need to talk at all. They just had to wait, them and the crew of *Hole Card*, Tank H47, fifty meters to the north in a parallel gully.

The plan wouldn't have worked against satellites, but the Holy Brotherhood had swept those out of the sky the day they landed at New Carthage on the north coast, the Federation capital. The Brotherhood commanders must've figured that a mutual lack of strategic reconnaissance gave the advantage to their speed and numbers . . . and maybe they were right, but there were ways and ways.

Buntz grinned. And trust Colonel Hammer to find them.

"Hey Top?" Lahti said. "How long do we wait? If the Brotherhood doesn't bite, I mean."

"We switch on the radios at local noon," Buntz said. "Likely they'll recall us then, but I'm just here to take orders."

That was a gentle reminder to Lahti, not that she was out of line asking. With *Herod* shut down, she had nothing to see but the sky—white rather than really blue—and the sides of the gully.

Buntz had a 270° sweep of landscape centered with the Government firebase thirty klicks to the west. His external pickup was pinned to a tree on the ridge between *Herod* and *Hole Card*, feeding the helmet displays of both tank commanders through fiber optic cables.

There were sensors that could *maybe* spot the pickup, but it wouldn't be easy and even then they'd have to be searching in this direction. The Brotherhood wasn't likely to be doing that when they had the Government battalion and five Slammers combat cars to hold their attention on the rolling grasslands below.

The Placidan troops were in a rough circle of a dozen bunkers connected by trenches. In the center of the encampment were four 15-cm conventional howitzers aiming toward the Spine from sandbagged revetments. The trenches were shallow and didn't have overhead cover; ammunition trucks were parked beside the guns without even the slight protection of a layer of sandbags.

According to the briefing materials, the firebase also had two calliopes whose task was to destroy incoming shells and missiles. Those the Placidan government bought had eight barrels each, arranged in superimposed rows of four.

Buntz couldn't see the weapons on his display. That meant they'd been dug in to be safe from direct fire; the only decision the Placidan commander'd made that he approved of. Two calliopes weren't nearly enough to protect a battalion against the kind of firepower a Brotherhood commando had available, though.

The combat cars of 3d Platoon, G Company, were laagered half a klick south of the Government firebase. The plains had enough contour that the units were out of direct sight of one another. That wouldn't necessarily prevent Placidans from pointing their slugthrowers up in the air and raining projectiles down on the Slammers, but at least it kept them from deliberately shooting at their mercenary allies.

Buntz's pickup careted movement on the foothills of the Spine to the north. "Helmet," he said, enabling the voice-activated controls. "Center three-five-oh degrees, up sixteen."

The magnified image showed the snouts of three air-cushion vehicles easing to the edge of the evergreen shrubs on the ridge nearly twenty kilometers north of the Government firebase. One was a large armored personnel carrier; it could carry fifteen fully-armed troops plus its driver and a gunner in the cupola forward. The APC's tribarrel was identical to the weapons on the Slammers' combat cars, a Gatling gun that fired jets of copper plasma at a rate of five hundred rounds per minute.

The other two vehicles were tank destroyers. They used the same chassis as the APC, but each carried a single 9-cm high-intensity power-gun in a fixed axial mount—the only way so light a vehicle could handle the big gun's recoil. At moderate range—up to five klicks or so—a 9-cm bolt could penetrate *Herod's* turret, and it'd be effective against a combat car at *any* distance.

"Saddle up, trooper," Buntz said softly to Lahti as he dropped down into the fighting compartment. "Don't crank her till I tell you, but we're not going to have to wait till noon after all. They're taking the bait."

The combat cars didn't have a direct view of the foothills, but like Buntz they'd raised a sensor pickup; theirs was on a pole mast extended from Lieutenant Rennie's command car. A siren wound from the laager; then a trooper shot off a pair of red flare clusters. Rennie was warning the Government battalion—they couldn't be expected to keep a proper radio watch—but Buntz knew that Platoon G3's main task was to hold the Brotherhood's attention. Flares were a good way to do that.

The Government artillerymen ran to their howitzers from open-sided tents where they'd been dozing or throwing dice. Several automatic weapons began to fire from the bunkers. One was on the western side of the compound and had no better target than the waving grass. The guns shooting northward were pointed in the right direction, but the slugs would fall about fifteen kilometers short.

The Brotherhood tank destroyers fired, one and then the other. An ammunition truck in the compound blew up in an orange flash. The explosion dismounted the nearest howitzer and scattered the sandbag revetments of the other three, not that they'd been much use anyway. A column of yellow-brown dirt lifted, mushroomed a hundred meters in the air, and rained grit and pebbles down onto the whole firebase.

The second 9-cm bolt lashed the crest of the rise that sheltered the combat cars. Grass caught fire and glass fused from silica in the soil sprayed in all directions. Buntz nodded approval. The Brotherhood gunner couldn't have expected to hit the cars, but he was warning them to keep under cover.

Brotherhood APCs slid out of the shelter of the trees and onto the grasslands below. They moved in companies of four vehicles each, two east of the firebase and two more to the west. They weren't advancing toward the Government position but instead were flanking it by more than five kilometers to either side.

The sound of the explosion reached *Herod*, dulled by distance. A little dirt shivered from the side of the swale. Twenty klicks is a hell of a long way away, even for an ammo truck blowing up.

The tank destroyers fired again, saturated cyan flashes that Buntz's display dimmed to save his eyes. Their target was out of his present magnified field of view, a mistake.

"Full field, Quadrant Four," Buntz said, and the lower left corner of his visor showed the original 270° display. A bunker had collapsed in a cloud of dust, though without a noticeable secondary explosion, and there was a new fire just north of the combat cars. The cars' tribarrels wouldn't be effective against even the tank destroyers' light armor at this range, but the enemy commander wasn't taking any chances. The Brotherhood was a good outfit, no mistake.

Eight more vehicles left the hills now that the advanced companies had spread to screen them. Pairs of mortar carriers with pairs of APCs for security followed each flanking element. The range of Brotherhood automatic mortars was about ten klicks, depending on what shell they were firing. It wouldn't be any time before they were in position around the firebase.

Rennie's combat cars were moving southward, keeping under cover. Running, if you wanted to call it that.

The Brotherhood APCs were amazingly fast, seventy kph cross-country. They couldn't fight the combat cars head-on, but they wouldn't try to. They obviously intended to surround the Slammers platoon and disgorge their infantry in three-man buzzbomb teams. Once the infantry got into position, and with the tank destroyers on overwatch to limit the cars' movement, the Brotherhood could force Lieutenant Rennie to surrender without a shot.

One of the Government howitzers fired. The guns could reach the Brotherhood vehicles in the hills, but this round landed well short. A red flash and a spurt of sooty black smoke indicated that the bursting charge was TNT.

The gunners didn't get a chance to refine their aim. A 9-cm bolt struck the gun tube squarely at the trunnions, throwing the front half a dozen meters. The white blaze of burning steel ignited hydraulic fluid in the compensator, the rubber tires, and the hair and uniforms of the crew. A moment later propellant charges stacked behind the gun went off in something between an explosion and a very fierce fire.

Two howitzers were more or less undamaged, but their crews had abandoned them. Another bunker collapsed—a third. Buntz hadn't noticed the second being hit, but a pall of dust was still settling over it. Government soldiers started to leave the remaining bunkers and huddle in the connecting trenches.

Flashes and spurts of white smoke at four points around the firebase indicated that the mortars had opened fire simultaneously. They were so far away that the bombardment seemed to be happening in silence. That wasn't what Buntz was used to, which made him feel funny. Different generally meant bad to a soldier, or anybody else in a risky business.

The tank destroyers fired again. One bolt blew in the back of a bunker; the other ignited a stand of brushwood ahead of the combat cars. That Brotherhood gunner was trying to keep Rennie off-balance, taking his attention off the real threat: the APCs and their infantry, which in a matter of minutes would have the cars surrounded.

Buntz figured it was time. "Lahti, fire 'em up," he said. He switched on his radios, then unplugged the lead from his helmet and let the coil of glass fiber spring back to the take-up reel on the sensor. The hollow *stoonk-k-k* of the mortars launching finally reached him, an unmistakable sound even when the breeze sighing through the tree branches almost smothered it.

The hatch cover swiveled closed over Buntz as *Herod's* eight drive

fans spun. Lahti kept the blades in fine pitch to build speed rapidly, slic-
ing the air but not driving it yet.

"Lamplight elements, move to start position," Buntz ordered. That
was being a bit formal since the Lamplight call sign covered only *Herod*
and *Hole Card*, but you learned to do things by rote in combat. A firefight's no place for thinking. You operated by habit and reflex; if those
failed, the other fellow killed you.

The fan note deepened. *Herod* vibrated fiercely, spewing a sheet of
grit from beneath her skirts. She didn't move forward; it takes time for
thrust to balance a tank's 170 tons.

A calliope—only one—ripped the sky with a jet of 2-cm bolts. The
burst lasted only for an eyeblink, but a mortar shell detonated at its
touch. The gun was concealed, but Buntz knew the crew was slewing it
to bear on a second of the incoming rounds before it landed.

They didn't succeed; proximity fuses exploded the three remaining
shells a meter in the air. Fragments sleeted across the compound. Because mortars are low pressure, their shell casings can be much thinner
than those of conventional artillery; that leaves room for larger bursting
charges. The blasts flattened all the structures that'd survived the ammo
truck blowing up. One of the shredded tents ignited a few moments
later.

Herod's fans finally bit deeply enough to start the tank climbing up
the end of the gully. Buntz had a panoramic view on his main screen.
He'd already careted all the Brotherhood vehicles either white—*Herod*'s
targets—or orange, for *Hole Card*. That way both tanks wouldn't fire at
the same vehicle and possibly allow another to escape.

Buntz's smaller targeting display was locked on where the right-hand
Brotherhood tank destroyer would appear when *Herod* reached firing
position. *Hole Card* would take the other tank destroyer, the only one
visible to it because of a freakishly tall tree growing from the grassland
north of its position.

"*Top, I'm on!*" shouted Cabell in *Hole Card* on the unit frequency.
As Cabell spoke, Buntz's orange pipper slid onto the rounded bow of a

tank destroyer. The magnified image rocked as the Brotherhood vehicle sent another plasma bolt into the Government encampment.

"Fire!" Buntz said, mashing the firing pedal with his boot. *Herod* jolted backward from the recoil of the tiny thermonuclear explosion; downrange, the tank destroyer vanished in a fireball.

Hole Card's target was gone also. Shrubbery was burning in semicircles around the gutted wreckage, and a square meter of deck plating twitched as it fell like a wounded goose. It could've come from either Brotherhood vehicle, so complete was the destruction.

There was a squeal as Cabell swung *Hole Card*'s turret to bear on the plains below. Buntz twitched *Herod*'s main gun only a few mils to the left and triggered it again.

The APC in the foothills was probably the command vehicle overseeing the whole battle. The Brotherhood driver slammed into reverse when the tank destroyers exploded to either side of him, but he didn't have enough time to reach cover before *Herod*'s 20-cm bolt caught the APC squarely. Even from twenty kilometers away, the slug of ionized copper was devastating. The fires lit by the burning vehicles merged into a blaze of gathering intensity.

Now for the real work. "Lahti, haul us forward a couple meters, get us onto the forward slope!" Buntz ordered. The main gun could depress only 5°, so any Brotherhood vehicles that reached the base of the rise the tanks were on would otherwise be in a dead zone.

They shouldn't get that close, of course, but the APCs were very fast. Buntz hadn't made platoon sergeant by gambling when he didn't need to.

The Brotherhood troops on the plains didn't realize—most of them, at least—that their support elements had been destroyed. The mortar crews had launched single rounds initially to test the Placidan defenses. When those proved hopelessly meager, the mortarmen followed up with a Battery Six, six rounds from each tube as quickly as the automatic loaders could cycle.

The calliope didn't make even a token effort to meet the incoming catastrophe; the early blasts must've knocked it out. The twenty-four shells were launched on slightly different trajectories so that all reached the target within a fraction of a same instant. Their explosions covered the interior of the compound as suddenly and completely as flame flashes across a pool of gasoline.

The lead APC in the western flanking element glared cyan; then the bow plate and engine compartment tilted inward into the gap vaporized by *Hole Card*'s main gun. As Lahti shifted *Herod*, Buntz settled his pipper on the nearest target of the eastern element, locked the stabilizer, and rolled his foot forward on the firing pedal.

Recoil made *Herod* stagger as though she'd hit a boulder. The turret was filling with a gray haze as the breech opened for fresh rounds. The bore purging system didn't get *quite* all of the breakdown products of the matrix which held copper atoms in alignment. Filters kept the gases out of Buntz's lungs, but his eyes watered and the skin on the back of his hands prickled.

He was used to it. He wouldn't have felt comfortable if it *hadn't* happened.

The lead company of the commando's eastern element was in line abreast, aligning the four APCs—three and a dissipating fireball now—almost perfectly with *Herod*'s main gun. Buntz raised his pipper slightly, fired; raised it again as he slewed left to compensate for the APCs' forward movement, fired; raised it again—

The driver of the final vehicle was going too fast to halt by reversing the drive fans to suck the APC to the ground; he'd have pinwheeled if he'd tried it. Instead he cocked his nacelles forward, hoping that he'd fall out of his predicted course. The APC's tribarrel was firing in *Herod*'s general direction, though even if the cyan stream had been carefully aimed the range was too great for 2-cm bolts to damage a tank.

As Buntz's pipper steadied, the side panels of the APC's passenger compartment flopped down and the infantry tried to abandon the doomed vehicle. Buntz barely noticed the jolt of his main gun as it lashed out. Buzzbombs and grenades exploded in red speckles on his plasma bolt's overwhelming glare. The back of the APC tumbled through the fiery remains of the vehicle's front half.

Half a dozen tribarrels were shooting at the tanks as the surviving APCs dodged for cover. The same rolling terrain that'd protected Platoon G3 from the tank destroyers sheltered the Brotherhood vehicles also. Buntz threw a quick shot at an APC. *Too* quick: his bolt lifted a divot the size of a fuel drum from the face of a hillock as his target slid behind it. Grass and topsoil burned a smoky orange.

The only Brotherhood vehicles still in sight were a mortar van and the APC that'd provided its security. They'd both been assigned to *Hole Card* originally, but seeing as all of *Herod*'s targets were either hidden or blazing wreckage—

Cabell got on the mortar first, so as its unfired shells erupted in a fiery yellow mushroom Buntz put a bolt into the bow of the APC. The side panels were open and the tribarrel wasn't firing. Like as not the gunner and driver had joined the infantry in the relative safety of the high grass.

The mortars hadn't fired on Rennie's platoon, knowing that the combat cars would simply put their tribarrels in air-defense mode and sweep the bombs from the sky. The only time mortar shells might be useful would be if they distracted the cars from line-of-sight targets.

The Brotherhood commando had been well and truly hammered, but what remained was as dangerous as a wounded leopard. One option was for Rennie to claim a victory and withdraw in company with the tanks. In the short term that made better economic sense than sending armored vehicles against trained, well-equipped infantry in heavy cover. In the longer term, though, that gave the Slammers the reputation of a unit that was afraid to go for the throat . . . which meant it wasn't an option at all.

"*Myrtle Six to Lamplight Six,*" said Lieutenant Rennie over the command push. "*My cars are about to sweep the zone, west side first. Don't you panzers get hasty for targets, all right? Over.*"

"Lamplight to Myrtle," Buntz replied. "Sir, hold your screen and let me flush 'em toward you while my Four-seven element keeps overwatch.

You've got deployed infantry in your way, but if we can deal with their air defense—right?"

Finishing the commando wouldn't be safe either way, but it was better for a lone tank. Facing infantry in the high grass the combat cars risked shooting one another up, whereas *Herod* had a reasonable chance of bulling in and out without taking more than her armor could absorb.

Smoke rose from a dozen grassfires on the plain, and the blaze on the hills to the north was growing into what'd be considered a disaster on a world at peace. A tiny part of Buntz's mind noted that he hadn't been on a world at peace in the thirteen standard years since he joined the Slammers, and he might never be on one again until he retired. Or died.

He'd been raised to believe in the Way. Enough of the training remained that he wasn't sure there was peace even in death for what Sergeant Darren Lawrence Buntz had become. But that was for another time, or probably no time at all.

While Buntz waited for Myrtle Six to reply, he echoed a real-time feed from *Hole Card*'s on a section of his own main screen, then called up a topographic map and overlaid it with the courses of all the Brotherhood vehicles. On that he drew a course plot with a sweep of his index finger.

"*Lamplight, this is Myrtle,*" Lieutenant Rennie said at last. The five cars had formed into a loose wedge, poised to sweep north through the Brotherhood anti-armor teams and the remaining APCs. "*All right, Buntz, we'll be your anvil. Next time, though, we get the fun part. Myrtle Six out.*"

"Four-seven, this is Four-two," Buntz said, using the channel dedicated to Lamplight; that was the best way to inform without repetition not only Sergeant Cabell but also the drivers of the two tanks. "Four-two will proceed on the attached course."

He transmitted the plot he'd drawn while waiting for Rennie to make up his mind. It was rough, but that was all Lahti needed—she'd pick the detailed route by eyeball. As for Cabell, knowing the course allowed him to anticipate where targets might appear.

"I'll nail them if they hold where they are, and you get 'em if they try to run, Cabell," he said. "But you know, not too eager. Got it, over?"

"*Roger, Four-two,*" Cabell replied. "*Good hunting. Four-seven out.*"

Lahti had already started *Herod* down the slope, using gravity to accelerate; the fans did little more than lift the skirts off the ground. Their speed quickly built up to 40 kph.

Buntz frowned, doubtful about going so fast cross-country in a tank. Lahti was managing it, though. *Herod* jounced over narrow, rain-cut gullies and on hillocks that the roots of shrubs had cemented into masses a hand's breadth higher than the surrounding surface, but though Buntz jolted against his seat restraints the shocks weren't any worse than those of the main gun firing.

The fighting compartment displays gave Buntz a panoramic view at any magnification he wanted. Despite that, he had an urge to roll the hatch back and ride with his head out. Like most of the other Slammers recruits, whatever planet they came from, he'd been a country boy. It didn't feel right to shut himself up in a box when he was heading for a fight.

It was what common sense as well as standing orders required, though, Buntz did what he knew he should instead of what his heart wanted to do. When he'd been ten years younger, though, he'd regularly ridden into battle with his torso out of the hatch and his hands on the spade grips of the tribarrel instead of slewing and firing it with the joystick behind armor.

"*Boomer Three-niner-one, this is Myrtle Six,*" Lieutenant Rennie said, using the operation's command channel to call the supporting battery. "*Request targeting round at point Alpha Tango one-three, five-eight. Over.*"

Herod tore through a belt of heavy brush in the dip between two gradual rises. Groundwater collected here, and there might be a running stream during the wet season. The tank's skirts sheared gnarled stems, and bits that got into the fan nacelles were sprayed out again as chips.

Hole Card fired. Buntz had been concentrating on the panoramic screen, poised to react if the tank's AI careted movement. Now he glanced at his echo of Cabell's targeting display. The bolt missed, but a Brotherhood APC fluffed its fans to escape the fire spreading from the scar that plasma'd licked through thirty meters of grass.

Cabell fired again. Maybe he'd even planned it this way, spending the first round to startle his target into the path of the second. The APC flew apart. There was no secondary explosion because the infantry had already dismounted, taking their munitions with them.

A shell from the supporting rocket artillery screamed out of the southern sky. While the round was still a thousand meters in the air, a tribarrel fired from near the predicted point of impact. Plasma ruptured the shell, sending a spray of blue smoke through the air. It'd been a marking round, harmless unless you happened to be exactly where it hit.

Herod had just reached the top of another rise. The APC that'd destroyed the shell was behind a knoll seven kilometers away, but Buntz fired, Cabell fired, and two combat cars on the east end of Rennie's wedge thought they had a target also.

None of them hit the target, but Buntz got a momentary view of a Brotherhood soldier hopping into sight and vanishing again. He'd leaped from his cupola, well aware that it was only a matter of time—a matter of a short time—before the Slammers' concentrated fire hit the vehicle that'd been spared by such a narrow margin.

Lahti boosted her fans into the overload region to lift *Herod* another centimeter off the ground without letting their speed drop. The side slopes were harsh going: the topsoil had weathered away, leaving rock exposed. Rain and wind deposited the silt at the bottom of the swales, so the Brotherhood troops waiting on the other side of the hill would expect *Herod* to come at them low.

Buntz'd angled his main gun to their left front, fully depressed. The cupola tribarrel was aimed up the hill *Herod* was circling. He saw the infantry on the crest rise with their buzzbombs shouldered. Before his thumb could squeeze the tribarrel's firing tit, his displays flickered and the hair on the back of his neck rose. The top of the hill erupted, struck squarely by a bolt from *Hole Card*'s main gun. Cabell's angle had given him an instant's advantage.

Twenty-odd kilometers of atmosphere had spread the plasma charge, but it was still effective against the infantry. There'd been at least six Brotherhood soldiers, but when the rainbow dazzle cleared a single figure remained to stumble downhill. Its arms were raised and its hair and uniform were burning. The fireball of organic matter in the huge divot which the bolt blasted from the hilltop did most of the damage, but the troops' own grenades and buzzbombs had gone off also.

Cabell'd taken a chance when he aimed so close to *Herod* at long range, but a battle's a risky place to be. Buntz wasn't complaining.

Herod rounded the knob, going too fast to hold its line when the outside of the curve was on a downslope. The tank, more massive than big but big as well, skidded and jounced outward on the turn. The four Brotherhood APCs sheltered on the reverse slope fired before *Herod* came into sight, willing to burn out their tribarrels for the chance of getting off the first shot. The gunners knew that if they didn't cripple the blower tank instantly they were dead.

They were probably dead even if they did cripple the tank. They were well-trained professionals sacrificing themselves to give their fellows a chance to escape.

Two-cm bolts rang on *Herod*'s bow slope in a brilliant display that blurred several of the tank's external pickups with a film of redeposited iridium. The Brotherhood commander hadn't had time to form a defensive position; his vehicles were bunched to escape the tank snipers far to the west, not to meet one of those tanks at knife range. Three vehicles were at the bottom of the swale in a rough line-ahead; the last was higher on the slope.

Buntz fired his main gun when the pipper swung on—on *anything,* on any part of the APCs. His bolt hit the middle vehicle of the line; it swelled into a fiery bubble. The shockwave shoved the other vehicles away.

The high APC continued to hose *Herod* with plasma bolts, hammering the hull and blasting three fat holes in the skirts. That tribarrel was the only one to hit the tank, probably because its gunner was aiming to avoid friendly vehicles.

Herod's main gun cycled, purging and cooling the bore with a let of liquid nitrogen. Buntz held his foot down on the trip, screaming with frustration because his gun didn't fire, couldn't fire. He understood the delay, but it was maddening nonetheless.

The upper half of the APC vanished in a roaring coruscation: the explosion of *Herod*'s target had pushed it high enough that *Hole Card* could nail it. Cabell wouldn't have to pay for his drinks the next night he and Buntz were in a bar together.

Two blocks of *Herod*'s Automatic Defense Array went off simultaneously, making the hull chime like a gong. Each block blasted out hundreds of tungsten barrels the size of a finger joint. They ripped through long grass and Brotherhood infantry, several of them already firing powerguns.

A soldier stepped around the bow of an APC, his buzzbomb raised to launch. A third block detonated, shredding him from neck to knees. Pellets punched ragged holes through the light armor of the vehicle behind him.

Herod's main gun fired—*finally*, Buntz's imagination told him, but he knew the loading cycle was complete in less than two seconds. The rearmost APC collapsed in on itself like a thin wax model in a bonfire. The bow fragment tilted toward the rainbow inferno where the middle of the vehicle had been, its tribarrel momentarily spurting a cyan track skyward.

Lahti'd been fighting to hold *Herod* on a curving course. Now she deliberately straightened the rearmost pair of fan nacelles, knowing that without their counteracting side-thrust momentum would swing the stern out. The gunner in the surviving APC slammed three bolts into *Herod*'s turret at point-blank range; then the mass of the tank's starboard quarter swatted the light vehicle, crushing it and flinging the remains sideways like a can kicked by an armored boot.

Herod grounded hard, air screaming through the holes in her plenum chamber. "Get us outa here, Lahti!" Buntz ordered. "Go! Go! Go!"

Lahti was already tilting her fan nacelles to compensate for the damage. She poured on the coal again. Because they were still several meters above the floor of the swale, she was able to use gravity briefly to accelerate by sliding *Herod* toward the smoother terrain.

Buntz spun his cupola at maximum rate, knowing that scores of Brotherhood infantry remained somewhere in the grass behind them. A shower of buzzbombs could easily disable a tank. If *Herod*'s luck was really bad, well . . . the only thing good about a fusion bottle rupturing was that the crew wouldn't know what hit them.

The driver of an APC was climbing out of his cab, about all that remained of the vehicle. Buntz didn't fire; he didn't even think of firing.

It couldve been me. It could be me tomorrow.

Lahti maneuvered left, then right, following contours that'd go unremarked on a map but which were the difference between concealed and visible—between life and death—on this rolling terrain. When *Herod* was clear of the immediate knot of enemy soldiers, she slowed to give herself her time to diagnose the damage to the plenum chamber.

Buntz checked his own readouts. Half the upper bank of sensors on the starboard side were out, not critical now but definitely a matter for replacement before the next operation.

The point-blank burst into the side of the turret was more serious. The bolts hadn't penetrated, but another hit in any of the cavities just might. Base maintenance would probably patch the damage for now, but Buntz wouldn't be a bit surprised if the turret was swapped out while the Regiment was in transit to the next contract deployment.

But not critical, not right at the moment. . . .

As Buntz took stock, a shell screamed up from the south. He hadn't heard Lieutenant Rennie call for another round, but it wasn't likely that a tank commander in the middle of a firefight would've.

Six or eight Brotherhood APCs remained undamaged, but this time their tribarrels didn't engage the incoming shell. It burst a hundred meters up, throwing out a flag of blue smoke. It was simply a reminder of the sleet of antipersonnel bomblets that *could* follow.

A mortar fired, its *choonk!* a startling sound to a veteran at this point in a battle. *Have they gone off their nuts?* Buntz thought. He set his tribarrel to air defense mode just in case.

Lahti twitched *Herod*'s course so that *Herod* didn't smash a stand of bushes with brilliant pink blooms. She liked flowers, Buntz recalled. Sparing the bushes didn't mean much in the long run, of course.

Buntz grinned. His mouth was dry and his lips were so dry they were cracking. *In the long run, everybody's dead. Screw the long run.*

The mortar bomb burst high above the tube that'd launched it. It was a white flare cluster.

"All personnel of the Flaming Sword Commando, cease fire!" an unfamiliar voice ordered on what was formally the Interunit Channel. Familiarly it was the Surrender Push. When a signal came in over that frequency, a red light pulsed on the receiving set of every mercenary in range. *"This is Captain el-Khalid, ranking officer. Slammers personnel, the Flaming Sword Commando of the Holy Brotherhood surrenders on the usual terms. We request exchange and repatriation at the end of the conflict. Over."*

"All Myrtle and Lamplight units!" Lieutenant Rennie called, also using the Interunit Channel. *"This is Myrtle Six. Cease fire, I repeat, cease fire. Captain el-Khalid, please direct your troops to proceed to high ground to await registration. Myrtle Six out."*

"Top, can we pull into that firebase while they get things sorted out?" Lahti asked over the intercom. *"I'll bet we got enough time to patch those holes. I don't want to crawl all the way back leaking air and scraping our skirts."*

"Right, good thinking," Buntz said. "And if there's not time, we'll make time. Nothing's going to happen that can't wait another half hour."

Herod carried a roll of structural plastic sheeting. Cut and glued to the inside of the plenum chamber, it'd seal the holes till base maintenance welded permanent patches in place. Unless the Brotherhood had shot away all the duffle on the back deck, of course, in which case they'd borrow sheeting from another of the vehicles. It wouldn't be the first time Buntz'd had to replace his personal kit, either.

They were within two klicks of the Government firebase. Even if they'd been farther, a bulldozed surface was a lot better to work on. Out here you were likely to find you'd set down on brambles or a nest of stinging insects when you crawled into the plenum chamber.

As Lahti drove sedately toward the firebase, Buntz opened his hatch and stuck his head out. He felt dizzy for a moment. That was reaction, he supposed, not the change from chemical residues to open air.

Sometimes the breeze drifted a hot reminder of the battle past Buntz's face. The main gun had cooled to rainbow-patterned gray, but heat waves still shimmered above the barrel.

Lahti was idling up the resupply route into the firebase, an unsurfaced track that meandered along the low ground. It'd have become a morass when it rained, but that didn't matter any longer.

There was no wire or berm, just the circle of bunkers. Half of them were now collapsed. The Government troops had been playing at war; to the Brotherhood as to the Slammers, killing was a business.

Lahti halted them between two undamaged bunkers at the south entrance. Truck wheels had rutted the soil here. There was flatter ground within the encampment, but she didn't want to crush the bodies in the way.

Buntz'd probably have ordered his driver to stop even if she'd had different ideas. Sure, they were just bodies; he'd seen his share and more of them since he'd enlisted. But they could patch *Herod* where they were, so that's what they'd do.

Lahti was clambering out her hatch. Buntz made sure that the Automatic Defense Array was shut off, then climbed onto the back deck. He was carrying the first aid kit, not that he expected to accomplish much with it.

It bothered him that he and Lahti both were out of *Herod* in case something happened, but nothing was going to happen. Anyway, the tribarrel was still in air defense mode. He bent to cut the ties holding the roll of sheeting.

"Hey, Top?" Lahti called. Buntz looked at her over his shoulder. She was pointing to the nearest bodies. The Government troops must've been running from the bunkers when the first mortar shells scythed them down.

"Yeah, what you got?" Buntz said.

"These guys," Lahti said. "Remember the recruiting rally? This is them, right?"

Buntz looked more carefully. "Yeah, you're right," he said.

That pair must be the DeCastro brothers, one face-up and the other face-down. They'd both lost their legs at mid-thigh. Buntz couldn't recall the name of the guy just behind them, but he was the henpecked little fellow who'd been dodging his wife. Well, he'd dodged her for good. And the woman with all her clothes blown off; not a mark on her except she was dead. The whole Quinta County draft must've been assigned here.

He grimaced. They'd been responsible for a major victory over the rebels, according to one way of thinking.

Buntz shoved the roll of sheeting to the ground. "Can you handle this yourself, Lahti?" he said. He gestured with the first aid kit. "I can't do a lot, but I'd like to try."

The driver shrugged. "Sure, Top," she said. "If you want to."

Recorded music was playing from one of the bunkers. Buntz's memory supplied the words: *"Arise, children of the fatherland! The day of glory has arrived. . . ."*

Sea Air

BY NINA KIRIKI HOFFMAN

Nina Kiriki Hoffman's first solo novel, *The Thread That Binds the Bones* (1993), won the Bram Stoker Award for first novel; her second novel, *The Silent Strength of Stones* (1995), was a finalist for the Nebula and World Fantasy Awards. *A Red Heart of Memories* (1999), part of her Matt Black series, nominated for a World Fantasy Award, was followed by sequel *Past the Size of Dreaming* in 2001. Much of her work to date is short fiction, including the Matt Black novella "Unmasking" (1992), nominated for a World Fantasy Award, and the Matt Black novelette "Home for Christmas" (1995), nominated for the Nebula, World Fantasy, and Sturgeon Awards. In addition to writing, Hoffman teaches a short story class at a community college, works part-time at a B. Dalton bookstore, and does production work on *The Magazine of Fantasy and Science Fiction*. Nina's next YA novel, *Spirits That Walk in Shadow*, will be published by Viking in 2006, and her next adult novel, *Fall of Light*, will be published by Ace in 2007.

Hoffman wrote the first draft of "Sea Air" many years ago. "I visited my friends Kim Antieau and Mario Milosevic," she said, "who at that time lived in a tiny Oregon coast town called Bandon. We walked to the beach one night, between huge hedges of gorse—an imported plant from Scotland that people said grew so rapidly and oilily it had twice caused the town to burn down; in fact, there used to be a Phoenix Festival in Bandon every year to celebrate the town rising from its ashes. I found the night quite spooky. We had to carry big sticks to fend off roaming Doberman pinschers. The atmosphere started the story working in my brain."

Hoffman lives in Eugene, Oregon.

"**It's like Michael's** allergic to seawater," Mom said. She offered Lizzie a plate of chocolate chip cookies, and Lizzie grabbed two.

"Shut up," Michael muttered.

For the eighth time in thirteen years, he and his adopted parents had moved into a new house in a new town. For the eighth time in thirteen years, Michael had to start life over, find new friends.

Mom didn't make it easy.

Lizzie lived in the house next door, but right now she was sitting on the couch in the new living room between Mom and Michael. Lizzie looked about sixteen, Michael's age. She had frizzy brown hair, yellow-brown eyes, and a wide, friendly smile; she wore a baggy brown sweatshirt, tight jeans, and duck shoes. The hem of one of her pantlegs had crept up. Michael saw she wore socks with animal tracks on them.

The moving van had unloaded everything the night before and left. Michael and his parents had been so tired after driving to Random, on the Oregon coast, from central Idaho that they had only unpacked enough things to sleep on last night. This morning they'd walked to the beach, then come home and worked all morning to set up the house the way Mom had planned it back in Idaho with a graph paper layout and little paper cutouts of the furniture.

After Dad and Mom and Michael had unrolled the carpets, set up the furniture, and put things away, Lizzie had appeared on the front stoop, hands buried in her pockets, questions in her mouth. Dad had met Lizzie before he raced off to meet his local boss for a sales lunch.

Lizzie balanced a teacup and saucer on her knee. She smelled like vanilla. She snitched a third chocolate chip cookie from the plate Mom had set on the coffee table.

"It's funny, because Michael came from a coast town, which is about all we know about his life before we adopted him. We've never lived in a seaside town before," Mom continued. "I love the beach. But I took Michael there this morning, and he wouldn't go near the water."

Lizzie turned her gaze to him. "Why not?"

"I don't know. It just bothers me." Michael didn't mention the way his flesh crept, the strange shuddery feeling of not wanting even the wet breeze on his skin. The rolling rush of waves had terrified him. He had felt as though fingers of sea were seeking him.

"When he was little, he was like that about *all* water. When we first adopted him, it took both his father and me to get him into the bathtub, and he was only three years old."

"Shut up," Michael whispered under his breath. He loved Mom, but why did she have to tell everybody weird stuff about him before he'd had a chance to make his own first impressions?

"Don't worry," Mom said. "He bathes regularly now."

"I can tell," said Lizzie. She smiled at him.

"Mo-om," said Michael.

Mom smiled—the tender look that frustrated him because it made him feel like he couldn't get mad at her. She had done so much for him, how could he even think about being angry with her?

"Right," she said. "I'm talking too much. Lizzie, what's your favorite subject in school?"

"Mo-om," Michael muttered again.

"My favorite subject isn't at school," said Lizzie. "My uncle's a marine biologist, and sometimes I get to go out to sea with him. I want to be a marine biologist when I grow up. Hey, Mike, what do *you* like?"

Of all the dorky conversations to have with his mother in the room. But if his mother wasn't in the room, what would they end up talking about? Probably nothing. Michael was a master of the uncomfortable silence, even though he didn't want to be. "Music," he said.

"Oh? That's cool. I've been taking flute lessons, but I never practice. Do you listen to music, play it, or both?"

"Both." He hoped she wouldn't ask him about his favorite bands. He had a very small CD collection, all of them by people most kids his age had never heard of. He was picky about music. He earned the money to buy CDs by babysitting, mowing lawns, whatever work he could drum up from neighbors. He spent hours at the CD store listening to whatever was open, and only bought CDs when he liked all the tracks. He couldn't pinpoint why he liked the things he liked, which ranged from thirties blues albums to compilations of Celtic music in languages he didn't speak.

"What instrument do you play?" Lizzie asked.

"Just piano. Not very well."

Mom sighed. "We had a piano a couple years ago, but when we

moved, we couldn't bring it with us. Michael's had to make do with singing and pennywhistles. Does the high school have piano practice rooms, Lizzie?"

"No, all the funds for the arts got cut." Lizzie sipped tea. "Hey. How about this, though? Mrs. Plank, two houses past mine, has a piano. She never plays, but she might let you practice on it. She's pretty nice unless you step on her flowers."

Michael looked at Mom. It had been so long since he'd played a piano he was afraid his hands had forgotten everything he knew.

"Okay," said Mom, "we'll bake some cookies and go visit. Do you know if she likes cookies, Liz?"

"It's never come up in conversation," said Lizzie. "She's not the type to invite people over. Mostly she just says, 'Lizzie, you have a well-behaved dog, not like some people I could name,' and 'Has the mailman come by yet?' "

"We can but try," Mom said. It was one of the ways they met new neighbors, at least in towns where they planned to stay for a while. Mom baked a big batch of cookies. They made up gift plates and dropped them off at nearby houses in the evening when people were home from work and school. It was a quick way to take the emotional temperature of a neighborhood.

Dad never came with them on these expeditions. Michael used to think this was because he wasn't interested, but lately, now that Michael was six feet tall, he noticed that doors didn't open as easily to him and Mom. Dad was a big man. Maybe Dad thought he would scare the neighbors. When Dad was home, he did all right with the neighbors, once Mom and Michael had made first contact and invited them over for backyard barbecues or card games or shared video rentals.

Michael had taught himself to slouch.

"How'd you find out about Mrs. Plank's piano?" Michael asked Lizzie. His fingers were already twitching.

"I saw it when I trick-or-treated at her house."

"We can but try," Mom said again. She watched Michael's fingers play inaudible scales on the couch cushions. "I didn't realize how much you missed it, hon. If this doesn't work, we'll find another way."

"Well," said Lizzie, "aside from not playing the piano, what do you do for fun?"

"Read," Michael said. Oh no. Way to brand himself as an utmost geek. He needed a save. "Walk around and look at things." Jeez, almost as dorky.

"Do you walk at night?"

"Sure."

"Don't do that here. Lots of people have big dogs here, and they let them loose at night."

"Aren't there any leash laws?" Mom asked.

Lizzie frowned. "Well, that's the thing. People are encouraged to let the dogs loose at night, because there's other things that come out at night." She sucked on her lower lip, then said, "Okay, we don't usually mention this so soon after you get here, but I like you guys, so I'm going to tell you right up front. Things come up through the gorse at night. They make noises. They do nasty things. Stay inside, okay? People disappear at night. If anybody asks, we say the riptides carried them away, but that's not what happens. We lose people here every year."

"Heavens," said Mom. "You're not pulling our leg, are you, Liz?"

"I'm not serious about much, but I'm serious about this. Michael, Mrs. Welty, don't leave the house after dark, unless it's to go to your car and drive someplace with lights around it, like the supermarket or a restaurant. Don't let Mr. Welty wander around after dark either, okay?"

"You went trick-or-treating," Michael said.

"Halloween's different. All the kids go out in big groups, and we make a lot of noise, and take dogs and grownups with weapons with us. We scare the Strangers off that night."

Michael and Mom exchanged glances.

Lizzie set her teacup on the coffee table and stood, dusting off her pants. "Ignore me if you want," she said in a flattened tone.

"No, wait, Lizzie," Michael said. He followed her to the front door. "Give us another chance. We're new. We don't know what's going on around here. Thanks for warning us."

Lizzie turned the front doorknob, paused with the door open. She stared at him without expression for what felt like ten minutes, then, finally, smiled. "Hey. I'll take you to the library. How about that?"

"That would be great."

Lizzie darted back and grabbed another handful of cookies. "Thanks, Mrs. Welty."

"You're welcome. Thank you for the introduction to the neighborhood. I'm going to bake now, kids. Michael, be home before five, okay?"

"Sure, Mom."

Michael left his bedroom window open a crack that night. He lay in the dark and listened to the pulse of the waves beating against the sand. It took him a long time to fall asleep. The waves' murmur terrified and thrilled him, the same way the smell of the salty air here had affected him when Dad had turned the station wagon off the highway and into town. He had smelled and tasted the sea, and his heart speeded; his skin tingled, hairs rising, bumps goosing. Even now, two blocks from the ocean, sea sound, sea scent kept him awake.

Was there a voice under the surface of sound, whispering his name?

Dogs barked in the street outside. He turned over and put the pillow over his head. More barking in the distance, and then the sound of a chase.

A town where he and Mom couldn't go out after dark? One of the things they did to learn about new communities was to wander the streets in the dark and study uncurtained windows, talking over the lives they glimpsed. Living rooms with lots of pictures of family on the walls always gave Michael a strange lost feeling; he hadn't told Mom about that. They had a few pictures of the three of them on the wall at home, mostly taken when Michael was six, seven, eight. Nothing recent. Dad was gone so much, traveling his sales territory, signing up new accounts, servicing the old ones. He was so successful the company kept moving him into territories where other people had failed. In fact, he had already gone on another trip, leaving Michael and Mom to unpack. They were used to that.

Once while she was talking to Dad on the phone, Mom had said it didn't matter if they moved with him, since he was never home anyway. Then she had gasped and covered her mouth with her hand, glanced at Michael to see if he had heard. He pretended he was so engrossed in his comic book he hadn't, but it had haunted his mind ever since.

Only the three of them, together, more or less, everywhere they went. No pictures of Mom's or Dad's parents, siblings, cousins, aunts, uncles. Were Mom and Dad orphans too?

"Michael," a voice whispered at his window.

Michael sat up. Who—

"Michael."

It was hard to recognize a whisper. Who did he know in Random who wasn't already in the house with him? Only Lizzie, and a few people she had introduced him to. Lizzie said she never went out at night. Was that just a dodge to keep Mom from suspecting that Lizzie wanted to invite Michael out for a midnight walk?

"Lizzie?"

"Michael."

Michael pulled on his robe and crept to the window. "Lizzie?"

The window slid wide and a face peered at him over the sill.

In the semidarkness, he couldn't really see the face, but he smelled a wet, salt, fish smell, nothing like Lizzie's vanilla scent.

"No," whispered the face.

"Who are you?" Michael took two steps back, reached for a weapon. He couldn't find a thing. Most of his possessions were still in boxes. The floor was chill under his feet; a worm of cold twisted in his stomach. Something about the person, the face, the whispering voice, something was not right.

"A friend."

"Come back during the day if you're really my friend," Michael said. He darted forward and slammed the window shut, then ran out into the hall, slamming his bedroom door behind him.

His mother rushed out of her room. "What's the matter?"

"Something at my window," he said, his breathing ragged.

"Should we call the police?" She took his arm and tugged him toward the master bedroom.

"I don't know."

Mom dragged Michael into her room and shut and locked the door, then got the baseball bat from the floor beside her bed. Her breathing was harsh in the darkness. "Tell me," she said.

"It was a person, Mom. I left my window open a crack, and someone called me. Whispered my name. Mom. . . ."

He felt her hand tremble on his arm. "All the doors are locked, right?" she asked.

He nodded. When Dad wasn't home, which was most nights, it was Michael's job to check every door and window before he and Mom went to bed, and he had never forgotten since the night they had a break-in, back when they were living in Los Angeles. Everything was so much scarier when Dad wasn't home. Someone had come into their apartment, but Michael had heard him and run to Mom's room, where they locked themselves in the bathroom and screamed until one of the neighbors beat on the wall and another called the police. By the time they came out of the bathroom the intruder had fled. He had taken Mom's jewelry box, but he hadn't taken anything else.

The jewelry box was where Mom had kept the things that reminded her of her life before. Michael remembered playing with her "pretties" when he was a little kid. She had let him take one piece of jewelry out at a time and look at it. She had had a charm bracelet with tiny gold sea creatures on it, some of them as strange as monsters from outer space. His favorite of all the things she had had, gone now.

Ever since, Michael had been compulsive about checking doors and windows nightly, sometimes checking three or four times to make sure. On nights when he felt particularly restless, he had to get up after a while and check again. Tonight he remembered the particulars; it was always that way in a new house the first few times he made his rounds.

"The doors were all locked. My window was only open an inch," he said. "There was this voice."

"The voice of a person who knew your name?"

"Yes. He said 'Michael, Michael.' I asked if he was Lizzie, and he said no. He said he was a friend."

"Was it someone you met when you were out with Lizzie today? How did you know it was a man?"

"I'm not sure." He thought back to the day they had just had. Lizzie had taken him to the library, where they met her least favorite librarian, and then over to Bob's Burger Grill, where she said the high school kids went after school, and sometimes during school. She had introduced him to Bob, a genial bearded man who had welcomed him to the community and shook his hand so hard his fingers felt crushed. After he squished Michael's hand, Bob had introduced Michael to a few of the kids in the restaurant, most of whom had acted completely not interested.

Lizzie told Michael later that most of the kids their age were gone for the summer. Off for obligatory time with noncustodial parents, summer camp, visiting relatives, camping, Disneyland—everybody was trying to get in one last spree before September crashed down on them. Everybody still in town was some kind of loser.

Michael had carefully avoided looking at Lizzie when she said that. They were climbing onto their bikes, anyway, so he had an excuse to focus on something else. They rode half a block before she burst out laughing and nudged his shoulder. "You were supposed to give me this look," she said, "or make an L on your forehead, you know? You're no fun!"

"Oh, yes I am!" He surprised himself and her with how loudly he spoke. He had lived in too many different places, started over too many times. He knew these early impressions set in cement, locked around his feet; he'd be dragging them around with him the rest of the time he lived here, especially if they only stayed half a year. He wouldn't have time to change people's minds. "Well, okay, that's no way to prove it," he said, "so never mind. Give me another shot."

"Maybe," Lizzie said in a teasing voice. "Anyway, everybody at Bob's was in the Ick Clique today. I'd introduce you to some of my real friends, but they're all gone this weekend. Let's go to the beach."

"The beach," Michael muttered.

Lizzie, ahead of him, had glanced back. "Oh, yeah. Your mom said you don't like the beach, huh? We could just go to the park and *look* at the beach."

"Okay."

They rode on a pitted street between looming, dusty hedges of yellow-flowered scotch broom. She took him to a wayside where tourists' cars could pull over and people could look at the beach without going down to it. There were wonderful standing stones on Random Beach, many like giant black teeth sticking up out of the sand and the water, a rock with an arch in it that looked like a *Star Trek* prop for a dimensional portal, another flat rock a little way offshore covered with fat slug-shaped creatures Lizzie told him were sea lions.

Then, of course, there was the water.

He had thought he'd be all right, standing on the cliff above the sea, far out of the reach of waves. The gulls cried as they circled in the air above, or swooped down to search tourist garbage. The waves whooshed, foaming, to the shore, then pulled away again. People walked and ran on the sand below, some tossing things for dogs to chase. Lizzie had pushed past him and taken a path out along the tops of some rocks, but Michael stayed at the viewpoint and just watched the water, wondering why he was afraid of it.

A thud had tripped in his chest, a thump, then another, slow footprints of something walking through him. His sight wavered: the sun-shod surface of the water vanished, and beyond it he saw—curls and currents, abysses and clouds, depths and darkness and flying creatures, a whole hollow world outlined by sound pulses—

He rubbed his eyes furiously until he could open them and not see it. "Lizzie!" he had yelled. "I'm going home!"

She had come back then, and they rode home.

He hadn't spoken to anyone but her at the wayside.

Nobody from their visit to Bob's would consider him a friend yet, right? He doubted anybody he had met there would even remember his name. Well, except maybe Bob. Bob had a great memory for names, Lizzie said. Was Bob the type to cruise around after dark and speak to people through barely open windows? Michael didn't think so, but he didn't even know the guy.

"I don't think it was anyone I met today," he told his mother.

She picked up her baseball bat. "You get the big flashlight. Let's go check it out."

He got the four-cell flashlight from her closet. They crept through the house in darkness, Michael going a little ahead of his mother. With her at his back, he wasn't so afraid, even though he knew that didn't make a lot of sense. Well, she had the baseball bat.

They eased open his bedroom door and waited, staring toward the pale square of curtained window beyond his bed. No sounds. No voice. They sneaked up to his window and looked out. Ambient light revealed that there was nothing outside but dark lawn and bushes.

Michael switched on the flashlight, opened the window, leaned out. Footprints patterned the soft dirt of the empty flowerbed below. He swept the beam over the dirt. Something was wrong with the footprints.

Mom leaned out the window beside him. "That's odd," she said.

"What is?" Michael focused the light on one clear print.

"The toes," said Mom. "They're—they're too long, and what's that between them?"

They stared at the ground. Michael moved the light, shifting the shadows, and the strangeness in the footprint vanished.

"We'll look at it tomorrow," Mom said. "For tonight, let's lock the window, and you spend the night in my room."

He lay on the floor in his parents' bedroom, zipped into his mummy bag, and stared at the ceiling. Mom had left one light on. She tossed and turned in the bed. They didn't speak. He wasn't sure whether she slept before dawn lightened the windows beyond her curtains, but he knew he didn't.

Morning came. They headed for different bathrooms, then went to his room again together.

When they opened the window to look out, the soil of the flower bed had been swept clean.

"We could board up your window," Mom said as she buttered toast.

"I couldn't live in a room with boarded-up windows." He always felt restless and panicky in enclosed spaces.

"Well, okay, put shutters on them. You could open those during the day."

"We could do what Lizzie says everybody else here does. Get a dog."

Mom sat at the table across from him. Michael ate a big bite of cereal. He knew he should have kept his mouth shut on that particular topic. Mom was giving him the thousand-yard stare she always unleashed when he mentioned something unforgivable. He had asked for a dog many times over the years. She had gotten tired of telling him that they moved too much.

Finally, Michael said, "Okay. How about a burglar alarm?"

"Stronger locks. Let's go to the hardware store and get stronger locks. I'll get you a baseball bat of your own, too. I guess the other thing would be that for now, you sleep in my room."

"Ouch," he said. His back hurt this morning. A hot shower had helped, but not enough.

"We could pick up an air mattress for you."

"What about talking to the police?"

"There's no evidence that anyone was ever here."

"We could ask them if there's peeping Toms."

Mom turned away, munched meditatively on a corner of toast. She never liked to talk to police. "How about we go to the Chowder House for lunch and talk to Gracie?" she said. Gracie was the restaurant manager. Mom had met Gracie when she and Dad drove over from Idaho to buy the house. "Gracie knows everything."

"Okay," Michael said.

Lizzie went with them to lunch. She said she was a chowder hound. Michael was glad she was still speaking to him after spending an afternoon with him.

"Gotta have the slumgullion," Lizzie said when a waitress named Dani had seated them at a picnic table by the window. All the tables at the Chowder House were picnic tables, with benches. They could seat at least twelve people. Often in the height of summer, strangers sat together, Lizzie said. She liked that part. She'd met people from Pittsburgh and Montreal and Florida. Maybe one of her hobbies was collecting out-of-towners, Michael thought.

"What's slumgullion?" Mom asked.

"Chowder with a bunch of shrimp thrown in."

Michael ordered a cheeseburger and fries when Dani came back. Mom and Lizzie ordered slumgullion and garlic toast.

"Come on, Michael, gotta taste it," Lizzie said, holding out a spoonful of her chowder to him.

"Michael doesn't care for seafood," said Mom.

"Sure, has he ever tried it? Are you one of those guys who looks at something and says, 'Never had it, don't like it'?"

He grinned at her because he knew he had said that.

"Open your mouth."

His insides squirmed at the thought of sharing a spoon with her. On the other hand, she was a girl he liked, and maybe her willingness to share her spoon was a sign she liked him back. He opened his mouth and accepted the spoon.

The dense white flavor burst across his tongue: cream and potato and melted butter, but more than that, the chewy, salty meat of the clams, the slightly squeaky texture of the shrimp, and something else, something primal that made him gasp after he had swallowed. He wanted more. He felt as though he had found the One True Food. He grabbed Lizzie's bowl and drank from it, emptied it in rapid swallows, set it down, and licked the last of the chowder from his lips.

"Michael!" Mom said. Lizzie stared at him, wide-eyed.

The flavor opened something inside him, a pulsing feeling in his center that reached outward to his skin, a second heartbeat that pumped power through him. After a moment it subsided. He shook his head. "No," he said. Then, "Oh, God. I'm sorry, Lizzie. You were right, I never had that before. I didn't know how much I'd like it. I'm sorry. You want the rest of my burger?"

"I can order more," she said, her voice doubtful. "You want more?"

"I don't think I better." It was too intense. Plus, what had that weird reaction been? A heart attack? The roaring appetite for more scared him. He had to ignore it, the way he ignored other things.

He took a bite of cheeseburger to chase the chowder taste out of his mouth, and the world settled back to normal.

Lizzie ordered another bowl of slumgullion but didn't offer him any. He tried not to smell it from across the table. His stomach wasn't hungry, but something in him was.

They had reached the crumbs-and-cold-salty-ends-of-fries stage of their meal when Gracie slid onto the bench beside Mom. "Howdy, Caroline. How you doing?"

"I'm glad you asked," said Mom. "We were wondering about something."

"Yeah? What?"

"Do you get a lot of peeping Toms in this town? Liz warned us about this yesterday, but we weren't sure. Someone came right up to Michael's window last night and spoke to him."

Gracie and Lizzie flinched.

"I thought peeping Toms were only interested in watching women,"

Mom went on. "But Michael's light was already out when this one approached the house. So watching doesn't seem to be the motive. What did it say to you, Michael?"

"It said my name, and that it was a friend."

"It left bare footprints in the flower bed, but when we went back to look this morning, they were gone. Is this a common occurrence around here?"

"It spoke to you?" Gracie asked after a moment of uneasy silence.

"Yeah," said Michael.

"They don't usually talk."

"What do they usually do?" Mom asked.

"They hiss until you run for a shotgun, and then they slip off. If you go outside to chase them, though . . ."

"What?" asked Mom. "Michael and I are often alone in the house, and we need to know how to protect ourselves."

"Don't ever leave the house at night," Gracie said. "They can't hurt you if you don't go out to them."

"Who are they, Gracie?"

"The Strangers."

"The Strangers," Mom repeated. "What's that supposed to mean?"

"People disappear every year," Gracie said. She glanced around, as if looking for listeners. "We blame the tide. It's usually the newcomers who vanish. We try to warn everybody, but most don't take us serious."

"What are the Strangers?" asked Mom.

"Don't rightly know," said Gracie. "Anybody who really knows is gone. Been a plague on the town for ages. One came to my window when I was a girl. Thought it was my boyfriend, and almost went outside, but glory be, my mother stopped me. They haven't come by my house in twenty years. They always know when someone new moves in, though."

"So you have this conversation a lot?"

"Try to," said Gracie.

"Does anybody ever do anything about these Strangers?"

"Not anymore. Had a sheriff back in the seventies who tried to ambush 'em. Set up traps, with guns and dogs and floodlights. They never came, no matter where he set up. Always knew somehow. Minute he moved the trap away from a newly occupied house, they'd show up and hiss at people if they left a window open, even a crack."

"As long as we stay in the house, we're safe?"

"Far as I know," Gracie said.

"How about yard lights?" Michael asked. "Motion detectors?"

Gracie shrugged. "Couldn't hurt. But nobody I've ever talked to has caught a clear sight of them, even with good lights. They move like shadows."

"Nobody knows what they are? Nobody? And you just go on living here?" Mom asked.

Gracie shrugged. "Whatcha gonna do? We know how to deal. So there are Strangers around and they hiss at you. Occasionally a chihuahua or a cat disappears. We still got the beach and the tourist trade and the balmy weather. And the threat of the Strangers cuts way down on petty crimes; burglars don't go out at night around here. Now you know, and you can be safe here, too. All right?"

Mom beat her fingers in a gallop on the tabletop, staring at the bucket of saltines on the table. Her mouth firmed. "I guess," she said. "But we're getting those lights anyway."

"Don't sleep with the windows open," Lizzie told Michael.

It wasn't a hiss, he thought, but he didn't say anything.

At the hardware store, he bought some plaster of Paris and threepenny nails. Together he and his mother bought fancy new yard lights with motion detectors to turn them on. They picked up an inflatable bed and a foot pump, too. Lizzie showed them where the baseball bats were, and Mom bought a nice heavy aluminum one so Michael would be armed too. "But you won't be able to hit them," Lizzie said. "Nobody ever has."

"What do they want?"

Lizzie shook her head. "Just treat it like bad weather you won't go out in. Shadow weather. That's all. We have the day, and that's enough."

Back home, Michael and Mom rigged the lights and the motion detectors. They inflated the new bed, and Michael lay on it, bounced on it, wondered if he could sleep on it. Better than the floor, anyway.

Michael took his bag of supplies, went into his room, and threw the window all the way open. It was still afternoon; he was safe enough. Cool salty air blew in, ruffling the curtains and fluttering the edges of the comic books on his desk. Outside, sunlight shone, bright and cold. A bird he didn't recognize called a sharp sweep of notes.

Lizzie had followed him into his room.

"It spoke to you?" she muttered. "Never heard of that before."

He set the jar of nails on the windowsill and went to get the hammer. Maybe if he nailed the window so it couldn't open more than an inch— sound could travel in and out of his room, but the thing couldn't come in after him.

"It said it was a friend?" Lizzie asked.

"I thought maybe it was you."

"That's crazy. I don't go out after dark."

He slid the window almost shut and positioned the nails on the sill above it. He wasn't ready to make the change yet, though. It was still broad daylight. He put the nails back in the jar. "Except on Halloween."

"Right."

"But they never go in houses."

Lizzie came and stared at the small dimples he had pressed into the paint of the windowsill with the tips of the nails, marking the places he planned to hammer them into later. "It's better if the window's closed all the way."

"I want to hear what it has to say."

"You don't."

"How do you know, if they've never talked to people before?"

"What if they have? What if they talked to the people who went outside at night and never came home? What if that happens to you? I don't want that to happen to you." She paced around the room, picked up one of the superhero comics from his desk, put it down. "See," she said, "I want you to be my neighbor. The last people who lived here were awful. I was so glad when they moved away. Then when I saw you guys moving in yesterday—I thought . . ." She paced between the door, the desk, and the bed, avoiding the stacks of boxes. She kept her gaze directed at the rag rug on the floor. "Okay, you know, the other kids think I'm weird. You know?"

"Why?"

"Well, because I *am* weird. I like school. I read more than they do. I hate video games. I don't like shopping. I don't wear makeup. I don't have a cell phone. I like to dissect weird, smelly things I find on the beach." She paused, watched him, anxious. "Don't you think that's weird?"

"Yeah. So what?"

Some of the tension left her shoulders. "See. That's what I was hoping for. You're a little peculiar yourself, so I thought maybe we could get along. But if you start obsessing about the Strangers—I might lose you before I even find you." She turned her back on him. "God. I'm sorry to be so lame."

"What's lame about that?"

"I'm pretty sure I'm not supposed to talk about anything substantial until we've known each other for weeks and weeks."

"It's all right." Michael opened a box marked "Electronics" and rooted through stray electric cords and adapters and various small devices, some of them broken, until he came up with his handheld, voice-activated cassette recorder. There was a cassette in it already. He rewound it a little and listened, realized the last thing he had taped was an anime theme song from TV, and it was fuzzy and tinny. But the batteries were still good, and there was still half the tape to go. "I want to find out what it wants. I'll try to tape it tonight. It might not leave footprints, but maybe I can catch its voice."

"Okay," Lizzie said, her voice shaking a little. "If you can be scientific about it. But don't let it—hypnotize you."

He stared down at the tape recorder. "I want proof that it was even here." He dug the sack of plaster of Paris out of the hardware store bag and turned it to read the instructions. "If there *is* a footprint after it leaves, I want to make a cast before it comes back to wipe it away."

"Don't. You'd have to go outside at night to do it. Don't go outside like a walking all-you-can-eat buffet."

"Do you really think they're eating people? Did anybody ever find body parts left over?"

"No!" she cried. Then, "No," a little less certainly. "I don't know," she said at last. She paced faster, then glanced at him. "When I was eight, my best friend was this girl, Beth, who used to live in this house. That was before the horrible neighbors came. Her family wasn't local. We told them about the Strangers right after they moved here, but I could tell they didn't believe us. But nothing happened for a couple years, except Beth was my friend."

He watched her jitter across the room. She said, "She was just the greatest girl. Fearless. She ran everywhere. It was hard to keep up with her. She was excited about everything. When I was with her, I'd get all excited, too. She loved the beach. We went every day when the tide was out. She had books about sea life, and she taught me the names of things in tidepools. And then—well, she wanted to go to the beach at night, to see the phosphorescence she read about, where you stamp sand and it lights up. I kept telling her not to. But she didn't believe me."

Lizzie stopped, placed her hands flat on the window glass, her brows deeply furrowed. "I'm going to be a scientist. Then I'll figure out how to catch a Stranger. I'll study it and find out . . . what really happened to Beth."

Mom knocked on the open door. "Hey. Another batch of cookies is ready. I need some tasters to make sure they're safe. Any volunteers?"

Michael set the tape recorder on the windowsill and followed Lizzie to the kitchen.

There was just enough daylight left to take the plates of cookies around to the neighbors' houses. Lizzie went with them, another new experience for Michael, already knowing someone who lived here. Mom and Michael met Lizzie's parents: Lizzie's mother was short and wide, with the same frizzy brown hair and tawny brown eyes Lizzie had, and her father was tall, wispy, and washed-out looking, with pale blue eyes and thin, blond-gray hair.

Lizzie's mother smiled up at Michael. "Oh my," she said, her low, pleasant voice flavored with the honey tones of the south. "Now I see why Lizzie's been gone so much."

"Mo-om," said Lizzie in the same tone of voice Michael had used on his mother the day before.

"Aw, honey." Lizzie's mother patted Lizzie's shoulder. Michael couldn't help smiling back at her, feeling a strange confusion inside at what she seemed to be saying: Lizzie was interested in him, and Lizzie's mother didn't mind.

"I'm Caroline, and this is my son, Michael," Mom said. "I'm afraid my husband Dan is away. He travels a lot on business."

"I'm Rosie, and this is Wagner. Welcome to the neighborhood. Don't let Lizzie make a nuisance of herself. Send her on home if she's irritating you."

"On the contrary," said Mom. "She's terrific. It's like having a native guide."

"Mama, look, Caroline made cookies for you. They're great."

"You're a baker!" said Rosie. "Something we have in common! Well, Caroline, I'm so glad you and Michael are here now." Rosie peeled the

HandiWrap off the plate of cookies, offered them to Wagner, who took one, bit it, and grinned. "What a sweet way to say hello. I see you have other deliveries to make, though, so don't let us keep you. Stop by afterward for tea if you like."

"Or tomorrow," said Wagner. "Dark's coming on."

"Or tomorrow," Rosie repeated. "Lizzie will give you our phone number. Let's make a date."

"Thank you, I will."

They trooped round to every house on their block. Lizzie already knew everyone, and introduced them, but rushed them, too. They lingered only at Mrs. Plank's house, where Lizzie broached the subject of the piano almost before the introductions.

Mrs. Plank, gray-haired and stern-looking, pursed her lips and studied Michael. She nodded decisively. "Come in and give it a whirl, boy," she said, gesturing him in, then leading them all to the front parlor, a room with comfortable-looking couches, tall lamps over the armchairs, a futuristic fifties coffee table in aluminum and glass, and a baby grand piano painted white.

Michael checked with her again, and she nodded. He sat down on the piano bench and lifted the key cover, rested his fingers on the keys. "It's been two years," he said.

"I won't expect virtuosity, then."

He stared into her gray eyes, then looked down and let his fingers go. Chopin emerged, startling him: a waltz. He didn't remember practicing it, but there it was, in his hands' memory if not his mind's; he played through to the end without stumbling, took a deep breath, let it out, and met Mrs. Plank's gaze again.

She nodded. "Come by between three and four on weekday afternoons if you're so inclined."

He stood up. "Thank you."

"That's all right. Couldn't have stood it if you were a rank beginner, but I can put up with a lot of Chopin."

By the time they'd reached the final house across the street, the sun was streaking the clouds with rose and amber. The young couple greeted them, grabbed the cookies, and slammed the door almost in their faces.

"Yeah," Lizzie said, "better get home."

She separated from them in the street and dashed to her front door. Michael and Mom, infected by everyone's urgency, rushed home and locked themselves into the house.

A breeze was coming from Michael's room; he'd left the window wide. He went in and shut it almost all the way, then hammered the big nails into the sill so the window wouldn't open more than an inch, but he only tapped them in a half an inch so he could pry them out again tomorrow. He grabbed the cassette recorder, said, "Test. It's the night of August 26 in Random, and I'm maybe expecting company tonight. Anything further will be the voice of a Stranger, with any luck." He tossed the recorder on his bed and met Mom in the kitchen, where they put together dinner and verbally dissected their new neighbors.

"Despite the weird night stuff," Mom said, "I feel like this is the best neighborhood we've lived in for a long time."

"Me, too."

They spent the evening unpacking boxes in the living room and setting up the bookshelves in the hall. Mom made up the inflated bed on the floor in the master bedroom. "Brush your teeth and check the locks," she said. "I'm going to turn the lights out in about half an hour."

Another thing he didn't like about sharing a room. In his own room, he could read himself into exhausted sleep. "Can you leave a night light on for me? I have something to do first," he said.

"What?"

Should he tell her? She'd forbid him to try to tape the Strangers, he was pretty sure. It might be dangerous—though how it could be, when he had nailed the window shut, he wasn't sure. She wouldn't want to take chances even in the name of science and detection. "Just something."

She narrowed her eyes. "Leave the bedroom doors open."

He went through the house and checked every door and window to make sure they were closed tight and locked. He checked the stove: all the burners were off. Then he slipped into his bedroom, leaving the door ajar and the lights off, grabbed the little tape recorder, and sat on the rug by his bed, a couple feet from the window. He had left the curtains open. Cool, damp, salty air flowed in through the crack.

Time inched by. The curtains fluttered as a damp breeze played with them. Outside was faintly lit by an orange street light. What if the Strangers didn't come? What if it was all some big hoax, some weird way to welcome newcomers to town, scare the crap out of them and laugh later? Quite a collaboration, though, with Gracie in on it, and Lizzie, and everybody on the block who had hesitated to answer their knock tonight, then ducked back into their houses a little too quickly for politeness.

"Michael."

The silhouette of a head showed in the window against the copper-edged night. Michael startled, then pressed the Record button on the tape recorder.

"What?" he said in a low voice.

"Michael." It was a whisper. Maybe it was too faint for his recorder to pick up.

"What?"

"Come here."

"I don't think that's a good idea. People have been telling us about you."

"What did they say?"

Michael wished it would speak with a voice instead of a whisper. He couldn't tell if it was male or female.

"They said you're Strangers and you lure people to their deaths."

The shadow laughed. It turned sideways. Its profile was strange. Something spiky lay along the top of its head.

It turned back. "Sometimes we do," it said.

"What do you want with me? I don't want to go to my death."

"We want you to come home."

"What?"

"Come home, Michael. You've been so long away."

Cold crept through his gut, arrowed up his spine.

"We lost you long ago. We couldn't reclaim you until now. Come home, Michael."

"What are you saying?" Michael whispered. He crept closer to the window.

"Come outside and we will show you." Then it hissed something, louder than its whisper, but not a simple hiss, something that divided into syllables and tones. Galvanized, Michael straightened. A hiss, but words, and he could almost translate—

Another hiss, a stroke, a caress. His name, but not Michael.

"Come back to us," whispered the voice, followed by the hiss Michael almost recognized.

"Michael!" Mom's voice was a yell from his doorway.

Mom switched on the light, and Michael dropped the tape recorder. Something pale, with spots of green glow where eyes should be, stared in through the window at them; then it was gone.

He rewound the tape recorder at the kitchen table while Mom made cocoa.

There was a lot of hissing silence on the tape, interrupted by his own voice, saying, "What?" "What?" "I don't think that's a good idea. . . ."

"How could you?" Mom asked. "What were you thinking?"

"I wanted to find out what it wants."

"Why?" She brought filled mugs to the table, set one in front of him.

"What are you saying?" Michael's voice said from the tape recorder. A murmur that he could almost hear, and then a burst of hissing that was definitely loud enough to record—

"Is that its voice?" Mom asked.

"Shh!" Michael rewound and listened to the hisses again. Rewound, listened again. Again.

He pressed the stop button and sat with his hand on the tape recorder.

"What is it?" Mom asked.

The time and the chance for change has come again at last. Come back to us, Ssskzz. Come home.

Michael shook his head.

"That's it, isn't it? That hissing? Gracie was right. When I turned on the light and saw that face, oh my God, Michael, oh, my God, and you were *talking* to it?" The resurgence of her hysteria swept over them both. She had babbled like this just after she had looked into his room; it had taken him fifteen minutes to calm her. "We can't stay here. We can't stay here. No matter how nice the neighbors are, we can't stay here. It's a good thing we didn't finish unpacking. I'll get a U-Haul tomorrow morning and we'll head inland. We could go back to Idaho. Things like this never happened there, and our house hasn't sold yet. . . ."

"Mom," Michael said.

She took three gulps of cocoa and a few deep breaths. "I'm going to call your father." She went to the phone, stared at the itinerary Dan had printed out and taped on the wall before he left on his trip, and dialed. "Daniel Welty's room, please. . . . Hello? Who *is* this? What? What? Is Dan there? He is? Tell him it's his wife on the phone, and I don't care what kind of meeting he's in, I need to talk to him right now." She held the phone away from her ear and muttered, "Sales associate, my ass."

Michael turned down the volume on the recorder, rewound it, and played it again, holding it up to his ear. There were nuances in the words that a simple translation couldn't catch, a strain of loss, a thread of opportunity, a breath of hope and longing, a whisper of welcome.

"Don't even bother trying to explain, Dan. I don't care what bimbo you're with. Michael and I are in a crisis here. We can't stay in Random. We're moving tomorrow morning. What? No. Why does everything have to be about you?"

Michael stood up and eased out of the room. His mother's back was to him; he was sure she didn't notice he was gone. He went to the front door and slid the chain sideways, eased it off, then opened the deadbolt. He clicked up the pushbutton lock on the doorknob and stood, his hand wrapped around the doorknob, and waited.

How could he leave her? Dad had been leaving Mom more and more, in increments, leaving them both for longer trips, with shorter visits in between, moving them around like knights on a chessboard, then leaving them behind. Mom and Michael depended on each other. He couldn't leave her.

He had to find out what the Stranger had been talking about. Did it really know who he was, where he came from? Could it tell him? He had to—

The doorknob turned in his hand. He eased the front door open and stepped out onto the porch.

But what about Gracie, and Lizzie, and all the new neighbors? What about Mrs. Plank, and permission to play the piano? What about a whole town that knew it had strange neighbors, and worked around them? What if the Strangers really ate people, and everything it said had been designed to lure him out of the house and into the open air, where it could net him, gut him, and take his fillets home for its children to snack on?

What about Mom?

It stood to his left before he noticed its approach, a tall, shadowed figure that smelled strongly of fish and brine and dripped on the boards of the porch.

"Wait," he said. "I just want to talk."

"We want to free you," it whispered.

"From what?"

"From the chains of this limited existence. You've suffered enough."

"What do you mean? I'm not suffering."

"Aren't you? Trapped in this thin atmosphere that can't even support you? Glued feet downward to this dirt? Deaf to the feel of sounds? Come home, where every breath is a taste and every movement a touch. Come home. Your family longs for you."

"I can't leave Mom. I don't even know you. Everyone here says you hurt people. How can I trust you?"

"Look in your heart. Walk with us, Michael, and we will teach you how to fly."

"Michael," said another. He glanced over and saw a second shadow. Three more materialized at the foot of the front porch stairs. They all peered up at him, slender forms with wrong-shaped heads. He felt it, then, the beat of a second heart in his chest, the thud of another system inside. It started slowly, but it accelerated as he stood among them.

"Michael!" Mom screamed from inside the house. "Michael! Where are you? Michael!" She flung open the door, letting house light fan across the creatures, and then she screamed, a loud, high, mindless shriek, heavy with woe.

"Come. Come quickly," said the one beside him, as the others melted into the darkness.

"No," Michael said.

It touched his left hand, and its wet touch burned, seared him like magnified sunlight. The burning spread across the back of his hand, sank down into his flesh all the way to his bones. The pain was excruciating; tears spilled from his eyes to cool on his cheek.

The creature vanished. The pain faded too.

"Mom." Michael turned and pushed his mother back into the house, shut the door behind them.

"Michael." She clung to him and sobbed.

He held her with his right arm. "Come on, Mom. Come on." He walked her back to the kitchen, where the phone's handset hung from the wall, a voice still squawking from it.

Michael eased his mother into a chair and picked up the phone. "What is it?" cried his father's voice. "What's going on? Was that a scream? Caroline, are you all right?"

"Dad, I'm hanging up now," Michael said.

"No, wait! Wait, Michael! What's going on there? What's wrong with your mother?"

Michael cradled the handset and sat down in a chair facing his mother's. He took her hands. Her breath hitched. Her face was pale, and her hands trembled in his grasp. She stared down at their hands, snatched her right hand out of his grasp. He looked down.

His left hand had stopped burning, but it had changed. The skin had bleached from tan to shiny gray-blue, and its texture had gone from callused, with hairs on the backs of his biggest knuckles, to smooth, almost rubbery. Worst was what stretched between his fingers: drooping flaps of skin. He spread his fingers and watched the flaps tighten. His hand looked like an abbreviated bat wing; even his fingernails had changed, darkened and hardened into claws.

He gasped and shook his hand as though he could shed the change like a glove.

His mother had covered her face with her free hand, but she grasped his normal hand hard in her other hand. She was still crying. She straightened, lowered her concealing hand, caught a deep breath, hiccuped her way through a brief flurry of sobs, then rose from the chair and pulled him to the sink. "Maybe it'll wash off," she said. She gripped his altered hand and thrust it under a stream of warm tap water.

The flow of water across the new skin was strange and exciting. Its touch mesmerized him; he could feel the flutter of current, sense the braided pulses of it. He spread his fingers, and the soft water stroked across the webs between. He knew if he cupped his hand a certain way so that water would push on it, it would carry him—

Mom turned his hand under the water, scrubbed at it with dish soap and the soft side of a sponge. It didn't change. Gently he pulled his hand out of her grip and turned off the faucet, went to the cupboard, grabbed a glass, filled it with water, and handed it to her. She blinked tears, then drank half the glass. She offered him the rest. He took it in his good hand and drank, felt his own bumpy breathing grow steady again.

"Should we go to the hospital?" she asked him.

He hid his new hand behind his back, then sighed, pulled it forward, and stared down at it. He turned it so he could study the palm, spread his fingers. A few creases defined where it could bend, but the intricate whorls of his identity had been erased. He closed it into a fist. The extra skin made his fist into a new kind of gesture, bulbous, with pale pleats separating the fingers, not a hitting hammer but something else. Mom ran her fingertips over the outside of it, stroked the folds of new skin. He moaned with delight, and she stopped, startled, stared at him.

He hid the new hand behind his back again.

"Does it hurt?" she asked.

"Not anymore. Mom—the hospital—I don't know. I don't think it's that kind of injury."

The phone rang.

They stared at each other.

She swallowed. "Probably Dan," she said. "What do we tell him?"

His stomach churned. Had Dad really been with some woman when Mom called? What did it mean? Maybe it was innocent. It sounded like Dad had said it was. But he was gone so much. Family meant Mom and Michael now.

"It's up to us," he muttered.

Mom picked up the phone. "Hi," she said. "Oh! Hi. It's Rosie, Liz's mom," she told Michael, then spoke to the phone. "No, we're all right." She listened, covered the phone's pickup with her hand, spoke to Michael. "They heard me scream, but they couldn't come over. They tried to call, but the line was busy." She listened, her gaze on the ground. "Yes," she said. "They were here."

She listened. "Yes. Well, it's complicated. We don't understand it ourselves yet." She touched Michael's new hand, cupped her hand around it. "Maybe. We don't know. Yeah, thanks for calling. I appreciate it. Thanks. We'll talk to you tomorrow." She let go of Michael's hand, fetched the shopping list with its pencil on a string, and wrote something down. "Thanks, Rosie. Good night." She hung up.

They sat in silence side by side at the table. At last Mom sighed. "We never knew where you came from."

"You always said a coast town."

"Yeah. We didn't go through regular channels to get you. Dan and I had been trying for years to have a baby of our own, but we couldn't, even with medical help. One night one of Dan's friends came over. Uncle Mike, remember? He'd just got home from a sales trip. He had you with him. You were so solemn and quiet, and you had such big eyes. You were the most beautiful little boy. Mike said you were his nephew and your parents were dead, but he couldn't keep you, and he knew how much Dan and I wanted a baby. I just said yes, yes, yes, and you were ours. Dan handled the paperwork." She looked toward the stove, then shook her head. "Mike said you were born in Seaside. I always figured there was something suspicious in how he got you, but I didn't want to know. I wanted to keep you. But I was always afraid somebody would come after us and take you back. That's why I haven't minded moving so often. Guess our luck ran out this time."

She rested her hand on the back of his new hand. "How did this happen?"

"It touched me. It was wet. It burned."

"When they were hissing at you, could you really hear words in it?"

"Hissing?"

"Hissing. I was screaming, and I—but one of them made these hissing, clacking sounds before they all—and you answered."

"Hissing." He reached for the tape recorder. He rewound it and played the first thing the Stranger had said that he understood. *Come home.* "I do understand it." Had his whole conversation on the porch been in this language?

"Those are your people," Mom said, her voice incredulous. She laughed. And then she let out a little sob, and rubbed her eyes.

"Mom." He wrapped his right arm around her shoulders, hugged her.

She struggled, then subsided. "I'm so tired."

"Me, too."

———

Michael changed into pajamas in the bathroom. He studied his new hand. The change in his skin had traveled past his wrist, raggedly up his forearm; it was not as though a circle delineated one part of him from another. He ran water into the sink and flapped the new hand around in it. He felt vectors, movement, change, powers. Once both his hands were like this, he would be able to—

He drained the water quickly, brushed his teeth, slipped under the blankets on the air mattress in Mom's room. She turned out the light. "Please," she whispered in the darkness. "Don't leave without saying good-bye."

He thought about sneaking off to his room to talk to the Strangers, but eventually he slept instead.

When he opened his eyes, Mom was sitting near the mattress, hugging her knees and watching him. The curtains were open, and morning light slanted across the floor behind her, touched her graying hair and a small patch of her cheek and brow. She smiled when she saw he was awake.

"What are you doing?" he asked.

"It's a mother thing. How's your hand?"

He slid his left hand out from under the blankets, and they both studied it. It was still changed. He sat up, using both hands to balance. Together, they supported him. He glanced at Mom. Her face wore a mixture of sad and worried and tired.

"What do you want for breakfast?" she asked.

Usually she let him get his own breakfast. She only asked on special occasions, like on the birthday they'd chosen for him.

"Pancakes."

She stood. "Do you even have a swimsuit?"

He couldn't follow her mental jumps. "No." Open water had always terrified him.

"Guess you won't need one. I don't think they were dressed." She left the bedroom, and he got up, wondering. The new hand worked as well as the other one, with only a few minor awkwardnesses when he snagged his webs on things.

In the kitchen, she set a plate of pancakes in front of him, and he grabbed his knife and fork, then stared at the new hand. The fork didn't feel natural in it. He switched the fork to his right hand and used it to cut, abandoning the knife. He tried pouring syrup with his left hand, and managed to get most of it on the plate. Mom watched behind a blank face.

Lizzie knocked at the kitchen door when they were halfway through their first plates of pancakes. She stared in at them. Michael hid his hand in his lap as Mom got up to let Lizzie in.

"What happened last night? Are you all right?" Lizzie asked as she came inside. "Mama said you were okay, but I saw the Strangers on your porch. What happened? You're still here. Oh, God."

"Where do the Strangers come from, Liz?" asked Mom.

"The sea."

Mom's shoulders sagged. "Yesterday, you said the gorse."

"They come out of the water and hide in the gorse. That's what everybody says."

Mom sighed.

"What were they doing on your front porch last night? I've never seen so many in one place. We heard you scream."

"Do you want some breakfast, Liz?" Mom asked.

"I want some answers."

"Ask Michael. I have to go figure out where I packed the camera." She left.

Lizzie pulled out a chair and sat down beside him. "Hey," she said. "Come on. Tell me. What happened?"

"Mom's been weird ever since we woke up. I have to find out what's wrong with her." He pushed his chair back and stood up.

"Michael." Lizzie grabbed his wrist, then shrieked and released it. Then she grabbed it again, gripped it tight, pulled the new hand toward her, stared wide-eyed at the changes. "Michael!" she cried.

His throat closed. He couldn't breathe. He felt a ghostly fluttering on the sides of his neck, and then his throat unblocked, and he said, "I understand the Strangers. They talked to me, and I understood them. Mom couldn't. She thinks they're my real parents."

"What?" Lizzie stroked the back of his hand, uncurled his fingers, felt the web between them. "Your hand wasn't like this yesterday, was it? I would have noticed."

"One of them touched it, and that happened. But maybe that's what happens to anybody they touch." He wanted to pull away from Lizzie and go after Mom. Mom thought the Strangers were his real family. Mom thought—Mom assumed he was leaving with them. How could she think that? She was the one who had raised him. She was the person he loved best in all the world.

"I found it," Mom said. She raised the Polaroid. "Smile."

"Mom."

She snapped a picture, and the camera's motor raced as it spat it out. "Gotta try again, you weren't smiling. I know you hate having your picture taken, Michael, but won't you let me anyway, this time?"

"Sure." Heaviness sat in his chest, a hot, sour lump. He summoned up a smile for her. The camera flashed, leaving red ghosts across his vision. She dropped the pictures on the table and came to put her arms around him. He felt the silent sobs jerking through her.

"What makes you so sure I'm leaving with them?" he asked.

She shook her head against his chest. She took a deep breath, straightened, stepped away from him. "Orange juice?"

Lizzie still held his new hand. She stood uncertainly beside him, then put her own hand palm to palm with his. He could taste her skin with his hand, sense the blood flowing beneath its surface. There was a scent he didn't sense with his nose, something that meant Lizzie, everything about her; it came in through his palm, his fingers. How could that be? He felt like he would know her with his eyes closed now, just from a touch. Heat brushed his face. She wasn't running away in horror because of his deformity. He curled his fingers around her hand, and she clasped his. Then she let him go.

Mom studied the two Polaroids, then showed them to him. He grimaced. He hated pictures of himself; he always looked dorky and weird, not the way he imagined himself. In the first picture he looked irritated, his mouth halfway toward a word. Lizzie, beside him, was arrested midrise, and she, too, wore an expression between one emotion and the next.

In the second picture, he smiled too wide, and Lizzie stood beside him, holding onto his hand, smiling, too, a very fake smile that tried too hard and looked like a smirk.

"I'm such a lousy photographer," Mom said. "It's a curse. Liz, are you any good at this?"

"Actually, yeah." Lizzie picked up the camera. "The light's awful in here. Let's go outside."

They followed her out into the morning. It was a cool, sunny day, the sky high blue with hurrying clouds, the breeze damp and salt. "Stand together," said Lizzie. "Move sideways a little so the door isn't behind you. Yeah, that's good. The siding makes a better background, less distracting. Michael, do you want to show your hand?"

A peculiar heat pierced his chest. He shuddered, then shook his head. "Why not?" he said. He rested the new hand on his shirt below his collarbone, spread the fingers so the webs stretched. Mom stood to his right, the top of her head about level with his nose. When had she gotten so short? She leaned her shoulder against his right arm.

"Both of you, relax. Smile like you're thinking about your favorite dessert. That's good. Hold it. Hold it." Lizzie pressed the button, and the camera stuck out a picture like a tongue. "Okay. Another one just to make sure? Lean a little toward each other, relax, just smile." Michael put his arm around Mom's shoulders, hugged her to him. She reached across, rested her hand on his chest beside the new hand, her little finger overlapping his little finger. He felt heat behind his eyes, a tightening in his throat. "Good. In fact, that's great, you guys. Smile just a touch more. Hold it." The motor raced.

He and Mom sighed simultaneous sighs. Michael's shoulders sagged. Lizzie snapped the camera again without warning. "Well, that ought to do it—at least one of them will be good," she said.

"Thanks, Liz."

They went inside. Lizzie put the pictures, with their green-gray-blue windows of mystery, side by side on the table, away from the food. Michael picked up his fork, stared at his pancakes, now soggy with syrup, and set the fork down again.

"Do you want more?" Mom stood by the stove, one hand around the handle of the batter pitcher, the other ready to move the frying pan back over the heat.

Michael shook his head.

"Is it time?" she asked.

"Time for what?"

"Time to go to the beach."

"Mom."

She rubbed her eye with her knuckle. "You know that's coming."

"I don't."

"You can't—" She pointed to his new hand. "I love you."

"I know, Mom."

"If that's who you really are—"

"I don't even know those guys."

"Something in you does."

He stood up, a rage of confusion inside, and slammed out of the kitchen in search of his jacket. When he found it—saw the little heart pin on the left side that Debbie, a girl he knew in school in Idaho, had pinned on his jacket when they'd gone to some dance last year—he was so angry he turned around, grabbed his dictionary, and threw it on the floor. It made a satisfying thud, so he did it again.

Did she *want* to get rid of him?

He sank down onto the bed and dropped his head into his hands. The left hand tasted the salt of his tears; there was a burning in his wrist, and he dropped his hand to look, watched the blue-gray slickness of the new skin spread half an inch up his forearm.

Inside him, a door closed. This change was coming, and he couldn't stop it or reverse it, at least not with anything he knew now.

Michael shrugged into his jacket, zipped it closed, and buried the new hand in his pocket. Mom hadn't come because he threw a book. Wasn't she even going to fight to keep him?

He went to the kitchen, found breakfast cleared from the table and Mom and Lizzie finishing dishes. Mom turned a pale face to him, then left the room and came back with her jacket and knit hat on. The beach had been windy yesterday and probably would be again today.

"I need my jacket too," Lizzie said, and then, "Is it okay if I come?"

"I—" said Mom. She looked at Michael.

He turned away, then said in a low, rough voice to Lizzie, "If I don't come back from this, Mom's going to need friends."

Lizzie nodded and ran out the back door.

Michael looked at the pictures on the table. All three of the ones Lizzie had taken were good. He saw a smile on his face he had never seen even in a mirror, tender as he stared down at his mother, who faced the camera with a sad smile, her hand touching his new, strange hand on his chest. His face looked innocent of the knowledge that the world as he knew it was about to end.

He glanced at Mom, smiled, and she smiled back. "I love you no matter what," she said.

"I know. I love you, too."

"Oh, good."

"Will you be all right?"

"Yes. I'll manage. I always do. Maybe you can visit."

"Dad," he said, and that was when she cried.

The sobs were great, gulping ones, the cries of someone who had lost everything in some kind of natural disaster. She wailed, and he didn't know what to do. Finally he hugged her, wishing she would stop it, this disturbing, wordless noise that grated on his heart. She clutched at his jacket. A little while later, she stopped, sucked in breaths, muttered something, pushed away from him, went to the sink, and drank a glass of water. She was rinsing her face by the time Lizzie came back, dressed for wind.

"Well," Mom said, "I'll slap your father around and see what happens. I'll find out whether he's really leaving me. I'm not sure what I want right now. A job, anyway. I checked the local paper. There were some possibilities in the want ads. I have a good feeling about this town."

"We'll take care of you," Lizzie said.

Mom smiled at her.

The beach was two blocks away, two blocks past other weathered houses, hunched trees shaped into waves by prevailing winds off the ocean, cars rusting from the salt air. As they walked, the wave sound grew louder. They reached the stairs down to the beach, and Michael stood at the top against the endless push of the wind and looked out over blue-gray motion and standing stones like the Earth's teeth rising from the sand and water. Was this really home?

Wind carried sand in low, scudding sheets before dropping it.

Lizzie clattered down the stairs, and Mom followed. Michael went down after them. At the base of the cliff, they sat on a drift log tossed high by a winter storm. Michael unlaced his tennis shoes and socks and hid them behind the log.

Seawater. He'd been wary of it for as long as he could remember, and even before, according to Mom. He still felt the shadow of terror at the thought that it was only feet away from him. He stood and drew in deep breaths until his heart slowed. Beside him, Mom took his plain hand and squeezed it.

"Ready?" she asked.

"Almost." He took three more breaths.

Lizzie looked up and down the beach, nodded, led the way left. "There's a cove this way that's closed off when the tide's high, but we should be able to get to it now. Not that many people go there."

They followed her along the beach. Gulls cried above them.

At last they came to a stretch of sand without many lines of footprints across it. Lizzie led them up over a spine of dark rock that stretched from the cliff to the water, and then they were in a cup-shaped cove, protected from the wind.

Mom still gripped his hand.

The three of them walked to the edge of the dry sand. Michael let go of Mom's hand and knelt, new fingers and palm against the wet sand. He felt the scorch of change rise up his arm.

He looked over his shoulder at Mom, who smiled at him. He touched his right hand to the wet sand. At the kiss of salty water, change attacked his palm and flared over his skin.

Water swamped his clothes, icy and aggressive and burning. He struggled out of them. Change twisted and worked through him.

The wave rushed out, beaching him on sliding sand in a haze of burning pain. Mom, her jeans wet to the knees, stared down at him, mouth open, eyes wide. Lizzie screamed and ran up the beach.

Mom dropped to her knees beside him. She closed her mouth and blinked three times, then reached toward his chest.

He lifted what had been his right hand.

Mom set her hand on his chest. He felt his second heartbeat pulse under her palm. "How do you feel?" she asked.

"How do I look?" he asked, but what came out of his mouth was a string of clicks and hisses.

She blinked rapidly, licked her lips.

He touched her cheek. She said, "Your eyes are golden now."

Something hissed behind him. He turned. There was nothing opaque about the ocean now: shafts of light plunged down into it, showed him the others, floating just offshore.

He struggled to his feet. Already that felt like a huge, uncomfortable effort, something his body wasn't made to do. He held out a hand to Mom, who took it. He hauled her up and wrapped his arms around her.

She hugged him, pressed her head against his chest.

"Love you," she whispered.

"Love you," he said, but it came out hissing. She smiled as though she understood and stepped away from him. A wave came up and he fell into it, grateful, and let it carry him out to where the others waited. The sea spoke along his sides and over his chest and belly, against his soles, under his palms. All around him spread a swaying world of light and distance, mixing with sand below and sky above, the standing rocks off shore like slices of mountains cut off at top and bottom, windings of seaweed beyond, and small living creatures flying toward him and away.

The others came to him.

He followed them out past the place where waves gathered and broke, out where the bottom dropped, deeper, where light grew dim. The others traveled around him, some darting close to brush along him, others teasing, sending patterns through the flow of water. Clicks and chunks and hisses flowed around him, and tastes filtered through his mouth, most of them unknown but somehow communicating. Joy thrummed in his chest.

A brief thought of something left behind, an image of sunlight on a face, a fading trace of longing and sadness. One of the others nudged his shoulder, and it was gone.

Afterword

Why Elemental?

December 26, 2004. The day the wave came. We all saw the images on our television screens though at the time we simply couldn't appreciate the magnitude of what we were witnessing. We were left feeling numb as we looked at images of Phuket and Banda Ache and watched the number in the corner of the screen ticking forever upward as the death toll rose—only then did it begin to sink in and we were engulfed by a collective grief unlike anything I have experienced in my lifetime. We were suddenly aware; we knew what tsunamis were, we knew how they were formed, and we knew, in sound and vision, the devastation they left in their wake. It is the dual gift and curse of the media generation, we cannot help SEEING things, and that immediacy affects us. These were real lives, real families, not episodes of glitzy television shows. Like the wave itself, the media coverage was relentless, and with good reason: this was a disaster on a worldwide scale.

I am lucky, I know good people—good people who know even more good people—which is how this book came about. For every one of the writers in here two more sent messages of support for the project and put us in contact with people who threw themselves body and soul into helping with the project. We owe the editors, the production teams, the marketing departments, the buyers, the reps, and the designers, absolutely everyone who had a hand in making *Elemental* real. You see, the science fiction community is exactly that—a community—and it banded together in the form of this book in a way that made me proud to be a part of it and call these people my friends. These people inspired me with the way they responded to the challenge and they humbled me with their generosity.

I saw the images of destruction on the television in a hotel room in London, but it wasn't until I retuned home to Stockholm that the shock wore off and the numbers really started making a sick kind of sense. On January 11, 2005, everything changed for me. I was walking down the corridor to the classroom where I taught fifth grade at the English School in Stockholm, ready for another day of the same old same old, when the school psychologist grabbed me and asked if I had heard. The way she said it stopped me cold. Six of the children had been there, two were still unaccounted for, and one of my own eleven-year-olds, Nikki, had stood on the beach in the middle of it, surrounded by corpses. She was all right. Her family had returned with a young boy who had lost his entire family on that beach. Then, with it right there in my face, I started to think and for a moment felt utterly helpless against the sheer force of nature I was up against. I got home and I called Alethea and asked if she was up for doing something stupid—my way of saying *I've had another one of those huge ideas; think we can pull it off?*

She said yes.

Suddenly the ball was rolling. Over the next few weeks, *Elemental* was conceived, a collection of stories showcasing the various elements of speculative fiction, hence the wide variety of stories presented here, from space opera and Vonnegutesque absurdity to high fantasy, magical realism, and the shadowy fringes of dark fantasy and slipstream. I wanted it all, in one book, unified because in itself *Elemental* represented the way the entire community banded together to help.

There was never any question that the money raised by the project should go to help the children left behind, so it was a natural choice to donate all proceeds to Save the Children's Asia Tsunami Relief fund.

The disaster may have slipped from the front pages of our newspapers and been replaced by celebrity gossip on our television screens, but before I go, I want to leave you with some of the cold hard facts.

As of today:

INDONESIA: 122,232 people dead, 113,937 missing
SRI LANKA: 30,974 people dead, 4,698 missing, and over 100,000 families have been displaced
INDIA: 10,776 dead, 5,640 missing—5,554 on the Andaman and Nicobar Islands
THAILAND: 5,395 dead, 2,993 missing
SOMALIA: 150 dead
MALDIVES: 82 dead, 26 missing
MALAYSIA: 68 dead
MYANMAR: 59 dead
TANZANIA: 10 dead
SEYCHELLES: 3 dead
BANGLADESH: 2 dead
KENYA: 1 dead
AUSTRALIA: 13 dead, 349 missing
AUSTRIA: 6 dead, 500 missing
BELGIUM: 6 dead
CANADA: 4 dead, 87 missing
CHINA: 15 dead (10 from Hong Kong; 3 from the mainland, and 2 non-Chinese residents of Hong Kong), 29 missing
CZECH REPUBLIC: 1 dead, 7 missing
DENMARK: 7 dead
FINLAND: 5 dead, 214 missing
FRANCE: 22 dead, 74 missing
GERMANY: 60 dead, 668 missing
ISRAEL: 5 dead, 5 missing
ITALY: 20 dead, 310 missing
JAPAN: 8 dead
NETHERLANDS: 6 dead, 30 missing
NEW ZEALAND: 2 dead, 64 missing

NORWAY: 16 dead, 908 missing
SINGAPORE: 8 dead, 31 missing
SOUTH AFRICA: 11 dead, 4 missing
SOUTH KOREA: 11 dead
SWEDEN: 52 dead, 1,838 missing
SWITZERLAND: 23 dead
TAIWAN: 3 dead, 45 missing
UNITED KINGDOM: 51 dead, 1,083 missing
UNITED STATES: 18 dead, 472 missing

In total, 170,125 people from 36 countries lost their lives, with another 134,012 people missing, the majority of whom are now presumed dead. Over one-third of these were children. These figures don't include those who were injured, those who lost their homes, those whose families were swept away.

On Christmas Day 2004 these weren't just numbers, they were people with families. Twenty-four hours later they became statistics in one of the world's worst natural disasters.

It seems fitting to write this closing paragraph today because it is the six-month "anniversary" of the school psychologist stopping me in the corridor. Six months gone by in the blink of an eye for me, but not, I suspect, for those left behind in the wake of the wave who still need food, shelter, clothes, an education, things we all take for granted. In buying *Elemental* you have gone a little way to helping rebuild these children's lives. It's a small step, but small steps can change the world. I thank you with all of my heart.

Steven Savile
June 11, 2005